FAMOUS

FAMOUS NOVEL-ONE

Kahlen Aymes

Cover designed by Sarah Hansen, Okay Creations

Formatting by Cassy Roop of Pink Ink Designs

Cover Art: ©shutterstock_132068789 & © istock_00024419708

Published by: Telemachus Press, LLC
http://www.Telemachus.com

Visit the author's website: http://www.KahlenAymes.com

ISBN: 9781942899037

For
Bob & Jaymie

You'll see why...

FAMOUS

Famous Novel-One

Prologue
Lights, Camera, Love

Brooklyn

LAST NIGHT WAS amazing.

Cade and I had holed up in my hotel room to work on one of our love scenes. Could anything be more beautiful, exciting, arousing ... or so *painful?* I mean; it was fucking excruciating. This was one time that being an actor might really pay off. We were completely in sync with each other; we practiced the scene ten times when we didn't need to practice at all. I could feel my skin flush with heat and excitement. We both knew what we were doing; which was finding *any* excuse to touch each other, to just be in the same room together. He made me tremble even without touching me, and I completely melted when he did.

I'd never wanted anyone so much in my life. Never wanted to hear a voice, feel a touch or see a face so much before. *Ever.* I'd seen some of his other work, did the research necessary to get familiar with his acting chops before we met, and I was worried. He was a huge star, and I was basically nobody. Even knowing how amazing he was going in, I wasn't prepared for how he'd affect me once we'd met. I was seriously screwed. Sure, he was drop dead beautiful; more in person than on screen, but it was the chemistry between us that was turning my world upside down.

The first time our lips met was life changing and the pull between us became this exquisite agony I craved, even though it hurt. I never wanted to stop kissing him, and I sensed the tension building within Cade as well. The pain of the scene was a shallow echo of the real ache growing between us. We were living this, even if we didn't intend to. I certainly didn't mean to care about him, but I couldn't help myself. He was so real and down-to-earth, and not how I'd expected a major movie star to act. I tried to convince myself over and over that this was just the movie, nothing real, and we were just really getting into our roles. But, sucked in by those blue eyes, sexy mouth, and strong jaw... I was lost, and, more than that, Cade *got me*. He understood me better than my boyfriend ever had. I never dreamed a connection this intense was even possible.

David was sweet and giving but didn't excite me with the same degree of desperation. I wanted Cade... I dreamed about him. I was falling in love, even though I tried my hardest to tell myself these feelings were manifesting from the characters and were convoluting reality. The yearning and wanting to give in with wild abandon went way beyond the characters we were playing. I knew it, and so did he. That was the scariest part.

I mean; I loved David—I still loved him. He was a great person, and we were comfortable together, but Cade... he was like a dream come true, like a flash fire that left me burnt to a crisp. A living, breathing fantasy.

Conflict ate away at my insides. I had so much guilt over my feelings for Cade—guilt because I wanted him and felt unfaithful to David, and because I'd probably hurt them both or, at least, one of them. I couldn't find a way around it or a way to change how I felt. I was miserable, but it didn't matter. I didn't really want it to go away. How could I? It was intoxicating, suffocating, completely consuming.

Cade was already suffering though it was amazing that he'd even notice me. We were both struggling. It was so tangible; I wondered if the whole world could see it. It was in the way he looked at me, the way the electricity shot through me each time I was near him, and when he touched me: well I was done. When we kissed, it was amazing; like nothing I'd ever experienced. I never wanted it to end. The way he smelled and tasted. It was addicting and unexpected.

Uhnnnng, God! My thoughts troubling, I ran a hand through my long hair in agitation.

Earlier in the day, during the shoot, each time we kissed it got hotter and hotter, beyond what the script called for, and the director kept correcting us. Cade was the one who knew what he was doing on set. I'd barely worked in the industry thus far, and his fame was already ridiculous. I tried to follow his lead, and he seemed immersed in the scene.

It was more than difficult not to shove my tongue down his throat, but this script called for those damn tortured, held back kisses. It was painful to the extreme. Well, check, check, check; we had the same thing working in real life. I could tell by his breathing; Cade was having difficulty holding back, too.

Finally, it was too much, and we both lost our fragile grip on the restraint. My tongue came out to lick his lip, and he began to push me backward on the bed, his open mouth sucking so slightly on mine, and pulling my lower lip into his mouth. I was dying for more and my hand fisted in the front of his blue button-down. It was the closest we'd come to French kissing and I wanted to go there badly.

Now, we were in my room on the pretense of running lines for tomorrow's scenes, though it was a joke. He was sheepish when he called and suggested we get together, but I didn't have the strength to say no, and it wasn't long before we were making out in full force, but this time, tongues were involved. It felt so good to give in, to feel his hard body pressed, full-on, into mine. Somehow Cade found the strength to stop, taking my shoulders with both hands and pushing away to put space between our bodies, then pressing his forehead to mine, his breath leaving his body in a whoosh. "Brook... I need to leave. I have to go, *now*." Both of our chests were heaving with excitement.

"Ugh... No. No, Cade, don't go," I protested, my hands moved up his chest to clutch at the nape of his neck. God, I never wanted him to leave. Whether it was wrong or right, I needed him.

"I absolutely *have* to. I'm... you have to know how I feel about you, Brook. I'm in hell. The situation is killing me and yet, I can't stay away from you. This isn't about the film. It never was." There it was; the truth that had hovered between us for weeks. And now we'd crossed the threshold, I wanted to cross the finish line.

Hearing his struggle, the pain in his voice squeezed my heart in a way that I'd never imagined it could. I reached up to touch his face and the soft, dark golden stubble scratched against the tender skin of my wrist. He turned and pressed his face into my hand and kissed the palm. "I'm working hard to be your friend and I'm not doing a splendid job of it."

"Does this happen to you a lot? Uh, I mean—" I stammered, "— things getting out of hand with costars?"

His eyes whipped to mine and held. He shook his head. "Sex, sometimes. I'm not going to lie to you, Brook. But, I care about you."

I opened my mouth to speak, but the look in his eyes stole my words away. He disentangled himself from my arms and moved off of the bed to sit on the edge.

"What are you doing for your birthday? I'd love to take you out." He ran a hand through his glorious mane of dark blonde hair and I wished it were my hands touching it. I was always aching to feel it, tug on it and thread my fingers through the silken strands. When I didn't answer, he continued, though it seemed a struggle. "You know, with the whole cast to help celebrate. Anywhere you want to go. My treat."

My heart fell. David was planning on coming to location for my birthday and I found myself resenting him and searching for any excuse to keep him away. That was completely unfair, but I was feeling protective of the little world where Cade was the center and protective of the limited time we had left. Suddenly, I couldn't breathe.

The fact was; I never wanted this shoot to end and the clock in my head was counting down with sickening speed. Sure, it was my first movie and I was excited about the actual filming, but my sadness that it would end was all centered on him.

The wrap was getting closer, looming like terminal cancer. Six weeks left, tops, and then he'd be gone and I wouldn't see him until it was time to begin promoting the movie. Months. The thought made me feel weak; sick that I couldn't control my feelings, and already miserable at the thought of him being so far away from me. I felt completely out of control of everything and I fucking hated it. I dropped my hand to his shoulder as he faced away from me and slowly ran it down his back because I couldn't help myself. He shivered a little and I longed to continue touching him. I lowered my head and swallowed.

"Uh... um," I glanced up and saw the understanding dawn on his beautiful profile, the pain flashed across his face before he tried to hide it. He stiffened and moved away from me, leaving me feeling cold and empty.

"Oh, right. How bloody silly of me. I should have known David would come for your birthday. It's completely ridiculous of me to think that you would want—" He was suddenly pensive and withdrawn from me. I found myself wanting to reach out to him, pull him to me, and rewind the clock to ten minutes before when we were kissing on the bed.

I nodded and bit my lip, my throat aching. *How in the hell am I going to get through this?*

"I'm... I still want to be with you. With all of you if... that would be okay."

His chin jutted out and I could see him swallow. It would be hard for both of us, but I couldn't bear to tell him no. His brow dropped and he nodded ever so slightly before bending to scoop up his script where it had fallen carelessly on the floor. "Yes, sure."

"Cade..."

"You don't have to say anything. This is my own fault."

My eyes widened as he walked to the door of my hotel room and I followed. "It's no one's fault. You didn't—" I stopped, searching for words. "I mean we didn't *plan* this." I reached out to touch him as he waited by the door for me to finish what I was saying. My hand hovered over his back and then fell in silence to my side.

Cade put his hand to his head and clutched at his hair on the right side of his head. "Goddamn it!" he groaned. "I should have been more careful. When I found you disarming at the audition, I should have been more on guard. I know this is just a job and that you've got a life and… *people*… waiting for you in L.A. You have a *real* life. Not just movie after movie like me. You're very lucky, Brook. Sometimes I hate this goddamned business."

I felt tears well in my eyes, afraid to blink or they would roll down my cheeks. I wanted to scream that I didn't want to go back to real life! I wanted to be as we were; constantly together and to stay that way forever. I wanted this never to end and I wanted every second of the time we had left. Panic started to well up within me, unfamiliar and frightening. I'd never been this confused.

"Cade…. Cade, don't leave—"

"I don't want to, but I have to. I'm doing this for you. Goodnight, Brook," he said softly and turned to brush his thumb across my chin. "See you tomorrow on set. Um… I might lose it slightly, so please forgive me. I'll apologize in advance since I know I won't be able to bloody help myself."

"Cade… We can still hang out. Cade!" I pleaded. With that, he was gone, and I was left gasping, staring, as the door slowly closed after him. I realized my body was shaking, and I couldn't breathe because, what had become a part of me, was walking down the hall and away from me.

Caden

I WAS TORN. I never wanted the day to end and yet, I couldn't wait to retreat to the safety and sanctity of my room. Being so close to her, feeling her breath on my face as we hesitated, our face only inches apart, and then our lips met and I finally pressed her into the bed, my hands exploring her body… I'd dreamt about it endless times and it was driving me bloody mad that it couldn't be real. I'd never wanted anyone as much as I wanted Brook. But, what did I fucking expect? I was in love with someone who was already involved. I was a ridiculous fool, but it wasn't like I even had a choice in the matter. And it was crazy. I'd never gotten close to an actress I'd worked with before. Not like this. I wasn't even sure why or how it happened. I was taken by complete and utter surprise, left stupefied and unable to do a damn thing about it.

Bloody hell! I was wound tighter than a drum. My body was aching the entire day and there was no way I could hide it from her. I felt her breath hitch. She clutched at my face and the back of my head, pulling my mouth closer, her body arching up to mine as I fell between her open legs. She was pulling and I was pressing ... God. I closed my eyes and tried to swallow the dryness in my mouth. It was brilliant.

"I've dreamt about touching you like this, for so long." My character's words echoed my own thoughts.

We'd reshot the scene over and over and I'd lost track of how many damn times or how many hours we'd been stuck in this small space, filming the first time our characters made out; just the two of us, and eight other people. I let out my breath in disgust. Not the way I'd fantasized about finally being in bed with her. I knew it was wrong to even want it for real, but every cell in my body screamed with it. It was so strong; it physically hurt.

We'd spent so much time together and gotten too close to remain objective or unmoved. It didn't matter that I'd been able to stay personally stoic on ten other films with ten other actresses, but Brook wasn't like them. She wasn't plastic; she was real. I felt incredibly blessed to have the opportunity to know her and learn about her life. We were so alike; with many of the same interests and she was so fucking smart. She wrapped around my mind like no one ever had and she was funny, confident and strong. She knew what she wanted, where she was headed, and she trusted herself completely. She didn't care about making it big, and that in itself was brilliant. She was in it for the experience, and really cared about the quality of the film. Not the bloody fame.

I loved the way she stood up to the director when she didn't agree with something. Brooklyn and I had very specific thoughts about the characters and we argued with Martin for days about how they should be portrayed. Finally, Brook had it out with him, telling him she wouldn't do the film if we couldn't play it the way we were feeling it. I smiled to myself as I thought about it.

"Look, this is about the pain, Martin. Don't you get it? I've read the script ten times! I've read the novel! I feel this situation and I know Cade does, too!" She had thrown down her journal on the table. We'd tried to calmly discuss it with the director all through dinner and were getting nowhere fast. *"Ryan and Julia have too many obstacles, too much distance and time to overcome to make it easy. Every move, every kiss... it has to hurt. It has to be pulled out of them both!"*

"It's my film. You work for me, so you will play it as I direct. The budget is too small for all of these reshoots." Martin refused to concede and I watched Brook's face tighten. I leaned forward on the table. Brook was unknown and even though we were halfway in, he could cut her and recast the role. I doubted he would, but I couldn't take that chance.

"Martin, we just ... we've worked on this for months before we ever came to set, and we both have the same ideas on how it should

be played. I agree that a film can't depict everything the book does, and that makes it even more important to get it right. The pain is as tangible as the love. Don't you get that? There are a lot of things that we can do, and to do it justice, we should. Wouldn't you agree?" I'd tried to reason with him.

Martin Deering was an up and coming director, who had been nominated for an Oscar already. I respected him and his vision, but as Brook insisted, and maybe because it was her and me, we had to play it the way it felt and it fucking devastated us both.

"I'm through discussing this. I think you guys are great people and wonderful actors, but I need you to act the way I tell you to act," he said, anger tightening his mouth and jaw.

Brook huffed and leaned heavily back in her chair, staring at Martin for a long moment. "No. I can't speak for Cade, but I will not play it that way. I'll drop the film if it comes down to that. I feel it's an injustice to the fans to sell out like that. I know I'm new, but I won't do films for the experience of acting. It's about telling the story, and I know the author wouldn't want it like this. I want to tell the fucking story and I won't make it into a joke, and I won't let you make either one of us into a joke. They bleed. We have to bleed." She was calm as she stood up and picked up her script, phone, and journal. She turned to me. "Cade, call me later when you get finished here." And, with that, she walked out, leaving me sitting there with a stunned Martin.

It was so fucking hot, watching her take charge like that. I felt a grin breakout on my face and my chest filled with pride. I tried to hide it from Martin because I didn't want to seem disrespectful, but the girl just hammered him. I watched Brook's retreating form until Martin's voice broke into my thoughts.

"Cade, talk to her," Martin finally said. "It's obvious she listens to you."

I shook my head with a smirk. I wouldn't try to convince Brook of something I didn't believe in myself. "We discuss things and we don't always agree, but um, we both feel the same way about this. Martin, we don't dictate to each other, it's about respect. You know, Brook is very mature for her age and it's really bloody incredible to see her stand up for what she wants." I laughed. "I mean, look at her! I agree that this is right for the film, and for all of us." I could see the anger and frustration in his eyes as a red flush began to creep up under his skin.

"You know, Caden, if she walks it puts this whole thing on hold. You've got another film to think about, are you sure you want to threaten me?"

I offered a small smile and met his gaze steadily. "What? I'm not threatening you. I'm just saying that I know how this is supposed to go down and I won't work with anyone other than Brook. It wouldn't feel right. So, if she goes, I do, too," I said quietly. "So, the schedule on my other film won't suffer. Why don't you just let us go with it for a scene or two and see how we do?"

I could see how pissed he was and I felt sorry for him, in a way. After all, this was his film and he was responsible for the end result. "Production costs money, Cade."

"Yes, I know. If we have to redo the scenes, I'll reimburse you from my salary."

"Are you sure this is about the film? I warned you about staying away from her and you've done a piss-poor job of it."

I stood up and pushed my chair into the table. "We all want the movie to be the best it can be. Just give us a shot to show you in one *scene. As far as Brook is concerned, she's an amazing person, a very good actress, and we've become close friends. Beyond that, it's really none of your business."*

Martin had no choice but to listen and the next day we proved our point.

I knew at the audition and then throughout the three months before pre-production began, that Brook and I were going to be tight. We'd been in contact on a regular basis, delving into the characters for weeks before we'd arrived in Canada to begin filming. We were good friends before we ever hit the set, and now, infatuation had turned to some sort of burning love. At least, it had for me. I felt palpable tension with Brook whenever we were together and couldn't deny myself the small hope that she could be feeling the same thing. But, at this point, it was a dream that was slowly slipping between my fingers as our time together dwindled. I was starting to feel a constant veil of desperation hanging over me at the pending loss of her presence in my life.

Now, after we'd played it and replayed it, take after take, I sat on the edge of the bed trying to get control of my errant body and labored breathing. I was shaking as I turned away from Brook and tried to get a grip on myself. She sat on her knees on the bed, waiting while Martin spoke to the production manager about the lighting and camera angles. Both of us were sitting in stunned silence. The last take of the scene had gotten so bloody hot. Ryan had finally touched Julia intimately in the story, and that meant I had touched Brook. I could feel her heat on my fingers, seeping through her clothes, feel how slippery the flesh beneath the fabric of her sweats had been. I'd had a raging hard-on all day and I was unsure how much more I could withstand. I felt so ridiculous and embarrassed, afraid of Brook's reaction. She felt it, too. I felt the tangible proof.

"Cade..." She scooted toward me. "Last night—and just now—I'm sorry," Brook said softly, but knowingly.

"Please don't, Brook. You didn't do anything to apologize for." I shook my head and kept my eyes averted, staring at the fake window in front of me. I couldn't look at her. She had so much skin showing, more than she ever did when we were alone in one of our rooms practicing and it was more than I could take, regardless of the others around us.

"I just—" she struggled for words and sat down fully on the bed, crossing her legs in front of her. "I don't like this strain between us. You're... well, you're one of my best friends. Maybe the best friend I've ever had."

Best friends fighting the love, like the characters we were playing. *Well, I'm bloody in love with you,* my mind screamed.

I threw my head back and looked at the ceiling. It was about twenty or thirty feet above us: just bare steel and girders of the warehouse where they built the interior set of the Boston apartment. "Brook, I'm just trying to get through this scene and remember what the hell the truth is. I'm sorry if I seem distant. It's the only way I can deal with it and how I'm keeping the thin grip on the little control that I have left. As you can tell from this last take, I'm not as strong as I need to be."

She brought both hands to her glorious hair and threaded her fingers through it on each side of her head. "Do you think it's any different for me? I'm just—"

The director had a great sense of timing and called to us from the edge of the set, a smirk firmly in place on his pudgy face, and inwardly I groaned. "Can you guys clear out for a minute? Get a drink or something while they redress the set for the next take."

I spoke before I could help myself. "How many damn takes do you need? How many ways can we do this for Christ's sake? We *have* it," I spat at him. Brooklyn swallowed and her face fell as she sat there, clutching the sheet around her. Instantly, I was filled with regret at my words. "I thought you were so worried about the budget," I said, more softly now, imploring him to stop the torture.

Martin stared up at me and crossed his arms across his chest. Brook was looking down at her lap as she started to move to the edge of the bed. I stood up and walked around the end of it and past Martin.

"I just want to shoot it with a tighter camera one time and then if it's all good, we'll be done with this scene. I also want to film some stuff that may get used for the other love scenes," Martin said impatiently, at the same time I turned to leave the set.

"Like what?" Brook asked hesitantly, trepidation clear on her beautiful features.

"Well, I just want a tighter shot of the kissing." He looked between the two of us for a second. I knew that would mean even less clothing between us.

"Christ," I said as I stormed off the set.

"Ten minutes, Cade," Martin called sternly after me.

Brooklyn's hurried footsteps followed me as I walked away and despite myself, I knew she'd find a way to lighten the mood and ease this bullshit I was feeling. I took a deep breath and walked outside of the warehouse, turning the corner and went around to the west side. The sun was starting to set and it was getting cold.

It was late March and we still had weeks of filming to go. As much as Martin frustrated me, as much as being around Brook when I couldn't act on my real feelings for her, hurt me, I knew that the day we were done filming would kill me. There were two more books, but who knew if they'd get made. These things depended on box office receipts alone. I lit a cigarette and leaned against the side of the building and blew out with force. A habit I knew Brook abhorred, but I needed something to calm me down.

"Cade," I heard Brooklyn's voice before she appeared around the corner. She'd put on a robe over her skimpy costume and shoved her feet into her sneakers. Still I was worried she wouldn't be warm enough. After she found me, she didn't say anything. She just leaned up against the building beside me, and reached for my hand, her cold fingers closing over mine.

"Are you warm enough?" I asked softly. When she nodded, I looked away from her face. I didn't want to see confusion or pain there and I knew I would. I should have felt elated, but instead felt empty and lost.

We stood there in silence, and soon my thumb was rubbing the top of her hand that was entwined with mine. The quiet comfort of her touch gave me center and focus. When it was just the two of us, I was fine. It was easy to push back the strain and pretend she didn't have a boyfriend or that this wasn't all going to end soon. I felt so connected with her and that connection was all that mattered to me.

"I suppose Martin will have our asses if we aren't back soon," I lamented after I finished my cigarette. I bent to press the butt into the ground to make sure it was out then popped a candy mint into my mouth. "Can he be any more annoying?" I offered her one.

Brooklyn shook her head.

"He budgeted a whole day for this scene, so he is damn sure going to use it up, even though he was whining about it before. God forbid he lets us off of the hook early," she agreed with a soft smile, her hand tightening around mine. I knew she was silently asking if things were okay between us, and I finally let myself look at her face and returned the pressure to reassure her. She was beautiful with her darkened hair flowing and those green contact lenses, but I longed for her bright blue eyes. Those gorgeous eyes claimed my very soul during all of those hours of running the scenes. When I'd met her, she was blonde, but she was beautiful either way.

I silently chastised myself. *Who was I kidding?* I let my breath out in disgust, which drew her gaze quickly to my face.

Both of us were very good at memorization, so if we were honest, we had no need to run and rerun the lines, *or* the kisses the night before. The painful kisses were all that were possible, and they left me aching, and wanting more. It was torture that I willingly subjected both of us to, and not just because of the script. Martin reminded me every other day that Brook was younger and more inexperienced than me and I wanted to scream every time he did. Did he think I was a bloody idiot or that I didn't comprehend what he was fucking saying? I think that was the main problem I had with him, and why I resented him so much. That, and he operated in a constant state of chaos. Chaos on occasion was healthy, but he drove me crazy with it.

"Look, Brook, I'm sorry about before. This scene is difficult for me." I felt embarrassed because surely she felt evidence of my arousal pressing against her when I'd pushed her back on the bed, but she didn't mention it. She had too much class for that, and I silently prayed that she didn't think it was just lust I was feeling. It became extremely important that she understand I wouldn't be aroused in a similar circumstance with anyone else. It was all about Brook.

"For me, too," her voice was low and aching.

"I'm... I'll never be sorry that we met, though. I mean, I'm glad that we're friends. I hope we can stay this way after the movie is finished. You're the first person I want to talk to every morning," I said honestly.

She turned toward me and wrapped her arms around my waist. After a stunned moment, I followed suit, enfolding her in my embrace. "Yes. I'd like that," she murmured softly against my shirt.

I felt a moment of relief. At least, I could be certain that we wouldn't lose touch after I went back to London, even if it wouldn't be the instant satisfaction of having her near me all of the time. "We'd better get back. The production assistants are probably scrambling around looking for us." I rubbed her back a couple of times before I let go of her, but slid my hand down her arm to take her hand as we started walking back into the building, and toward the set.

"Let's kick the shit out of this take, huh?"

"Yeah, okay." I decided I'd let myself pretend that this take was Cade and Brook, and not the characters we were playing. I decided to grant myself this one small gift and allow myself to really feel with her. Maybe today would be one of the last chances I'd have to kiss her, and I was going to savor every second no matter how much it would kill me later. "It's a tough job, but somebody's got to bloody do it," I teased gently. She smiled and shook her head the way she always did when she was embarrassed by a compliment.

As we drew near the set, I dropped her hand and she shoved her hands into the pockets of the robe. "What do you want to do tonight?" Brook looked up at me expectantly. My heart swelled within my chest, and contentment settled over me like a blanket, a smile spreading across my face. For now, I could forget about the outside world and just concentrate on what I felt flowing between us. I knew she'd been fighting whatever was happening between us. We both were, but it was there: tangible, palpable, and alive.

"Whatever you want. We could order pizza and invite the others in to play music or a movie, or go out for dinner." I loved it when we played music, and how Brook always watched me. It didn't escape my notice that her eyes lingered on me more than anyone else, and it created such pure happiness, I had difficulty bottling it up inside. She could play guitar fairly well because she was learning it for another audition, but she didn't have a guitar of her own. I smiled to myself as I thought of the pure mahogany one that I'd ordered for her, and would give to her on her birthday in a couple of weeks. I loved that she enjoyed the same music that I loved and playing together was something that could bring us even closer to each other. One thing that was just ours; that I could be certain she didn't share with the boyfriend. I was more accomplished at it than she was, of course, since I'd been playing for years, but it gave me immense pleasure when she'd asked me if I could give her lessons.

"Music and pizza sounds really good."

"Yeah, it does."

Brooklyn

IT WAS MY birthday and the day had been busy. Cade and I spent the entire day downtown, filming from early in the morning. I was tired, and cold as I arrived back in my room. The whole cast was taking me out for the evening, but Cade organized the whole thing. My heart tightened in my chest as I walked down the hall that led to my room. My manager, Jeanne, would have arranged for David to get a key from the desk, and no doubt he'd be waiting inside. If only I wanted to see him. I'd tried to dissuade him from coming, knowing what a grueling day I'd have, and how tired I'd be, but he'd insisted. Guilt crept over me. Being tired had nothing to do with not wanting him to come up from L.A. and I knew it.

He was a good guy, and we had a history, but there were times when I felt like I was talking to a wall and it didn't matter what I said. When he got something in his head, it was over. Done. Everything was starting to feel superficial, and I knew why. I beat myself up because I was constantly comparing him to Cade; the sensitive, intelligent, funny, gorgeous and gifted, deep thinker.

I'd been rushing so I'd have time to take a hot shower before meeting everyone at the party, but as I got closer to my room, my pace slowed. I wasn't sure what felt more filled with lead, my feet or my heart.

I took a deep breath; as much air as my lungs could stand, and ran both hands through my hair as I walked the last few steps to the door. My fingers curled through the strands, and I wanted to pull them out by the roots. I hadn't seen David in a month, and a year ago I would have been anxious and excited at the prospect. Three months ago, even. But... not today.

I knew tonight was going to hurt the shit out of Cade, and I dreaded it. He was so open with his feelings and more and more; it was eating at me. My heart hurt every time I saw the adoration in his eyes, and I was dying to tell him I was falling for him, too. As much as I'd tried to fight it, I knew I wanted it as badly as he did, and that made it inevitable. He could have played the movie star role so easily and brush David aside to get what he wanted, but he didn't. He was caring of other people's feelings, and of mine, and that made him all the more special.

So now, tonight, I had the man who had loved me for more than three years, and the one who loved me without measure, in a way that felt fucking celestial; both of them, together in the same room. I didn't know if I was strong enough to handle it. I didn't know if I was a good enough actor to pull this shit off.

I dug in the back pocket of my jeans for the keycard to my room. I tried to steady myself and shoved it in the slot. The lights flashed and the lock clicked before I pushed open the door. David was lying on the big king-size bed, watching television. All I could think about was that the night prior, Cade and I were *practicing* on that very bed.

"Hey," his face lit up, and he jumped up from the bed. "There's my girl! Happy birthday, Brook!" he said as his arms enfolded me warmly. I lifted my arms to loosely surround him as well, but my heart felt distant and involuntarily, I knew I was putting up a wall. My stomach lurched. I'd hoped that seeing David would vanquish the confusion I'd been having, but if anything, it only compounded it. And, the guilt was huge.

"Thanks. How long have you been waiting?" I pulled out of his embrace and kicked off my shoes. I knew I sounded less than enthused as he moved to take me back into his arms and press a kiss to my mouth. I tried to respond, but these were not the lips I wanted. I couldn't help myself from comparing the two men. Cade was tall, with dark blonde hair and deep blue eyes, David was part Mexican with swarthier skin, dark hair, dark eyes and stocky. He was handsome, but couldn't hold a candle to Cade.

I am so fucked.

My chest tightened as he moved his hands over my back and ass like he'd done a million times. It was familiar, but now it was empty; panic rising inside me. His hands pressed me to him and I felt his erection pressing into my stomach.

"Forever. It's been so long, babe. Let's do it before dinner."

I pushed away from him. "How romantic. You just swept me off of my feet," I said coldly. He didn't deserve my hostility, but I didn't want his hands on me, his mouth pressing me for kisses. His face fell a little, and I regretted hurting him. None of this was his fault.

"I'm just really wiped out. I need to take a shower and get ready for dinner. The cast is taking us out."

"Brook! You knew I was coming up here! Why do we have to go out with all of those people? You see them every goddamn day! If you're tired, we should just stay in," he said harshly.

I went to dig through my clothes and picked out jeans, a button-down shirt, and clean underwear without saying anything. I knew whatever I said wouldn't be what he wanted to hear.

"Well?" David demanded.

"*Well*, these are my friends. They've become like my family. I'm isolated up here and we've gotten pretty close. I want to spend time with them tonight. They've gone to all this trouble and this may be the only birthday I'll ever get to celebrate with them. Don't make a big deal out of it." I shrugged.

"Who exactly has gone to the trouble, Brooklyn?" David's perception was not something I felt up to dealing with right now. His dark hair fell haphazardly over his icy gray eyes and he pushed it back impatiently.

"The entire cast wants to celebrate with me."

"Yeah, sure," he said skeptically. I averted my eyes for fear he'd read the truth there. "I wanted to be alone. We haven't had sex in months."

"Guh! *Really?* Happy birthday, I see that you're dead tired, but let's fuck?" This was not new behavior. He'd always been direct about wanting sex, but this time it offended me. Something had changed. I knew what that something was, but I tried to push it back and swallow the emotion rising up in my throat.

"That's not what I meant. I miss you."

"I'm sorry. I've missed you, too." I gave him a quick hug. "We've got time later, but now I need to get ready or we'll be late. I'm going to take a shower." I turned and went into the bathroom, locking the door behind me. I didn't want him coming in there while I was naked in the shower and I didn't want more interrogations either.

By the time I got into the shower, silent tears were falling down my face and I raised my face into the spray, trying to lose the tears in the rush of water raining down. How could things have changed so drastically in such a short time? My whole world had been turned upside down by a shock of golden hair, a set of amazing blue eyes, and a disarming smile; but it was more than that. Cade touched me on a deeper level. He and I shared a connection that couldn't be defined or articulated, and there wasn't anything I could do to stop it. Jesus, I was going to miss him. I closed my eyes as pain swept through me again. The guilt I felt for the man on the other side of the bathroom door wasn't helping, yet, it felt if I let David touch me, I'd be cheating on Cade and I couldn't do it. My heart twisted painfully in my chest.

Truthfully, I wished David would disappear and I could spend the evening alone in my room. I needed sleep and I wasn't up for what I knew would follow. I didn't want to deal with his confusion at my obvious distance, or to watch the pain that I knew I'd see on Cade's beautiful face all evening. A huge part of me was hoping that he wouldn't show tonight, that he would choose to stay away to protect himself, but I knew him better than that. He would be there for me, no matter how he felt himself. I leaned on the side of the shower and bowed my head as I struggled to pull it together.

***

WHILE DAVID AND I were in the cab that took us to the sushi restaurant where Cade had arranged my party, he pulled me close and I leaned on his shoulder, seeking comfort and to ease a portion of the guilt that was nagging me. David had been with me since the ninth grade and we'd always had an easy, no-pressure relationship. Only now, I was feeling pressure big time, but it wasn't because of anything he was doing.

"What did your family send you for your birthday?" I felt uncomfortable with the small talk, and would have been content with the silence.

I inhaled and sat up, moving away from him slightly. "Um, my mom sent me some clothes and my dad and brother are going to visit later in the month. I hadn't really thought about it, and I don't need anything. There isn't anything that I want," I said absently, looking out the window as the lights of the city flashed their reflections on the glass. Vancouver was a lot like New York, bustling; the streets crowded, people walking everywhere, but on a less intense level.

"Well, I thought we could take a trip to Cabo when filming wraps. Would you like to do that?" He was holding my hand and it burned my flesh like acid. It was all I could do not to pull away from him.

"Yeah, sure. That sounds good."

"Brook, what is with you tonight? I'm here with your *friends*; like you wanted, so what gives?" His sarcastic emphasis of the word made me want to smack him.

"I told you. I'm just really tired. We're going twelve to fifteen hours a day and today we were outside the whole time. It was cold and it's exhausting, David."

"I'll talk to Martin and tell him to take it easier on you, okay?" I rolled my eyes but he couldn't see me since I was still looking out the window. Like he'd have one ounce of pull over Martin because he'd had a small role in one of his films.

Yeah, right.

"No. Please don't. I can fight my own battles. Besides, this is a job and the tight schedule is required to bring it in within budget, and deadlines. It's just worse, now that we're winding down."

As we pulled up to the restaurant, I was grateful we were surrounded by others so I'd be able to avoid the personal conversation. He knew me very well, and clearly realized something was bothering me. Pretty soon, he'd be asking more direct questions that I didn't want to answer, but I didn't want to lie either.

The rest of the cast was already there when we walked in and all the guys stood. My eyes searched for a certain beautiful face that was conspicuously missing, and David noticed. He glanced at me to gauge my reaction. Over the past couple of months, he'd accused me of spending too much time with Cade, and he was skeptical when I told him it was mostly for the film.

I pulled away from David's hand, and went around the table and hugged everyone. "Thanks for being here, you guys. It means a lot to me."

"Hey, David," Wendy said and pointed to two open seats that she had saved beside her. She and I met at an audition for another movie the year before, and she was a friend to both of us. David took the one closest to her because he'd worked on that film, and I hadn't been cast. I silently hoped that she'd keep him occupied so I could talk to the others. Another wave of guilt rushed over me as my eyes searched the entrance to the restaurant, looking for Cade. My heart fell. Despite how I knew this would affect him, I realized how much I wanted him to be there. I always wanted him close.

We ordered the first round of drinks and my eyes glanced at the empty chair at the end of the table.

"Brook." Ethan Ranfeld caught my attention. He played the brother to Cade's character in the film. "How was it today? I talked to Cade, and he said it was an ordeal. What a way to spend your birthday." His handsome face was relaxed and he smiled.

"Yeah. It was cold and one of the production assistants fell off a curb and broke her arm. The sidewalk was slippery and her legs just flew out from underneath her."

"Was that the concert scene?" Jennifer asked. Jennifer was a pretty girl with dark hair who was cast as my best friend in the film.

"Yeah. Cade and I were running too close to the edge, I guess. The assistant moved backward to make room, and didn't watch what she was doing. I felt really bad for her."

"Speaking of Cade, where is *the man* tonight, Brook?" Wendy shot out, and nudged David in the shoulder. I stiffened slightly. She had the hots for Cade and didn't bother to hide it.

"Um, not sure. I thought he'd be here." I hoped the disappointment wasn't evident in my tone. "We were both exhausted, so maybe he decided he'd rather sleep."

David leaned into me, and whispered, "Why the hell does Wendy think you'd know where he's at?"

Shit.

"Well, probably because we worked together today," I said

impatiently.

"Sorry, I'm late. I fell asleep." As if on cue, Cade walked toward me, took my hand, and pulled me up from my chair for a hug. "Happy birthday, Brook," he said softly before letting me go and moving toward the open chair between two of the guys. David shot me a dirty look as I retook my seat, then his eyes followed Cade as he moved away from me.

"I would have understood if you wanted to keep sleeping. I almost did, too," I smiled at him from across the table.

David flung his arm around me and pulled me close so he could kiss my temple. My eyes were on Cade and he glanced away, trying to talk to Ethan. I couldn't hear what he was saying, but I wanted to. Ethan's eyes glanced at me, then back to Cade's face as he nodded.

Dinner progressed with David hanging all over me, and Cade doing his best to keep his eyes off of us. On the occasions that I'd catch him looking toward me intently, and his jaw visibly stiffened when David would call me baby, or pull me in for a kiss. I felt very uncomfortable; it wasn't like David to be the doting boyfriend, and I knew it was his frail male insecurity that was putting on a show for Cade's benefit. My stomach clenched and started to ache, causing me to pick at my food.

Cade's expression was painful. He hid it well and the others were oblivious to the tightness around his mouth, or the way he looked down with a frown as he listened to the casual conversation. But, he couldn't hide it from me. Even though he was good at laughing and trying to seem as if he didn't have a care in the world... I knew. Maybe it was the movie, or maybe it was residual shit that was carrying over; the problem was, I wasn't certain. I didn't know for sure at this point, but I knew that hurting him; hurt me. It was eating me alive.

We were almost finished with dinner when Cade abruptly stood up, his chair scraping across the wooden floor, after David had nuzzled my neck one too many times. "Um, I'll be back in a bit," he said, and turned to leave. He was stressing, so I knew he'd be going out to have a cigarette. At least, I *hoped* he wasn't leaving. Suddenly, I knew I needed to find him.

David's arm was heavy as it lay across my thighs and I lifted it off of me, and took a drink of my soda. Jennifer was watching me, and I could tell by the look in her eyes that she understood what I was going through.

"I'm going to use the restroom, David. I'll be back."

"Do you want me to come with you?" Wendy asked expectantly.

"No, thanks." I quickly got up and went to find Cade, hoping the others wouldn't notice that I walked right past the bathrooms. I went out the side door, and found him in the courtyard sitting on a bench with his back turned in my direction. It was pretty with a lot of trees, and a few tables with candles on them. The white lights that were strung in the trees were the only lights, and it left the atmosphere pretty dark and romantic. He didn't hear me approach as he pulled on his cigarette, and ran his hand through his hair. He was agitated.

"Hey..." I said softly and he turned, his clear blue eyes widened when he saw me.

"Hey, I didn't mean to make you leave your party, love."

"Well, you're part of my party, and I wanted to talk to you."

His face lit up with a lazy smile. "Yeah? You were with me all day, so aren't you sick of me yet?"

I laughed softly, and sat down beside him. "You wish."

"Not at all. Never," he answered ruefully, looking away. I could see the muscle working in his jaw. "Today was grueling, huh?" he sighed and blew out a stream of smoke.

The scene had both of us crying our guts out, and my eyes were still swollen. It was a big part of the exhaustion we both felt. I nodded.

"I'm sorry David is acting like a jealous ass in there."

"I understand. I'd be doing the same thing if I were in his place. If you were mine, I couldn't keep from touching you either. I mean... uh—"

My heart thudded in my chest, and I was sure he must hear it pounding. "Cade. You shouldn't say things like that to me. I'm..." I struggled for words. "Well, I'm just... really confused about stuff right now."

He reached out and took my hand, bringing it up to brush his lips on the inside of my wrist. "I know. I'm sorry." His expression was serious as he searched my face. I couldn't hold his gaze because I knew I'd get lost in his eyes. "I don't mean to confuse you."

"I know, but you do," I said softly. So softly, that even I almost didn't hear my own voice. I felt my throat constrict painfully. The emotions I felt with Cade, around Cade, and for Cade; were all over the fucking place. He could infuriate me like no one else could, make me burst out in hysterical spasms of laughter, make me want him so bad my skin vibrated. I felt his pain as deeply as if it were my own. Hell, maybe it was *my* pain. There were times when I couldn't tell where he ended, and I began. It terrified the shit out of me.

Cade turned to contemplate my expression, and his eyes softened; his lips quirking slightly at the corners, as he let out his breath in an amused huff.

"So... I told Martin we were meeting at a different restaurant." His shoulder nudged against mine gently; his voice full of laughter. "I didn't think you'd want him here tonight." His attempt to change the subject worked.

"Uh uh! No, you didn't!" I said incredulously, and laughed. "Cade!"

"What?" A beautiful smile split across his face. "I didn't think you'd want him bloody crashing your party, right? Isn't fifteen hours of listening to his incessant, mindless rabble enough for you?" he chuckled, and I started giggling. This was the best I'd felt all night.

"Oh, my God, yes! You're right. So what? You sent him somewhere else? He's gonna be soooo pissed!" I was still laughing. "You're amazing."

His face sobered as he touched my chin with his fingers. "There's the smile I needed to see on that beautiful face. You should be happy today. Let's go eat cake, shall we? It's my favorite part of birthdays."

I longed to take his hand and press it tighter into my cheek, to lean into him and close my eyes. Instead, I nodded. "Okay." I nudged his shoulder with mine lightly; repeating the gesture written for our characters, which had now become part of us. "This, *right now*, is my favorite part so far," I said quietly. His eyes lit up, and he leaned into me in return. "Thank you for the party."

"Anything for you. You know, I have a gift for you, too, but I want to give it to you when we're alone. How long is David staying?"

My heart fell at the mention of David's name and my little illusion fell around me in shards. I swallowed and licked my lips, dropping my gaze to the ground.

"Uh, I think a day or two. Truthfully, I didn't ask him."

Cade nodded as he stood up and held out a hand to me before leading me back into the restaurant. "Well, then, in the next few days, yeah?"

The lump in my throat threatened to choke me. "Um... sure."

***

I SAT ON the bed as David moved around me, taking off his clothes as he went. He was talking, but I wasn't registering one word he was saying. I stared off into space, not seeing or hearing anything, as my mind replayed the look in Cade's eyes as we said goodbye before David led me out of the restaurant. The way his fingers fisted in the back of my shirt, as he hugged me and kissed the side of my face, told me everything I needed to know.

Of course, Cade and I weren't lovers, but there was a high degree of desperation in that embrace.

"Hey, Brook." David was waving a hand in front of my eyes as my hand absently played with the bedspread, my unseeing eyes finally focusing on his almost nude body. Leave it to him to get right down to business. "Where the hell are you?"

I stood up, removed my jacket, and kicked my shoes into the closet. "I'm sorry. I'm just so tired," I said wearily. I prayed that he would just let me crawl into bed and fall into a blissful sleep. One where I wouldn't dream of Cade's tortured expression or the strain of that last embrace when he whispered, 'Happy birthday' against my face, with his hot breath washing over my skin.

"It's no wonder, they work you like a dog. Where was Martin tonight? I was going to talk to him to see if he had any jobs on his other films."

I smiled, flopping down on the bed. "Hmmph! I, uh, guess he must have gotten lost. He was invited." I could barely contain the laughter. If David really knew the truth of what happened, he would be furious with Cade.

"Are you going to let me in on the joke? What's so damn funny?"

"Nothing." I tried to keep a straight face, and failed. David's expression tightened.

"Aren't you going to get ready for bed?" David lowered his voice and crawled up next to me. He propped on one elbow and used his other hand to start unbuttoning my shirt, but my hand came up to cover his.

"Yeah, I'll do it," I said, and got up from the bed. David sat up and pulled his knees up to rest his elbows on them. I glanced at him out of the corner of my eye and found him studying me intently.

"What's going on, Brook?"

I was digging in my drawer, looking for some sweatpants and a t-shirt, when my hand came across one of Cade's shirts he'd left here after one of our all-nighters. I quickly shoved it under some others, and pulled out a long sleeved Henley to wear with my sweats.

I stiffened at his words. "Nothing. I told you five times, I'm tired."

"Yeah, well, I could see the way Carlisle was looking at you all night, like he was a starving man sitting in front of a huge steak dinner."

I rolled my eyes and walked into the bathroom, hoping he wouldn't follow. "Don't you think you're being a little over dramatic?"

"No, I sure as hell don't. Wendy told me how he follows you around like a dog, and that you let him."

I pulled my shirt up over my head and donned the one I was planning to sleep in. David showed up in the doorway to the bathroom and leaned on the doorframe. I could feel the heat rising up under my skin, and knew it would be flushing red.

"Wendy should mind her own fucking business," I said sardonically. "And, you shouldn't be gossiping about me behind my back. She has ulterior motives. Jesus!" She obviously wanted Cade and wanted him bad. "If anyone should be following anyone, I should be following *him*!"

"Something's different. You've changed."

I dropped my jeans, not caring that he was there. He'd seen me naked numerous times. I pulled on the sweats.

I nodded, grabbed a scrunchie, and wound it in my hair several times to secure it in a knot at the top of my head. "Yeah, maybe I have." I shrugged. "People change." I knew the tone in my voice was disinterested, disengaged and maybe if he didn't have that accusatory tone to his voice, I would have given a damn.

"Is *he* the change? Are you fucking him?" he asked forcefully. His face was angry and flushed. He was breathing hard with his fists clenched at his sides. I knew my next words were going to make him even more pissed, but figured it wouldn't matter what I said. He and Wendy had already judged me.

"Look, you need to relax. You're going to have a coronary," I said dryly, and went about pulling out my toothbrush.

"Brooklyn! Are. You. Fucking. Him?" he yelled at me.

"Yeah, right. Well, I'm sure you and your little partner in crime have already decided what I've done, so why does it matter what I say? I don't particularly feel like answering right now, so why don't you go ask Wendy? She seems to know everything." I shrugged and loaded my toothbrush with too much toothpaste. My indifferent demeanor was only making him more furious.

"He wants you, you know."

I shrugged, getting into the game now. He was pissing me off, making me feel more justified in building the wall between us. "Yeah, I know."

"Why are you being such a cold bitch? I came up here to be with you, and you couldn't care less that I'm here. You're more concerned with him than me!"

I sighed heavily, my anger finally coming to the surface and I threw my toothbrush into the sink. "Fuck you, David. In all the years we've been dating, shit like this has never come up, so why now? Frankly, I'm fucking tired of the little conspiracy theories that you and Wendy have cooked up." I turned, storming past him into the other room, then whirled around. "Are you sure you two still aren't in junior high? Yes! Cade and I spend a lot of time together, but we are the two principals in this film. Yes! We're friends. Yes! We care about each other. No! We aren't having sex! Satisfied?" I was breathing hard, tears of frustration welled up in my eyes. David came toward me and tried to put his arms around me, but I pulled away.

"Please don't touch me right now," I said, my eyes looking straight into his. I could see the regret flash across his face when he reached out to put his hands on my shoulders.

"Brook," he began, but I backed out of his arms. "I'm... Look, I'm sorry. I don't mean to be jealous but something about that bastard just makes me crazy." My heart hardened at his use of the derogatory name for Cade. "I love you, and all I want is to make love with you right now." He came up behind me, and pressed his pelvis into my ass. I could feel him getting hard against me.

I felt sick to my stomach, and the last person I wanted touching me now was David.

"You're kidding, right? You were screaming at me thirty seconds ago and now you expect me to roll over with my legs in the fucking air? Not likely."

I turned, and pushed him away. He looked at me with stunned eyes.

"But, it's been months."

"So what? I don't feel like it right now! In fact, I just want to be alone." I went to the end of the bed where he'd left his clothes, picked them up, and thrust them in his arms.

"What the fuck? You're kicking me out?"

"I guess. Just go back to L.A. We'll talk when I get back." I walked back into the bathroom, slammed the door, and picked up the toothbrush I'd thrown in the sink. I took a deep breath, and turned on the water. My chest was tight and, with the breath I'd sucked in, a sharp pain shot through me.

I rinsed the brush and put new toothpaste on it, and stared at my reflection. My eyes were wide, and there was a bright red flush on my skin. I was so screwed up, and David was so insensitive. Pawing at me all night, and in between that, buying into Wendy's lies.

Stupid Bitch. If she wanted Cade, she shouldn't have been causing problems between David and me, I thought.

I brushed my teeth and decided to take a shower, hoping that when I went back out into the other room, David would be gone. Thankfully, he was. My body started trembling. I didn't want to hurt David, but I just couldn't stand the thought of sex with him. He'd accused me of changing; maybe he was right. I'd hurt both of the men I cared about tonight, but I felt out of control of everything.

I glanced at the clock; it was almost midnight. Cade and I had been up for eighteen hours, and I was tired, but the look on his face when I left with David haunted me. My instincts told me what he'd been thinking, and I couldn't let him think that; not if there was the slightest chance it caused him pain.

I went to my jeans, and dug out my phone. It rang three times when he finally answered.

"Hey, are you okay?" he asked anxiously. "I didn't expect to hear from you anymore tonight."

"I'm fine. What are you doing?" I sat on the floor at the end of the bed, leaning up against it.

"Ethan is here. We're just having a drink and talking. What about you?"

"I just wanted to call you. David left," I whispered into the phone. I wasn't sure what I was expecting for a response, I just knew I needed Cade to know.

Silence.

"We got in a fight."

"I understand if you don't want to tell me, but um… what about?" He was hesitant and pensive. I could almost see his face just by the sound of his voice; the low tenor of it flowed like silk through the phone. He was so fucking sexy. "Uh, I mean, you looked… he was very attentive tonight."

"I guess he was too attentive for my tastes. We argued about a few things."

"Like what, Brook?"

"Apparently he and Wendy had a little soirée, and talked behind my back. I was tired and didn't want sex, and just…. *You*," the last word ripped from me.

"Oh." I could hear him breathing, and the sound of Ethan calling him from across the room. "I'm sorry."

"Hey, you didn't do anything, so don't apologize. Will Ethan be there long?"

"Not sure. Why? Do you need me?" The velvet timbre of his voice dropped another level, and it made me catch my breath.

My heart leapt in my chest. *You have no idea.*

"I don't want to interrupt you guys, but if he's leaving soon, can you—?"

"Yeah. I'll be right there."

"How—?"

"I just will. Ethan knows… well, he'll understand. Can I bring your birthday gift?" he asked hopefully.

I smiled, ran a hand through my hair and pulled a knee up to my chest. Leave it to Cade to make me feel better, with his sensitivity and thoughtfulness, once again. This was why I found David lacking now. After Cade, he seemed so much less than before, even though it wasn't his fault. Caden Carlisle was a damn tough act to follow… or precede. *Whatever*.

"Okay."

"Be right there." With that, the phone went dead.

Caden

I FLIPPED THE phone off, quickly pulled on a dark blue button-down over my rumpled T-shirt, and went to the bathroom to dampen my fingers and run them through my hair. God, there was nothing for it. I shrugged. Brook wouldn't bloody care anyway.

"You're leaving?" Ethan looked at me incredulously. "What the hell?'"

"That was Brooklyn," I said, as I bent to tie the laces on my Nikes.

"No shit. Why else would you be high-tailing out of here like your ass was on fire?" he raised an eyebrow and smirked. Grabbing the remote, I tossed it to him since he'd just started a beer.

"Yeah, I guess David left. Feel free to stay as long as you like."

His eyes widened at me. "What does that mean?"

I shrugged, trying not to get my hopes up. "I don't know. She just said they had a row."

"A what? What the hell is a row?"

"A fight, okay? An argument. Jesus," I laughed. "You should get out more."

"The hell I should. This is America! Talk *American*," Ethan teased.

I went to grab the guitar case from behind the chair in the corner. "No, it isn't. It's Canada, you wanker," I shot back, and Ethan grinned.

"Did she say what it was about?"

"Uh, no." I decided to keep it to myself. Brook didn't need anyone else to know unless she decided to tell the story herself.

"Well, it's her birthday, but you just got a gift from heaven. Have fun."

I shook my head at him in disbelief as I headed to the door. "It's not like that. We're friends."

"Yeah, sure you are. Who are you trying to convince?"

"No one. We *are* friends. Cheers," I said, and with that, I was out the door. It was chilly in Vancouver, since it was only early April, but I hardly noticed as I walked the two blocks to Brooklyn's hotel. Another of Martin's futile attempts to make sure I didn't cross the line. *What a bloody joke.* We were together constantly.

I walked through the lobby, and the concierge nodded at me. "Good evening, sir," he said. He knew me well enough. I was here more than I was at my own hotel.

"Good evening, Trent," I smiled as I rushed into the elevator. "How are you?"

My heart started to beat faster as I got closer to Brook's room, and finally I was at her door. I set the guitar to the side so she wouldn't see it when she opened the door, and then knocked very softly.

I could hear her coming to the door, and when she opened it, a big smile split her face. Suddenly, I found my arms full of her. I wanted to crush her to me, but restrained myself, and just hugged her back gently. She smelled all Brooklyn... shampoo, a light dusting of musky perfume and something slightly sweet. I turned my head into her neck, allowing myself the small pleasure of breathing her in.

"Thanks for coming. I hope Ethan wasn't mad," she said sheepishly as she moved backward into the room.

"Who bloody cares? It's your birthday, not his."

She smiled, and pushed her hair behind her ear on one side. "So are you going to stand in the doorway all damn night, or what?"

I reached to my right, and pulled the guitar in with me. I had a big red bow tied around the neck of the case, and her eyes lit up.

"Oh, my God! Really?"

The pleasure I felt at the look on her face was beyond words. My heart swelled with the love I felt, and her obvious joy at the gift, and she hadn't even opened it yet.

I walked toward her, and handed it to her. "Open it," I said softly.

Her right eyebrow raised and she bit her lip as she took it. "Well, it's either a guitar or you're totally creative in wrapping whatever it is."

I burst out laughing, and shoved my hands in the pockets of my jeans. "No, it is a guitar," I said stupidly. "I thought we'd be able to play together, and you said you wanted me to teach you some stuff, so I just thought..."

She'd moved to the bed and set the case down, flipped the locks and pushed open the red velvet lined case. The guitar was mahogany and very dark, with the wood grain visible on its shiny surface. It had been delivered to me, only two days earlier by Federal Express.

She raised her eyes to mine, as her hand went to her mouth. "Cade! Oh, my God, it's gorgeous!"

"More importantly, it sounds amazing. I tuned it for you." I sat down next to her, and she reached out to touch my cheek, so gently that I wanted to close my eyes. Her eyes were glassy and filled with tears.

"It's just... perfect," her voice sounded thick.

"Yeah. I wanted to give you something that you wouldn't get from anyone else."

She blinked a couple of times to push back the tears, and shook her head. "Only you would take the time to listen to me enough to understand what I really wanted. Thank you."

She took the guitar out of the case, and strummed across it. The perfect chord filled the room.

"You don't have to play it now. I know you're tired."

"Are you tired?"

I nodded. "Yeah, beat. Today was rough."

"Too tired to play a song for me?" she asked hopefully.

"You want me to play it before you do? It's yours."

"Yeah, but somehow it feels like it's *ours*, so yes, I'd love to hear you play. Just one song?"

I smiled, shedding my coat and kicking off my shoes, as was my habit when we hung out together. I pushed back on the bed until my back was resting against the headboard, and reached for the guitar.

"You know I can refuse you nothing." My words were telling, and a little too revealing. I tried to cover. "It is your birthday, after all."

"Nothing?" she said softly, and my heart thumped in my chest. She'd just had a fight with David but who knew how she'd feel in the cold light of day. I felt it best to ignore the comment and try to distract myself from the implied meaning of her question.

I softly strummed the guitar, and watched Brooklyn's face. She looked thoughtful, like she was thinking about something, and I longed to know what it was.

"Do you want to talk about what happened with David? I'll listen if you need to talk about it," I said over the chords I was playing; then started to pluck out some individual notes. Her eyes came up to meet mine, and she took a breath.

"Um… it's not that important. Just, I guess I was just tired, and I didn't want…" Brook bit her lip and went to the little refrigerator, pulling out a soda.

I nodded silently as I watched her back. She brought me a beer. I stopped strumming, and cracked it open to take a long pull. I felt a measure of satisfaction knowing what she was implying: it was as if a huge weight had been lifted from my chest, and I could suddenly breathe again. She told me on the phone that the argument also had something to do with me. I could only guess that he could sense the connection Brook and I shared, and was jealous. I couldn't bloody blame him, but knowing he had a right to be with her, only served to put me in hell. I decided not to press her, mostly because I didn't need the details to add to the torment I felt whenever he was in town. My imagination was bad enough.

"What should I sing? Something soft, so you can relax, and sleep?"

She crawled onto the bed next to me and curled up on her side, her head resting on the pillow next to me. "That sounds good."

Here was a golden opportunity. Brook and I connected with music, and this was a chance to tell her how I felt. I'd use the song to communicate what I couldn't talk to her about. I knew she was trying to push down her own feelings, and *close her eyes* to what was happening between us. I knew what I wanted to say, and which song to sing.

I picked out the first few notes of the bluesy tune, and then started to sing... words that said *I know you don't want to love me, and even though I know it, I can't stay away...*

I felt Brook's hand come out to rest on my leg just above my knee, and she moved closer to me on the bed. My heart started to jump around inside my chest, but I kept on singing. These were words I couldn't speak to her, even though I was dying inside.

She was closing her eyes every time she chose to ignore or fight the feelings I knew deep down in my gut that she had for me. I knew she was fighting falling in love with me. It would be easier not to, and I knew that, too, but she needed to know I would still be in her life... always waiting and hoping; no matter what.

When the last of the notes died out, I slid off the bed and moved to put the new guitar back in the case. I felt her eyes watching me until I came back to the bed and resumed my position next to her, only this time I laid down, and turned on my side toward her. I could drown in those deep blue eyes and I wanted to. I wanted this to be my life... not David's or any other man's. In my heart, she belonged to me.

I picked up her hand and brought it to my mouth, barely brushing my lips across the top of her knuckles. Her eyes became liquid as she looked at me. "I know you don't want to see it, but I know you can feel what's happening between us, Brook. It's real."

She slid the hand I'd kissed across my stomach, and snuggled in tighter, resting her head on my shoulder. She didn't utter a sound for at least ten minutes. I tightened my arms, and turned my face, so my lips were resting on her forehead. I kissed her softly and she nodded against my mouth.

"I know, but I'm scared."

"You don't need to be. You know, if you're going to marry me, you'll have to trust me," I said softly, waiting with bated breath for her response. I'd asked her to marry me before, but always in a flirty or teasing way. This time, I was serious. Seeing her with David, once again, had a way of strengthening my resolve. The seconds ticked by in silence before she finally spoke.

"I do. I trust you more than anyone in my life. That's part of the reason I'm scared."

As I drew in my breath, my chest rose and fell beneath her head. I ran my hand lightly down her arm, then back up to cup the back of her head, her luxurious hair sliding around my fingers. "It's late; I should go," I murmured quietly after a while.

"Why? I mean… we've spent lots of nights asleep together… so will you stay?"

Those were the most beautiful words she'd ever said to me, and I knew she wanted to fall asleep in my arms. A great river of contentment flowed through me.

"Okay, but let's get you beneath the covers before you fall asleep." She nodded, and moved from me to pull the covers back and crawl under them. I did the same, but first removing my button-down and my socks, but leaving on my jeans and t-shirt. I was there to take care of her, to make her feel safe… to offer comfort.

I flipped off the lamp, and she curled back into me when I gathered her close.

"Cade, thank you for everything today," she said softly in the darkness. "The guitar is very beautiful. I love it."

"You're welcome, love." I turned my head to place a soft kiss on her forehead. "My pleasure."

I felt my lids getting heavy as sleep came up to consume me. Brook's breathing was already soft and even, rushing against the skin of my neck as she slept. Now it was safe to tell her the words my heart was screaming... the most profound truth in my world.

"I love you... more than anything, Brook. I love you."

Chapter 1

It's a Wrap

Brooklyn

THE LAST WEEK of filming wrung me out emotionally... I didn't know whether I'd be capable of putting on a happy facade or if I'd get through the evening at all. This was my first movie and going in, I didn't know what to expect, but I did expect to fall apart. I kept telling myself to hold it together, but my insides were like jelly, and I felt like I would lose it at any moment. I'd still see Wendy, Jennifer, Ethan, and the rest of the gang in L.A., but I wouldn't see the one who mattered most. Cade would be halfway around the world.

I could feel my chest tighten, physically tighten like iron bands were winding around me. Considering the advances in modern communication, it would still feel like a million miles after all we'd been through together. I steadied myself as my boyfriend and I walked into the restaurant, then meshed into the throng of the familiar faces that had become like a second family.

David was here. Of course he was. He was stamping his claim on me as he always did; more so in the past months, especially when Cade was around. I closed my eyes and tried to steady my breathing.

Cade.

Coming to terms with the fact that I wouldn't see his gorgeous, encouraging face every day as I had for the past five months of production and pre-production, was more than difficult. I was failing miserably. He and I had become each other's lifeline in what was a somewhat terrifying experience to both of us. He was more experienced than I was, and I looked to him for what to expect and how to navigate this completely new world.

The fact that in a few short hours I'd be saying goodbye to him, made it hard to breathe. David's hand in mine offered no comfort as my eyes scanned the room for Cade's gaze. I noticed Jennifer by the bar, and wanted to talk to her.

"David... um, I'm gonna get a drink with Jen. Be back in a minute." I could see that he wanted to stick to my side like glue, but his presence had me feeling suffocated. I wished he wasn't here at all. Not tonight. I left him standing alone in the middle of the room as I moved toward her.

"Hey, Jen. Hard to believe it's really over, huh?" I could feel my voice catching as tears threatened to choke me.

She nodded, then hugged me. "Yeah, I love all of you guys, and sure, we will miss this, but we'll see each other all the time. Ethan is already planning our next get together! Game night will happen, but in L.A."

I swallowed the pain in my voice, and blinked my eyes several times to keep from making a huge fool of myself. I probably wouldn't be attending any parties for a while. Not until I had acclimated a little better to Cade's absence. Being around everyone would be a very painful reminder, and I was sure it would take me some time to adjust.

"Is everyone here?" I hoped she wouldn't understand what I was really asking as I searched for blue eyes in the crowd.

"I haven't seen Cade or Martin yet, but otherwise, yeah, I think so."

"Hmmm. I just want to get a chance to thank everyone, and you know, say a proper goodbye." I felt like an idiot as the babbling words fell from my mouth; uncomfortable with my lack of control over my emotions.

She looked at me knowingly, hesitating a bit before continuing. "Yeah, I think I do know, Brook. Everyone can see how much you and Cade mean to each other. You don't have to hide it. It's only natural that you'd get close to each other through this."

My breath caught, and my eyes filled with tears. "Everyone falls in love with him, don't they?"

She nodded. "Yes, but working so closely with him..." Her words trailed off.

"Yeah, we shared a lot of good moments together." My voice wavered despite my best effort. "I couldn't have done this without him; he's an amazing actor." I paused for a moment, not sure what else to say. He was a huge star and everyone knew how talented he was, I didn't need to reiterate.

"And, he's crazy about you," Jen said, squeezing my hand. "Distance won't change that."

I nodded, my chin jutting out as I swallowed tightly. "I didn't realize how much I'm going to miss him." I tried to brush the tears from my cheeks quickly so no one else would see. But I did realize. I'd been aware of it from very early on. "I wish David wasn't here tonight. I don't think I'll be able to really say goodbye to Cade properly with him hovering around like he does. This thing between us has been so unfair to Cade."

She looked at me for a moment before she spoke. "You didn't know he'd fall in love with you; it's not your fault, and I'm sure Cade doesn't blame you. Whatever it is between you, everyone noticed. There was no stopping it." Her eyes were watering, too.

I nodded as I looked at the ground and ran my hands through my hair. I couldn't look at her. *Cade in love with me?* I was nobody, and he was amazing; every girl's dream. Everyone wanted to be with him.

"Brook, try to get a moment alone with him. You'll regret it forever, if you don't. But, I'm sure you guys will keep in touch after this is over, and there is one more film." She smiled as she tried to reassure me. The books were a trilogy, and we'd for sure have one more movie, but we weren't sure about the third. That one fact was the only thing keeping me sane. But filming didn't begin for more than six months.

I was fidgety, standing next to Jen at the bar, when I saw David coming toward me. "I really care about him very much." My voice was uneven as I continued in a low, rushed tone. "I've known what was happening," I shrugged, "but I guess, didn't know how to stop it." I tried to speak quickly before David intruded on us.

God! Could he let me be with my friends for five fucking minutes? I'd gotten more and more impatient with him, the closer I got to Cade, and then, the guilt ate away at me.

Didn't he understand that tonight was going to be painful? He couldn't know how hard it was going to be, but still, I knew he didn't care. I tried to swallow the tightness in my throat, and blink back my tears so that he wouldn't see. He should know me better. I felt like my misery was shining like a beacon on my face.

"Hey, there you are, hon."

I tensed as he approached.

"Hi, Jennifer," David said.

Jen nodded to him. "It's nice to see you again, David. Brook, I'm gonna mingle. I think I just saw Cade come in over there by Dawson." She pointed toward the far end of the restaurant.

David tensed at my side, and his face tightened as he glanced down at me.

Just what I needed; his pissy mood would only make things worse. *God*, I asked myself, *why did he have to be here?*

My eyes scanned for Cade across the room. The last couple of times on set with him had been so emotional I wasn't sure either one of us would make it to the wrap party. But, when it came down to it, he was really the only reason I was here.

David or not, I had to talk to Cade before the end of this thing. I had to let him know what our time together meant to me. He made no secret of his feelings for me even though I'd struggled to keep mine at bay the entire time. But now, at the end, I couldn't let him believe I didn't care, or that being away from him would be easy for me.

The problem was, how was I going to tell him all I needed to say? Even if I could get away from David long enough, could I get through it without completely breaking down?

As I looked around for Cade, my mind wandered back on the last week or so. Knowing our time together was ending, it was weird, as if neither one of us knew how to act. We'd both been a little distant and uptight, on and off set. I guess we were both preparing to walk away from each other. Neither of us ever quite managed to come to terms with it, and I had been dreading this moment for weeks.

Up until recently, Cade and I had such an easy coexistence. We were both passionate people so we did have our little tiffs throughout filming, but neither one of us could stay mad at the other for long.

I mean, he'd become my best friend. It was only natural we'd argue sometimes because we were never afraid to piss each other off, but his presence alone could take the edge off of any situation that had me agitated. I felt comforted knowing I'd see him every day, and no matter what shit Martin threw at us, we'd get through it together. And, he accepted absolutely everything about me.

Unconditionally. It was mutual.

We gravitated toward each other constantly. When one of us was tense over an upcoming scene, we'd get dinner or just hang out. It was always Cade I wanted around. We even ended up falling asleep together in one another's rooms a few times after a long night of running lines. The most recent, being the night of my birthday; the same night I sent David packing.

Cade and I were comfortable and natural around each other. It was easy, despite the incredible sexual tension that flowed like an electric circuit between us. It didn't escape my notice how acutely aware of each other's discomfort we both were when David was around, but though David ranted at me, Cade understood. Every woman in the cast and crew ogled him, and he was completely oblivious to it all. He'd become a huge force in my life and now I didn't know how I'd cope with going back to my life in L.A., and being so far away from him, knowing if I called, he couldn't come over.

Jesus.

How would I be able to hide the pain or the loss? I didn't know if I was strong enough.

David was talking, and I didn't register what he said. "Hey, earth to Brooklyn! What's your deal? You're acting like you couldn't care less if I'm here!"

My eyes locked on Cade's face. He was staring straight back at me, and I could see my pain mirrored in his eyes. My heart thumped in my chest so loudly, I thought everyone around me could hear it. He looked so sad, and I was aching.

"Um... huh?" I asked, tearing my eyes away from Cade to look at him.

"Hullo?" David was angry which pissed me off. He was just going to have to fucking understand. What the hell was his deal anyway? He'd been a production assistant but was now an actor himself. Mid-list maybe, but still, he'd been in a couple of films so he should understand how close you get to people you practically live with for months on end. I didn't go all ballistic on him when he was on location so he could just back off.

"Look, I'm really sorry, but tonight is about saying goodbye to a lot of people who have become like family to me. I'm going to need to talk to them, and I may not be able to spend every second with you tonight. I'm sorry!" I glared at him. "I just wish you would have called before you flew up here. You should have just waited in L.A. Jesus, I'm going home tomorrow!"

He looked more pissed off than hurt by my words. If we were both being honest, he was more like a friend than a boyfriend. Maybe that isn't how he saw me, but especially during these last few months, that's how I was starting to see him.

These last few months... My mind screamed, and my face burned.

I met David when I was very young. I was infatuated with him at the time, but lately, I realized it was nothing more than a child's crush. He'd made it into more, but I was unclear if he really wanted me, or was more interested in all that went with being near my family. My aunt was a Hollywood agent with big connections, and he wanted them. End of story.

I withdrew my hand from his with a hard tug. "I'm going to talk to my friends. I'll find you later."

He huffed angrily as I walked away. But I didn't care. "Brook, this is bullshit!" he almost shouted, and stormed off in the opposite direction.

I was already looking back toward the bar where Cade had been the last time I'd seen him. He was gone, and my heart dropped to the pit of my stomach. I wandered through the crowd, mindlessly chatting with Ethan and the others, continually searching yet trying to not be obvious.

My mind wandered back to Cade's last night in Vancouver. I still had some scenes to shoot with Wendy and Jennifer, so he was finished a few days before me.

He'd been short tempered and upset all night, and after we finished shooting one of the more emotional scenes, he'd retreated into his trailer. I recognized his brooding mood, and knew he'd need to talk.

I went to find him after I'd changed out of my costume, and he opened the door immediately when I knocked. There were tears in his eyes, as he pulled me into his arms and close against his chest. He buried his face in my hair and inhaled deeply.

"Are...are you okay? Are you mad at me?" I whispered as his arms tightened around me.

"No Brook, I'm not mad." His face turned into my neck and buried his face in my hair. "It's just, I guess I'm feeling lost because we...well, this is almost over."

My heart ached, and my eyes closed.

"I know, me, too. I'm gonna miss, uh, everyone, so much." We both knew we were talking about each other, and nothing more.

I hugged him back hard, my hand moving up to hold the back of his head and play with the soft strands of his hair there. He smelled like heaven, his scent now so familiar, and I inhaled deeply.

"Let's watch a movie. Comedy? Action? Dark? What are you in the mood for?"

I gave him a quick, playful shove as we fell onto the sofa together. It brought a smile to his face as he looked at me. I leaned into him to rest my head on his shoulder as the movie started, and his arm fell easily across my knees.

"It doesn't matter as long as you're here," he murmured softly, as he used the remote to start the movie.

We snuggled closer as we watched a movie we'd watched ten times before on nights just like this. It was bittersweet and sad, as the memories washed over us, but I wouldn't trade a minute of it for anything in the world. I was going to lock those memories away in my heart to hold on to when we were apart.

We had a way of making each other feel better. We'd watch old movies, play guitar together, listen to music or talk well into the morning hours. The time we spent developing our characters and how they should relate to each other, became hard to distinguish from reality. It was a love story of epic proportions, but filled with a lot of angst and sexual tension. Cade had rewritten every scene from Ryan's perspective so he could draw on real emotions.

He was amazing.

At the audition when I read for Julia, I'd been so nervous. It was my first reading up against a big Hollywood star and I was literally on the verge of a panic attack. I'd read the books and wanted the part so badly. I wanted the emotions to be raw, and with Cade, it was easy. It was like we became those characters, we lived and breathed them the minute Martin said "action." The script was intense, and so was our connection. It just felt right. Meant to be. Right before I left, he grabbed my hand and met my eyes. *"You've got this,"* he'd mouthed, his back turned so the director wouldn't see.

I felt more in sync with Cade than I'd ever been with anyone in my life, and the vulnerability necessary for the film came easily. I literally cracked myself open. We both did. Cade was worried if we didn't dig deep it might come off as cheesy, and neither of us wanted that. We had to really trust each other to be that raw. *Raw*, I thought with a sigh. That was how I felt in this very moment.

I chewed on my lower lip as I watched the cast and crew laughing, and milling around the restaurant. I knew I should join them, but I wasn't feeling happy or sociable.

The end of the shoot had been hanging over me like a huge storm waiting to drown me for the past two weeks, and I was still feeling its effects.

Just three days ago, during the last rehearsal of the park scene, watching Cade, it stabbed me in the heart. He was screaming, and crying. My breath stopped. It was like the crew all disappeared, and there was no one on set but us. At the end of it, I was the one sobbing my eyes out. I couldn't stop. I wanted him to feel for me, the depth of emotions he was portraying for my character. This was the end and an uncontrollable sadness washed over me. I couldn't stop crying. When the scene was done, Cade heard me and rushed to my side. His own face damp with tears as he pulled me into his strong arms, which only made me cry harder.

"Brook, what are you doing here? What is it?" he asked desperately, his eyes searching my face. I felt so out of control, like something inside me had burst, and I just cried my heart out.

Cade touched my face, trying to wipe away the tears. "Sweetheart, tell me what's wrong!" His face was filled with pain as he searched my eyes with his.

I couldn't speak. All I could do was clutch his shirt and sob into his chest. He took me away to one of the trailers so he could console me in private. When the director tried to follow us, Cade put up his hand to stop him. "Martin, I'm sorry; please give us a few minutes. I'll be back if we need another take; I'm sorry," he said again.

"Is she okay?" he asked

"I'll take care of her," Cade said as his arms tightened around me again, but his words had me sobbing even harder. "She'll be fine."

When we got inside, he pulled me onto his lap, and wrapped his arms around me. He rubbed my back, stroked my hair, and kissed my forehead, over and over again, as I clung to his chest, sobbing softly into his shirt. We didn't speak, but after some time, I got control of myself and my sobs subsided to small hiccupping gasps.

"Cade, I'm s-sorry... your s-shirt." I sniffed.

His arms tightened slightly, and he sighed. "Love, you can drown me in your tears whenever you want." Then he kissed me so sweetly, so softly that I thought my heart would burst. He'd called me 'love' before. That sweet British-ism that was commonplace in his culture but made my heart stop each, and every time.

Afterward, we never talked about what had happened that night or why. We didn't need to. He knew why I was breaking, and it was clear he felt the same way. His strong arms around me, his kiss in my hair, the patient way he rubbed my back, told me all I needed to know.

Get a grip, Brooklyn, I told myself. You're never gonna make it through tonight if you keep this up.

I sat down at the bar and ordered a Coke. Gavin, the actor that played the father to Cade's character, was there. He smiled, came over, and put his arm around my shoulders. Though he'd only been on set for the last two weeks of filming, I'd gotten to know him pretty well. He was handsome, with a warm smile and sandy brown hair. He always had this look of understanding and compassion behind his blue eyes.

"How you holding up, honey?" he asked.

"Oh, you know," I attempted a weak smile, "I'll muddle through. I guess I wasn't prepared to feel so sad. I hope we'll stay in touch after we leave Vancouver." I felt my voice catch, and the tears begin to burn the back of my eyes again. I swallowed hard to try to maintain some semblance of control.

Gavin smiled, and rubbed my arm. "We will, Brook. How will you live without my gourmet pasta dinners?" He laughed. His character only had a couple of scenes in the first book, though the entire cast was on set to prep for the second film, and he'd made dinner a few times for those of us working. Every time it was pasta, and Cade came to call him 'Chef Boyardee.'

"No clue," I smiled softly through my tears, and took a sip from my glass.

"It's natural to feel sad at the wrap of a film that has been in production for a few months, and this being your first one, it's probably even more pronounced. Um... Brook?" He hesitated, and I heard the concern in his voice.

"What is it?" I wanted to know, but a feeling of dread washed over me.

"Well, I probably shouldn't say anything, but Cade seems..." Gavin paused. "Well, he's a complete wreck, and has been his last week on location. He won't talk to me, but I think he'll tell you what's bothering him." He cleared his throat. "He really needs y—" He broke off mid-sentence, and looked at me seriously. "Is Cade at your hotel this time?"

I flushed. He was, but since they put us in different hotels during filming, we didn't really tell anyone. I nodded.

"I'm surprised. I think he only came back to talk to you. Wrap parties are nothing special after so many films."

I frowned. Yes, I knew what was bothering Cade, because it was bothering me, too.

"Okay, Gavin," I shook my head, and touched his arm. "I'm pretty sure I know what's wrong, so yeah, I'll find him. I only saw him for a minute across the room when he first came in. Do you know where he went?"

He nodded slowly. "Out to the patio. I hope you can bring him back into the party."

I wasn't sure that was what Cade needed, but I smiled at Gavin regardless. "I'll do my best. Bartender, may I have a Heineken, please?"

I took my Coke and the beer in hand, then turned to walk outside, but paused to look back.

"Gavin, can you do me a small favor? David isn't keen on me spending any time alone with Cade, and he doesn't understand our relationship, so could you... um... keep him occupied?" I hesitated; my brow knitting. "Make sure he doesn't follow me out so Cade and I can talk?"

Gavin smiled knowingly; as if he knew exactly what I was trying to say. "Sure thing, sweet pea," he said.

"Thanks, I'll see you later," I said, heading back.

Cade was leaning over the balcony of the rooftop, looking out over the city. Lost in thought, he didn't hear me approach. My breath caught at how absolutely beautiful he was.

My Cade.

My heart was racing, hammering against my ribs like crazy. I knew it was selfish to think of him as mine and that I had no right, but I couldn't help it. Surely Julia would think of Ryan as hers, and honestly, it had all become a blur of emotion, and the implications were clear. Would I ever get through the coming days without seeing him, without being able to talk to him, or find excuses to touch him? I realized how his easy smiles, gentle wit, and calming presence had become such a big part of my life. And, how I always looked forward to seeing him every day.

Each time he was near, my heart raced. This wasn't the first time, but it was the first time I was trying to separate us from the characters we played on film.

I walked up quietly beside him, and nudged him with my shoulder, trying to speak but failing. The nudge. It was part of our script, but it had become us, as well.

Cade didn't look at me, so I tried again. "Hey you, what 'cha doing out here all by yourself?" I asked softly.

He shrugged ever so slightly, but still didn't say anything.

"I brought you something." I offered him the beer, and he took it, being careful not to touch my hand. I felt his misery without him saying one word.

"Cade, I didn't invite David tonight." Knowing his misery the night of my birthday, Cade should know I'd never invite David on our last night together.

Silence.

"Um..." I began, "he just showed up at the hotel right before I was leaving. Wendy must have told him about the party. I'm sorry." My heart ached when he didn't answer; just kept staring out over the edge of the balcony. "I'm very upset that he's here; I didn't want him here..." I let the words drop off as I stared at his profile. After a minute or two,

I couldn't take it anymore. "Say something." I turned my face toward him again. "Please, Cade."

"He has a right to be here."

"Then why does it feel like he's intruding?"

He turned to me, his expression was guarded, but intense. I knew him well enough to know that with the slightest push, it would all tumble out of him like water from a burst dam. His expression softened as he looked at me.

"You look beautiful tonight." His voice was like a caress.

The dress was a deep shade of blue that I knew he particularly liked on me. I had taken extra effort with my hair and makeup. This was the last time he'd see me before the promotional stuff started, and at this point we had no idea when that would entail. I wanted him to remember me like this.

Clearly, I wouldn't be able to keep my feelings from showing on my face, so I drew in a shaky breath and tried to calm myself, but looked straight ahead, over the rooftop's edge. "I wore this for you," I whispered. My throat was aching, and I knew Cade heard it in my voice.

Finally, I turned and had the courage to look into his eyes. His face twisted in pain.

"God, Brooklyn. I just... I can't do this!" He took a deep breath, his voice thick with emotion. "I can't say goodbye to you tonight. I don't want this to be over."

He shook his head in defeat as he looked at me with those deep blue eyes. My heart skipped a beat as his words hung between us. I couldn't bear to see his pain. I knew, in my heart, I was in love with him; so in love that it stole the very breath from my lungs. Still, I couldn't bring myself to tell him so. I wasn't sure if the feelings we felt throughout this whole process were really Brook and Cade, or just shadows of Julia and Ryan. I wanted, and needed, to be certain before we turned our lives upside down. All I knew for sure was that sadness was suffocating me, and I felt everything he'd just said.

"Why do we have to?" I asked achingly, as one tear slowly slipped from beneath my lashes. He lifted his eyes to mine hopefully, then reached over to wipe the tear away. I caught his hand with mine to stop him. If he touched me like that, I would crumble.

"You're right. This isn't the place for us to say goodbye."

"Uhhmmmm." I tried to clear the tears out of my voice before continuing, but my heart was breaking as they threatened to overflow. I couldn't let that happen. The tears would come in torrents tomorrow, but not now. Not here. "Why don't we go back in there and try to have a good time, like we always do? Then tomorrow, before my flight, I'll come to your room so we can talk." I reached out for his hand again, and he took mine between both of his. Electricity shot through me at his touch.

He stared at me unflinchingly, his heart pouring from his eyes. I could see he wanted to hold me, and I wanted to be in his arms more than anything. Others were watching us through the wall of glass between the restaurant and the patio, so all I could do was lean on him a little, and hope he knew I wished for more.

Even through all of this sadness, the pull palpable, the connection undeniable. Always undeniable.

"Yeah, we can do that. So much has been on my mind lately; I know I've been distant. I'm sorry. I should have stayed here last week, but to say I've been struggling is putting it mildly." His hand ran down the length of my arm and then rubbed the top of mine in a soft caress, and I nodded in silent understanding. "So you'll come by in the morning?"

"I promise."

Cade raised his hand to my face, his thumb brushing back and forth on my cheekbone as I pressed into his hand. I'd just postponed the hardest moment of my life for a few more precious hours.

He let go of my hand as we walked back into the room full of our friends. We were soon swallowed up, and surrounded. I actually had a decent time after I got control of my emotions, but caught Cade looking at me several times throughout the evening. He would give me a small, sad smile whenever his eyes would catch mine.

Yes, we had postponed the moment of our goodbye, but we both knew it was coming much too soon.

Chapter 2
If You're Not the One

Brooklyn

THE HARDEST PART of the evening came when Martin got up and asked Cade to sing a song or two. It wasn't bad enough he was beautiful, built and sensitive, he could act, and write music. Lethal, especially when he was so unaware at how incredible he was.

Everyone cheered as he asked Cade to come to the front of the room. My heart swelled; I was proud just to know him. He was very talented, and deserved every bit of adulation he was getting, and more. The lead singer from the band that had been playing moved off to the side as Martin took the microphone.

"Let's give our boy some encouragement, and maybe he'll do a song for us! Come on up here, Cade!" Martin encouraged him, motioning to bring Cade on stage. In my gut, I could feel how uncomfortable it made him to be the center of attention, and he resented Martin putting him on display. Especially after our talk, I knew the stage was the last place he'd want to be.

The room erupted with applause, and cheers as Ethan and Dawson pushed Cade forward. Dawson played a character named Harris, the boyfriend of Jennifer's character, Ellie. He'd become a good friend to both of us over the past months, and he was also a musician, so he and Cade had jammed at some of our cast parties. I was pretty sure Cade had confided many of his feelings about me with Dawson.

"Thank you. I'll sing, but just one, and not one of mine." He picked up a guitar, fastened the strap around his body then leaned back to talk to the band.

He turned back to the mic and looked out over the room. "Um, I've been on a few sets but many of you have become some of the best friends of my life, and this experience has meant the world to me. So, thank you. I'll never forget you." His eyes searched my face, and I held my breath. At least I'd get to look at him unhindered, without being obvious or ridiculed by David.

"This song is called," he cleared his throat, and hesitated. "Well, it's called," he paused for another second, "'If You're Not the One'."

I felt my heart stop.

Choosing to sing with just his acoustic guitar, he began, the soft sounds of his voice calling out to me. Jennifer came up to me and grabbed my hand. She squeezed as the strains of the song and Cade's soulful voice rose above the room. My eyes started to tear up as I listened to the words, and the intricate strains of the notes he plucked and strummed on the guitar.

Cade's beautiful voice filled the room as everyone fell silent. The words of the song spoke to me, and it was clear why he chose it. It asked the question, "If you're not the one, why do I love you so much? Not knowing the future, I wouldn't change it." My heart was screaming inside my chest, and I was certain I was visibly shaking.

"My God, Brook," Jen said, as I took a shaky breath. Clearly she knew he was singing to me, and probably so did most everyone else in the room.

As he sang, I was sure he could read the pain in my face as my eyes glossed over. My hand clutched at my chest like it would help me breathe. I listened as if my life depended on it, unable to tear my eyes from Cade's. Tears fell, and I didn't care who saw them. My hand went to my heart to try to stop the pain. I couldn't breathe; it hurt so badly.

A small sob escaped me as I struggled not to break down. Jennifer put her arm around me and leaned her head against mine, as many eyes looked between Cade and me. It was clear to everyone in the room that he was singing just to me. For the first time, I didn't care. My throat ached as I fought the pain.

I closed my eyes as more tears fell from my lashes. I knew I was going to break down any second. Still, I was frozen in place.

"If you're not made for me, then why do I feel this way? Why do I feel this way?" As the song faded out, it was like time stopped, and it was only Cade and I in the room. But it was Cade and I, and three hundred others.

Stunned silence.

Then the applause broke out, and I tried to join in, but I felt every pair of eyes on me.

I have to get out of here, I thought. *Now.*

That song said everything I knew we were both feeling. It told of Cade's anguish over David and not being able to be with me, crying out the agony of our impending separation, and the loss of not being able to be together in a moment that was killing us both. I wanted to die. I wanted to go to him, but I couldn't.

I ripped my eyes away. "Jen," I said as I turned to her. "I have to get out of here for a minute. I'm sorry," I said softly.

"I completely understand, Brook. Go."

As I hurried to the bathroom to collect myself, David came toward me with a pissed look plastered across his face. Jen stepped in to stop him, placing a hand on his arm. "David, Brook isn't feeling well. Give her a minute," she said sternly. I didn't wait to see his reaction as I took off.

I drew in several deep breaths to steady myself, went into one of the stalls, then sat down and put my head into my hands. *Breathe*, I thought. I just had to make it through a few more minutes. I tried to inhale, but it hurt.

I blinked back the tears, and prayed to God for the strength I needed. Finally, I was able to go to the sink, splash some water on the back of my neck, and take a few deep breaths to steady myself. I knew I had to get back to the party before anyone noticed I was gone. Before David's reaction got worse and he made a scene; if he hadn't exploded already.

As I made my way out of the bathroom, Cade was waiting in the hallway, leaning with his back against the opposite wall. He didn't say anything, but as I walked past his hand brushed down my arm. When his fingers reached mine, I let mine close around his for a few seconds, letting him know I understood the message he sent with the song.

My eyes met his for a brief second, and I knew I'd rather die than to see that pain on his beautiful face. He raked his hand through his dark gold hair, turned abruptly, and walked away. I stood frozen in place for a minute, finally making my way back into the crowd, and doing my best to appear normal when, in fact, I was shaken to the core.

For the remainder of the night, I talked to everyone I needed to talk to, and made sure to tell Martin thank you for giving me the opportunity to work on the movie. "Thank you for having faith in me,

Martin. I hope I didn't let you down." Both Cade and I had argued with him over and over, which, given this was my first movie, I would never have had the guts without Cade's support.

"Of course not, honey. You and Cade were better than I could have hoped. I'm grateful you two insisted on trying new things with some of the scenes. I owe you, big time." He was a little drunk, and though not affectionate by nature, hugged me goodbye before stumbling out the door to a waiting cab.

Everyone was filing out, and for the last time, through all of the goodbyes to others, my eyes searched for Cade. I hugged Ethan, Gavin, Wendy and Dawson goodbye. Dawson whispered in my ear as I hugged him.

"How you holding up, Brook?" I just looked at him, and gave a small shrug. "Find a way to talk to Cade. He is losing it."

I nodded slightly, my heart seizing again. "I have. I will again, I promise. Thank you for everything, Dawson. I'll miss you." He leaned in to kiss my cheek.

"Bye, Brook."

David was tugging me out, knowing full well I hadn't said goodbye to Cade. I saw him watching us from across the room, and I wanted desperately to go to him. He held my eyes, and pushed away from the bar he was leaning on to move toward us.

"Hello David, sorry I wasn't able to talk to you much tonight. Thanks for letting us borrow Brook these last months. It wouldn't have been the same without her." Always the gentleman, Cade said what was politically correct and included David in our conversation. As he spoke to David, his eyes were on me, only flickering to David's face once or twice.

Cade let out his breath as the corner of his mouth twitched in a half smile as his eyes came back to my face. It didn't go unnoticed by David, and I could sense the tension building between the two men. David couldn't wait to leave; evident by the way he was pulling on the back of my dress.

Not to give up our secret meeting in the morning, Cade made the pretense of telling me goodbye for the others' benefit. Everyone was watching us to see how it would go down, our on-set chemistry something that was speculated by many of the cast and crew to be an off-screen romance as well.

Cade took me in his arms and when he held me tight against him, his arms tight around my back, it felt like heaven. Breathing in his scent, I clung to him, my arms around his waist. *All I need are his arms around me*, I thought. He kissed me twice, once on the side of my face, and then my temple.

"I'm really going to miss you. Try to keep in touch if you can."

I felt my stomach lurch and my heart drop. Tears stung my eyes despite the fact that I would see him in the morning. I hugged him closer to me not wanting to let go. I nodded, the top of my head brushing his chin. "You have to know I'll miss you, too, so much," I said into his chest. I'd been close to him a lot over the past five months, held in his arms, kissed him, held on for dear life, both on set and off.

I took a trembling breath and forgot David standing behind me, forgot everyone but Cade, as I looked up into his deep blue eyes. "I couldn't have done this without you," I whispered. "Cade, the song, was so beautiful. Thank you." My voice cracked as he drew me back into his embrace.

"Oh, Brook," he whispered softly, so only I could hear. I felt his breath in my hair as he breathed me in, and his hand at the back of my head as his hold on me tightened. My hands clutched at his back and shoulders of their own volition, my fingers winding into the material of his shirt. Behind him, Sarah, who played his mother, Elyse, was crying softly, as she watched the two of us clinging to each other.

Slowly, Cade pulled my arms from around his waist, lightly kissed me on the mouth, and then each of my two hands. "Take care of yourself, love," he said.

I couldn't speak, but could only look at him with pleading eyes. I nodded, not able to tear my gaze from his. Cade kept my hand in his as David finally hauled me out, following behind us to the curb where the car waited. Cade's reluctant fingers fell away from mine as David shoved me inside.

I was shaking so hard, I thought my bones would break. Tears slipped from under my closed eyes and melted down my face. I turned toward the window, away from David as my heart broke. Hopefully, he wouldn't see the depth of my grief, as I struggled to get control of myself. I didn't need to worry. He was totally self-absorbed.

"Glad that fiasco is over! Do you think he slobbered you up enough?" David laughed in disgust. He tried to put his arm around me, and I hedged away from him. For God's sake, couldn't he see how badly I felt? I was breaking, and he didn't care why, though he could've been a little understanding.

"Please—just stop! I'm sorry, I wasn't prepared for any of this."

I was so mad at him for ruining the last night that I could spend close to Cade, which I knew wasn't fair of me. He was, after all, my boyfriend. I looked back at the curb as we drove off. Cade was standing in the street, staring after us with his arms wrapped around himself. The look on his face nearly killed me. Gavin walked up and put his arm around Cade's shoulders, but he remained frozen in place. I hated seeing him in pain. It was like a knife in my fragile heart, and I couldn't breathe. After a few minutes, I was able to collect myself enough to speak. "David," I cleared my throat, "I really want to be alone tonight. I have to pack up my things, and my flight leaves pretty early. I need some sleep. I'm wiped out." I found myself thankful that my manager had booked my flight long ago, so David and I wouldn't be on the same plane.

He looked at me with disdain. "Brook, I wanted you tonight," he said. "After the fiasco on your birthday."

Ugh! I thought. I couldn't bear the thought of it. It had been months since we'd been together like that, since before I started spending all of my time with Cade. Now, even though Cade and I had not touched like lovers, at least while not filming, I couldn't bear the thought of anyone else's hands on my body. So, what the fuck was I going to do now?

"Not tonight, David. I didn't expect you to be here, and frankly, it made things harder. This was very difficult for me, and your attitude only makes it worse." I could see this was going to be an argument, but I didn't care. "Driver, can you stop by Mr. Walker's hotel first, please?" I asked.

"Sure thing, miss," he answered.

"What? Are you saying I ruined your night with your costar?" His voice was taking on an ugly tone as he almost sneered at me. I tried to dismiss him. I put my head down, shaking it, and sucking in my breath.

"I'm not up for this tonight. If you care about me at all, you'll let me have some time to regroup. I'll be fine in a couple of days, but I'm emotionally spent, and really just need time to myself." I looked at him pleadingly. "Please try to understand."

"Are you meeting him tonight?" he yelled at me angrily.

"No, I'm not, but I can tell you one thing! If I told him that I needed some time to myself, he would give me what I asked... without question!" Cade always knew what I needed without me saying a word. "He respects me, values my mind, and really cares about what I want, he's interested in what I think about things!" I knew the pitch of my voice was rising so I tried to calm down. "You could learn something about how to treat women from him. I won't stand for you cutting him down. He's brilliant, talented, and the most decent human being that I know. He would have been a great friend to you, if you'd given him a damn chance," I retorted angrily. Now I was really pissed but at least I wasn't crying anymore.

"So sorry, I can't measure up to Mr. Perfect, Brooke. Sorry, I can't be friends with some prick who's trying to fuck my girlfriend behind my back! He's not some superhero... he's just a regular guy," he hissed at me.

Hardly, I thought. We'd pulled up to his hotel, and the driver was waiting. I took a deep breath and sighed deeply. What the hell was I doing trying to make him understand, anyway?

"Yeah, well, I'm *just a girl* who doesn't want to be with you tonight." His eyes widened and his face turned a mottled red. "I'll call you after a few days back in L.A. Goodnight." He stared at me for a few seconds, and huffed at me. "I said *goodnight*." As I glared at him, he finally got out of the car.

I put my head in my hands, and the tears started all over again. "Are you okay, Miss Halloway?" the driver asked with concern.

"Yes, thank you. It's just the end of a movie shoot, and I'm really going to miss these people. I've come to love some of them."

"Yes, we see a lot of you movie stars in Vancouver. Many get weepy at the end." He nodded in understanding and took me back to my hotel.

I went in through the back entrance by the kitchen on the off chance there would be fans waiting at the front. I was a complete unknown, but sometimes Cade was with me so normally there were at least a few. I couldn't take a confrontation with the fans or the press, especially not tonight.

I went straight to my room. Wendy texted, trying to get me to come to the bar for a drink or two, but I just needed to be alone before I completely fell to pieces. She probably wanted to talk because we hadn't had any time at the party, but I needed to be alone.

I shut the door behind me and shed my clothes, dropping them carelessly on the floor on my way to the large bathroom. I turned on the shower and stepped under the hot spray, letting the memories of Cade and the past months flood my mind and heart, as the water ran over my body. Soon, my tears were streaming down my face to mingle with the shower, and I was bracing against the shower walls sobbing.

Oh, God, help us be strong enough to get through tomorrow... and, however many days or months it will take to ease this loss, I prayed. It was hard to walk away from someone when he thinks he's in love with you especially when your heart is screaming that you're in love with him, too.

I had to put some space between us so I could figure out if these feelings were real. We had to be Cade and Brook... not Ryan and Julia. "Help us be us, just us. Let him love me for real. Please," I begged through my tears.

When I got control of the crying, and out of the shower, I put on my old sweats, and started to pack my bags, picking up my discarded clothes from the floor and shoving them into my suitcase. I looked around the room and couldn't help remembering all of the happy times Cade, me and the other cast members had spent in this hotel during filming. This room had been my home for five months. It was stupid, but it was all part of letting go, and it hurt.

My eyes were swollen and sleepy from all the tears, so I hoped I would be able to sleep without dreaming tonight. My phone buzzed, and I didn't want to see another hateful text from David or one begging me to come to the lobby from Wendy. Ping... Ping... it kept on pinging.

As I lay back on the bed after t was finished packing, I grabbed the phone, prepared to tell David to go straight to hell. I hesitated for one minute, and then when I looked at the phone, my heart stopped. The text wasn't from David.

It was from Cade.

Immediately, I flipped open the phone, anxious for his words.

I wish I could have spent more time with you tonight. I was only there for you, anyway. Will you still come to me in the morning?

I texted him back.

Of course, I'll be there. Nothing will keep me away. Thank you for the beautiful song.

I put the phone down and held my breath, turning out the light and crawling under the covers. How was I going to leave him tomorrow, when all I wanted were his arms around me forever?

Ping... Ping.

You were the most beautiful thing I'd ever seen tonight. Thank you for that memory and the dream I'll have when I close my eyes.

I felt new tears trickle down my cheeks as I curled into a ball on the bed. Fuck, I had to stop crying.

Why did he have to be so damn perfect? I didn't have the answer, but he was.

He was perfect. He could lift my heart out of my chest, whenever he wanted.

Chapter 3
Declaration

Brooklyn

THE SUN CAME up to find me tossing around in my bed. My heart was so heavy anticipating this last meeting with Cade, I'd hardly slept all night. Sure, there would be press junkets to promote the film, interviews, and several months from now, various premiers that we would both have to attend. But, what would happen to our relationship in those long months apart? I didn't want things to change, but that seemed an unrealistic expectation. I didn't even have a right to call it a relationship. I felt sick to my stomach.

I opened my phone about 7:30, and texted Cade.

> ***Hey, I'm up. My plane is at 10, and***
> ***my car is taking me to the airport***
> ***at 9. When do you leave?***

Within a minute my phone pinged.

Forty minutes. Can you come now?

My heart plummeted. I should have gotten up earlier.

I'll be down in a couple minutes.

This was it.

I picked up the gift I'd made for him, struggling one last time with whether I should give it to him or not. Maybe he'd think it was sophomoric and silly. It was a photo album and scrapbook of our time as Ryan and Julia. It included things from the parties we went to, cast jam sessions, and pretty much any picture I could get my hands on. There were matchbooks from restaurants we went to, napkins we'd written some script changes on, and ticket stubs from events we'd attended together. Even though it was hard for me to let go of some of those precious things I loved, it was my desperate attempt to make sure he didn't forget me.

I took a couple deep breaths and glanced at myself in the mirror. I looked as much like myself as possible, considering my sleepless night and river of tears. I ran my hand through my hair one more time, grabbed my sunglasses, and went to his room.

When I got there, I leaned my head on the door trying to center myself. I didn't want to let him see how badly this was affecting me, cause him more pain, or make him uncomfortable.

Slowly, I knocked on the door, and it opened within seconds. There he was.

A little dark under the eyes, but still gorgeous in jeans, a long sleeve black button down with the sleeves rolled halfway up his strong forearms. He was delicious; his hair tousled in the way I loved.

Distinctly, Cade. He's so fucking beautiful. My thoughts were full of him.

I didn't think I'd ever get enough of looking at him, especially since we had only minutes left. I tried to soak up everything, memorize every line of his body, and perfect features on his face. His eyes were just as hungry as he looked at me, but there was sadness there as well. He pulled me into the room and into his arms in one motion, which was where I wanted to be. Cade was where the world felt right.

"Brook..." he began.

"Shhh..." I whispered. "Just hold me. Please?"

I felt his arms tighten, and his lips press into my hair. "Whatever you want. I'll give you anything you want."

I just wanted to be close to him. To feel him breathe; take in his scent, feel his heart beating, and his strong arms around me. I tried to lock every single thing about him inside my heart one last time.

After a minute or so I pulled back, and looked up into his face. His eyes looked right through me like only he could do. I leaned up on my toes, and brushed the tip of my nose across his jaw and softly kissed along it. It was bold, and not something I'd have done before this, but I needed Cade to know how much I cared about him. "Mmm, you smell yummy," I said, and smiled at the obvious pleasure my words caused.

He smiled. "Hmph." He huffed in the way he always did when he got compliments. Like he didn't believe it really, but it still made him happy.

"Do you have a couple of minutes?" I asked. "I need to talk to you."

I paused for a second then took his hand before I pulled him down to sit beside me on the edge of the bed.

Cade didn't say anything, just looked down at our entwined hands, and rubbed both thumbs softly over my skin. Every little brush of his fingers on mine was like a thunderbolt, and I could tell he felt it, too.

His brows dropped over his eyes, and his mouth pursed as he slowly nodded. I drew a shaky breath at his expression. There was so much pain, and my heart constricted. I kept his hand in mine, rubbing my thumb along the top of it, and turned to look into his face.

"Cade." I took stock of my trembling voice and shallow breathing as I struggled to get the words out. "First, I want you to know that no one has ever touched my heart, or my soul in the way you have." I swallowed at the tightness in my throat. This was so hard.

My gaze dropped to our hands nervously, tears threatening to fall from my eyes, and my voice thickened with emotion. I'd never poured out my feelings to anyone like this before, but after the many times he'd told me he cared for me, he deserved to know how I felt about him. It didn't matter that it would have consequences for both of us.

"You're brilliant in so many ways; as an actor, and musician. It's been the greatest privilege of my life to work with you on my first film. You are so, so talented, and you've taught me more than I ever thought I needed to learn. I'll never be able to repay that." I cleared my throat in an effort to keep from full-on bawling.

"I know your career will only get bigger, and I'm going to follow all of it." I put my free hand over my eyes as I struggled with my emotions. I bit my lip to stop it's trembling, and continued. "Jesus, this is so hard." Cade squeezed both of my hands gently. "I'll always be watching you."

He moved a little as if to say something, and I put a finger to his lips as a tear fell from my eye. "I couldn't have done this with anyone else. You... brought me to life. Not just the character, but me. I've felt things with you, that... that I..." I stumbled over the words and shook my head, "...didn't even know were possible. I care about you more than you know."

I struggled to continue because I was crying softly. I sniffed back the tears as his hand tightened on mine again. "I'm really going to miss you." I felt a sob well up within my chest, threatening to break free. "I'll miss you, every day. I... um, I h-hope you'll al- always remember..." My voice caught, and to keep from sobbing I had to stop for a minute. I took a ragged breath, my throat seriously aching.

He brought my hand to his mouth to kiss my palm, his breath hot against my skin. "Oh, Brook..." he sighed. "This is the worst bloody moment of my life. It's hell."

I nodded. "I brought you something to remember me by, but please don't open it until you get back to London," I said, wiping away my tears with my free hand. I offered him a tumultuous smile, but I could barely manage it through my misery.

He took the package, and placed a hand lovingly on the top. His eyes closed, and he sighed heavily.

"I don't need anything to remind me of you. I won't forget a single detail, not a single second of our time together here," he said softly. "But, thank you for wanting to leave me with some part of you. It means the world to me."

When his eyes opened, he set the package on the bed then knelt down in front of me. One of his arms wrapped around my body, and the other came up to cup my face, his thumb caressing the line of my jaw. My skin tingled where he touched me, and my heart ached at the tears in his eyes. My shoulders started to shake with silent sobs. It hurt so fucking bad.

"Brook." His beautiful blue eyes stared right into my heart. "You've always been stronger than me. You control your feelings so much better, than I." The corners of his mouth lifted in a sad smile as his fingers brushed along my jaw.

I gave a little laugh through my tears. "I'm not feeling very strong right now, Cade." I took a shaky breath. "The only way I'm gonna get through this is to believe that we'll still keep in touch with each other. I feel so close to you. I don't want to lose that." A tear slipped from my lashes, and slid down my face.

"There will be things we'll need to do to promote the movie, so we'll be together again for some of it." His eyes searched my face as he spoke.

"I'm holding on to that. You're so important to me." I swallowed hard, and bit my lip against the pain.

"We will be together again, I promise. I don't know how I'll survive without seeing your beautiful face every day." I blushed at his words, and gave a shaky laugh, though my tears fell like rain.

I thought of my photo album gift, and knew now it was just what he would want.

"As the whole world will agree, you are the beautiful one." My eyes rose to his face. His strong features were flooded with a mixture of confusion, sadness, and denial.

He would never believe how extraordinary he was. He couldn't see that he was amazing to everyone who met him and even millions who hadn't. "I've always found you beautiful. From afar, I mean. When I watched your movies. But, who you are inside," I placed my hand on his heart, "is the most beautiful part of you." I tried to brush a tear away with the other. "I expected you to be so different then you turned out to be."

Suddenly his arms went around me, and my hands came around his forearms as we stared into each other's eyes.

"My God, Brook. I know you don't want me to say it, and I know

I have no right, but if I don't, it feels like I'll die right here." His voice broke on the words, and my heart stopped. "I'm *so* in love with you." He searched my face, trying to find an answer in my eyes. Tears were streaming down my cheeks as I put my hands up to hold his face.

"I love you…" he whispered, "and I don't care if I'm going to hell for saying it out loud." I could see how urgently he needed me to believe it. My heart thundered inside my chest, and my breath caught as I read the truth and emotion in his dark blue eyes.

"Cade." At that moment, he was the only thing that existed in my world. I breathed his name as I kissed his eyes, his nose, his cheeks, and forehead so softly. I opened my eyes, and moved my mouth down to his lips, hovering over his mouth.

Our kisses had always been so restrained. While passionate, so much was held back. We never really let ourselves kiss each other like I knew we both wanted to. I placed a feather light kiss on his lips, and I felt him draw in his breath, as his lips moved gently with mine. The moment of hesitation was wondrous: a pivotal moment in the fabric of my life, the precipice. If I jumped off, it either could kill me, or fill my wings and lift me up to heaven.

I knew this was the time to let Cade see my true feelings, and to take what I could of him while I had the chance. I could feel my body and my voice trembling, as I finally asked for what I'd been wanting for months.

"Cade, will you kiss me goodbye? As you… not Ryan," I whispered against his lips.

He understood what I wanted, and his mouth crushed down on mine instantly, our lips parted, our tongues melding in deep, slow perfection. It was everything… and it wasn't enough. As we kissed, we held each other tightly, our arms moving up and down each other's bodies, and into each other's hair, as our mouths devoured each other.

It was heaven. I never wanted the moment to end.

He pulled me closer, and I kissed him back so deeply that surely we would melt together. My tears and Cade's mingled on our cheeks. Our kisses softened, still passionate and reverent. We couldn't bear to separate, and continued to hold each other still placing little lingering clinging kisses on each other's mouths as his hands cupped my face and he brushed my tears away with the pads of his thumbs. He took my lower lip between both of his and sucked on it lightly. I sighed into him, our breath meshing as he rested his forehead on mine.

I didn't want to fight it anymore. I couldn't.

How could I have ever questioned my feelings for this man? I loved him so much it stole my breath.

"Jesus, Brook, you are so incredibly amazing. I'm so blessed to have met you and to have this time with you. You make me happier than I've ever been in my life." He paused when his voice thickened. "Leaving you is just... fucking killing me."

There was a knock on the door. "Mr. Carlisle, your car is downstairs."

Cade's hold tightened, as a sob broke free from my chest. He lifted his head, and paused to clear his throat. "Thank you, I'll be right down." He made his voice loud enough so the bellman could hear him on the other side of the door, but his hand stroked the back of my head as he kissed me on the temple, and placed several more soft, velvet kisses to my mouth.

Please don't go, my heart begged.

He leaned back on his haunches, and took my hands in his, kissing the insides of my wrists, then looked intently into my eyes. His eyes were sad and glassy.

"I've gotten you a gift as well. It's in the bedside drawer. Take it with you and open it on the plane, will you?" He brushed my hair back from my face and continued. "Know that we will always be connected, no matter what." He kissed my lips once more and caressed the side of my face with feather-light fingers. I pressed my cheek to his palm, tears squeezing out of my closed eyes as my shoulders started to shake, the sobs becoming too hard to quell.

"Brook, my love, please don't cry." His thumb brushed across my jaw. "I can't bear your tears."

He stood, turned from me, and put his hand up to cover his eyes as he cleared his throat again. I could see Cade struggling; could hear the tears in his voice. I watched him thread his fingers through his hair. After a moment, he picked up the package I'd given him then walked to where his bag and guitar waited by the door. He opened his carry-on, and placed my package inside before zipping it back up. He shrugged into his black leather jacket, and shoved his sunglasses on as he looked at me, the muscle visibly working in his jaw, his mouth tight as he took a deep breath.

"Cade, wait!"

I flew to him and he crushed me to his body. He kissed my mouth deeply, slowly; then softly sucking and nipping, as our mouths separated for the last time, his breath fanning out over my face. We clung to each other like we couldn't get close enough. I felt like my world was ending.

I rose up on tiptoe to kiss his jaw to whisper in his ear. "You are everything to me... and perfect. You're my perfect Ryan," I said as a final farewell, my voice breaking.

His arms tightened around me as he breathed in my scent and placed one last kiss in my hair. "And, you're forever, my beautiful

Julia. We'll always have this between us. Nothing or no one can take it from us." Then, he let go of me and went out the door before I could stop him.

I stood frozen in the spot he left me for what seemed like forever, my suddenly empty arms aching to hold him. Tears were streaming silently down my face, as I felt like the most important part of me had just disappeared.

I walked quickly to the window so I could catch one last glimpse of him as he left the hotel. I could see the limo waiting, and a minute later Cade was walking out to the car. He stopped as if he knew I was watching, and looked up at the window. He raised his hand to his lips and then toward me in a silent kiss as he got in the car.

The mass of fangirls who screamed his name didn't really know him, or that his kiss was meant for me alone. They'd built an illusion of him that wasn't who he really was. This was the first time I'd seen Cade ignore their pleas for pictures or autographs as he got straight into the car. A sure sign of the pain he must be feeling.

I watched until the car pulled out of sight, then fell on the bed as silent sobs racked my entire body. My hands dug into the bed covers, and I pulled in his scent from the pillows and sheets. I poured my broken heart into them. A few minutes later, I finally dragged in a tortured breath. "Oh, Cade," I cried, my shoulders still shaking with my grief.

If I needed any more proof that I was in love with him; this unspeakable sadness at losing him was enough.

Chapter 4
Circle of Us

Brooklyn

I MOVED, REMEMBERING the gift in the bedside table. I opened the single drawer to find a small box tied with a white ribbon. There was no card. I took it, and went back to my own room to gather up my bags. My flight was leaving in an hour, and I was cutting it way too close. There was a chance I'd miss my plane.

Wendy was waiting downstairs as I got out of the elevators.

"Hey Brook, you just missed Cade." She pointed over her shoulder toward the large revolving door that was the hotel entrance. I had my sunglasses on so she wouldn't see my red, swollen eyes. Her words hit a strange chord since he left almost forty-five minutes earlier.

"Yeah, I should have gotten down here earlier, but we said goodbye last night at the wrap party."

She looked at me, and raised her eyebrows. "Yes, we all saw *that*." The emphasis she put on the last word pissed me off. No doubt she'd be reporting back to David.

"Hmph." I snorted, trying to appear like it didn't matter if I missed Cade's departure. "Well, I'll text later to apologize for not being downstairs this morning. How did he look?" I eyed her cautiously for her expression.

Wendy had had a crush on Cade since before any of us hit the set, and I sometimes wondered if they'd hooked up once or twice during filming. She never came right out and said it, but I could see it in the seductive way she looked at him and was constantly asking where he was. I knew she was jealous of all the time he and I spent together, and tried to invite herself along on numerous occasions. Cade was too nice to deny her, but there were times he was clearly annoyed.

I noticed when I had scenes that didn't include Cade or voice-over work to do; she'd invited him to go out to eat, to a club, or shopping without inviting any of the rest of the cast. Cade hadn't done that more than once or twice, and always ended up inviting one or some of the rest of the cast to join them.

She'd always invited him out when I was within earshot, and I wondered what she was trying to prove. The guilty pangs of jealousy I always felt were doubly troubling. I was with David, and so I could hardly begrudge Cade being with someone else; even though my heart ached at the thought.

"He didn't say much, but well, he looked gorgeous, of course. He *is* Caden Carlisle," she gushed.

Seriously, DID she really just say that? Gag! I smirked a little. "Yeah, that he is," I said. And, he's mine, I thought selfishly, only to be nagged by that same thought about being tied to David.

But, Cade was the one I loved. I had no doubt anymore. The realization settled over me like a warm blanket despite the complication it caused with David. My thoughts were a mess as Wendy and I made our way out of the hotel to the car that the studio had sent to take us to the airport.

Wendy's obvious infatuation with Cade caused my stomach to churn, and I silently prayed I wouldn't have to listen to her blather on and on during the entire flight.

She was David's friend before I even knew her, and it hadn't bothered me when we all hung out together, or even if they'd done something together, but I was feeling weird now, like maybe there was more between her and Cade than she let on. I'd just admitted to myself that I was in love with him, which made me over sensitive to her sickening adoration.

The plane ride to L.A. was uneventful. I was itching to open Cade's gift but wanted to wait until I was completely alone. I knew whatever it was it had to be extremely personal, and no doubt would reduce me to a tearful mess, given the fragility of my emotions. I didn't want to risk breaking down in front of Wendy. I was cursed because my emotions showed easily on my features, and I wasn't strong enough to fight it right then. I'd have to wait until I was home.

She didn't need to know about it anyway. Wendy was fun to hang out with, but we didn't have one of those friendships where we confided every secret to each other. I wasn't sure if I could really trust her not to run right to Cade with anything she thought would rile up trouble. There were only two people I trusted that much, Cade and my brother, Nathan. I was shocked by my thoughts. I didn't trust David as much as I did Cade though I'd known him for years, and until five months ago, he was the closest person to me.

As the plane landed, I figured Cade was somewhere over the middle of the United States, like Chicago, and each passing second took him farther away from me. My head ached, my chest felt empty. I had to call my manager when I got back to see what she had lined up for me. Aso, my publicist would have worked out my promotional schedule. The best distraction would be to dive into more work, so I hoped Jeanne had some other auditions lined up. Another role or whatever it took to pass the time until I would see Cade again. Perhaps Martin would let us use some of the rushes to submit for other roles.

I did know there was a script waiting for me for some pop culture biopic that I'd need to read. Jeanne was adamant that I needed to audition for that one so I promised myself I'd do my best to delve into that in the next day or two. Tonight, I just wanted to hug my parents, walk my dog, and open Cade's present. My heart sped up a little at the thought. I closed my eyes as the memories of this morning in the hotel room overwhelmed me.

My phone vibrated in my bag causing my heart to lurch, anxious to see if would be Cade, but it was only David.

U back yet?

How romantic, I thought.

I had to find a way to distance myself from him, mostly because I was uncomfortable whenever we were together now. I didn't want to hurt him because he'd been a good friend over the years, but we really needed a break. He was a good person, but somewhere along the line, infatuation had been replaced with indifference, and sometimes, even irritation. I needed to figure out how to deal with David in a way that would facilitate us both moving on and yet, remaining friends. My parents and brother adored him, and that would pose a problem. I dreaded hurting him, and knew he wouldn't take it well.

No.

I sent a reply. I hoped he wouldn't bug me all night.

After the car dropped me at my house, I went inside, and took my bags up to my room. "Hey, Brooks!" I smiled at my brother's nickname for me. "Glad to have you home. Wanna go for a dip with me?" Though he was my brother, Nate was one of my best friends. His presence would be nice today. He'd keep me from worrying and feeling sad.

"Yeah, just give me a few minutes to get settled. Can you grab my other suitcase off the landing and bring it upstairs, please? Leave it by the door, and then I'll meet you out back, okay?"

"Sure, Sis!" He bounded out to the stoop to retrieve my suitcase.

I was thankful for the sunny weather. It rained so much in Vancouver, and the overcast skies felt gloomy. It was beautiful there, though, and I liked nothing more than taking walks by the water or taking the ferry to Granville Island. Cade and I spent some special moments doing that.

I ran up the stairs with my dog, Molly, following close on my heels. I threw my bag on the floor, and bent down to hug her and ruffle her black fur. She was a mutt; the vet said some sort of mix of Black Lab and Chow. She had fluffy jet-black hair, and her tail curled over the top of her butt like an umbrella.

I couldn't wait a second more so I sat down on the bed and pulled the small box with the white ribbon from my bag. My heart was jumping around in my chest so badly it almost hurt, but I was excited. I struggled with the little bow, my trembling fingers making the job even more difficult. The box was from Tiffany's. Whatever was inside was going to be precious.

I started to shake, and my eyes welled up as I opened the box, and peaked inside. My breath caught in my throat at the sight. Nestled inside was solid white gold bracelet inlaid with seven diamonds, and the initials R and J. It was an exact replica of the bracelet from the book series we were filming, and a similar one would be used on the promotional materials. No doubt, this one was the real deal. A million facets of light reflected off the beautiful stones, the center one being the largest. I wasn't a good judge of gem sizes, and I didn't care. The brilliant diamonds threw rainbows of reflection all around the room as I took it out of the box.

I took a shaky breath as I held it in my hand. It was heavy; solid white gold, and diamonds. He communicated with me on so many levels, no words were even necessary. Obviously, he couldn't give me one with our initials on it, but this was just as special to me. I knew the meaning behind it. And, I'd be able to wear it without questions from anyone, including the press.

Cade's words came back to me. "We'll always be connected." I closed my eyes, as my eyes welled up.

Cade. God, he was so incredibly perfect.

I went to my phone to send him a text, even though I knew his phone would be off as he flew across the country.

I love the bracelet. It's almost as beautiful as you are. I'll keep it with me always. I miss you so much already.

I grabbed a tissue, and told myself to pull it together.

I scrubbed the tears from my face. I couldn't cry continuously for the next six months, so I needed to get a fucking grip. I'm an actor! I'd better start acting, and now, I told myself. I smiled wryly at the irony of it. My character was easy, I could love Cade in the open, but now, as myself, I had to bury it deep inside, and it wouldn't be easy.

I set the box on top of the dresser, and dug through the drawers to find my bikini. I might as well enjoy some time with my brother. He was my best buddy, and I loved him dearly. We were fraternal twins, but he had different dreams than I did. Soon, he'd be going to UCLA for an engineering degree. He liked to build stuff and always had.

I donned my suit, grabbed a towel, and some sunscreen, then ran outside to find him.

"Hey! It's great to be home!" I started to lather up with the 40 SPF and then remembered that I didn't have to be pale anymore now that the movie shoot was finished. The movie was set in Boston, so they didn't want any of us, too tanned. A little color was fine, but not the deep tans that the California sun afforded. I could actually get some sun if I wanted to. I set the lotion down next to the lounge chair I settled down on.

Nate was lounging by the pool as I relaxed and turned up the music. He had on an indie rock station, which suited me. I lay back, realizing how exhausted I was... and my eyes were tired. Maybe I'd get a little sleep.

"Brook, how are you holding up?" he asked.

I lifted my head, and looked over at him. "What do you mean? I'm good, just really wiped out," I replied. It was the truth. It's amazing how exhausting crying gallons of tears could be.

"How was the party last night? Wendy called and said you were pretty messed up, and that you and David got into it."

My mouth thinned as I looked over at my brother. "Why would she do that?" I barely spoke to her last night; I thought, and I didn't openly fight with David until we were in the limo on the way back to the hotel.

"She didn't have a clue how I was last night we hardly even spoke at the party. I think, all things considered, that I made it through pretty well." I frowned behind my glasses.

"Hmmm. Um, how was it saying goodbye to Cade?" Nate asked hesitantly.

I was surprised, and my eyes opened wider. "What?" I asked.

"You heard me. Sorry if it's a sore spot, but I was a little worried about you. I didn't think you'd want David around for that party and was surprised when you asked him to come up there. Was it so you wouldn't have to be alone with Cade?"

"Nate." I was miffed. "First of all, I didn't ask David to come up to Vancouver; he just showed up. I would've rather he weren't there at all. He hung on me like an old shirt. And, yes, it did make it hard to get any time alone with anyone, let alone Cade." I put my glasses back on and tried to move on from the conversation.

"Okay, sis, I get it. You don't want to talk about Cade." He was very perceptive. At times, I was glad he had that ability, but not today.

"Look, Nathan," I used the long form of his name on purpose. "I love you, but what the fuck are you getting at?" I was exasperated.

"Nothing, I guess. I just figured you'd be a hot mess after that. It was obvious on my trips up there how close the two of you are."

I shrugged my shoulders and sighed. "Okay, you want to know the truth? I'll tell you." I sat up a little and looked at him. "Cade is a great actor and an amazing person. We developed these characters together. We didn't just read lines from the script. We worked really hard to make them everything they could be with all of the layers of pain and love that were needed to bring the book to life. I think that we did a damn good job of it."

Nate watched me with narrowed eyes.

"In the process, we learned a lot about each other, and we did get close. What do you want me to say? I can't pretend I don't care for him! He's one of my closest friends."

Nate's eyebrows raised, and he leaned his head back on his chaise, no longer looking at me. "Yeah. Sure, Brook. I thought you were going to tell me the truth," he mocked.

"I did. Are you asking if it was hard to say goodbye?" I could feel the emotions overwhelming me again. "Yeah, it was horrible. It was harder than anything I've ever had to do. Satisfied?" I lay back on the lounge chair, swallowed the pain and prayed he'd drop the subject.

"How did Cade take it with David there?" Nate kept pushing, and I realized he knew that David was a big issue last night.

I sighed. I could see Nate wasn't letting go of this until I spilled my guts.

"The whole thing was really hard, but we got through it. Barely. It was hard on Cade, too, and yes, it was difficult to say a proper goodbye with David there. Cade wasn't expecting him to show up, and I didn't even know to warn him. Isn't that what David intended; to keep Cade away from me, and stamp me with his brand? I was pissed, but Cade was a complete gentleman to David. Cade was hurting, but it was David who acted like an asshole. I felt like scratching his eyes out."

I kept my glasses on and my face toward the sun as I spoke. I sighed, and said more softly, "Nate, I care more about Cade than I ever intended. My whole world has revolved around him for the past several months, and I only began to realize how important he'd become toward the end of the shoot. I'd be lying if I said it was easy to leave him, it wasn't. It was hard for both of us." I turned on my side toward my brother.

"What happened?" Nate asked. He was contemplative, and didn't seem judgmental, so I kept talking.

"We arranged to meet privately for a while this morning." I could feel the emotion thicken my voice again, and I hated it. "We held each other and cried, okay? I'm not strong enough yet to really talk about it, but please don't tell David the details. I'm not sure how I'm feeling about things right now, and I need some time to sort it out."

"Cade's in love with you, Brook."

My eyes popped open, and my heart beat faster.

"You think?" I asked. Okay, here goes nothing. I decided to put it out there with my brother so I could be myself when I was with him. "I hope so, Nate. I hope so. The truth is, he's a huge star, and women are throwing themselves at him all the time. You should see it. It's embarrassing to watch."

Nate's eyes widened as he stared at me. I knew he expected me to slough that off with a laugh, but I couldn't. I just needed to get through the next months as best I could, and that meant I had to have at least one person close to me that knew the truth. Someone I trusted, and someone I could talk to about my feelings without feeling judged. That was my brother... he had always been my confidant. Even though he was a friend to David, blood was thicker than water.

Ping... Ping...

I hesitated to pick up the phone because I figured it was David or Wendy bugging me to go out somewhere. I just wanted to stay at home for a few days, absorb all that had happened, and if I were honest with myself, think about Cade. When I reluctantly looked at my phone, I saw Cade's name on the face of the phone.

Hey, just landed in New York. Another 8 hours until I get to London. Miss you more than I can say.

I smiled. It seemed silly to think Nate could hear the hammering of my heart, but it felt like he should be able to.

As I went to my room to get ready for bed, I thought about how tired Cade would have to be. The eight-hour time difference was just another painful reminder of the distance that separated us. He'd just be getting in, and it was morning in London. Tomorrow he would have serious jet lag if he didn't stay up for at least eight more hours.

***

IT WAS AFTER midnight when my mom came into my room to say goodnight. Nate and I both still lived at home. We were just eighteen, and while he was going to college, I hoped to do more films, though now, I wondered how weird it would seem without Cade.

"Hey baby," Mom said. "I saw your light was still on. Can I come in? We haven't had a chance to talk since you came back. It's been a long five months, and I've missed you."

"Oh, hey. Mom, yeah, sorry, it's just been an overwhelming few days. You know how it is. I didn't mean to hole up in my room, but I'm tired." I wasn't ready for one of her heavy discussions.

"Have you spoken to David since you've been home?" The bed gave way next to me as she sat down on its edge.

I sighed, and rolled my eyes simultaneously. "No. I really think I need a break from him, Mom." I saw her face tighten. She loved David like a son because he'd been around so much for the past couple of years.

"What does that mean, Brook? You guys have been together for a long time," she said.

"So what? Who do you know who ends up with their high school boyfriend? Besides, I'm confused over feelings I have for someone else," I said, more snark in my voice than I wanted. I stopped to look at her.

"Cade," she stated without a second thought. My eyebrows lifted as I watched her face for further reaction.

"Yeah. He's just so—" I couldn't find words good enough to describe him, "—amazing, I guess."

"I know he's handsome, Brook, but he's a huge star with women throwing themselves at him. How will you deal with that?" She watched my features intently as I got up and nervously moved around the room, pretending to put my things away.

"David's been in movies. Why haven't you lectured me about him, then?"

"Because you've known him and we know his family. Also, he's not from another country."

I groaned, and sat back down on the bed. "That crap doesn't matter at all, Mom."

"What makes Cade so amazing, anyway?"

So many things. I bit my lip as I tried to articulate his magnificence in a way that didn't make me sound like an idiot.

"He's just..." Again, I struggled for words. Whatever was between us seemed so personal, I wasn't ready to talk about it with my mother. "He's incredible. He's not full of himself like you'd expect. He's kind, brilliant, and so talented. Musically he's unbelievable and he's an amazing writer." I shrugged, and sighed the grinned. "He's tall, hot, and British. He's gorgeous."

She looked up at me with pursed lips. "Beauty is only skin deep, baby."

"Being beautiful is only a small part of him, and he doesn't even see himself like that. He's deep, you know? He has a very old soul, and he's taken the time to really know me. He cares about me, and took the time to get to know me better than anyone else in my life. It doesn't matter that I've only known him for six or seven months. I seriously think I'm in love with him, Mom."

She looked thoughtfully into my eyes, and rubbed my arm. "How does he feel about you? Did he say?" she asked. I knew she was skeptical. We had numerous talks about 'Hollywood men", and her misgivings about their intentions.

"Mom…" I was pacing back and forth, and I stopped, shaking my head and shrugging at the same time, "You'll never believe how difficult these last couple of weeks have been, knowing that we'd be leaving each other after filming ended." I stopped to clear the rising ache in my throat.

"Last night, he was so broken. We couldn't say goodbye because David showed up just before the party and I didn't have time to warn him. Cade is such a good person; he didn't get angry that David was there. He was so gracious, and it was David who acted like a jerk." I knew my mom didn't want to hear anything bad about David, but I continued anyway.

"Martin asked Cade to sing a song, and he did, but in a room of two hundred and fifty people, he was singing only to me. He found a way to communicate, even though David made it impossible for us to talk." As I looked up at her, my eyes were soft. She grabbed my hand and squeezed.

"This morning, I went to his room a few minutes before he left for the airport. Mom…" I looked at her as my voice cracked, "He told me he was in love with me. We hugged and cried, and honestly, I… I didn't want to let him go." Tears were running down my face now. "It felt like I was dying. Then, I get back here and I realized I didn't tell him I loved him back." I wiped at the tears with the back of my hand. "I'm such a bitch."

"Brook, you are obviously overwhelmed by all of this. Take a few days and see how you feel. This may all be a residual from your characters. Have you thought of that?" she asked softly.

A little sob escaped me. "Yeah, I have. That's what's holding me back from saying it. I want to make sure, but my heart is just breaking right now. It's like nothing I've ever felt, and I have to trust that."

"Give it some time, honey. And, maybe some space from him." She put her arm around me and gave me a hug.

"Isn't half the planet enough space?" I asked, anger replacing my sorrow. "Are you saying I shouldn't be in contact with him at all?" I couldn't believe she would suggest such a thing. "I can't do that to him, Mom. I won't make him feel like I don't care about him, it would kill him right now."

Ping...

My phone went off.

*Just landed at Heathrow. I'm in the car on the way home,
looking at the gift you gave me. It's perfect.
You're so beautiful. I miss you, love.*

My heart thumped in my chest as I returned my eyes to my mother.

She looked at me with sad eyes. "What will you say to David?" she asked, as she handed me a tissue.

"I'm not really sure, Mom." My lips tightened, and I shrugged. "But things have been really strained between us for quite a while. I feel guilty because I know I've backed away as I've gotten closer to Cade. After I have time to figure things out, I'll probably just tell him the truth. He has to realize that our feelings would change over the course of all this time as we've both grown up. I never thought I'd say this, but what I feel for Cade I can't imagine feeling for David."

I really wanted to call Cade. After a couple of minutes, I hinted that my mother should leave me alone. "Mom, would you mind? I really need to crash. I'm so tired; emotionally wasted."

"Sure, honey. I understand. I love you." She kissed me on the forehead then began to walk from the room, holding the door open as she turned back to me. "It's really good to have you back home."

When she left, I picked up my phone, and immediately pushed one on speed dial. "Hey, love," Cade answered on the first ring.

"How are you doing? I bet you're exhausted." I hoped he couldn't hear my stuffed up nose that was residual from the conversation with my mother.

"Yeah. Thank you for your gift. I love it." I could picture a soft smile on his gorgeous face.

"What did you do today?"

"Just flew home with Wendy. I couldn't open your gift until I got home. I didn't want to fall apart in front of her."

"I'm sorry, baby. You shouldn't have to fall apart. I love you, you know."

"Thank you for the bracelet. I loved it. It made me cry all over again. How did you get to be so perfect?" I wondered if he could hear the love pouring out of my voice.

"I'm not perfect. I wanted to use our initials, but I figured the Paparazzi would have a field day. I just didn't want you to forget me."

"Cade, you know that's not possible. I'll never forget you. It's just beautiful. I'll always wear it," I said, my voice thick with emotion as I wiped a tear off my face. "Um... did Wendy bother you in the lobby?"

I tried to change the subject so I could keep it together. The last thing he needed was me being a slobbery mess on the telephone.

"Not too bad. She wanted to get some coffee, and tried to hug me a lot." Cade laughed. "I couldn't get out of there bloody fast enough. Did you see me from the window? Were you watching?"

"Of course. I got my kiss. Thank you." I was smiling into the phone.

"Brook, speaking of kissing; the kisses today in the room were... *wow*." His voice was soft and husky. "I wanted to make love to you. I still do."

"Yes, I couldn't get close enough to you. I really want you, too." My breath caught at saying the words out loud.

"God, Brook. Tell me this is going to happen for us, or I'm going to go crazy," he said. I could tell from his exasperation he was running his hands through his hair.

"It's complicated, Cade..." I began.

"If you aren't going to be with me, I can't keep going through this hell. I can't bear more of what I've endured these past months. Don't you see that?"

"I never meant to put you through anything. I'm sorry. It's just... not that easy." My voice was wavering. I wanted to tell him that I loved him and end his suffering, but I couldn't before I figured out how to handle my relationship with David. I couldn't be with Cade until it was officially over with David.

"I know you didn't mean to hurt me, Brooklyn, but I just need you to make a decision; especially after yesterday morning. I know you love me, but if that isn't enough to make you leave him, it isn't. From my perspective, it's bloody inevitable." His voice was conflicted. "I don't have any choices when it comes to you."

My chest was tight, and I was having trouble breathing. I hated hurting him. Those words were in the script. *I don't have any choices when it comes to you.*

"Cade, I'll figure it out, okay? I promise." I had tears on my cheeks, and I wished I could crawl right through the phone to him. "Just give me some time."

"I'm sorry. Just - not knowing when we'll see each other next, it's unbearable." He sighed loudly. "Jesus, I'm so fucked up with this."

"I know, me, too." My voice caught on the words as I wiped at my tears. I felt panic rise inside. He could have anyone, why did he need to wait around for me to make a decision? "It hurts so much. Would it be easier if we didn't talk every day?" I heard his sharp intake of breath and I knew he misunderstood so I scrambled to continue. "I've considered that we might take a little space until we get acclimated to being away from each other. Otherwise, every time we talk, I'm going to cry all over again." God, I felt like someone had punched me in the stomach. "I know you're suffering, too, and it's killing me." A small sob broke from my chest before I could stop it.

"I don't know what the right thing is. I do know that I love hearing your voice, but yeah, it bloody hurts as well." Cade sighed heavily. "Don't cry, honey."

"I'll figure this out, Cade, okay?" I promised. "You need to get to bed, sweet boy. I'll be dreaming of you tonight," I whispered softly.

"Ugh, God, Brook!" he groaned, and I could tell he didn't want to hang up. After a short silence, he said, "I love you, babe, and miss you so much."

"Yeah, I miss you, too. You're all I think about. Sleep tight." As I hung up the phone, I knew he was probably hurt that I didn't say I loved him in return, but it didn't feel right to do it over the phone. I crawled into bed, and wrapped my arms tightly around my body. As I tried to push back the loneliness of not having Cade within minutes of me, tears slipped from my closed eyes.

Chapter 5

Misunderstood

Brooklyn

TIME PASSED AS it always does.

A week after I got home, Cade sent me a song for my iPod called "Gravity" by Sara Bareilles, without any message connected to it. But, the message was clear: I don't want to love you if we can't be together, but I can't fucking help it, and I will love you until I die. Cade was a musician, and music was a form of communication he excelled in, and he'd made his point, yet again.

The song was beautiful. I listened to it constantly. My heart swelled and started aching each time. I learned to play it on the guitar he'd given me for my birthday two months before. It had a way of calming me down, and closing the distance between us.

One thing was clear; I had to break up with David because of my longing for Cade. He'd been with me for such a long time, and it wouldn't be easy. Right or wrong, I was putting it off, and was to the point of avoiding him completely since my return from Vancouver. It was obvious he was getting agitated, which would only make things worse.

I kept busy with my friends, my agent, and managers. The studio people sent a list of promotional activities and photoshoots that would be done in the months leading up to the premieres. Cade and I had a few interviews, some together and some separately. We had the MTV award show at the end of May, the Entertainment Weekly Photoshoot in June, and then Vanity Fair photoshoot and Comic Con in July. I'd heard that Comic Con was a madhouse, and would be our first taste of the fans' reaction to the trailers for the movie. It all felt like a dream or someone else's life.

I knew I had to deal with the David situation before Cade came back to the States.

He and I kept in touch through phone calls or texts at least once a day. We Skyped a couple of times and it was those times I lived for. Cade being in the news, all over Twitter, and Facebook was becoming a problem for me. All I did was Google him. I wanted to know about him, but I was beginning to feel like a stalker, and some of that shit hurt. So I stopped. It was hard, but I forced myself to do it.

Every time either of us went anywhere, there were Paparazzi trying to shoot photos of us, and my agent warned it would only get worse. I should have been stoked for the attention. This was my first taste of fame, but after talking to Cade for hours, and hearing his disgust about how those people were so ruthless, stopping at nothing to get a photo op, and constantly twisted the truth, my opinion did a one-eighty.

When I'd signed on to the film, I knew nothing about the books or story at all, but through filming, it became more and more popular. Now it was freaking everywhere I looked.

Finally, three weeks after I returned from set, I gathered my courage and met David out for lunch to talk to him. He was grinning when he first arrived, but that didn't last long.

"How have you been Brook? It's good to see you, finally. I've missed you." He reached for my hand from across the table, and I let him take it.

"Thanks, David. You look good, too. Anything new with you?" I was hedging, struggling for a way to begin. The waitress came by for our order, and after she left, we sat looking at each other and after a few minutes of small talk, the strain between us elevated. Finally, I dove in.

"David, you've always been good to me, and you know I love you, right?" I reached for his hand again, and forced a small smile to my lips. Right in the middle of it, the Paparazzi popped up from behind a wall and snapped twenty shots in about half as many seconds. *What the fuck was that?* I blinked.

Great, this was just what I needed; the breakup scene on national magazine covers. I shook away the thought. I wasn't even popular. No one cared about me beyond that I was in a movie with a few big names.

"Yeah, I love you too, Brook, you know that." He smiled at me, and rubbed my fingers with his thumb. "I'm so glad you got over your infatuation with Carlisle. What a womanizer he turned out to be, huh?"

I tried to ignore the pain David's comments caused, but the truth was, I'd seen some photos of Cade out in London with his friends, and there were always willing women waiting in the wings. If I were honest, it made something hurt deep in pit of my stomach when I saw it. I glanced at my wrist. This would be the last time I didn't wear the bracelet Cade had given me. I pulled my other hand free of David's.

"He's not the source of our conversation today, okay?" I paused to organize my thoughts. "David, I don't know how to say this, so I'm just going to come out and say it." I took a deep breath. "You've been such an important part of my life, and I'll always care about you."

He put his hand up to stop me. "What the fuck is this Brook?" He exploded, causing people at other tables to glance at us. "You're dumping me?" he asked incredulously, then measurably lowered his voice. He was almost laughing, like it was such a ridiculous thing. "I should be the one dumping you for parading that peacock around in front of me like you've done. You humiliated me, and yet, I stayed with you."

I felt my face flush hot. "I wasn't parading him anywhere at all! He was, and is a good friend of mine, as you are." I stopped and looked in his eyes, but ended up shaking my head. "I hoped you'd also realized we have just grown apart, David." I looked at him with sadness in my heart. "What we had was more of a crush, and not really love. I wasn't old enough to do some of the things we did. I'm very sorry. I care about you, and I still want us to be friends." He looked angry, not broken, so hopefully he wouldn't suffer from this. "That's what we have been mostly. Friends."

His face was red, and I could see that he was ready to bolt out of the restaurant.

"Friends who fucked, you mean?" he spat.

I sighed. "David! There are Paparazzi around, so let's not make a scene, please. Bad press won't help either of us and aren't you in negotiations for a new movie right now?" He hesitated then visibly relaxed. "Let's just finish our lunch, and hug goodbye like we normally would. Please?"

His voice was bitter when he said, "I guess I shouldn't expect dramatic tears, and crying for this goodbye, right? Should I sing you a song?" he asked sarcastically.

I felt bad he was hurt, but he was starting to piss me off. "Stop acting like an asshole! It isn't going to change the way I feel." I sighed, softening my voice. "I'd still like to be friends. I never wanted to hurt you. Please believe that. I'm sorry."

He didn't say anything else as we finished our lunch, though neither of us ate much of anything. "I'm not sure how I'm feeling, or if I'll be able to be friends. I'll have to let you know after some time passes," he said. I was shocked at his change from rage to quiet contemplation.

"Okay, I respect that. Thank you for being so understanding." I reached out toward him to touch his cheek. He smiled weakly when I got up from the table. "Do you want to walk a little? I'm meeting Wendy for shopping. Why don't you join us? I really meant it when I said I wanted to stay friends."

David looked at me for a second then shook his head. He put on his sunglasses. "No. I better just go."

He stood up, and I stepped in to hug him goodbye. When I tried to give him a kiss on the cheek, he grabbed my head and turned to kiss me full on the mouth. Click, click, click, click went the cameras, faster than lightning. When he released me, he smiled an evil smile. *It was a fucking set up!* My mind shouted.

"Thanks a lot, David." I said, my lips tight when I jerked away from him. "You're such a prick!"

"My pleasure," he stated smugly. "Hope Mr. Wonderful enjoys those pictures. Let's just say they're my parting gift to the two of you."

"So much for being friends, I guess. You really make me sad." I scowled at him for a couple of seconds, upset by his actions. Of course, no paparazzi blitz was going on now. "Goodbye, David." I walked out of the restaurant, leaving him standing beside the table.

Of course, there would be photos on the Internet by that evening. I could see it now. "Julia forgetting Ryan with long-time boyfriend!" in the rag headlines. I groaned. Stupid, stupid, stupid!! I was furious with for getting into that position in the first place.

Cade hadn't pressed me to officially break up David since the first conversation when he asked me to make a decision, however, I knew he was anxiously waiting for the day when he could be open about his feelings.

He was spending a lot of time with his friends in London working on his music, and as the hype over the film grew, we were both in the news more and more. It was tough seeing each other's lives happening from a distance. I couldn't help it, from time to time, I still followed Cade online, and I knew he did the same. I just hoped he would have a sense of humor over these new photos. Ugh! I hated this feeling of dread that felt like it weighed a thousand pounds.

I decided to nip it in the bud, so took out my phone to text him. Not that he had ever pressured me for explanations, but I didn't want to hurt him.

Hey, you... miss you. Can we talk tonight?

I pressed send. I waited for about two hours before a response showed up on my phone.

Have a gig with a couple of my mates, so I can't talk now.
Call you when I can.
You're always on my mind.

It seemed to take longer for the responses lately. I reminded myself that it was 9:30 PM in London, so he was probably on some stage. My stomach always got tight wondering what Cade was doing with his evenings without me. He was a hot commodity; a lot of women wanted him. Why would he want me when he could have anyone? I fought back the feelings that made my stomach and my head ache and then told myself that he loved me. I replayed our last moments together, over and over in my head. Even looking forward to the nights when I could crawl in bed, wrap my arms around a pillow, and think of him without the intrusion of anyone or anything else.

The next day, I still hadn't heard from him, and I was starting to really panic. It wasn't like Cade to leave my messages unanswered, and I couldn't help feeling nervous and worried. My brother was the only person who knew about Cade and me besides my mom, so I went to find to him. I needed to talk.

He was in his room playing his Xbox, and looked up from the TV when I walked into his room. "Hey, sis, what's up?"

"Nate, I really need to talk about Cade. Do you have a few minutes?"

"Sure, Brooks." He put down the game, and patted the sofa next to him. I sat down beside him, absentmindedly flipping my phone around in my hands. I accidentally dropped it to the floor, and Nate stretched to pick it up.

I began to fiddle with the strands of my hair, still dark from filming. "You know Cade and I have been keeping in pretty close contact since he left. I guess this distance thing isn't very easy on me."

"Yeah?"

I tried to get to the point. "A couple of days ago, I met David to tell him I wanted to break up, and even though I didn't tell anyone about it, there were Paparazzi there." I hesitated.

A frown dropped Nate's brow. "Is there a point in here somewhere, Brook? You're going to have to get used to the media blitz. It will only get worse if you're lucky." He smirked at me.

I sat there wringing my hands, and he put one of his over them to stop me. I didn't give a shit about the movie, the possible fame, or anything else beyond Cade's misunderstanding.

"The point is, that at the end of it all, I tried to kiss him goodbye. I meant to kiss him on the cheek, but he twisted his head, and kissed me on the mouth."

His eyes got wider in realization. "Oh, I see. So, now there are pictures of you 'kissing' David, and you can't get Cade to answer you, right?"

"Yes, exactly." I got off the sofa to pace around the room. I couldn't get rid of my nervous energy. "Like I said, Cade and I never really defined our relationship, but I know those pictures will hurt him, Nate. Do you think he would distrust me that much, that he won't even call to ask me about it?"

"It depends. There is a history with David, Brook. Cade knows that."

Deep down, I knew he was right. Cade would immediately assume I'd changed my mind.

"Oh, God, I feel sick," I moaned, and I sank back down beside my brother.

"Why don't you text him? I guarantee he'll at least read it. Not sure if he'll answer." He reached out to touch my hand. "It depends on how upset he is. Brook, you really love this guy, don't you?"

"Yes," I said as I nodded. "More than I even want to. I'm agonizing over that he may be hurting or mad at me, and I didn't even do anything." I could feel the tears prick the backs of my eyes. "What should I say?"

"Just be honest. That's all you can do."

I struggled with what I'd say to Cade as I took out my phone.

How could I say it so he'd hear me? My life had gotten so much more complicated, and probably for the first time ever; I actually cared what someone thought about me. If someone had told me I'd be acting like this about someone else's reaction, or give away that much power over how I felt, I would have laughed.

Cade, we need to talk. I miss you. I'm worried. Please respond in some way.

I read the text to Nate, and after his nod of approval, hit send.

Soon my phone vibrated, and I could feel the blood rushing to my head, pounding until my brain hurt. My face felt hot, and my hands trembled. I was afraid to read it.

I saw that you made your choice, Brooklyn. Let's not make it harder than it is. I understand, but I'm not ready to talk. I don't know if I ever can.

My heart lurched in my chest.

"Oh no, Nate!" My heart sped up so fast I thought it would fly right out of my chest. The heat in my face began to hurt, and my lungs constricted. "He thinks I decided I didn't want him! How? How can he do that without talking to me?" The pain and panic were clear in my voice.

My brother seemed to be at a loss for words, and he just looked at me, in shock.

Cade, don't do this. It's not what you think. Let me explain. Please.

I couldn't ever remember feeling this flustered or filled with panic in my life.

Nate put a hand on my shoulder. "What's he saying?" he asked.

"He won't let me explain," I said softly, my eyes welling with tears.

Not long after, my phone vibrated in my hand again.

Brook, let's not drag it out, please.
I understand it was only
about the movie for you, but it was so much
more for me. I need some space to deal. Sorry.

Chapter 6
Damage Control

Brooklyn

I STARTED SHAKING so badly that Nate stood up to take a hold of me. His arms around me were the only thing keeping me from falling. *What was I going to do?*

Damn David for doing this, and damn Cade for not giving me a chance to explain!

I felt angry and frustrated; the type of frustration that made tears impossible to hold back. I pulled away from my brother to frantically pace around his room. My mind was racing, my heart pounding, as I struggled to figure out what to do. Then it dawned on me.

"Nate, I have to find him. Now. He's thinking the wrong thing and he won't answer his freaking phone."

"You're going to England?" His face held a stunned expression. He followed me into my room, and watched me pull my suitcase from my closet. "Isn't that kind of drastic?" Nate asked.

No, it was necessary.

I was so mad, but it was more than anger, I was desperate to make

Cade understand the truth of what happened. I ignored my brother, and called my manager. She would book me a flight to London right away. When the call ended I pulled out my suitcase, and started packing.

"Will you tell mom and dad where I went, please?"

He looked at me as if I was crazy. "Hell, no, I won't! Dad would kick my ass if I let you run off halfway around the world by yourself. I'm coming along. Call Jeanie back and have her get me a ticket, too." He left the room in whirlwind. I stood frozen for a minute after he rushed out to go pack his own bags. He was amazing, and I couldn't ask for a better brother.

On the long flight to London, I tried to sleep, but I was too jacked up. I worried over how I'd find Cade once I got there and what his reaction might be. If I called him, chances were he wouldn't answer, so how would I find him? I bit my lip as I considered my options. Gavin could help me because he and Cade had become good friends. When we landed I called him from the customs line.

"Gavin, it's me, Brooklyn."

"Hey, Brook! It's good to hear from you, how have you been?" His voice was warm.

"Not so great. I have to find Cade. I don't want him to know that I'm in London, until he sees me here." I spoke too fast, and couldn't hide the desperation in my voice.

"Brook, you're in London? Is something wrong?" His voice was laced with concern.

"I'm sorry, Gavin. I don't have time to tell you the whole story, but to summarize, Cade thinks I was kissing David and he won't let me explain."

"David... your boyfriend?"

My heart sank. This is the same thing I'd face with Cade if I found him. "I was breaking up with him! Paparazzi took some pictures, Cade saw them, and now he won't answer his phone. He texted and said he needed space."

"I guess a lot has happened in the last few weeks, huh? Maybe that's what he needs, love," he said quietly.

"But... he doesn't know the truth. You know how stubborn he can be. After I tell him, then I'll give him all the damn space he needs, but I can't have him thinking that I would do that." I felt defeated. Jesus, he has to listen to me. "Not after... how we left things." I could feel my throat start to thicken as I put a hand to my forehead. The customs line was moving and the people weaving around were watching me tear up. Eyes were anxious, and I was thanking God news about the film hadn't hit the UK yet.

"I'm a huge mess, aren't I?" I said in disgust.

"Because you're in love, Brook," Gavin said quietly.

"Is it that obvious?" I tried to joke, but my heart wasn't in it.

"It has been for quite a while now, sweetie," Gavin replied.

"Yeah, but I haven't told him how I feel. It's been a huge mistake, and I need to find him and make him understand. I can't lose him, Gavin." My voice was shaking, my eyes closed in pain. I was certain I sounded desperate, and I didn't care. God, he was never really mine, but I felt like I lost him. "Please, will you help me find him?"

"I guess I can text him and ask him where he'll be. Maybe tell him I'm coming to London and want to see him." Gavin was a little hesitant.

"Would you? Can you say you're already here? I don't want to wait another twenty-four hours to get to him. I'm sorry for involving you, Gavin, I just..." I took a shaky breath. "I seriously didn't know what else to do."

"Are you there alone? It's a big, scary city."

"No, my brother came with me. He's my best bud." I smiled a little.

"Okay, Brook. I'll call you back in a few minutes. Let me see what I can do."

Soon, we were through customs and Nathan was getting the bags from the claim area. I took the time to run to the bathroom. When I looked at myself in the mirror, I knew I'd have to pull myself together and look somewhat normal when I went to find Cade. I didn't want to seem shaken and worried, or worse, clingy. I had to be matter of fact, and just make him see the truth. It would work out. It had to.

I ran my hands through my hair. I looked horrible; pale with dark circles under my eyes and my hair all messy. I groaned and went to find Nate. I managed to make it through the airport without anyone recognizing me, again thankful this was London and not L.A. A couple of girls followed us out, trying to walk beside me to get a better look at my face, but I lowered my head and hid behind my hair until we got in the taxi.

My phone rang and I picked up Gavin's call. "Hey," I said as I answered.

"Brook, Cade said he and his friend, Daniel, are going to open mic night at a pub called Harrington's in Hampton tonight. Do you know where that is?"

"No, but we're taking a cab, so maybe the driver will know. I have to find a hotel where I can clean up first. Um... did he say what time they'd be there?" I asked. My heart sped up knowing that in only a few short hours, I'd see Cade.

"He said not before ten." I looked at my watch. It was a little before six, so I had some time. In L.A. time was only 10 am. "Try to get a nap today, okay?" Gavin said in a very fatherly voice.

"I will. Thanks, Dad," I said, and smiled into the phone. "I really appreciate your help, Gavin. You're a life saver and a good friend."

"I hope Cade isn't pissed at me." He sighed. "But I'm only doing it for his own damn good." He laughed.

"Thanks. I'll let you know what happens. Love you," I said.

"You too, honey."

I told the driver to take us to a nice hotel in Hampton, and was relieved when we finally arrived. Nathan checked us in, and helped me take my bag to my room. I was restless, and though I needed rest, I didn't feel calm enough to nap. Nate went to his own room, and I wasn't able to lie there staring at the ceiling for hours without going completely nuts. I bolted off of the bed and out of the hotel room to explore the city around the hotel.

There were a variety of trendy shops nearby, and I decided to spend the time buying a new outfit, and getting my hair and makeup done. If nothing else, it would boost my confidence and give me a shot of much-needed courage.

I found a little fitted, sexy, black dress, a black leather jacket with three quarter length sleeves, and some strappy heels. I wanted to look amazing. I needed to knock him flat on his ass. I smiled a secret smile to myself as it occurred to me that if things went well, we'd be together tonight. Finally.

The afternoon passed in a blur. I found myself staring at my reflection in the mirror just minutes before it was time for Nathan and I to go to the club.

My hair was done in a wild style with more curls than I normally wore, and fuller. It looked like it was windblown, and sexier.

Sexy bed hair. I smiled to myself. That was my personal description of how Cade's hair always looked. My make-up was more pronounced, smoky eyes; heavy on the liner, with darker lip gloss, and flushed cheeks. The darkness of my lashes and hair made my aqua eyes pop.

When I opened my room door for my brother, he stared at me for a few seconds. "Wow! You look great, sis! Cade doesn't stand a chance." Nate whistled, and then winked. Okay, that wasn't weird at all, but I knew he was just trying to make me feel good about myself.

"Thanks, dude," I said. "I need all the confidence I can muster." I looked at myself critically in the mirror one last time, and tried to see myself as Cade's would when he saw me.

The dress was low cut, showing the top swells of my breasts clearly visible above the top of the bodice. The short skirt along with the high heels made my legs look really long. I had on black hose and the fitted leather jacket pulled in at my waist, emphasizing my hourglass figure. And, the precious RJ bracelet was securely fastened around my wrist. I definitely look like a woman tonight, I thought with satisfaction.

"That's some bracelet, sis," he said, pointing to my wrist. "Are you sure it's safe to wear it?"

"Well, it's safer to wear it, than not. Tonight anyway," I said quietly as I touched it lovingly. "Besides, I never take it off. Cade gave it to me."

Nate lifted my hand and looked at it. "The letters are wrong, right?"

"No. It's from the movie. It represents our characters."

Nate raised his eyebrows as an expression of astonishment over took his features. He mouthed the word 'wow' but no sound came out.

I felt my stomach flutter. *Could I really be this nervous?*

This is Cade. He knows me better than anyone, and he loves me. He'll understand. I took a deep breath.

"Nate are you ready? It's 9:45 and I want to get there, already." I grabbed my clutch purse, and walked to the door. "I'm jumping out of my skin." I smoothed my dress and let my hand rest on my fluttering stomach.

Harrington's was hopping and bigger than I expected. The crowd was an eclectic mix of all ages; boisterous and loud except when someone was on stage. My eyes scanned the crowd for Cade, but I didn't see him. My heart was in my throat. I was nervous, but my plan was to crawl onto his lap, and tell him I loved him. Just him.

Simple, right? Yeah.

We made our way to the bar and ordered a couple of drinks. I wasn't sure what the drinking age was in London, but the bartender didn't even hesitate to serve us. Men were looking me over, and one came up to me and put his hand on the back of my waist.

"Hey, love, can I buy you a drink?" He was attractive but I hardly noticed; my eyes kept scanning the room for Cade.

"Um... no thank you, I'm with someone." I smiled at him, and turned to move away.

"Well, he's a lucky bloke," the man mumbled as I left him.

Then I saw Cade.

He was moving up to the stage getting ready to sing, and the crowd was screaming. I sat at the back of the bar, and watched as they quieted down when he began his song. He was singing a song he'd been working on during filming, and playing acoustic guitar. I'd heard him sing it before, but this time, he seemed more emotional about the song. He seemed sad. Looking at him like that, tortured artist that he was, I loved him so much I couldn't even breathe.

Jesus, he's beautiful.

My heart thumped in my chest as I watched, knowing that in minutes, I would go to him.

After he finished, the entire place erupted in a huge mass of applause. I was amazed that even though he was who he was, no one treated him like a celebrity. That wouldn't happen in L.A. Cade put down his guitar on the side of the stage, and went back to a table near the front. I'd met Daniel Mayfield and his girlfriend when they made a trip to Vancouver to see Cade a few months into filming. Both guys were at the table along with a couple of other women I didn't recognize. One of them immediately stood up to hug and kiss Cade when he made it back to the table. While he didn't stick his tongue down her throat and yank her to him, he didn't exactly push her away.

My heart stopped, and I felt sick to my stomach. I literally thought I would vomit.

So, this is what I get for coming all the way over here to pour out my heart?

My whole body began to tremble, as I bowed my head, trying tried to get control of my emotions.

Nate sensed me tensing up, and he'd also witnessed the scene at Cade's table. "Brook... maybe we should just go."

"*No.*" My head came up to look into Nate's worried face. I shook my head. "No, I came here to confront him, and that's what I'm going to do. He needs to at least see that I'm here." I swallowed hard, trying desperately to clear the lump of emotion rising in my throat.

I set my drink down, and made my way through the crowd. Men were checking me out, and many were trying to speak to me, but I kept moving toward the table at the front of the room. Cade was laughing and talking to Daniel, and one of the women at the table, so he didn't see me coming. I walked right up to his table, and stopped directly in his eye line.

I waited until he noticed me.

He stopped mid-sentence and stared at me, completely stunned.

"Brook?" He gaped at me. "What are you doing here? You look… incredible." He started to rise when the woman to his right grabbed his arm.

My eyes went to her face and then back to Cade's. My jaw jutted out against my will. I could see the panic behind his eyes when he realized what was going through my mind. "Brook…" he began. I put up a hand to stop him.

I swallowed. "Um… apparently what I'm doing, is seeing things I needed to see."

He looked all kinds of uncomfortable. The woman next to him looked me up and down, and put a hand on his arm possessively. She was pretty, a blonde, but bitchy looking.

"Who is she, Cade?" she asked him.

I raised my eyebrows in challenge. "Yeah, who am I, indeed?"

He was speechless, frozen in place, as he met my gaze unflinchingly.

"Can I borrow your guitar for a minute?" He continued to look at me, his eyes burning into me. It was almost as if he was touching me. His brow creased as he struggled to speak. "Okay, I'll take that as a yes," I murmured, tearing my eyes from his and turning away.

I walked closer and picked up his guitar, then taking it with me, up to the stage. I asked the MC if I could play a song, explaining that I wasn't able to stay long. He nodded, and moved me up the list and motioned for me to sit down on the bench sitting in the middle of the stage. I looked back at Cade as I readied the guitar on my lap; he was taking in my dress, my legs in the stockings and high-heeled shoes.

When he brought his eyes back to mine, he stared straight into my face without wavering.

The look of shock on his face would have been amusing if the situation wasn't what so fucking heartbreaking. The woman next to him was trying to get him to talk, tugging on his arm. He shrugged her off, and continued to look at me. It was as if he'd never seen me before.

The crowd silenced when I adjusted the microphone down to my level. It whined and screeched with feedback, making me wince. A few men whistled and hooted at me, but I barely noticed.

"Hi." I didn't feel it necessary to say my name. "Um… I'd like to play a song for you called 'Gravity'. It was written by a new American artist, Sara Bareilles, and it's about not having choices when it comes to love. Someone I care about introduced it to me, and the lyrics have real meaning in my life." I cleared my throat as emotions began to flood my heart.

Cade's eyes widened when I said the name of the song and he swallowed hard. He leaned back in his chair, and brought his hand up to his chin.

My heart thumped in my chest, and my stomach twisted into knots. My hands were shaking so badly, I wasn't sure if I could play. "I hope you like it."

I didn't know if I'd be able to get through it, but I had to try.

I strummed out the first six bars of the introduction, and looked directly at him as I started to sing

He never took his eyes off me for the entire song. I could see the pain in his face, and it hurt me. My throat ached so much that I could hear tears in my own voice; so much, I had to look away a couple of times to keep from breaking down.

Cade frowned while he watched, the muscles along his jaw clenched as he listened to the words he knew only too well. It was clear he was upset because he kept running his hands through his hair. Usually, I adored it when he did that.

It became harder and harder to get the words out as the song progressed, and *as* the final few notes were fading out, and I felt a tear slip from my lashes and slide down my cheek. I wiped at it with the back of one hand

"Thank you," I said and began to set the guitar down. The applause was thunderous and people were on their feet, shouting.

I couldn't tear my eyes away from Cade.

I'd risen, and he was trying to rush through the crowd toward me, but was having a hard time making his way around all of the people. Part of me was thankful for that. I felt trapped, like I'd die an absolute death if I didn't make an immediate escape.

I needed to get out of there fast, or soon, I was going to be a sobbing mess. I could feel the misery welling up and threatening to overflow.

I pushed my way through the crowd toward the other end of the bar, toward the entrance and away from Cade.

"Brook!" he called. "Brook, wait, please!"

I kept going, my eyes on Nathan a few yards in front of me. My vision blurred with tears, but I stumbled through the crowd, pushing my way toward him.

"Brook! Bloody hell! Stop!" Cade was beside me, and grabbed my arm. "Stop... Just wait a second, please." His voice lowered as he looked at the tears running down my face, his scent enveloped me. Finally, I had the courage to meet his eyes but my face crumpled, and I cried hard.

"Cade, just please, let me go. It's obvious that coming here tonight was a big mistake." My voice broke, and more tears slipped from my lashes. I bowed my head when my shoulders began to shake. I couldn't stop them from doing that, and it felt humiliating to be standing here, in the middle of a bar, in a place I'd never been, with a couple of hundred eyes boring into me... and worse, to witness what I'd just seen.

"Tell me why you're here," he commanded softly, his finger lifting my chin so I had to look him in the eyes. He looked sad and anxious. "When I saw you, I couldn't believe my eyes." His eyes searched my face, trying to read my mind. "I felt like the earth opened up to swallow me alive."

I tried to speak, but nothing came out. I opened my mouth, closed it, and then shook my head. "It just... It doesn't matter now." I tried again to pull my arm free.

"Goddamn it, Brooklyn! Tell me *why* you're here!" he pleaded, and grabbed my other arm, which completely prevented me from looking away from his face. We were both breathing hard; standing motionless; as if there was no one else in the room.

Finally, I looked away as I struggled for strength to control the tears in my voice.

Maybe if I tell him the truth, he'll let me go.

I turned back to him. "I came here to tell you that what you saw in those photos wasn't real, and that I was ending things with David. That you are who I want to be with." I started to shake, my face crumpled. Cade took me by the shoulders, and pulled me tightly to his chest.

"But from the looks of things, you're doing just fine. It didn't take you long, did it?" A small sob escaped, as I resumed in earnest. "I thought I was going to surprise you for your birthday, but it looks like I'm the one getting the big surprise." I was angry and hurt; my heart shattered into a million shards that ripped through my flesh and left me bleeding. I renewed my struggles to get free of him, but he was too strong. He moved me away a little to look in my eyes, his brow low over his eyes and his mouth tense.

"Brook, what was I supposed to think? You never said you were mine. How was I to know? Those pictures were like reliving the entire last year as I watched you with him when I wanted you for myself!"

"After the way it was between us... the way it felt! You saw how my heart was breaking when you left. After that, how could you doubt me? You don't trust me at all."

I felt the walls were crashing in around me. I tried to push against his chest, but he only held me tighter, his arms going around my back.

"Go back to your... girlfriend!" I said the words softly, but inside I was screaming. His eyes were wide, and he was breathing fast when he looked at my tear stained face

"Brook, this is so fucked up! Please listen to me. Until twenty seconds ago, I thought you were with David!" His voice was thick with pain, as he tried to stop my struggles.

My useless struggles quieted, and defeat filled my voice. "Cade, I beg you, please let me go. Don't make a scene that neither one of us can afford. We don't need the rags telling the wrong story to the world. Please, I just gotta get out of here." I struggled against him again, and this time his arms dropped to his sides. He stood in front of me, staring in stunned disbelief.

"Please don't follow me." I turned and ran out to the street, and to the taxi Nate had waiting at the curb.

"No, Brook! Brook! Don't go. Please!" He was following close behind me, and people in the crowd looked at us as we ran out of the bar. Cade's friend, Daniel Mayfield, came up beside him, but everyone else left us alone. I was thankful his celebrity madness hadn't reached the same intensity in England as it had in the States. I didn't see a single cameras flash.

Nate was on the curb by the cab, ready to help me make a fast escape. "Nate, please, let's just go. Now!" I could feel the last part of my reserve crumbling. Still crying; I rushed into the sanctity of the cab.

"Don't tell him where we're staying. I just want to go home." I could see Nathan blocking Cade from coming in. He was trying to talk to him.

"Just give her some time, man. I'm sure she'll come around."

"Nathan! For fuck's sake! Let me talk to her! She's got the wrong idea!"

"Oh, you mean, like you had the wrong idea about her and David?" He paused, and shook his head. "Look, man, you know that I really like you, but Brook is my first concern right now. Just let me get her taken care of and then I'll see what I can do, okay?"

Cade's shoulders hunched in defeat, and he ran his hand through his hair, attempting to glance past Nathan into the back of the cab. I turned from him to huddle in the corner. The sobs were gone, but the tears were still leaking from my eyes. I put both hands over my face, and bent over my lap as I cried.

"Please arrange for us to talk before you leave London. You know I had reason to believe those bloody photos!"

I could see their reflection in the window as they talked; Nate's back to me, but Cade facing the cab. He grabbed my brother's shoulder desperately. "Jesus, Nate, you have to know what she means to me." His voice was soft, defeated, his eyes tortured.

"Yeah." Nate nodded and then looked in at me, then turned back at Cade.

Chapter 7

Never Stop

Brooklyn

"BROOK, WE NEED to talk." Cade looked miserable.

My brow furrowed. "*Now* you want to talk? Just go away. I can't do this right now. The time for talking is over." I tried to shut the door in his face.

Cade's arm held the door open, as he pushed his way into the room. His arms went around me so fast I didn't know what hit me; then the sound of the door banged as it closed heavily behind him. He lifted me off the ground, and I lost my breath, as my feet dangled off of the floor. Cade wound his arms around my back and used one hand to hold the back of my head.

He buried his face in my hair as he spoke. "I'm so sorry, Brook. Please, please talk to me. I love you so much. If you really *are* mine, I can't lose you," he said. His lips were moving on my neck, jaw, eyes, cheeks, and finally found my mouth.

His lips hovered above mine. "I was a bloody fool. Will you forgive me?" He brushed my hair away from my face, and looked in my eyes.

Tears filled my eyes; still frozen, unmoving. My emotions conflicted between wanting to melt into his arms, and pushing him away. I wanted so much to believe his words. I closed my eyes; every breath I took was tortured.

"If you don't trust me, how can you say you love me?" The words ripped out of my throat. I bent my head and rested my forehead on his shoulder, tears falling from my eyes. I could feel the sobs begin to rack my body, so deep no sound could escape, my shoulders shaking in violent silence.

"I came here to tell you that I loved you..." I gasped out the words. "I knew the pictures would hurt you, and I couldn't b-bear to let you believe that I w-wanted someone else..." I was gasping for air. His arms tightened around me, and he let out his breath. "And, to find you k-kissing another woman..." My voice broke, cutting off my words; and my cries filled the room around us.

"Brook, you *have* to listen to me." One hand came up to brush my tear-dampened hair off of my face. "I couldn't bear the thought of you with David, not after our goodbye. I love you so much; my heart is breaking with it... it physically hurts, and it's stunned me. The pain I felt these past months on set, seeing you with him when he visited, and yet, denying my feelings..." His strong arms were still holding me tight. "It fucked up my judgment. It was killing me." He kissed my neck, pausing a moment, to stroke the back of my head with his hand.

"Try to understand. I couldn't bear to think of him *touching you* like that again. I want you to be all mine, only mine, *forever*." The anguish in Cade's voice; that beautiful voice, couldn't be denied as he held me tightly against to his body.

I sniffed, hiding my face in the hollow between his shoulder and neck, finally able to get a bit of control over the crying. "How could you let that woman kiss you? I wanted to r-run to you and throw my arms around you, b-but then I saw you with her, and something died inside. You don't know w-what that did to me." I was still shaking with hiccupping sobs.

"Yes, I do, Brook." He stopped for a moment, and then took a deep breath. "That's how I know you love me. That's *exactly* how I felt each and every time I had to see you with David. When I saw those pictures; I felt like the wind was knocked right out of me. I should have let you explain, but I'd just started to hope after that last morning in Vancouver. After seeing those pictures, I was afraid you'd tell me you'd changed your mind. I didn't want to hear that voice I love, telling me you didn't want me." He kissed the side of my face and my temple. Still he held me off the floor, his arms didn't allow even an inch of space between us.

"How could you think for one second that I didn't want you?" I asked softly. "The whole world wants you. I tried to tell you how I felt!"

Cade brought his mouth close to mine, and this time, as he moved to my mouth, he took it for all he was worth.

I kissed him back like I was starving for him. My arms slid up his chest, and around his neck, into his hair of their own volition. I pulled him closer still, and we were wild with each other. His hands on both sides of my face slanted my head so he could take my mouth in deeper and deeper kisses.

Finally, he placed another soft kiss on my mouth, catching my top lip between both of his, he gently tugged on it, reluctant to separate. "Love, I'm so sorry. I've been a bloody idiot." His hot breath mingled with mine, his warm scent was so delicious, I felt faint.

I pulled back to look into his eyes. I didn't want there to be any question about the sincerity of my words. My voice was thick with emotion, and tears clung to my lashes. "I didn't mean to fall in love with you... but you've wrecked me," I whispered.

A happy smile slid across his gorgeous mouth, his brilliant teeth flashing as he placed a hand on the side of my face. "Oh, Brook, I've dreamt of hearing those words, since the moment we met. I've loved you all this time." His blue eyes melted into mine. He could stare right into my soul, and there was nothing I could do to stop it. I couldn't fathom how I could deserve him, but I was flying and giddy; my heart was racing.

"I should have told you before, but I wanted to make sure it wasn't just residual feelings from Ryan and Julia. I wanted it to be real; to be us. The night before we said goodbye, after the party, I prayed that you would love me as me, and not Julia. I missed you so much I ached with it, and we weren't even apart yet," I said between kisses.

"My God," he breathed. "I love you more than my life." I gasped at the gravity of Cade's words and the emotion in his expression, my fingers tracing lightly over his jaw and the side of his face. We held each other and kissed for a long time. He lifted his head and rubbed my back. "Are you okay, baby? I still can't believe you're in London, in my arms like this." He walked to the bed, sat down and pulled me onto his lap. "It's paradise," he whispered against my temple.

"I'm perfect now." I snuggled in and laid my head on his broad shoulder, my hand resting on his chest right over his heart. I could feel his muscle definition underneath my fingers, and I longed to explore his body further.

His beautiful eyes looked down at me in wonder. "Brook," he took a deep breath, "how did this happen? How are these feelings even possible?" He brought his mouth to mine for another kiss and his sweet breath fanned out over my face.

"You tell me. You're the one with all the experience."

"I don't have experience with this. I can't believe anyone has ever loved someone this much before." He looked at me for a long moment, my mind flashing to a place in the script when Ryan said the same words to Julia. "It's just—" he let out a little breath with a little shrug.

My hand came up to stroke his hair. "Overwhelming?" I finished it for him, and Cade nodded. "It's nice to know I'm not the only one who feels that way. You can twist my heart in knots and wring me inside out. There are no words."

A gentle smile tugged at his full mouth, then, he kissed my forehead. Cade continued to knead my back as my head nestled on his shoulder. We sat like that, holding each other for a while, each of us soaking up the other, and basking in the glow of the love we felt. *I felt so safe*. I never wanted to move.

"Were you going to run a bath? You must be tired. How long since you slept?" he asked.

I considered the time since I boarded the plane in L.A. "Um, I guess about thirty hours, but it doesn't matter now. I don't want to sleep now that you're here with me." My hand rose to his face, and he covered it with his.

"I don't have to go anywhere, love." He kissed the inside of my wrist, and I wondered if he could feel my pulse racing beneath his lips. "Why don't you let me run your bath, then I'll tuck you in, if you want." A devilish smile split his face.

I raised my eyebrow at him and bit my lip. Cade laughed. "Hmmm... sounds like heaven," I said softly.

"Okay, I'll be back." He lifted me as he stood up, laid me back down on the bed and touched my chin softly before he turned and went into the bathroom. The rush of the water started in the tub.

I got up from the bed and found a hair clip in my bag. There were also some candles I'd brought from home in case we'd get the chance to spend the night together. *Turns out it wasn't just wishful thinking.* My breath caught as I took two of them out of my case, then twisted my hair up, securing it on top with the clip.

I was nervous, even though I'd dreamt of this moment over and over for so long. Months, if I was honest with myself. We spent many nights together during the shoot, running lines, watching movies, falling asleep together, even cuddling sometimes, but now we'd admitted we loved each other. That was huge. It was the biggest moment of my life. Butterflies fluttered in my stomach at the thought of finally being able to consummate that love.

I put a couple of candles around, lit them, and turned out the bedside light that was on. The room was bathed in a soft golden glow with shadows falling all around, the vanilla scent wafting into the air.

The door to the bathroom opened, and Cade walked up behind me, his hands coming up to rest on my shoulders. "Wow, this is perfect," he said. " Brook, you're exhausted. I just want to take care of you, get you into your bath and I'll be happy to hold you all night." He brushed a soft kiss on my neck, and his hot breath made my skin tingle. "Just holding you is enough."

He was telling me he didn't expect us to make love, always the gentleman. I smiled to myself, turned, and raised my eyes to his. He was so flipping perfect.

"What if I don't want sleep?" I asked softly. I watched him take off his jacket, leaving only his black shirt between my fingers, and the smooth, hard muscles of his chest.

"That's okay, too. I'm yours; anything you want." He put his hands on my shoulders again, and ran them down the length of my arms to my hands. He pulled one up and kissed the inside of my wrist, his eyes never breaking connection from mine.

His words held a deeper meaning to me. I reached up to touch his handsome face.

"I want you. Forever," I whispered. I reached my hand up to the back of his head, drawing his head down to kiss him, but his lips hovered over mine.

His hand lifted, and he brushed his knuckles against the side of my face.

"Forever," he reiterated, and I nodded. "That may not be long enough," his other hand slipped behind my waist, and he began kissing hotly down the column of my neck. It felt beyond delicious, shooting a series of shudders to rack through me. I closed my eyes at his words, and the feel of his mouth on my skin. My hands explored down his chest reaching inside between the buttons. It was euphoric, something of dreams. Cade was a huge movie star, and while that mattered when I first met him, now, while he was still sexy as hell, all of that star stuff wasn't who he was.

He trembled at my touch, then struggled with something he was trying to say. I just looked up at him and waited, knowing love had to be pouring out of my eyes.

"Brook. Can I just... *look* at you?" he asked, as he ran a hand through his gorgeous mane. "I mean, I've been dreaming of you for months, and I just..." his words fell off as he lifted his eyes to meet mine and there was a faint blush to his cheeks. "I want to look at you, finally." He seemed slightly shy at asking, but I found it extremely sexy and endearing at the same time.

A small, secret smile came to my lips at his embarrassment. He was the last person who I'd ever expect to have this type of reaction.

"Cade," I breathed, and lifted up onto my tiptoes to finally place a soft kiss on first his mouth, and then his neck, sucking just a little with each one. He shivered at the touch of my tongue on his skin. "Take off my clothes," I begged.

He sucked in his breath, and then his mouth was on mine, slowly exploring, but full of passion as he unzipped my dress, and slid it down my body. The touch of his hands as they roamed over my back, and then followed the dress down, was so soft and sensual it set every inch of my skin on fire. I trembled in his arms. My mouth broke from the kiss as I stepped back a little.

My black bustier, bikini panties and thigh-high stockings still on, I stepped out of the dress. His eyes were hot on my body, roaming slowly over every swell and curve. I could see the love, and lust, burning there. He was the most beautiful thing I'd ever seen.

"Bloody hell, you are so damn beautiful, Brook. I'm completely fucking helpless." He bent, kissing first my shoulder, then the curve of my neck. His mouth was fiery hot, yet it sent waves of goosebumps rippling over my exposed skin. It felt so exquisite, sensual and very loving. Cade made my insides melt and heat pool between my legs.

"Oh, my God, Cade," I moaned. I was dying inside. I'd imagined this moment for so long. His hand tentatively slid along the top of my breasts above the lingerie, his fingers hovering and reverent; as if when he touched me I would disappear before his eyes. My head fell back and I gasped, but held his eyes with my own. I felt so good. All of my senses were soaring.

I took his hand, and kissed the palm with my open mouth, letting him feel the heat of my tongue. I walked back into the bathroom, carrying one of the candles and pulling him behind me by one hand.

The candle flickered all over the room, reflecting off of the sunken tub that was now full of bubbles and the mirrors. I placed the candle on the counter, and took in his smoldering gaze.

He took my breath away; just gorgeous in the flickering candle light.

I slowly took off my stockings, my eyes never leaving his face. He looked like a starving man, his eyes devouring me from head to toe.

I felt powerful as I realized that he wanted me more at that moment than he'd probably ever wanted anything in his life.

"Will you unhook the back?" I whispered. His eyes flickered with desire and the candlelight dancing in reflection. The golden light and dark shadows playing off the planes of his perfect features left me completely speechless.

I turned around and offered him my back. He unhooked the bustier, his hands tracing lightly over my shoulders and down my spine. I held the front of it in place, over my breasts. He kissed the back of my neck with his open mouth, sucking ever so lightly, as he lifted his lips away.

"Huuuuhh," my breath left in an unstoppable rush at the caress of his mouth. "I can't believe this is happening."

When I turned around to face him, I let the bustier fall away, my round breasts bare, my pink nipples taut and erect. I was standing only in my black lace string bikini panties. I waited, letting Cade look me over, my lips parted, my gaze wanton as it fell on him. *Oh, God. This is finally going to happen,* I thought.

"Brook... is this real? Are you really here with me now? You're so perfect." His voice was rough with emotion. "So beautiful and perfect."

"Cade, in times to come when distance and work keep us apart, I want you to remember this moment. Know that no matter where I am, or what I'm doing, know that I'd rather be with you like this."

He came forward and gathered me up in his arms. " I love you." He breathed out my name before his lips brushed mine. Then, the pressure increased as our mouths parted, kissing over and over, more and more deeply, as if we couldn't get enough of each other.

Cade left me breathless as I placed little kisses on his jaw, moved back up to claim his mouth and started to unbutton his shirt. His breathing was heavy as he pulled his mouth from mine.

His hands came up to cover mine. "Babe, I know how tired you are. I'm happy just to be with you. Get in the bath and I'll wash your back." He held both of my hands in one of his, as the knuckles of the other hand grazed the outside curve of my breast. I licked my lips and looked up at him with hooded eyes.

"For now," I whispered as I stood on tiptoe to curl my hand around the back of his neck and pull him in for another kiss. My mouth parted, and I ran my tongue along his. He groaned when I slid my tongue between his lips and teeth into the deep recesses of his mouth, his arms gathering me tight against him. His tongue came to meet mine and our lips were tasting, sucking, and savoring every movement.

Kiss after kiss after kiss, he was delicious.

Don't stop. Don't ever stop.

Chapter 8

As If In Dreams

Brooklyn

CADE FINALLY TRAILED his lips down my neck and over the top of my shoulder. I lifted his hand to my breast. "I want you to touch me," I breathed.

"I'm afraid you'll evaporate into thin air if I do. My dreams have been filled with this, and..." He tentatively reached out toward me. "I don't want to wake up, love." But his hand was warm as he cupped my breast, his thumb grazing over the erect nipple, and the other on my back, falling lower to the edge of my panties. His eyes, now dark and intense with desire followed the hand at my breast until finally lifting to my face.

"Mmmmm... " I moaned. " I love it when you touch me. Your hands are the only ones that I want on my body. Only you," I breathed into the skin of his chest.

"You have no idea what that does to me, Brooklyn. I've loved you from the minute our eyes met; and when we kissed... I was lost."

His hands were running down the sides of my body and came to the edge of my panties, they slid over my butt underneath the fabric, kneading my flesh and he groaned.

I was kissing his chest when his fingers slid them down to fall at my feet. His words were running like molten lava through my veins.

"You're so romantic; exactly what every woman dreams you are."

"Shhh, babe," he groaned against my mouth. "Get in your bath while I'm still able to let you." His mouth ghosted mine until he stepped back to let me get in the tub. I moved slowly in front of him, so my body was visible. His eyes were hungry as I slid down in the tub.

"This feels nice."

Cade watched me for a minute. He shook his head slightly and let the air out in a small huff. I'd become familiar with that huff, and I loved what it meant.

"Hmmph..." he smiled softly at me. "I feel like I'm twelve years old." The corners of his mouth twitched, "It's like I've never been with a woman before. You're the most beautiful thing I've ever seen. Absolutely breathtaking." Adoration radiated from his eyes.

I smiled as I remembered another time he told me that. "Better than the blue dress?" I teased with a seductive smile.

The corner of his mouth twitched and then broke into a grin. "Yeah, even better than the blue dress, although you were stunning in that as well, and tonight on stage, just so, so incredible. I loved watching you."

He sat on the floor next to the tub, dangling his arm over the edge, he picked up the sponge and begin running it over my body. I watched every move he made. He was so lithe; like some sort of caged cat and his shirt was unbuttoned halfway down his chest.

Something about him stopped my heart, but that was nothing new.

I paused; absorbing how much I needed this beautiful, complicated man. I knew in that moment; I'd never love anyone else this much for the rest of my life.

"You practiced your guitar." His eyes were thoughtful, as he smiled softly. "You were amazing tonight."

"It makes me feel closer to you when I play it. It was the only part of you I could touch on a daily basis," I said of the birthday gift he gave me a few months earlier. It was also intended to remind me of him after filming ended. I knew him so well. "It's beautiful. I really love it."

"The song was perfect," he said quietly as his eyes rose to meet mine. "It was like you reached right into my chest and squeezed my heart with your hand."

He moved the sponge down my body, his eyes following its progress as a small smile danced around his mouth.

"Cade," I whispered. He stopped running the sponge down my leg and looked at my face.

"Yeah, love?"

"You can *touch me.*" I softly removed the sponge from his hand. "You don't need this. I don't want anything between us anymore." I watched his face as he realized what I meant. His gaze darkened. My hand reached for his and pulled it to my bare body. "I don't want anything to come between us, ever again."

He lifted the other hand to cup the side of my face, his intense eyes tenderly searching mine. "Brook, you kill me. Just looking at you... *hurts so much.*"

He leaned in to kiss me softly and my heart beat faster.

He's absolutely perfect. Brilliant and talented, beautiful, sensitive, and so romantic. Everything I could ever dream of, and more. I couldn't fathom how I could ever hope to deserve him. I was nothing compared to him.

His hands ran over my body under the water. The suds making them slip easily over my skin. He touched my arms, legs, shoulders, and then slid his hand over my breasts and down my stomach. I caught my breath as his fingers brushed lower over the apex of my thighs, and then down the smooth skin of my leg. His eyes were greedy as they raked over every exposed inch of my body.

I could see him tense. I wanted to touch him too, and the heat in the pit of my stomach and between my legs started to burn and throb intensely. "Cade, take me to bed," I requested softly.

"God..." Cade groaned as his arms went around me in the water, and he kissed me deeply on the mouth. He lifted me out of the tub and stood me on the rug. Water sloshed on the floor, and onto him, as well. When he brought the towel around behind my back, he used it to pull me closer. I could feel how excited he was when his erection pressed against my stomach. His breathing sped up when our bodies touched. I wasn't sure how much of this I could take, but I let him take the lead.

He rubbed the towel gently over my skin, softly kissing the parts he'd just dried. When he got to my breasts, he took a nipple into his mouth and sucked on it gently. I couldn't help but arch toward him and let out a soft moan as pleasure raced through every cell.

"Oh, Cade, I love you," I said so softly I wondered if he could hear me.

"Say it again, Brook. I can never get enough of hearing you say it." He groaned against my breast, laving my nipple with his tongue, first one, and then the other, bringing more gasps out of me as he ran small feather soft kisses down the side of my breast.

I put my arms around him and pulled him up so I could kiss

him. "I love you more than anything. Always," I whispered against his mouth.

My hands slid up around his neck, and then my nails raked down his chest. He pulled my lower lip into his mouth and sucked on it gently. I wanted him to feel how much I needed him. I pressed against him, my hands touching anywhere I could reach. Feeling him, rock hard, big and straining against me, made my knees go weak.

He bent, and lifted me into his arms, carrying me to the bed, while never breaking the kiss. I dragged my mouth to his neck, sucking and nipping at it gently. He moaned at the feel of my teeth on his skin.

On the bed, I rose onto my knees and went to work on the remaining buttons of his shirt.

"Brook, we don't have to..." But his eyes were on fire as he watched my naked body move in the candlelight.

Desire burned between us.

"You said you'd give me anything I wanted," I reminded, my mouth against his skin. I ran my tongue from his collarbone down his chest to his left nipple; my mouth closed around it as I used my tongue and mouth to tease it.

His breathing and heartbeat sped up; I could feel it. I pushed the shirt off his shoulders, and Cade pulled the clip from my hair, allowing it to tumble over my shoulders and down my back. His long fingers threading through it felt incredible. He was so breathtaking, and the light hair on his chest, getting heavier as it disappeared into his jeans, made me wet with anticipation. My hands ran down his hard chest, feathering over his flat stomach until I found the button on his jeans. I made short work of it and slid the zipper down. He was full and thick, as hard as steel, yet soft as silk.

My hand reached inside as I stared up into his blue eyes.

He gasped as my hand closed around his flesh. "Jesus, Brook. Fuck, you're driving me insane. I don't have the strength to resist you."

I raised my head to look into his eyes again, my hand still moving on him. I loved the way he felt. I loved knowing I'd soon know what it felt like to have him inside of me. Finally, inside of me.

"Mmmm... I don't want you to," I said in a moaning whisper; the overwhelming love I felt making me bold.

Cade made a low growl deep in his chest. I thought he'd throw me down on the bed and take me, but he was so gentle. He bent to lick my top lip and then placed a soft kiss on the corner of my mouth.

The kisses, while still passionate, slowed and became more tender, his hands more gentle and light on my body. Worshiping with every pass.

I touched him, too; managing to start moving his jeans down his lean hips. My hands pushed down over his firm butt. I felt his naked desire press on my stomach, and I sucked in my breath.

"Oh, God, Cade." My heart was pounding, the wetness pooling between my thighs. "I've wanted you for so long." I sighed into his mouth.

"For fucking eternity." He took my mouth in a deep, soulful kiss. His arm tightened around my waist, my arms around his neck, hands in his hair, holding him, kissing him back deeply as he lowered me to the bed.

His knees pushed into the mattress on the sides of my legs, as he bent to slowly kiss my neck, shoulders and breasts. He had me panting with desire when his hands ran the length of my body, and he bent to suckle my breasts again. He sucked the nipple into his mouth and flicked his tongue over it as his right hand lowered to the spot between my legs that screamed for his touch. It was slow, sweet and exquisite torture.

"Uhh…" I panted as my hips surged to meet him.

"Bloody hell, Brook. You're so beautiful. I never want this to end." His mouth left my breast and moved down my body. He touched every inch of my flesh, softly kneading, as if he couldn't get enough. His hands spread my legs, and I held my breath.

I felt his breath on my inner thigh and ran his tongue from my knee higher up my leg. Feather-light kisses followed up and down both of my legs, my hips and on my stomach just below my navel. He had me writhing in anticipation. Then, his hands were on the inside of my thighs and sliding below my bottom as he brought his hot mouth down the apex of my clitoris.

"Oh, my God," I panted. I felt like I was dying.

"Mmmmm…" he groaned, sucking lightly. I was wound so tight that I was going to come too soon. The months of wanting, and fantasies about this very moment, coupled with the long slow build of the evening, made me so sensitive.

"Cade… Uhnggg, Cade…" I gasped out his name, my back arching, my head falling back and both hands clutching frantically at the sheets

"Just let it go, baby. I love you so much, Brooklyn. I want you to come under my mouth." His words made me gasp and writhe at the intimacy of it. Cade returned his greedy mouth to me licking and sucking until I thought I couldn't stand it, until finally, he lightened the pressure to bring my body back down. I didn't know how long it lasted, but he kept up the ebb and flow until I couldn't bear another second. It felt delicious and sensual and right. I lost myself in the sensations, until finally, my body tensed and shuddered as he brought me over the edge. My back arched, and I convulsed over and over again. His lips lightened on my body as the shutters wracked me. Oh, my God, he was so good. And he was all mine.

"Caaaddeeee..." I breathed his name. "Mmmmm...."

He moved up my body and kissed my mouth deeply. "Brook, you are incredible. You taste so sweet, and your scent; you drive me wild with wanting you." He nuzzled my neck, and then moved to kiss me deeply again, and I could taste myself on his mouth.

This was the most intimate I'd ever been with anyone; the closest I'd ever let myself get emotionally, too. It was so incredible. He was so beautiful; his passion and tenderness overwhelmed my heart.

I reached for his erection. I wanted to touch him, to bring him pleasure, to feel him inside me. He groaned under my touch, as my hand slid around him, and up and down his length.

"Mmmm... this has to be a dream. It's so perfect," he groaned.

My hands lightly skimmed his body, and I kissed his chest and neck, with my open mouth... "Let's not wake up," I said against his skin. He was salty and sweet, savory and sour, and I loved his taste.

I tried to push him back so I could taste him, but he stopped me. "Brook. I can't wait another minute to be inside you. I want to make love with you." Then he kissed me so passionately that it took my breath away, his tongue deep in my mouth, sucking on my lower lip between kisses.

I felt his knee go between my legs, and I moaned in anticipation, letting my legs fall open. I wanted him... now.

"Yes," I begged against his mouth as I arched up to him.

I felt the thick, round head of him press into my softness and begin to stretch me open. I was so wet that with a little push, he'd be deep inside. "My God, babe. You're so hot, so tight." He moaned as he pushed in all the way. I pushed up to meet him, stretching, feeling him fill me. Every sensation increased my desire.

"You feel so amazing," I murmured through the passionate haze.

He started to move within me, his hands reaching out for mine, our fingers interlacing and locking overhead as he continued to kiss me deeply on the mouth. He moved slowly, at first, savoring each long thrust. I couldn't believe the wonder of it as my mind fought to memorize every touch of his mouth on mine, his body pushing into mine, the way he sounded and smelled, his hands so tightly entwined with mine. I'd dreamed about this moment for months, but this was even more than I imagined it could be; more than I'd ever felt. This was making love, and it would leave its mark on me forever.

I raised my knees higher so he'd sink deeper into my body. I wanted to get closer and closer, still.

"Oh, God... oh, babe," he groaned from deep within his chest. I twisted one of my hands free and grasped the muscles of his ass to pull him in tighter.

Another orgasm started to build, slower, this time, as we moved together. His hands, his lips on my body, every inch of me screamed for his touch.

"Cade, I've never felt like this... it's never been like this," I moaned against his mouth as my body clenched around him. I wanted him to feel how much I wanted him, and what he did to me. One of his hands was stroking my leg from ankle to thigh, and he was sucking, and playing with my nipples with his teeth and lips.

"I know love, for me, too." His eyes closed as he moved inside me, with me, for me. "Brook, you're making me come ... I'm so close," he moaned. Suddenly his hands were on the sides of my face. He was breathing heavy as he stroked my hair back from my face.

"Brook, please. I need you to open your eyes," he demanded as he kissed my mouth softly.

My eyes opened to see him looking down at me as his body continued to surge within mine. He was slowing a little, but the pressure and depth of his thrusts remained constant, as our bodies pushed and pulled in opposite rhythm.

"Mmmmm... Uhhh," I moaned softly, the sensations still building within me. His eyes were dark with passion, but I could see the pain on his perfect features, as well. I reached up to lay a hand on his cheek.

"I've dreamt of this moment, when I'd feel your body writhing beneath me, clenching around me and pulling me in; when I'd hear my name on your lips, your voice thick with emotion as I make you come. And this is so much more incredible than I've ever imagined or dared to hope for." His voice was thick with emotion and his eyes liquid. "I love you more than anything in this world. Right now at this moment... I would die in your arms; just to finally be with you like this." His eyes were pools of love. He lowered his mouth to mine, kissing me deeply once again.

I felt myself start to tense and spasm in orgasm around him even as my heart seized at his words. Those beautiful words and his tender lovemaking brought tears to my eyes as emotion overwhelmed me.

"Uhhhh... Cade..." I said his name as if it were a prayer, my eyes closed and my back arched, my hands held the sides of his face, as a tear squeezed out from my lashes.

He kissed my mouth hotly, his tongue diving into my mouth and I sucked on it like my body was clenching, sucking on his, as he groaned giving in to his own climax. I felt him shudder and twitch inside me, and I was still clenching around him, milking every last drop and tremor of sensation from him. I wrapped my legs and arms around him, as I felt the tears begin to fall. "Oh, my God... Cade, I can't believe how much I love you." I cried, our bodies clinging together.

"Don't ever leave me, please." Cade's voice was thick and his eyes were wet as he looked down on me, slowly brushing my hair off of my damp forehead, skimming his knuckles in a soft caress across my cheek and chin, staring in wonder at my face. "You're everything that matters to me," he said softly. My arms tightened around him, as I sobbed into his shoulder.

He kissed my neck, forehead and shoulder as he collapsed into the pillows behind my head. I just held him tighter, kissing the side of his neck, and then his mouth when he finally lifted his beautiful face above mine. He was still inside me, and I never wanted to disconnect. We stayed like that for a few minutes, just holding and stroking each other.

I kissed his shoulder, temple and mouth.

He stared down at me, his eyes soft with the aftermath of our lovemaking, his skin glowing with a thin layer of perspiration, his breathing heavy. He kissed the tears off of my face as I looked at him.

"Don't cry, my love..." he sighed, as his fingers brushed my forehead then moved down the side of my face.

"That was... so beautiful. I'm *still* shaking." I felt him smile as he moved to my side and propped his head on his arm; his leg still tangled up in mine

He reached out to touch the bracelet on my wrist. "Forever entwined," he said in his velvet voice. I knew there was a double meaning in those words, as his eyes rose from the diamonds between his fingers to look into mine.

My hand came up to cover his, my eyes full of love as I looked at him. "I'll always cherish and protect it." I felt flushed and feverish. I was so happy.

My hands running through it had mussed his dark gold hair, his features were relaxed and satisfied; his eyes languid. "I wanted to get it made with our initials, but I wasn't certain you were in the same place as I was. With this."

His arm rested softly across my stomach as he gazed down at me, and pulled the sheet up over his hips and my breasts.

"I was." I looked at Cade in amazement. " Where did you come from? You've touched me in places I never dreamed existed."

He smiled at me as I studied his face in the candlelight

"I mean..." I searched for the right words. "You're everything, Cade. Perfect. You're like my own personal miracle."

"I've thought that about you, too, but never more so than in this moment." His eyes were thoughtful as he considered his next words. "Brook, I meant it when I said I love you so much that sometimes, I can't even breathe. I know you might be skeptical given my lifestyle. But I promise it's the truth."

Cade frowned a little as he looked at me, his hand lightly rubbing up and down my body.

It seemed something he was thinking was hurting him, and I needed to know what.

"What's wrong?" I asked, snuggling closer. We were lying on our sides facing each other, touching and softly kissing.

"I just don't ever want to feel like I've felt these past few days. Ever again. Losing you after this would be unbearable. I think it would literally kill me." His blue eyes burned into mine and I reached up to touch his face. That line was one from the next script. I wondered if he'd read it yet.

He rolled onto his back and pulled me onto his chest so I could rest my head over his heart. I listened to it thump beneath my cheek as my fingers drew figure eights on his chest.

How can I put him at ease? I considered it for a moment before I spoke, my gaze concentrating on my fingers as they drew figure eights on the skin of his chest

"We have to trust each other, and make sure that nothing comes between us again." I kissed his chest and put my hand up to touch his face as his arms tightened around my body.

"I agree," Cade answered. "No matter what anyone says to us or about us, or how the media tries to twist photos or headlines out of lies, let's promise that we'll always talk to each other and not jump to conclusions. Because I promise you, it won't *ever* be true. I'll never hurt you."

I stayed draped across his chest as my hand went up around his neck into his hair.

He touched my face and ran his thumb over my cheekbone.

As I lay in his arms, in this paradise, I voiced my thoughts. "I'm wondering what I did to deserve you."

He smiled. "Simple. You auditioned."

I laughed happily. "I was done for the minute you walked in for the first reading ... my heart recognized you, even then."

He laughed with me as his arms tightened around me. "You make me so happy, love. You've definitely convinced me you love me." He breathed with a devilish smile, but then his eyes turned serious. "I'll never doubt that again."

I sighed and hugged him close. "Better not," I teased.

"Not possible now." He breathed in my hair and kissed my head. "I know you're exhausted, honey. Try to sleep. I'll stay with you."

The lovemaking, the jet lag, and the soft glow of the candles in the room were lulling me to sleep. I was tired, but I had to make Cade understand one more thing before I let myself fall asleep.

"Cade?"

"Mmmm?" he murmured. It was clear he was also falling asleep.

"I have to tell you something." I raised my head to look into his face, my fingers running over his chest in a delicate caress. "You said tonight that it's killed you this past year thinking of me with David."

I felt him tense as he interrupted me, his eyes snapped open and his hand came up to cover mine.

"Brook, that's in the past. I don't want to talk about him, not tonight. I understand, and it wasn't your fault. None of that matters now that I know you're mine. It's over." He kissed my forehead.

I kissed his chest, as my head rested on it, and my fingertips traced circle patterns across his velvet skin. I would never get tired of touching him.

"No, you don't understand." There was an almost unperceivable shake to my head. "I need you to know something." My words dropped off as I felt him take a deep breath beneath me.

"What is it?" He hesitated. "You can tell me. No matter what it is, what it might cost, or even if you think it will hurt me. I always want to know what you're thinking," he said softly. His arms tightened around me, and his fingers brushed my cheek.

God, he was just so *Ryan*, I thought. Th*ose characters were* us.

I moved up on his chest a little so I could look in his eyes. My hand caressed the light stubble on his chin as I searched for just the right words. "Babe, what is it?" His eyes bore into mine, his voice gentle.

"I haven't let anyone else touch me like this, not even David, since the day of my audition. I need you to know that it's only ever been you." My eyes never left his as I spoke.

His eyes widened in astonishment, and he started to sit up a little, his mouth ready to speak. "Brook."

"No, I need you to know that all the pain you felt when I was with him, when you saw pictures of us, when you thought he and I were together—like this—all the things that tormented you, were only imagined. They didn't happen at all. It breaks my heart that it hurt you so much. I don't *ever* want to see that kind of pain in your eyes again. I'm so sorry." My hand was still stroking the line of his perfect jaw as my eyes filled with tears again.

He looked at me in amazement. "My God..." He stopped, putting a hand over his eyes as he fell back on the pillows.

Suddenly he pulled me on top of his body, his arms going around me and crushing me to him. He was dragging his mouth over my face pausing to kiss my cheeks, my eyes, and finally my mouth. "I could tell you that I love you a million times, but words can't even come close. It'll never be enough to express how I feel about you."

He put his head down and kissed my shoulder and my neck lovingly. He lifted his head and kissed my mouth with tears in his eyes. "Thank you for telling me that, you can't know how much it means to me."

He kissed me again, his kiss soft but turning passionate. His tongue slid into my mouth and stole my breath, as our bodies entwined again.

"Cade," I breathed against his lips as the kiss ended. "I'll never stop loving you. I'll die if I do."

Chapter 9

Proposition

Brooklyn

THE MORNING CAME, and I awoke to find Cade propped on his elbow watching me, his hand lightly playing in my hair. "Mmmmm... How long have I been sleeping?" I asked as I stretched.

"Um, I'm not sure what time we fell asleep, but I think about twelve hours." He gave me the crooked grin I loved.

"What?" My hands went to my hair as I struggled to keep my eyes open. "I guess I worried last night was a dream, and didn't want to wake up." I sighed as I looked at him. He was so beautiful. If I woke up with him every day, he'd stun me. "Why didn't you wake me, babe?"

"Last night *was* a dream, love. A ridiculously wonderful dream." He was serious as he looked at me, and I watched his eyes darken, the love in them shining like a beacon. I reached my hand out to touch him, my heart swelling in my chest.

I loved that damn accent. So delicious, it made my mouth water.

I grinned, and Cade's gaze turned playful, His mouth began to twitch with the start of a smile. He took my outstretched hand and kissed the inside of my wrist. "Besides, I like watching you sleep." He smirked at me.

I smiled to myself then placed soft kisses on his chest and down his stomach, and giggled a little bit. "How fascinating for you," I said wryly. Sleep left a person unguarded and vulnerable.

"Mmmm... " he said in response to my ministrations down his body. He put his arms around me to roll me over onto my back, his body pressing me into the mattress. "Something like that," he said, then he kissed me long and deep on the mouth.

I hugged him and touched his hair, brushing it off of his forehead. I could feel his body coming to life where it touched mine. I pressed against him, and he groaned.

"Last night was indescribable, Cade. I'll never forget even a single second of it," I promised. My thumb traced his jaw; a sexy stubble starting to appear, and I felt my insides begin to turn to jelly. He was so fucking *hot*.

"Brook, you're beautiful in the morning. All the time." He sighed as he stared into my eyes, and then his brow crinkled a little, his face getting serious. He continued to look down at me as he gently touched my face, his fingers lightly tracing my cheekbone, and then the side of my forehead. "Will you marry me?" A small smile played on his mouth, but his eyes were melting into mine, as he waited. Then he started to place little kisses all over my face, along my jaw and down my neck. "Hmmm?" He sighed between kisses. "Will you?" He chuckled a little.

My heart thumped wildly in my chest. I was sure he could feel it from his position over me.

He had asked me several times during filming if I would marry him, and it became a playful joke between us on set. I knew that he meant it, but had always laughed it off, flirting outrageously with him the whole time. He was expecting the same response now, but something stopped me from saying it.

I waited until he stopped kissing me, wondering about my silence, to look at me. My hands fluttered down his back and up again. His nose was nuzzling mine as he resumed his soft kisses on my face and mouth. I placed my hands on the sides of his face to stop him, so he'd meet my eyes with his.

The fingers of my right hand fluttered on the side of his face and down his jaw, before moving around to stroke the hair at the back of his neck.

"Yes," I answered softly. His blue eyes widened as I kissed his stunned mouth. "Yes, Cade," I whispered against his lips.

He stared at me. "Brook... God, is this real?" He waited, and I nodded, my eyes filling with tears.

"I love you more than air. I *have* to be with you. Always. You own my heart and soul," I whispered. "There is no other choice now, so, yes... I will." I shrugged a little and smiled through my tears. "Yes," I said one last time.

Cade looked down at me, his breath catching in his chest. A smile of sheer joy lit up his handsome face. His mouth came down on mine, softly at first, but the passion grew between us, his tongue sliding in to claim my mouth, and my hips moved against his as he brought my body to life. His mouth separated from mine softly and he licked my top lip before kissing me one more time.

"You make me so happy! I promise to love you forever. You're all I'll ever want," he said, his voice rough with emotion.

I smiled through my tears. "Every woman in the world is in love with you," I teased.

"Hmmph…" He smiled as his fingers brushed my cheek. "Even if that were true, the only one that matters to me is right here in my arms." He kissed me softly, and then he was staring at me again, his beautiful eyes making my heart beat faster. "I'm the luckiest bastard on earth."

Nope. I'm the lucky one, I thought.

* * *

THE WEEKEND FLEW by. Nathan and I only stayed in London for another day and a half.

Our time together wasn't long enough; Cade had a meeting with his managers to discuss the promotion schedule for a couple of films that he'd shot before ours, and I had to get back for that new audition Jeanne set up.

We decided to keep our relationship secret and not tell anyone who didn't already know. Our families and some of our closest friends from the cast were aware or at least, suspected, but we decided we didn't want it coming out before the premieree of our movie. Martin deserved that the focus of the coming months, be on the film. I didn't care if we kept it between the two of us. I even preferred it that way.

Cade rode with Nate and me to the airport in the limousine, and as the driver helped my brother unload and check our luggage on the curb, there were a few minutes Cade and I could spend alone before I had to exit the car and join Nate on the sidewalk. He pulled me onto his lap and kissed me deeply on the mouth. His arms were wrapped around me and mine around his neck, then into his hair as we kissed more deeply.

"God, this is hell," he moaned as he dragged his mouth from mine. "I love you, baby girl."

I sighed and placed another small kiss on his mouth. "I'm really going to miss you." I touched his face and fought the emotion swelling up to choke me. "I should go." My eyes were sad and began to fill with tears. "I don't want to drag out this goodbye; it's hard enough as it is." A lump was rising in my throat.

"Just know that I love you, and think about you all the time."

I hugged him again, my hand in his hair at the back of his neck and my face turned into him. "We have to avoid the press as much as possible, so maybe you shouldn't get out with me. They'll recognize you. My agent already called and ragged on me for coming to London. She said we had to meet as soon as possible after I get back. I'll call you and let you know what it's about, okay?"

He looked so unhappy; my heart squeezed in my chest. "I've waited an entire fucking year, and I still can't call you my girl. Bloody hell," he muttered.

"Maybe we can't tell anyone, but nothing has ever been more real to me." I placed a soft kiss on his mouth. "I love you more than anything, you sexy beast. That's never going to change, Cade." I brushed his hair back again and tried to smile.

His mouth twitched as he grinned, and his adorable dimples pressed into his cheeks. He leaned in to kiss me again; our mouths were hot on each other, tongues melding and meshing. I was fighting the urge to cry, so it was time to go. "I have to go, babe. Thank you for the beautiful weekend." I closed my eyes and lowered my forehead to his shoulder.

His arms tightened around me as he said, "Goodbye, my love. I'll ring you tonight." I felt his hand on the back of my head, as he turned his face into my hair, breathing in my scent. "Have a safe flight. I love you, Brooklyn." He kissed my hand as I turned and stepped out of the limo.

I stopped, put on my sunglasses, and placed my hand on the window one last time as it pulled away from the curb.

Oh, God, would leaving him ever get any easier? I wondered. This was our life now; we'd be saying goodbye over and over again.

I swallowed the hard lump of emotion in my throat, turning to walk into the terminal.

As Nathan and I flew home, I thought about the meeting with my manager, agent, and lawyer coming up tomorrow afternoon. This was probably a taste of what was coming. Suits, managers, and meetings. I loved the actual acting, but the business stuff might get tedious. Maybe it was something about my trip. Maybe someone was upset. I could worry for hours, and it wouldn't change anything, so I pushed it from my mind.

I texted Cade when we landed eight hours later.

Touchdown. Don't forget I love you.

I felt warm and giddy as I remembered our time together in London. I would miss him, but I was happy and solid with the fact that we loved each other. I wouldn't let anything come between us. Nothing.

* * *

WHEN I GOT back, the promotion schedule for the film was waiting for me at home. The good news was we had the MTV Music Awards, and Cade would be coming to L.A. It would include the first of our interviews together to begin promoting the film. *I can make it through two weeks.*

As I unpacked, I daydreamed about my time with Cade. My heart expanded when I remembered his tender lovemaking. *God... I can't believe that I fought my feelings for so long. I must have been insane.*

I called Jeanne when we landed, and she read me the riot act for hopping a plane to London, but said we'd discuss it in further detail at the meeting.

My phone brought me back to the present, as I threw my clothes in the laundry. It was Wendy. She wanted to shop and I used the MTV event as an excuse to agree. I didn't really care about how I looked for the event, but Cade would be there, so I suddenly had a new interest in being stylish.

When she picked me up the following morning, she was giddy and talked non-stop about a party she'd been to the night before and all of the hot guys. She noticed that I wasn't paying too much attention and gave me a quizzical look. I told myself to stop being such a rotten friend and to snap out of my daydreams.

We went to some of the poshest boutiques on Rodeo Drive, and she was all too willing to give me fashion tips. The problem was, her taste in fashion and mine, were two different things.

The awards were during the day and would have a lot of tweens and teens there, so Wendy said I didn't need the standard "red carpet" type outfit. This being my first event, I didn't have a clue what the "standard" was for any of it. After trying on several different ones, I decided on some black silk Capri pants and a simple white top.

"What do you think Wendy? Trés Chic?" I giggled a little bit. Wendy assessed my outfit.

"Kinda boring, if you want to know the truth." She raised her eyebrows and wrinkled her nose.

"I like it. It's simple but still dressy enough."

"What's with you today? You're positively *un*-Brook-like! Usually, you don't give a rat's ass about what you're wearing." She rolled her eyes at me. Most of the time, our shopping trips were all focused on her, so she was picking up on my new attitude.

"Yeah, well, I have a meeting with my suits tonight, and I'm sure they will be telling me to *start* caring." I shrugged. "I have a bunch of promotion to do for this film," I said casually. "We'll all have some."

I didn't want her to know that I cared so much about my outfit because I would see Cade. She inevitably asked if he would be joining me at the MTV Awards. She always wanted to know what he was doing. When I confirmed that he'd be there, she mentioned she wanted to call him to ask if they could hang out while he was in town.

Ugh! I hated to hear her ramble, but would I love to be a fly on the wall during that call. Of course, he would be otherwise occupied while in L.A., so I smiled to myself and let it drop.

We spent the rest of the day wandering around, and grabbed a quick lunch at a salad bar at an organic grocery near my house. A couple of hours later, the Paparazzi began trailing us, and it was time to call it a day.

Wendy thrived on the photographers and reading about herself in the rag mags. Again it was new, but the one time with David was enough to tell me that I hated it. *Ugh!* Cade was surrounded by the hype daily, but I cared about my career, not the glam sham. I didn't know how he did it and doubted I'd ever find it palatable.

When I got home, my mom was waiting. She was ready to go to the meeting with my agent, publicist, manager, and attorney, but I was dreading the entire thing.

We met them at a trendy bistro near my house where my manager had reserved a room in the back. "Wow, a private room. Either this is a real big deal, or I'm paying them *way* too much," I said. I was over eighteen, but I needed my mother's guidance.

"I think it's a big deal, honey." She threw me a somewhat disapproving look. "I'm sure it has to do with your little trip off to London last weekend, and also what's in store during the next months to promote your film."

"Yeah." My parents weren't too happy with me, and Nate, over the trip, either.

My stomach fluttered nervously. I was paying these people, but this felt like they were all ganging up on me.

The room was warm with Asian décor with deep red and gold tablecloths. The soft lighting was a sharp contrast to the brightness of the weather outside. I knew Jeanne picked the place because she used it for her other clients. It was notorious for keeping the press at bay, and we were less likely to be mobbed.

Ken, my agent, Joel, my attorney and Jeanne, my manager, were already waiting at the table. My publicist, Ruth, came in a couple of minutes after we got there. The restaurant management had placed some oriental screens on the south side to separate us from the rest of the room, which was weird, considering it was empty anyway.

"Hey," I murmured as I took a seat across from them. My mother took the one to my right.

"Hello, Brook. Diane," Jeanne said. "Can we get you something to drink before we start?"

"I'll just have an iced tea, thank you," I told the waiter, and then my mother ordered a gin and tonic. It was only four o'clock, so I raised my eyebrows at her and was repaid with a dirty look. She must be thinking it was going to be a fucking ordeal. I'd never seen her drink so early. I ran a nervous hand through my hair.

"So," I started. "What's this about?"

They all glanced at each other, and then Joel started the conversation.

"Brook, it's our job to advise and protect your interests, so that is what this meeting is about," he began.

"I'm listening," I said and took a sip from the iced tea the waiter had just left, raised my eyes to look at them and waited.

Jeanne waited until the waiter retreated and then she said, "This is partly my fault. I shouldn't have gotten you those tickets to London without asking what you were going for, so for that, I apologize."

I was getting flushed, the heat coming up under the skin on my face. "What I did in London is *my* business," I said. "I don't have to ask any of your permission to take a trip." I couldn't help but be defensive and angry. "You're saying you're sorry now after you bitched at me on the phone? I don't get it."

Ken spoke up. "Brook, you're under contract with Pinnacle," he paused.

"That's not news to me, Ken. So?"

My mom put a hand on my arm. "Brook, just hear them out. Relax." I glared at her. So now she was on their side?

"There are clauses in your contract that state that you will not become involved personally with any of your co-stars," Jeanne continued. "Clauses, I might add, we put in place to protect you. You *were* a minor when you started filming, and we took all the necessary steps to ensure that you'd be protected."

I was getting upset now. "Are you telling me that I can't make friends or socialize with my cast?"

Joel interjected by placing a hand on my arm. "No, of course not, Brook. You can socialize, but you are prohibited from becoming *romantically* involved with any of them."

"What is this? The sixteenth century?" I laughed nervously. *How did they already know?* I wondered.

They all just looked at me with serious expressions on their faces, and Joel took out a cigarette.

"What are the consequences? Are others under the same restrictions, or am I special?" I asked sarcastically. My inner bitch was rearing its ugly head. I was really feeling uncomfortable as my hand automatically covered up the bracelet on my left wrist. Even though I was keeping it hidden, it still calmed my nerves to touch it.

"No, the entire cast has the same clause. There could be some legal ramifications for not only you but for whoever is involved with you. These could include losing your fee, and future royalties, cancelation of the contract, or dismissal from any subsequent roles with the studio." He puffed away on his cigarette.

I took a deep, shaky breath. "I see." The ice in my mom's glass clinked as she took a drink of her cocktail.

Ruth, my publicist, spoke up next. "Brook, you really need to be more careful in the future, of everything. It's all so critical to your image. What you say, where you go, who you spend time with, and how you handle yourself. I know it isn't fair, but this is part of the *business.*" She handed me a photo.

The picture was of me, and Cade, as I struggled to get away from him at Harrington's Pub last Saturday night. I was crying, and we both looked upset, his hands on both of my shoulders, as I pushed on his chest with both of mine. What was going on in the photo was pretty obvious. My heart lurched in my chest.

"Oh, God..." I closed my eyes.

"This picture was taken on a cell phone," she continued. "With technology the way it is these days, you can't be too careful. Thank goodness no others have surfaced, and I've been able to shut this person up with some money, but we won't always be this lucky. *If* Pinnacle got a hold of this, you'd be in a lot of trouble." She pursed her lips. "So would Caden," she added pointedly.

"I *understand*. But, this conversation is a little *late*! Why didn't I know this before I went to Vancouver?"

"Well, you were with David, so we didn't think it would be an issue."

"Then why did you put it in the fucking contract?" I blasted back.

"It's standard language when a minor is involved. The entire cast and crew are bound in those cases."

"We've already decided to keep things a secret, won't that be enough?" I could feel the tears prick the backs of my eyes. They all just stared at me.

Jeanne shoved the picture at me again. "Obviously not."

"What are we supposed to do now?" I put my hand over my eyes as I struggled to swallow the tears. They all waited for me to continue, and I swallowed. "Have Cade's people told him the same things?"

Jeanne spoke to this. "We don't know. We thought it best just to keep it close to the cuff, so we haven't called them to find out. We felt the fewer people who know about this, the better. I'm sorry to point this out, but you two haven't done a great job of keeping it a secret up to this point. So my guess is that yes, they'll talk to him."

"We only just realized our feelings. This sucks." I shook my head in confusion.

Jeanne sighed. "Brook. It's *been* obvious how the two of you feel. Everyone can see how you are drawn to each other, and it will only get worse as the promotion gears up."

"Right, so?" I nodded in understanding. "I tried not to love him, I really did." Thinking of the pull I always felt around him, my desire to be with him when he wasn't around... *this is damn impossible.* I resented that I had to sit here and justify my feelings.

"Does it make any difference now that I'm no longer a minor and that the film is already in the can?" I asked.

"No. The contract was in place before you turned eighteen. It is binding and written for the length of the promotional tour. As I mentioned, the entire cast is subject to this clause. Pinnacle also indicated that should more of the book series go into production, the same rules will apply for the remaining films. They feel it is possible a relationship between costars may hurt the box office receipts."

"That's dumb. Surely, two romantic leads involved for real will only help ticket sales?"

"No. Particularly, if you broke up before the series was completed. It could injure your working relationship, and the promotional obligations would suffer. Another consideration would be that fans wouldn't 'believe' your love connection on screen if they thought you suffered a bad break-up in real life," Joel answered. "It's just better to keep it professional, and fans can let their imaginations carry them from the books into the films."

"There is also the matter of all the little girls and women screaming for Cade. They all want to fantasize that they'll end up with him, and that won't be possible if he's openly in a relationship with you," Ruth interjected.

"Good God," my mother sighed, and looked toward me. I took it all in, the skin on my cheeks began to burn. "This is a little ridiculous, isn't it?"

"Unfortunately, their concerns are valid. If the two of you did end your relationship and the publicity of your personal lives affected the box office take, they'd have grounds to sue both of you. If you blatantly disregard the confines of your contracts it could seriously damage the chances to work with any major studios in the future." Joel's face was stern and determined, but he sighed. "*Any* of them, Brook."

God, why do all these people have to make it sound like they are talking about a cardboard cutout? I'm a person. I have a life and feelings. And Cade... I shuddered at what this would do to him.

It was like Ken read my mind when he spoke up next. "I know you probably feel that your career can handle the controversy, Brook, you're you and just getting established so mostly, the contracts aside, the public would overlook it on your part. But, they may blame Cade. Surely, we don't want to jeopardize his future," he said softly.

Man, that was low. I was a rebel at heart, and I didn't give a flying fuck about the production company or their silly-ass rules... for myself. But, he knew if I cared about Cade, then I would heed their words and warnings only too well.

My mother was rubbing my shoulders and I sighed.

"Look, this isn't a fling. We're in *love* with each other. How are we going to hide it for several months, or freaking years?" I cried.

Joel's eyes widened, and Ken got up from his chair to pace around the room. Jeanne just looked pissed as she loomed over me. I'd known her the longest, and she always was very honest with me on all levels.

"We never *planned* this, it just happened." I stopped and put my sunglasses back on my head, using them to push my hair off my face. *Could this be any more unfair?* My heart hurt, and my head was pounding.

"Not flaunting it is one thing, but I can't promise that either of us can *hide* how we feel, and I can't speak for Cade. I do know I *won't stop seeing him...*" I trailed off softly.

"Keeping it a secret we can work with." Joel spoke again. "Brook, you'll have to convince him to go along with it. Who else knows?" he asked.

"My brother, Gavin Sims and Cade's friend; Daniel Mayfield, and probably Cade's family. Jennifer Briggs indicated to me that she is aware of Cade's feelings, but other members of the cast probably suspect as well, if what you said is true about the two of us being so obvious." I leaned my head on my hand.

"Is that it?" Ruth persisted as she raised her eyebrows at me. "We have serious damage control to do, Brook, you need to tell me everyone that might suspect."

I sighed. "Martin knows for sure. He warned Cade to keep his distance and remain professional after he saw our chemistry at the audition. David also mentioned a suspicion although I've never confirmed anything with him."

"You and Cade are both actors, so you'll just have to put on a damn good show. You should remain with David." Jeanne began. "Do you think he'd agree to be a beard?"

A beard was a stupid term that the press and industry used when one relationship was used to disguise another. I interrupted her angrily. "Wait! I don't want to use anyone! Is this some sort of game to you people? This is *my* life! Cade's *life*!" I leaned forward toward them all. I was so pissed.

"I can't put Cade through parading David around as if we're together again. It would kill him, even if we were only pretending. He's already endured all of that for months, and it's not fair to David either. I don't want to do that to either one of them," I cried.

"Honey, they are just trying to protect you both," Ruth answered. "You and Cade can still talk on the phone and sometimes we can arrange some meetings after the two camps take the necessary precautions. But the two of you cannot openly date or show affection in public. It's okay to go to cast functions, but you are not allowed to act like a couple in any way."

She sighed at the sadness obviously on my face. "Also, you'll have to be careful of how you act when the two of you are together for the promotion of the movie, and what you say at interviews. You'll need to arrive at and leave from everything separately, and you can't even hug him on the red carpets," she said, her face showing her concern. I put my head in my hands fighting the tears.

"Are you serious?" I protested. "This isn't fair."

"I'm so sorry, Brooklyn. We'll do what we can to help, and we'll script you on what you can say when you promote the film." Jeanne came to the chair on my left to sit next to me.

"Oh, God," I breathed. "I've watched Cade for the past couple of years. He's hugged or put his arm around his other costars. Why am I so different?"

Jeanne sighed. "As we've said, the chemistry you have with Cade is volatile. It's palpable, evident for the entire world to see. You have to tone it down."

"So, I can't ever let my feelings show for him unless I'm on set being Julia." The tears pricked my eyes as I shook my head. "I don't know if that is *even possible*." I wiped a tear away. I couldn't have the paparazzi seeing me cry with my staff because they'd know something was up.

"None of you have any idea how we feel ab—" I stopped myself mid-sentence, and took a deep breath to steady myself. "I need to talk to Cade, and I need to get the hell out of here. Thank you all for coming and for sharing your thoughts. I know you're just doing your jobs." I stood to leave.

My mother followed suit. "Thank you all, so much," she said. "I'll try to reason with her." Then, she followed me out.

* * *

I DECIDED IT would be too late in London to call Cade immediately, but when I opened my phone to send a text, there was one he'd sent three hours earlier already waiting for me.

Going to bed without you is torture. Mind, body, and heart, I'm aching without you.

I closed my eyes, my heart lurching at his message. I loved him so much. How were we going to get through this without being able to touch each other? How would I hide my feelings when I looked at him? How could we act like casual acquaintances? I didn't think I'd be able to carry it off.

I feel the same way. I miss you so much. Please call me tomorrow. I love you, always.

I sent my reply, then got ready for bed and mulled over everything that was said during the meeting as I cleaned my teeth. I didn't think anyone took a picture of us at the pub, but I'd been too overwrought with emotion to notice anything that went on around us. I sighed, and put my long hair up in a scrunchie, as was my habit before sleep.

It was after 10, so I was surprised when my phone rang. My new ringtone was the song he sang to me at the wrap party. I needed to talk to him more than I realized.

"Hey... aren't you supposed to be in bed?" I smiled into the phone.

"It's a lonely hell without you. I miss you, love."

"Me, too. I got my press packet today. That's good news, isn't it?" I asked him.

"Yeah, only twelve days, five hours and thirty-six minutes until I can kiss your mouth and wrap my arms around you." He was teasing me.

"Mmmm. Sounds like heaven to me," I sighed. "You're very sweet to me."

"Mmmm, is right." He sounded relaxed, which would be a good prelude to the conversation I needed to have with him.

I didn't know how to begin, so there was a pregnant pause that quickly rid him of his calm demeanor.

"Is something wrong?" He paused. "I can sense something's up. What happened during your meeting, Brook?"

"Wow. How do you know me so well?" I asked softly.

"Because you're part of me. It's like knowing myself, except you're *much* more delicious." I could picture the crooked grin he'd have on his face.

I smiled. "That's a matter of opinion. I find you very motivational." I told him with a little giggle.

He laughed, and I could picture his hand was running through his hair. "I missed you."

"Me, too, Cade."

"Okay, spill. Tell me everything."

"Um..." I began hesitantly. "You're not going to like it."

I heard him take a breath. "Just tell me what it is."

"I was informed about the confines of our contracts with

Pinnacle," I began. "Apparently, there's a clause in them that prohibits us from any romantic involvement."

"What? That's utterly ridiculous!" He laughed. "They can't do that!" he retorted.

"My lawyer told me they can, and they have." I could feel my eyes begin to tear and my throat throb. "I'm just in hell," I said softly.

"Did they give any specifics?" His voice was tense and angry.

"Yeah. They said that Pinnacle needs you to be single because of the fangirls' fantasies, and they have legitimate concerns about a possible split during the promotion of the first movie or filming subsequent sequels, that it could seriously damage box office. If that happened, they could sue us, cancel our contracts, and a bunch of other unpleasant shit." I started to cry softly.

"Brooklyn, don't cry, love. We'll figure this out. I'm not going to let anything keep us apart. I promise, okay?" But I could hear an edge of panic in his voice.

"Cade, the worst part is that it could damage your career, and I won't let that happen. I just have to believe that we'll survive this, that eventually we will be able to be together as we want."

"What about *your* career, Brook? This could be your *year*!" His voice was getting louder, angrier. "I was going to tell you I'd changed my mind about keeping it a secret. It's too much bloody work, and I'm miserable as fuck!"

"We have to. I'm sorry." I waited a minute to continue. "There's more." I sniffed back the tears and he sighed.

"Ugh!!!!" He yelled, but waited for me to tell him the rest.

"They said we couldn't be seen out alone together, that we can never arrive, leave or travel together. We even have to be careful what we say about each other in interviews and watch how we act when we're near each other. We can attend cast functions, but not together, we can't act like a couple... *ever*. If we're asked about our relationship, they want us to deny it... and... and..." My heart was breaking at telling him the next part.

"Honey, I'm sorry I got upset, it's just pissing me off, but we'll get through this. I'll do anything, wait however long I need too, to be with you. You know that."

"You might change your mind after this next thing," I moaned. His silence told me he was worried, so I just barreled on with it. "Um... Oh, God." My voice cracked. "They want me to get back together with David."

"*What? No!* This is just fucking brilliant, Brooklyn!" His voice rose as frustration overtook his words. "I can't go through that kind of hell again. I'm going to call my lawyer right now," he growled.

"Calm down. Believe me, I don't want this; I won't hurt you like that!" I paused. "We might have an option, but you need to have an open mind. Just remember how much I love you, okay?"

He sighed heavily. "I'm sorry, but I just *got* you, and now this fucked up mess! Bloody hell! I want to *kill* something!"

"Well, David is between jobs and might need money. What if I *hire* him to go to functions with me, hold my hand a little, but no kissing, or anything. I'll just have him there to keep the illusion the studio wants in place."

"And, all the while I have to stand there and *watch*? Smiling for the cameras, while my guts are ripped out? No! I *can't*! Don't ask that of me, Brook." I'd never heard him this upset. I waited as he calmed down. "Besides, he'll never agree to that. I know I wouldn't."

"It would only be for show. You know I'm with you now, and nothing would change between us, I promise," I whispered. "Please, just think about it."

"Except he'd be able to touch you, kiss you," I could hear the pain dripping from his words, "when I can't."

"I wouldn't let him kiss me, Cade. After what I told you in London, you should know I don't want anyone else touching me. I *meant* that. Trust me, please?" I begged.

"I do, Brook. But, this is going to be bloody unbearable for me."

"I know. It's killing me too, but I love you enough to do this. It sucks, but we don't have a choice. For us to get through this, I have to believe you're with me, okay?"

He took a deep breath and let out the sigh. "How did they know about us?" It suddenly dawned on him to ask. "I haven't told anyone."

"I didn't either. There was a photo that someone took at the pub while we were fighting. They sent it to my publicist, demanding hush money." My lips pressed into a taut line.

"Fucking people! Is this how it is going to be?" His voice was strained.

"I think it will get much worse before it gets better. Don't let this rip us apart, Cade. I love you." My voice broke on the words.

"I love you, too. I'll do anything for you; you know that." He took a shaky breath. "But, um..."

"Yeah?"

"Have you already *hired* David?" he asked.

"No." I tried to clear my throat. "I wouldn't do that without talking to you first, you know?" I hoped the love I felt came through in my voice.

"Thank you, love." I could hear his voice relax. I yawned, and he heard it. "You sound so tired, sweetheart. We'll talk about this tomorrow. Into bed with you, vixen, and *don't forget to remember me.*" His voice sounded weary.

I smiled when he repeated words from the script. It was the title of the second book, but already, he'd said during filming of the first movie.

"I wish I were right there beside you." He sighed. "I miss holding you."

"Mmmm... I miss you, too, and *you're burned into me.*" I repeated Julia's line that followed Ryan's, so Cade would know I caught it. "I'll let you know what he says. Don't worry, okay? I love you."

"Okay, I love you, more... Bye sweet," he said and hung up.

I crawled into bed, wrapped my arms around myself and shuddered at the situation.

I hoped to hell David wouldn't be a jerk and agree to help us. Cade was my future and we had to make it through this necessary charade.

Chapter 10
The Madness Begins

Brooklyn

AS I GOT READY for the MTV awards, my heart was beating wildly. I was worried about the interview, and what type of questions we'd be asked about our personal lives. Even though we hadn't been out promoting the movie together yet, there were tons of things online that focused on our relationship. Youtube and other sites had multiple fan-made videos focusing on our chemistry on set, and already the world already speculated if our relationship was real. The enormity of what could happen to us scared the shit out of me.

I had done my best to block all of it out, but if I were honest, many of the fans were spot on. When we did that MTV interview on the set last February, we'd both said several things that could be construed as personal. Even in jest, we basically blew our cover even before we knew how we felt ourselves. We played and goofed with each other *way* too much for mere co-stars. I'd been so naïve and oblivious to how those words would be interpreted later. When I'd watched the interviews, I could see what everyone was seeing between us. *But hell, we were friends then. We hung out; we goofed around. That's what we did,* my mind protested.

Damn it! I needed to get through this interview, and then get Jeanne to help me find a way to be with Cade.

It would be the first time I'd seen David since our break-up two weeks ago, and Jeanne and Ken had worked out the details with him. *Shit. He was going to receive a hundred grand every time he went somewhere with me. I only made two million on the entire fucking movie.*

I picked up my phone and called my agent.

"Hey, Jeanne, what's the schedule for today?" I really didn't care about any of it except how Cade and I were going to be together, afterward.

"Hi, Brook. The car will pick you up in twenty minutes. They've already picked up David. He's been briefed on what will go down and how he needs to behave. Cade should be there when you get there, so David and you will meet him there." She stopped for a minute as she contemplated her next words. "Okay, so hand-in-hand, arm-in-arm, I don't care how you do it, but the two of you need to show some form of affection as you walk up to Cade."

"This is going to be hard on Cade, Jeanne." I sighed.

"It's necessary, Brook. Cade will have his individual photo call, David will drop back, and they'll take photos of you by yourself, and then you and Cade will pose together."

"Can we touch at all during that time? Jeanne, you have to understand how seeing me with David is gonna affect him. I have to be able to let him know in some small way that I care about him."

"We'd prefer it if you wouldn't, Brooklyn, but if you must, then you can have your arms around each other for the pose. You know, lightly behind the back, no hugging, and no kissing. *None.*" Her voice was stern.

"Cade knows what this is about, and he's on board." I could tell she was sidetracked as she went through the itinerary. "Oh, and try not to look *adoringly* at each other, too. You guys suck when it comes to that. Focus, Brooklyn, focus." She was teasing, but I *was* not laughing. "This will be huge for your career. Being with Cade on any red carpet is notable. Known movie stars clamor to be next to him, and you're just getting started."

"Thanks for the reminder," I scowled.   I didn't really care about that crap, so it was a good thing that it was her job to worry about it. I rolled my eyes and nodded. "Okay, is the interview on the carpet or after the awards?"

"Right after the photo calls on the carpet. Keep it light when it comes to your relationship, but answer the questions about your roles, the characters and the books as you normally would. Except don't give up too many details of the film, only a taste to get them to the theaters, you know the drill." She sounded nervous, too, and she noticed my silence on the other end of the line.

"Do I?"

Jeanne sighed. "Look, Brook, I'm really, really sorry. I know this sucks for you guys," her voice pleaded with me for understanding. "But Cade's people are adamant that we have to keep your relationship under wraps. He won't blow out the box office if he gets tagged as trashing your relationship. Maybe when the movie gets closer to release..."

Oh, sure. When the movie releases and the studio exec's pockets overflow, then they'll want us to flaunt it. "It's okay, Jeanne. I know it's not your fault, and you're doing what you can. Will there be any way to see Cade while he's in town? It's been weeks since we've been together, and we need some time alone."

"I've already called Cade's agent, Denise Kirby, and we've arranged for me to bring him over to your place for a while tonight. Will your parents be cool with that?" Jeanne wanted to know.

I felt my pulse speed up. "Yeah, they're cool. How long will I have with him?"

"Until he calls her to pick him up, but it would be best if it were in the middle of the night that they come to take him back to his hotel. Less chance of photographers, you know. So, maybe ten or twelve hours."

My heart fluttered and the corners of my mouth lifted slightly. At least, I'd have a few hours with him. "Thanks, Jeanne. I really mean it." I hung up the phone and went to finish my makeup.

On the drive to the event, David didn't say much, so finally, I decided to break the silence. "Hey, David, it's good to see you. Thanks for doing this for me."

He looked straight ahead. "Sure, maybe someday you can return the favor."

"Yeah, of course," I said, even though I knew it wasn't likely.

"So things aren't so smooth with Mr. Perfect, eh, Brook?"

"David, do we really have to do this? This has isn't about Cade; it's about our commitments to Pinnacle Studios and promotion of the film. You and I have always been good friends, even more before we were a couple. I don't want to lose that, so can we just get past all this shit, *please*?"

He reached out and took my hand. "Okay. Look, I'm sorry. It's just not easy to know you don't love me anymore." His brow crinkled but he tried to smile at me as he squeezed my hand.

"I still love you, David. You've been a big part of my life. I haven't forgotten that, and I'm sorry. I never wanted to hurt you." I squeezed back.

"Okay." His other hand touched my chin. "Let's do this." I smiled, hoping that we really could be friends. *Cade might not like it, but he'd understand.*

The door to the limo opened, and the sun shone in. When I stepped out onto the Red Carpet, the crowd was already screaming. The throng of fangirls screeching at the top of their lungs made my ears hurt.

"Hmmph…" *The object of their desire, and my desire,* I thought. My heart was pounding in my chest as my eyes searched for him through the flashing cameras and over the heads of the hundreds of squealing women.

There he was. My heart thumped in my chest and my hungry eyes devoured him.

Gorgeous as ever in a dark gray jacket, black slacks and a lighter gray button-down and the classic Ray-Bans he always wore. His hair tousled adorably in a way that screamed to have my fingers to run through it. He was smiling brilliantly as he frantically signed autograph after autograph. "You're mine! *Mine!*" one of them screamed and the rest of them added their screams to the din. "Marry me!" "I love you, ahhhhh!" Hundreds of them were screaming at him. *Holy shit.* I started to giggle lightly. This was nuts. I mean, I guess I expected it; but it seemed silly.

"Hmmph!" I huffed and shook my head slightly as I got out of the car. *Get used to it Brooklyn.*

David took my hand and we walked up, cameras flashing. I tried to remember to smile but my eyes were locked on his. Good thing my sunglasses hid the direction of my gaze. I waved to the crowd and the screams amplified.

He stopped signing autographs when he heard the commotion. The girls were actually begging for my autograph as well. I was surprised as I signed my name next to Cade's scribble across one of the first released movie stills.

"What's it like to kiss the hottest actor in the world?" they screamed. I rolled my eyes behind my sunglasses.

"You're so lucky!"

"*Oh, my God*! Ahhhhhh!!"

"Is he a good kisser? Tell me!!" They kept screaming over each other at me, and I couldn't help laughing at the absurdity of it all.

Okay… seriously? I took the books and photos they offered and started signing. I'd never expected anything like this, and it was a little overwhelming.

"Well… um… sure. It's hot!" I smiled at them, feeling ridiculous as heat infused my cheeks. The women screamed even louder. "Sort of amazing." I nodded and bit my lip. More screaming followed, more shrill and concentrated than before, if that were possible. *Holy Fuck.*

I glanced at Cade and he was smiling from ear to ear and shaking his head in disbelief. *As if he'd never experienced this before, but it seemed like every woman in the world wanted him.*

After a few minutes, the producer came up and told the fans they needed to let us get to our photo calls and interviews. We stood separately as the photographers swarmed around us. What seemed like hundreds of flashes hurt my eyes as I waited for them to finish. Jeanne, who was standing off to the side waiting to move with me from one reporter to the next, motioned for me to remove my sunglasses.

Finally, they asked us to come together. As Cade's arm went around my waist, I wanted to melt into him, but did my best to stand there, smile and not stare up at him as much as I wanted. I did allow myself the occasional glance, and he leaned down to speak to me so no one would really hear him. "Love you, Brook. You look gorgeous."

My breath caught and my smile widened as cameras flashed at a frenzied pace. My hand squeezed his waist a little tighter.

The interviews went pretty well; Cade and I were standing close together, I held the microphone so he'd have to lean in a little to answer his questions. At least, we got to touch a little that way and I could smell his cologne; musky, salty and fresh. They asked about the filming, whether we were both aware of all of the *Dr. Ryan* hoopla, if we'd read the book series, what we thought about it and also how it was to work with Martin. *No problem. This is cake.*

"We heard that you might be working on some music for the score. Tell us about it," the interviewer asked. I held the mic toward his face, my other arm crossed over my body under the other elbow, as I waited for his response.

I remembered the day we sat on set for hours talking about music, and what artists we hoped would be involved in the soundtrack. I loved how much music was part of him, and it was just another connection between us.

"Oh, no. Maybe for one of the films, but it's not official. We've barely had a conversation about it." he finished his answer.

"What about you, Brooklyn? Have you heard him play?" she wanted to know.

"Oh, yeah. Um, I mean, sure. I've heard him play, and he's... spontaneously brilliant, so I hope we will get a song out of him." I glanced up at him, and he was watching me. His mouth lifted at the corner, and I knew my words brought him pleasure. If he wanted me to get through this damn interview, he'd have to stop dazzling me like that. "I'm sure it would be amazing, actually." I was flustered.

Then it happened, she asked the question we'd hoped to avoid.

"We've all heard about how hot your onscreen chemistry is and how that is what clinched Brooklyn's casting. Cade, you had input with the director, right? Is there anything going on between the two of you off screen?"

I couldn't speak at that exact second, so I held the mic up for Cade and waited. He was the experienced one, and so I just clamped my mouth shut and concentrated on not smiling.

"Oh yeah," he said. My eyes widened behind my glasses. "I liked her in the beginning. I even asked her to marry me a few times, but it didn't go anywhere." He tried to make a joke of it, but it wasn't, not at *all*.

"Oh, I'm so sorry about that. Well," she directed the comment to me now. "Maybe you'll reconsider?"

I flushed. *Fuck!*.

"Oh um, I've learned a lot from Cade, and he's become one of my closest friends." I stammered uncomfortably, pushed my hair back and glanced at Cade through my peripheral vision. He was looking away, behind my head and I felt my heart sink. "I hope we'll stay that way."

My words hurt him, even though he knew the game we were playing. With David standing less than ten feet behind us in the camera's eye line, I had no choice. I had to do what we'd agreed to do; to protect our contracts.

I tried to get him to look at me so I could convey something with my eyes, but he would never meet my gaze after that. He looked sad, and my heart was breaking that I couldn't clarify but surely he knew why I said what I did.

We went inside the awards venue and Cade, with his agent, were seated a few rows behind David and me. I could feel Cade's resentment radiate toward us. David kept holding my hand, occasionally leaning in to speak in my ear and at one point put his arm around me.

It was the longest fucking two hours of my life.

I could feel his gaze on the back of my neck like a white-hot poker, his resentment seeping through my skin. I couldn't wait to get out of there, to go home, be alone with him and try to soothe him in whatever way he would let me.

When I finally got to my house, I jumped on the phone to Jeanne. "Okay. When is he coming?" I asked, slightly out of breath.

"Listen, Brook, I'm not sure if he is. His agent said he was upset and wanted to go back to his hotel."

"Yeah, it was hard on him seeing me with David. I'm gonna try to call him," I said sadly.

"I'm really sorry. Didn't you guys talk about this? Surely Denise briefed him."

"Yes, but it's harder than we thought to carry this off. Listen I really have to call him. I'll call you back."

Cade didn't answer, so I texted him.

Get your *sexy ass* over here *now*! I love you and miss you so much. Please?

I pushed send. My nerves were shot and my hands were shaking as I waited for the response.

My phone buzzed about ten minutes later as I was pacing back and forth out by the pool.

Okay.

Apparently, he was still brooding, but at least, he'd be here soon.

Call Denise. She has this worked out with Jeanne. I'm counting the minutes until I'm in your arms.

I let out a huge sigh of relief as tears came to my eyes.

Okay, time to take his mind off all that bullshit.

I went upstairs and peeled off my clothes, piled my hair on top of my head, and put on a sexy black bikini with gold metal rings at the hips and between my breasts. This was the most revealing of any bikini I had ever owned, by far, so I pulled a black gauze sarong around my hips and tied it on the left. I had butterflies in my stomach as I wondered if Cade would like it.

My dad was out of the country for work, and I'd asked my mom and Nate to give me some time at home alone this afternoon with Cade, before coming back for dinner. I planned to make Pasta Carbonara for everyone.

My house was in a private neighborhood in Toluca Lake so that Jeanne would meet Denise, and on a side street in a nearby neighborhood, he would get in Jeanne's car and then she'd bring him to the back entrance to my house. Her car was often seen near my house, so the paparazzi would be much less suspicious that way. I was getting used to the attention, and slowly more aware of how to avoid them. I was still relatively unknown, but the minute the speculation of Cade and me together got a foothold, all bets were off and it was sometimes impossible to avoid the press.

My heart was beating so fast when they finally pulled up, and when the back gate in the twelve-foot brick wall around our pool opened. The path from the side door on the garage was hidden behind part of the wall, and it felt like it took them forever to open it.

Jeanne came through first, and then he followed her.

There he was, standing right in front of me, and all mine.

He took his sunglasses off and shoved them in his pocket. I could see by his tight expression he was still upset, but I didn't let that put me off.

I got up and walked around the pool to him, touched his chest as both arms slid around me. He took a possessive hold on me and it was what we both needed.

"Thank you, Jeanne. This means the world to me." My eyes never left his face as I spoke to her. I bit my lower lip as he looked into my eyes.

Then the talking was over, his arms turned my body to his and we were kissing as if we were starving, my arms going around his neck and into his hair, his arms around my back and one clutching at the sarong on my hip.

"Mmmmm... " I murmured against his mouth. Jeanne was getting a good show, but neither of us cared. "You taste so good. Not being able to touch you like this earlier, just hell." I wanted him to know that it was just as difficult for me as it was for him. "I've missed you so much."

He was still holding me tight, his face turned into my neck, breathing me in. For a long time, he didn't say anything, just continued to hold me and kiss the side of my face, shoulder, and neck. My hands went to his hair and I stroked it back off his face. "I'm sorry about before, babe," I said into the curve of his neck.

He kissed the top of my head and finally placed a finger under my chin to lift my eyes to his and he finally spoke. "I didn't like it. Seeing him touching you like that when I couldn't, hearing you say I was your 'good friend' was worse, and having to stand there and smile like some stupid sod through it all…" He trailed off, disgust in his voice. I saw the pain in his eyes, and my heart ached.

"Cade, you're here with me, David isn't. You know it's all for show, and besides, you *are* my friend." My eyes pleaded with him when his face tightened. "You're my best friend, my lover, the love of my life… you're *everything*."

I stood on tiptoe to kiss him. "Come on, don't you know that yet?" I heard the gate close behind Jeanne as she left, and felt some of the tension ease from his body.

"It's easier to believe when you're in my arms like this." He hugged me tight.

"Did you bring a suit?" I giggled as I yearned to get him, at least, semi-naked. "We can get a little sun now that the filming is over." The movie was set, mostly in Boston, which was a far cry from sunny L.A.

"I did. But I'd rather just look at you." His eyes were soft as he looked at me. "You're so beautiful, love."

"Well, now that it's finally *here*," A big smile split my face. "I want to *see* that *sexy ass*." I teased him. "Go change, and I'll get you something to drink." He started to walk away, but his eyes never left me, raking up and down my body. He grabbed me and pulled me back into his arms.

"How am I supposed to hang out with you all day, when you look good enough to eat?" He smiled then bent to shower my shoulders and neck with hot, openmouthed kisses.

"Ugh! You're killing me! Just change, please? My bedroom is at the top of the stairs, to the left. You can put your bag in there. *Go!*" I pushed him away and went to the bar on the patio.

He came back down after a few minutes and I had opened a beer for him, and gotten a soda for myself. He was in black swim trunks, his chest bare, and I couldn't wait to get my hands on him.

"Am I staying *with* you in there?" He was sheepish, a blush rising on his high cheekbones. "I really like being in there; it smells just like you." He stretched out on one of the loungers, and I looked at his body, he was so gorgeous. He was muscular and solid. *Mmmm*, I thought as desire made my heart beat faster.

"Unless you'd rather not?" I smiled as his eyebrow raised and he shook his head with a grin. He knew I was kidding as he shook his head. "My mom's cool. I've told her how madly in love with you I am," I was teasing him now. "She understands how difficult it will be for us to get any time alone unless we can be at home."

"I think I love your mum," he said.

"Hmmm. Well, I'm not great at sharing." I sat down next to him on the lounger and realized how stupid I was for saying that considering what had just happened at the award show.

"Yeah, I know the feeling." His mouth quirked with irony, and he ran a hand up and down my arm in a feather-light caress. I placed my hand over his as his eyes met mine. "It's bloody killing me."

"Hey. It's you and me now. Always." I leaned in to kiss him, my mouth open, gently sucking on his lips. Just as his tongue came into my mouth, I pulled back and sucked on it a little more, and then Cade groaned and took my mouth in a deep kiss, his tongue moving into my mouth and his hand around the base of my head, pulling me closer. *Oh, God... he tastes so good.*

"Mmmm... " Cade groaned as our mouths parted reluctantly.

"How did we make it through all of those months without all of this yummy stuff?" A full smile split my face. I was so content and happy to be with him.

"I died a thousand deaths, and you were blissfully oblivious!" He laughed at me, ruffling my hair as I hugged him.

"No, I wasn't. Not at all." My voice softened. "I was fighting it, confused by my feelings." A sad smile found its way to my face, and he brushed his knuckles along my jaw. "I'm sorry I wasted so much time."

"It wasn't wasted time." His eyes were soft on my face. "We were still together most of that time, and we became so close. However, I'm certainly glad you've finally had an epiphany." He grinned at me, and raised my hand to kiss my palm. "Are we alone?" he asked hopefully, looking into my face, his brows rose in the way I adored. "I can't stand not touching your body. You're sexy as hell."

"We are." I smiled as Cade's eyes widened a little. "Surprise!" I raised my hands and moved my fingers like they were a sparkly expletive, then reached down to touch the big bulge in his trunks. "Is that for me?" I teased as I felt it rise under my hand, emboldened because I knew he wanted me.

His eyes burned into me, and his mouth twitched into a little smirk. "Did I tell you how much I love you?" He was just so damn hot he made my body react just looking at him.

I felt my mouth fall open slightly as I stared in his eyes, my tongue darting out to run over my upper lip. I saw the desire and the love behind his lashes, and knew it had to be mirrored in my face. Want rushed through my veins, and my stomach tightened as I gazed at him through hooded eyes. I bit my lower lip.

"God Brooklyn, you drive me insane with wanting you." He put his arms around me and dragged me to lay over his body, his hand insistent on the back of my head as his mouth came down hungrily on mine. His other hand slid to my hip, grasping it to pull my lower body closer to his. *Oh, God*, I thought, as my hands slid around his body.

After a minute or two of kissing, he stopped suddenly. His lips twitched up with a mischievous grin, and then stood up from the lounger and swooped me with him in one movement. "You're going to get it for teasing me this way!"

Instantly, he rushed forward and jumped, plunging both of us into the pool. "No! Cade! Stop! Ahhhhh!" I screamed as I clung to him, just before we whooshed under water.

We surfaced, gasping and laughing, still clinging to each other. "Oh, now you're gonna get it!" I said, my arms still around his neck. I felt his hands slide down my back and shivers ran up my spine, but not from the cold water in the pool.

Our movements turned into slow motion. I was mesmerized as his eyes turned serious. My hands slid up to brush his hair back and then to the back of his head as he bent toward me. He was so beautiful as his blue eyes bore into me, his lids heavy, his lips hovering just above mine. The desire so potent, it made me gasp. I closed my eyes and reached for his mouth with mine. He brushed my upper lip with his lower one.

"Really?" he whispered against my lips. "Then please, please give it to me," he said, his eyes closing. His tongue flicked my upper lip and then sucked it in between both of his. "I beg you." His hands on my body felt like warm silk. "I want all of you, Brook."

His mouth opened over mine and I was lost. He was moving to the side of the pool without breaking the kiss, pressing me up against the side. His knee slid up between my legs to rub and press on the center of my desire, pinning me to the side of the pool.

"Oh, God. You're so hot," he breathed as he took my mouth in another onslaught of deep kisses. I couldn't get enough of him, couldn't get close enough to his body, but he moved slowly, making the most of every kiss, and every touch between our bodies. I trembled in his arms.

"Uhhhhh... It's you. You make me hot." I gasped as his hand moved to my breast, lifting the brief material of my bikini top aside to massage and tease the nipple. It was already taut, but I felt it grow in his hands. He groaned, and pressed against me as he took in the meaning of my words.

"Oh, God, Brook, I want to make love to you. Is it okay? Here? Right now?" His breath was coming in short bursts.

"Mmmm... Now..." I breathed as I raised my eyes to look into his. My lids were heavy, and I could see the same desire reflected in Cade's expression. He was intense, serious, and in love. My breath caught in my throat.

I knew my mother and brother wouldn't be back for a couple of hours. He hoisted my legs around his waist as I pressed my pelvis into his. I could feel his rock hardness against my burning softness, and I wanted him inside me. He lifted me a bit higher, his hands under my ass so that he could suckle my breasts. My hands buried themselves in his wet hair, and my nipples were screaming under his ministrations, until he had me gasping.

"Oh, I missed you," I whispered into the top of his head, as he bent to my breast. I felt his arm around my body tighten and the one under my rear, moving forward, searching, seeking for the flesh beneath the bikini bottoms. He pushed aside the material and slid two fingers into me. "Ahhhh... uhhh..." He had me gasping.

"Tell me what you want," he whispered against my skin. "I want to give you everything, love." He was sucking on my breasts and moving up to kiss my collarbone; upward to the column of my neck, his mouth was hungry for the taste of my skin. His fingers thrust inside me under the water and I wanted more.

As I sank to be on eye level, he took his fingers out of me, and started rubbing tiny circles on my sensitive flesh. "Oh, God." He had me gasping. "You're so good, I just want you so much," I whispered in his ear, and then drew the lobe into my mouth, sucking and nibbling. Mewling little sounds broke free as he continued to torment me.

"God, Brooklyn," he moaned. "You can't talk like that. I'll die if I don't have you."

I felt like I was on fire, and I wanted to feel all of him. He slid me down and I was pressed against his hardness, as he lifted me to rub our bodies together back and forth in delicious friction, his mouth locked on mine. My hands searched between our bodies for the string closure of his trunks, I wanted to touch him, feel him. I freed him from the confines of his suit, and my hand closed around his length. I moved my fingers up and down and gave a little squeeze with each downward motion.

"Oh, babe, I love you so much. These past two weeks have felt like fucking years," he said as he broke the kiss and lifted me, pulling the crotch of my bikini aside. I felt him slide into me as he settled me back down on him. He groaned against the skin of my shoulder and neck.

My legs wound around his waist, my arms around his shoulders and hands fisting in his hair as we made love. His hands slid under my hips to lift me up as he thrust into me, holding me as if I weighed nothing. He felt glorious, filling me to the hilt.

We kissed madly, straining for each other, moaning, I clenched my body around him as tight as I could, as he thrust deeper and deeper into me.

"Uhnn..." he groaned. "Whatever you're doing, Brooklyn... keep... doing it." Cade panted, his mouth moved like fire across the skin of my neck and shoulders, the top of my breasts and back to my mouth as he continued to move within me.

"Baby, does it feel good? What can I do to make it better?" he whispered against my skin, but the waves of pleasure had already begun deep within my body.

"Just don't stop loving me. That's all I'll ever need." I threw my head back as the orgasm wracked my body. "Uhhhhh! Oh, babe, come with me... please," I begged.

"Brook, I'm with you... Oh fuck," he gasped as I felt his body tense. He kept pumping into me until we were both left gasping, completely still except for the residual tremors that ran through us both. Spent.

My head rested on his shoulder, my arms wrapped around this man who meant more than I'd ever dreamed possible.

He stroked my wet hair down my back and kissed my shoulder softly, as our shudders lessened together. "Oh, Brooklyn. You are my life. I love you." My body was still trembling, my legs shaking uncontrollably.

"And, I love you," I said softly; then nuzzled his neck and then placed a wet, open mouth kiss on the throbbing vein I found there. We held each other for several minutes, not moving until he lifted his head and pulled my top back over my breasts, releasing my legs from around his waist as he slid out of me.

My hands found his trunks to pull them back into place. My hands curled in front of me between our bodies, as I kissed his chest. "I'll never get used to this."

"What?" he said, gently nuzzling my neck and side of my face with his nose. "I'll always be with you." He continued to rain kisses on my neck and shoulder, "And, it will always be this incredible, I promise."

"It's beyond words. I'm melting." I felt his smile against the skin of my shoulder. He raised his head, and kissed my open mouth softly.

"Mmmm, this is all amazing." He brushed his fingers on my face, and bent to give me one last lingering kiss. "I can't believe you want me."

"Goof!" He smiled incredulously, as the true male came out. "I'm starving, what's for dinner, woman?" He slapped me on the ass. I looked at him and burst into a giggle, as I turned and pulled myself out of the pool. Cade followed, chasing me into the house, both of us laughing out loud.

Chapter 11

No Screaming Please

Brooklyn

AFTER I SENT Cade up to my bathroom to take a hot shower and change, I called my mom. "I'm getting ready to start dinner. When will you be home?" I asked.

"In about forty-five minutes. How are things?" she asked. "Was Jeanne able to get Cade over there without any problems?"

"Yeah, we just hung out by the pool, went for a swim, and now he's in the shower. He's still on London time, so he's gonna wipe out early, I think, but it's just so nice to be here with him. I can't wait for you to get to talk to him, Mom."

"Nathan told me a lot about him. I'm looking forward to getting to know him, Brook."

"I know how much you love David, so I really appreciate that you're giving Cade a chance. You'll love him as much as I do, I promise."

"Okay, Brook."

"See you in a bit, bye."

Cade called me from the top of the stairs, "Hey, love, I'm finished.

Do you want to shower now?"

I ran up the stairs, undoing my sodden sarong and preparing to wring it out in the bathroom and hang it over the top of the shower. "Yeah, my mom is on her way home, so I'll just hop in quick." I watched him dry his hair with a towel; another slung low on his hips. Yes, I could get used to seeing this view on a regular basis.

I went up to him and drew my arms around his waist; running kisses across his strong back beneath his shoulder blades. I loved that he was tall. "I'm so glad you're here." I laid my head on his back.

His arms covered mine. "Me, too. It feels so good to be with you like this. Off to the shower with you, now." He brought my hand to his mouth to nibble a little, then turned to watch me strip and jump under the hot spray, a devilish gleam in his eye. My skin burned as if on fire where his eyes slowly roamed over my naked body.

"Mmmm... You're so gorgeous." He smiled his crooked grin at me and winked before taking a comb to his damp hair.

After we had both dressed in jeans and t-shirts, we sat in the kitchen as I began to get the ingredients together for our dinner. I was digging around for bacon and fresh peas when my mother and brother came in.

"Hi, Mom! Hey, Nate." I hugged my mom and took her by the arm to bring her over to Cade. "This is Cade Carlisle. Cade, this is my mom, Diane Halloway."

"It's a pleasure to finally meet you, Mrs. Halloway." Cade reached out to shake her hand.

My mother pulled him in for a hug. "Call me Diane. I feel like I know you already, Cade. Brooklyn and Nathan told me so much about you."

"Thank you, Diane. I'd be pleased to do so," he said, blushing.

I proceeded to make my carbonara sauce while they chatted together, sitting down at the table like old friends. I smiled as he recounted some of the stories he'd told me during our countless talks over the past year.

There wasn't anything my mother asked, that he hadn't already shared. I realized how well we really did know each other. I looked up occasionally and found Cade's eyes watching me move around the kitchen as I prepared the food. I raised an eyebrow at him once, and he smiled his big crooked grin.

"What?" I asked.

"Nothing." He shook his head as he kept on smiling.

"Hmmph..." I snorted, and he burst out laughing.

He came to stand behind me when I was chopping fresh herbs for the salad, his hands running up and down both of my arms. My skin tingled whenever he did that.

All evening, he would touch me gently at random moments. Raising my hand for a kiss to the inside of my wrist, he held it, trailing the fingers of his other hand lightly up and down my arm. Then he placed soft kisses on my temple or forehead, brushing my hair back, gently.

It felt so right, and I knew my mother noticed how happy we were together. My heart swelled in my chest as I watched him draw my mother in with his charming demeanor. *Irresistible.*

After dinner, we played Guitar Hero on Nate's Xbox. It was hilarious. Cade kicked all of our asses, of course, and watching my mom struggle on her turn was hilarious. Cade was great, attempting to teach her how to do it. He had her laughing so hard she was in tears. I was happy she liked him; my cheeks ached from smiling so much.

At the end of the evening, I took him upstairs and told him to make himself at home in my room. "I'll join you shortly," I whispered and placed a small kiss on his mouth.

"Don't be too long." His voice was low; his fingers entwined with mine. When I turned to leave the room he pulled me back for another hard kiss before he let me go.

I hated to leave him, but I was anxious to talk to my mother and see what she thought of him. Her light was shining into the dark hallway underneath the door to her room. I knocked and opened the door slightly to peek in. She was already in her bed, so I sat down on the edge.

"Well?" My cheeks flushed and my eyes sparkled with excitement.

"I can certainly see why you are so drawn to him, Brooklyn. He's a very nice young man. Very smart, respectful, and talented. Just as you said, honey." She was smiling cheekily.

"And funny, and beautiful, right?" I paused and smiled at her as she nodded with a grin. "I just can't believe all that stuff comes wrapped up in one person." I shook my head in disbelief. "He's so... *amazing*!"

My mother took my hand and looked at me warmly. "The best thing about him, Brooklyn, is that he loves you so much. It's very obvious. He touches you with such reverence, and I can see it's mutual. You're very lucky, even if this Pinnacle bullshit is a pain. I can see how difficult it will be for the two of you, but it'll all be worth it if you kids can stick it out." She smiled at me. "He *is* quite disarming, isn't he?" She sighed at me. I laughed along with her.

"Uh, oh. He's dazzled you, too." She winked at me.

I hugged her. "Thanks, Mom, Your support means a lot to me. Cade's really tired, so is it okay for him to sleep with me in my room? I don't want to miss a minute with him, even if it is only sleep. Jeanne said we would need to get him out of here around 4 or 5 AM, so that doesn't give us much time." I couldn't keep the sadness from my voice.

"Yeah, go ahead, honey, but behave yourselves." She shot me a warning look. "Goodnight."

"Love you," I said. Her meaning was clear as I left the room, but Cade wouldn't be easy to resist. I was lucky my dad was away on business or this would never fly.

"You too," she said, as the door to her room closed behind me as I left.

When I walked into my room; it was dark, except for the soft glow of the small light over the vanity in the bathroom that shone slightly through the crack in the bathroom door. He was laying back on my pillows, bare chest and flat stomach showing above the covers to his waist. He was sculpted and cut, even in sleep. The time difference was taking its toll.

If only he could be with me like this every night, I sighed.

I moved around the bed just looking at him. He was so perfect I couldn't breathe.

Thank you, God, I prayed silently to myself. *Thank you for letting us be us, for letting him love me, for bringing him into my life. I'll never ask for another thing even if I live a hundred years.*

I slipped out of my jeans and shirt then crawled under the covers in my bra and panties. I curled up next to him and just watched him for a while. I reached out to touch his chest and his hand covered mine.

"Brooklyn..." I waited. Was he asleep? "I love you." I settled on his chest, and his arms wrapped around me. *The earth could stop spinning in this moment, and I'd be fine.*

"I love you, too. So, much." I placed a few soft kisses on his chest and nuzzled into the light spattering of hair there with my nose. I sighed as I lay my head on his chest, his arms tightened around me and his legs entwined with mine. I drifted off to have my dreams filled with blue eyes, wild golden hair softly entwined through my fingers, and a perfect mouth molded to mine in passionate kisses. So sweet...

* * *

IT WAS DARK, and something was rousing me from my sleep. I felt a fluttering on my arm,

and a light kiss on my shoulder.

"Mmmm..." I felt Cade's length plastered up against my back as he ran his fingers up and lightly down my arm, punctuated with occasional kisses.

"It's 4 AM, love."

"Noooooo!" I turned to Cade, put my arms around him, and pulled him closer to me. "I don't want you to go," I whispered.

"I don't want to, either. I never want to leave you, Brooklyn." He kissed my mouth and his hand went to frame my face, his light touch already setting my senses and my body on fire.

The kisses were soft, but my arms tightened around him as he rolled me onto my back. "I'm so in love with you; I feel stupid. It's unreal. I can't bear to leave you even for a second." He made love to me with his words, and then his kiss deepened. My mouth was wild as I answered the urgency of the kiss.

"Do you have enough time to tell me what your schedule looks like?" I asked when he lifted his head and placed a series of small kisses on my nose, eyes and lips. I knew my voice was getting thicker, as emotion was threatening. "No matter how much we have to say goodbye, I'll never get used to it," I said as I stroked his hair.

"From what I understand, I don't have to be back in London for about two days, and then I have to do a couple of interviews in London and Paris for the film. Then back to L.A. in about a month for the Vanity Fair Photo shoot. Apparently, the entire cast is going to be hauled to some field in the middle of nowhere, but that's okay by me because I get to be with you." He was trying to cheer me up. "What do you have going in the next month, love?"

"I have a couple of auditions, some promotional radio, and TV morning show interviews with E!News. I think several of us have a couple of mall appearances during that same week of the VF shoot. It might be when we do Entertainment Weekly the following month; I can't remember exactly. Is it always like this?"

"Not for every movie. Just some of them."

My hands were rubbing, kneading his back and his butt muscles as he lay on top of me.

"Mmm... babe, that feels so good," he said as he started to kiss me again.

"Nice ass," I giggled and kissed him back. After a few mind-blowing kisses, I let myself ask the questions I had to ask.

"Do you really have to go, now? Is Denise waiting outside?" I whispered. "Can you stay until tomorrow?" My eyes widened as I thought of something Jen told me last week on the phone. "You know, Ethan is having a 'game night' party at his Condo tonight. Can you come?"

"It sounds fun, but not as fun as being alone with you. I guess it would be a good *test* of keeping our relationship a secret from all of them." He sighed, and I knew what he was thinking; that he didn't want to hide out. "Denise was going to pick me up when I called. I'll tell her that she and Jeanne will have to figure out another escape plan for me."

He rolled away from me and got up from the bed. His jeans were on the floor under the window, and he grabbed his cell phone from the pocket and dialed Denise. He was completely naked, and my eyes feasted on him as he moved. I was one lucky girl, I decided, as I rolled onto my stomach and placed my chin in my hands.

God, I want to lick your skin off. I smiled wickedly, and Cade raised his eyebrows questioningly. I shook my head at him and bit my lip.

"Hi Denise, it's Cade. Sorry, about the time, but I'm not ready to leave Brook's, just now." He paused to listen. "Yeah, yeah... I know that's what we said, but um, I'm not leaving right now."

He sat down on the edge of the bed and reached for my hand. He brought it to his mouth for a kiss as he listened to his manager on the other end of the line.

Cade was angled away from me, so I took the opportunity to slip out of my bra and panties, without his notice. I smiled to myself as I crawled over toward him, slid under his arm and halfway onto his lap. Facing him, I ran my hands down his chest and across his stomach.

"No, I can't, Denise. I won't!" Another pause followed while she talked... his eyes roaming over my naked skin, his mouth quirked at the corner. "Brooklyn said to call Jeanne and she'll help you figure another way to get me out of here late afternoon today. Yeah, I'll need to go to my hotel, change, and then Ethan is having a party at his condo that I want to attend. That won't need to be secret, will it?"

His hand was on my hip as he took in my bare breasts, the sheet falling to my waist. His eyes were like hot coals burning into me.

I kissed his stomach a few times, letting my tongue leave a wet trail behind and moved my hand to rub his thigh. I could see the rise start under the sheet and felt a wave of satisfaction engulf me as I realized again, how much he loved me and wanted me. "Mmmmm," I moaned softly; reaching out to touch his hard length.

"No, listen, I really have to ring off. Bye, Denise. "Yes, I have to go!" He shut off his phone and threw it in the corner, instantly grabbing me and pulling me full onto his lap.

He held the side of my face to his chest as he tried to calm down. "Brook, stop tormenting me. You know we can't make love with your mother and brother in the house."

"Why not? We'll just have to be quiet as mice..." I smiled softly as I kissed up his neck, over his jaw and then finally his delicious lips, my hand grabbing on to the part of him I wanted the most.

"I'm not sure I can be," he groaned. "Stop. You know what you're doing to me."

"Sure you can, my love. It's good practice for when we sneak away to the costume closet on the next film," I breathed. His large intake of breath stopped me. I looked at him, my eyes sparkling with laughter. "What?" My eyes widened in mock innocence. I laughed a soft, wicked laugh, and then his arms tightened around me.

"You're a witch," he breathed against my mouth, but I pulled back a little.

"I know." I smiled, and ghosted his mouth as I spoke. "Move to the top of the bed and sit near the headboard." I kissed his jaw and moved down to suck at the sensitive skin below his ear and throat. Soft, sucking, wet kisses. I felt him tremble under my hands.

He did as I asked and watched me crawl toward him. I threw one leg over him to straddle his lap, so I was on my knees in front of him. He bent to hold my breasts and lift one slightly so he could take it in his hot mouth. I grabbed his full erection, and my hand started moving. I loved how he felt. He groaned against my breast.

"Ugh! Brook, you're gonna kill me. I've never wanted anyone so much in my life."

"Shhhh…" I said as my fingers on my free hand raked through his hair, bringing his mouth to mine. I moved my hips, bringing my core over his erection, still held in my hand, as I started rubbing the head back and forth on my most sensitive places. "Mmmmm…" I whispered. "You feel so good."

His hands ran down my back and under my butt, where he squeezed a little. "I love your little ass." He smiled against my lips.

"Well, I love your big, ummmmm… mmmm… You're big, uh…" I let my words drop off with a grin.

"Oh, sweetheart, you're so damn beautiful," he said against my neck as he left a hot, wet trail of kisses down its length. "And *very, very* sexy."

His hand touched between my legs, parting the hot flesh and started rubbing in small circles. "Can you feel how much I want you, Cade?" I asked him as I ripped my lips from his, but he captured the bottom lip and held on with his teeth. He was so hot. Every fantasy I'd had about him, every time I'd seen him on screen, he was more.

"You're so wet. Oh, God."

I was gasping. "Only for you," I whispered.

He lifted me and slid inside, filling me easily. "You're so *hot*. You feel so bloody amazing." His head fell onto my shoulder as he started to move within me. My hips rose and fell to meet his, slowly, completely. Our bodies were made for each other. My legs curled under me, on the outside of his hips, and his hands held me as he guided my movements, forwards and back as our bodies vibrated and rocked together.

"Oh, Cade, God, it feels so good." Each thrust was long and

strong, and this position gave good pressure to all of the right spots, the friction between us delicious. I wanted to make it last as long as I possibly could.

I wrapped my arms around his shoulders while I sucked on his lips until our tongues came to meet each other's, and our mouths and bodies merged in beautiful unison. It was gentle and explosive at the same time, and unlike anything I could ever have imagined. I continued to move my pelvis against his, and he moaned deep in his throat. He let me play a little, but it got to be too much for him. He groaned, covering my mouth with his, his tongue and lips wild as they warred with mine. Then he was moaning my name over and over into my mouth as his arms wrapped around my body and pulled me closer. It was so hot to have him saying my name like he'd never get enough of me.

"Oh, God, Brook... Brook... Brook," he whispered with each thrust. "Oh, Jesus." His thumbs rubbing the peaks of my breasts as his hands held me around my ribs. My head fell back as I felt my body begin to tighten; ready for the inevitable fall into the glorious sensations he was creating in my body and my heart.

"Shhhh... Remember... Shhh..." I was panting, too, "Uhhh, Cade... you're making me..."

I was losing it as I felt the surge of pleasure begin to overtake me. He flipped me onto my back, our bodies never relinquishing each other, as he thrust into me harder, deeper. I felt him tense, but he didn't make a sound beyond increased breathing. "Ahhhh..." he moaned softly, then exploded within me, and our bodies jerked simultaneously.

Our bodies were covered in a fine film of perspiration as we collapsed together onto our sides, my legs still wrapped around his waist. He stroked my hair back. "Oh, babe," was all he said.

"Yeah, exactly," I said as I touched his beautiful face.

"Brooklyn." He began..,

"Uh huh?" My hand still lightly skimming his jaw with feather touches, I looked into his eyes.

"I just," he stopped again, his brow furrowing.

"What is it?" I was getting a little concerned.

"I don't think I can do it," he said finally.

"Do what?" I kissed his shoulder and neck below his ear.

"Pretend I don't love you, and not touch you when you're near. I just think it's impossible. I bloody can't!"

My arms went around him, and my hands went into his hair at the back of his head as I pulled his lips to mine. I gave him a long, deep kiss, and then a couple of smaller, lingering ones, our tongues sliding in and around each other. His fingers rubbed little circles on my lower back.

"Oh, Cade. It will be hard for me, too, but we have no choice right now. You know how much I love you. I don't know how I ever lived without you." Emotion filled my voice. He smiled, and brushed my hair back off of my face, tracing his thumb over my cheekbone. He kissed me softly again, his lips so sweet against mine.

"Me, too. You're my baby."

We just held each other for a while, not talking and then I thought of something. "Hey, since we have to keep it a secret, let's make it a game." He looked at me questioningly.

"Yeah, we'll come up with some sort of signal or series of regular words that mean something different, but just to us; like our own language. That way, we can tell each other we love each other, want each other, we're jealous, or whatever, and no one else will know what we're saying. It could be fun." I grinned at him. "Right?"

"Sure. Except I won't enjoy the jealousy part." He smiled, and his dimples appeared as his brow rose in that ridiculously sexy way it did when he was amused. "But we'll have to use them in complete sentences or else everyone will think we're sods." His soft chuckle was so contagious, I couldn't help myself, and I burst out laughing.

"Shhhh! My mother will come in here, so we'd better get some clothes on, in case." He laughed again. "Shhhh!" We fell over together in a naked, giggling heap on the bed.

We ended up snuggling in and sleeping for several more hours. I never wanted to leave this room or the safe serenity of his arms.

Chapter 12
Friends & Frenemies

Brooklyn

THAT AFTERNOON, JEANNE came over and drove her big SUV into my garage, where we loaded Cade in for his getaway behind closed doors. We'd spent a lazy day by the pool, ordered a pizza, and just talked and talked about everything. The little touches and kisses kept me at ease, as I tried not to think that he'd be going back to England tomorrow evening, and I wouldn't see him for a month.

Ethan's party was typical of him; Lots and lots of alcohol, video games, a karaoke machine and lots of laughing. Ethan and Dawson ribbed all the girls into doing karaoke, so we all three got up there and belted our version of "Girlfriend", by Avril Lavigne. We all took turns singing different parts, and it actually sounded really good. We were dancing around being silly, flirting and laughing at the men. Then Cade walked in, smiling brightly, as he took in the scene. He grinned as he glanced around, openly enjoying watching us.

Everyone was surprised to see him, and I tried to act just as surprised, waving at him in the middle of the song. Wendy stopped singing and ran over to where Cade was standing to throw her arms around him with a flamboyant squeal. *Ugh*, I thought. I could tell what tonight was going to be like.

The guys swarmed around him, which was ironic in a way. Cade wasn't someone who acted suave or conscious of how popular he was with women, which was amazing in itself considering how gorgeous he was. Still, the guys all worshiped him like he was a God in that department. He thought it was funny, but now that I'd made love with him several times, I smiled secretly to myself. He was very adept in that department. He smirked at me, clearly wondering what I was thinking. My eyes flashed at him, as I tried to stifle a smile.

The guys clapped and cheered for Jennifer and me as we finished up. Cade was staring, his gaze intense. I rubbed the back of my neck and lowered my lids to hide a glance in his direction. Dawson leaned in to say something to him, and Cade grinned. Wendy was still near him, grabbing his arm and trying to get his undivided attention. She was so fucking obvious, which was what I knew she was hoping for, and I was irritated. I was jealous, not because I thought he would fall prey to her blatant display, but because I couldn't be near him or touch him as she was doing. Pretending to be indifferent when I was so in love with him would be impossible.

"Hey. Glad you could join us tonight, Cade," I said to him a few minutes later. "Did you want a drink?" I was going to the bar. Wendy was sticking to him like glue, not that I was surprised. "I'll have a vodka martini, Brook!" Wendy called after me. Cade nodded to my question.

Great, I thought as I flashed her a dirty look. *I'm a fucking barmaid for his groupie, now?*

I was already feeling particularly snarky toward Wendy in anticipation of her blatant worship of Cade. Awww, hell! If I was honest, I wanted to scratch her freaking eyes out. I reached the bar at the opposite end of the room. I hoped she didn't notice that Cade didn't tell me what to get him since he knew I'd know what he'd want.

When I got there earlier in the evening, she drilled me about seeing Cade on the Red carpet. She wanted to know everything in minute detail. What did he say? What was he doing? What were his plans? Ugh! She creeped me out. I'd seen a little of this side of her in Vancouver, but then, I didn't have the right to be pissed. I guess I still didn't have that right since she didn't know Cade and I were together.

Wendy was in what she thought was a deep, meaningful conversation with him, her hand on his arm as she prattled on. He tried to lean toward her to hear her, but his eyes rose to mine as I simply handed him his beer, set down her drink in front of her, then faded into the background to observe. No one in the room was oblivious to how Wendy was fawning over Cade. Jennifer, who'd guessed the truth about Cade and me at the wrap party, came to join me.

"You look great tonight, Jen. Thanks for being silly with me on that song. It was fun," I told her, and smiled as I sipped my wine. She looked happy as if she was really having a good time. Ethan always joked around with her, and Dawson paid her a lot of attention. Why wouldn't they? She was a terrific person, and very pretty.

"Have you had a chance to talk to Cade? Wendy seems to be monopolizing him a lot." She looked at me with wary eyes. I think she was looking for some reaction.

"Yeah, I noticed. I'll find some time to catch up with him later. He seems to be enjoying himself a bit too much, though, doesn't he?" I said as jealousy tightened my stomach into a knot. I fucking hated feeling that way.

"Brook, he hasn't seen any of us for more than a month, and

everyone is clamoring to talk to him."

"Yeah, I know. Like I said, I'm fine. Dawson sure is all over you, tonight," I teased her, nudging her with my elbow, as I noticed Jack staring at her from his position on the couch next to Noah.

"He's always so sweet." Her eyes lit up when she talked about him.

"He's a great guy. Very talented, and very easy on the eyes, too." I leaned in so she could hear my low voice. "You could definitely do worse." I winked at her, and she giggled.

Wendy came over to join us, and shoved a glass of vodka in my hand. "You need a drink, Brook. You seem really uptight since Cade got here. He doesn't bite. Promise," Wendy touted.

I raised my eyebrows and wondered how I'd acted any differently. Didn't she see the glass in my other hand? I was socializing with Jen, and not threatening Wendy's position as center of attention at all. After her next comment, I decide she was being decidedly bitchy. "Maybe you need to get laid," she said, giggling. She'd had a little too much to drink and obviously had sex and CADE on the brain.

"Hmmmph…" I grunted, letting out my breath. I smiled at the complete irony of that statement considering the last twenty-four hours with Cade. "Yeah. Yeah, that must be it, Wendy," I said as I took a long pull from the glass, my left hand setting down the vodka, and going to the sleeve of my shirt to touch Cade's bracelet under the cuff. I rolled my eyes at her, and glanced toward him. His eyes were hot, intently watching what was transpiring between Wendy and me. A small smile danced on his lips as he noticed my hand wrapped around my left wrist.

"Cade is just so gorgeous, isn't he? I just wish I could get a piece of that." She sighed as she stared at him from across the room. I blinked.

He was talking to Ethan and started laughing at something,

completely oblivious to her stares. I wondered if this burning in the pit of my stomach was reminiscent of what Cade suffered when I was with David. It completely sucked. I wanted to know what had gone on during their earlier conversation.

"Have you tried to make it happen?" I asked cautiously, trying to keep my face as innocent as possible.

"Well, he has to know how absolutely hot I find him, but I haven't come out and said 'Cade, will you fuck me?'" My eyes widened in shock at her words. She was getting obnoxious, even for her. I felt my face infuse with heat, and my stomach turn over.

I cleared my throat as my forehead wrinkled into a frown. "Just a guess, but I doubt he'd find that approach irresistible." My voice was strained; laced with my discomfort.

"Well, I'm certainly going to make that my next project." She took a drink and leered at him over the edge of her glass. I wanted to smack that smirk right off of her face.

"Yeah, well, good luck with that." I knew my face was taut and annoyed, but damn it, I couldn't help it. She ignored my comment, and rambled on about some party she'd gone to the night before and who was there. I couldn't remember a word she said when she was finished. Sometime during her tirade, Jennifer had exited to the other side of the room. Couldn't say I blamed her.

Jesus, was Wendy always this boring or was I just being oversensitive tonight? I had to get away from her, and then got a gift from the Gods when she moved to leave.

"Hey Brook, I'm going outside for a smoke. See you in a minute." I watched her wander toward the balcony door; which, of course, was right next to where Cade was talking to Dawson, and Ethan. I turned away, not wanting to see her flirting with him. Even though I knew he'd brush her off, I didn't need to watch. I wished I was anywhere else but at this party, trying to act like Cade was only my friend.

I was lost in thought a few minutes later when I smelled his delicious scent behind me. My heart raced. "Hey you..." I heard his low murmur behind me. "Does this Pinnacle rubbish mean we can't even talk to each other at parties?"

"No." I shook my head. "I just wanted to give you some space to catch up with everyone." I turned toward him, and smiled.

"I'm missing you in my arms. You're the only one I want to catch up with, love."

"I know. Me, too." I knew my eyes had sadness behind them, as I searched the room to see if anyone was watching us. "This is going to be harder than I thought." His eyes were so mesmerizing; I didn't know if I'd be able to look away.

"When you were singing with the girls, Dawson told me that I needed to stop drooling." He laughed.

I was unable to quell the big smile his words brought to my face. "Hmmm. I think I'm in love with Dawson." I couldn't help but giggle as I raised my eyebrows. Cade grinned back at me, and took a big swig from his beer.

"Better not be, then I'll have to kill him." He was joking, but his eyes were serious as he looked at my face. "I love you, Brook." Cade's voice was quiet, but his tone, serious.

I met his gaze and nodded, my body screaming to be nearer to him, my hands aching to touch him. "You better, or I'd have to kill you." I smiled, and he grinned in response.

He crossed his arms across his chest as he leaned against the back of the couch. "Why don't you do another song?"

He grimaced as if in pain and nodded toward the other end of the room where Ethan was doing a sad rendition of "New York, New York." "Ethan's butchering the hell out of that, I think my ears are bleeding!" Cade laughed.

"Besides, you should practice. Doesn't that new film require singing? I could, at least, look at you." He sighed and gave me a half smile but his eyes were hungry.

He always knew how to melt me, but tonight I had to reign in my reaction.

"Sure. What should I sing?" I laughed, my hands aching to reach out and touch him. "Something just for me," he said softly; touching my hand and looking in my eyes.

"If I do that, they'll know..." I was drowning in his blue gaze.

"Shit, Brook, most of them know anyway, and frankly, I really couldn't care less. This," he dropped his gaze for a moment before bringing it back to my face, "hurts a little bit, doesn't it?" He let his breath out in a little snort. My heart thumped as his thumb caressed the back of my hand.

"Quite a bit, actually." I nodded as I looked down and licked my lips.

Wendy came up and interrupted our moment, and Cade dropped his hold on my hand before she could see. "What are you guys up to?" she asked as she openly glanced at his face; then mine.

"Brook is going to sing another song." He smiled as he took another drink of his beer. He knew he was cornering me. "Get her up there, Wendy."

"Yeah, Brook, you should. You've got a great voice." She gave me a little shove toward the karaoke machine on the other side of the room. *Oh no, that wasn't obvious! Not at all.*

"Hmmm, what to sing," I said as I moved toward Ethan, who was ending his song. "Hey, give me the mic, big boy!" I raised my eyebrows at him a couple of times. He smiled, and I laughed.

Ethan hugged me as he passed the microphone over. I looked at the discs that were out and I decided to do a cover version of "Soulmate." I smiled to myself as I thought about the implications, secretly hoping Wendy might get the message. Cade did, after all, ask me to sing just for him.

"Okay... well this song is dedicated," Cade's face snapped up to look at me, "to Ryan, from Julia." I smirked. Everyone shouted and laughed. "Yeah, I think it fits, especially if I get into character." I was openly teasing him, a big smile on my face. His mouth twitched and slid up on one side in a crooked half smile. Next to him, Wendy openly glared at me and her brow furrowed as she looked at him for his reaction. Obviously, she didn't like what she saw. *Keep dreaming, bitch, he's mine*, I thought.

The song started and I noticed her sitting on the arm of the sofa trying to keep Cade's attention. He put his hand up to stop her, and said something over his shoulder. He probably told her he wanted to listen to me sing because he was interested in hearing the lyrics. She looked upset, took her phone from her back pocket and started texting someone.

The music was playing and I was swaying. It had a slow rhythm, and the words were serious. I started to sing...

I tried not to let the words overwhelm me because I knew our feelings would show on both of our faces. I couldn't help letting some of it show.

Cade's eyes got serious as he watched me, and the music slowed even more in tempo. My voice got softer as the song ended.

My voice trailed off as the music faded and Cade clapped

exuberantly and whistled; as did the rest of them, save for Wendy.

I set the mic down and walked toward Dawson who said, "Wow, those lyrics are perfect for the movie, Brook. They should use that song on the track."

"Maybe a slower arrangement would be better. It makes it more painful, somehow. But, I'm sure the tracks are chosen by now." I allowed myself to glance at Cade out of the corner of my eye, and his gaze was hungry, following my movements. We both struggled to catch little looks at each other without being obvious. Ethan was saying something to him, so he ran his hand through his hair and turned his attention to the conversation.

There was a big commotion by the door as the bell rang, and in seconds, Wendy ran to answer it.

I couldn't believe what I was seeing, and I was pissed. It was clear who Wendy was texting as I sang. My lips compressed in a tight line. He must have had a rocket up his ass to get here so fast, or more probable, Wendy had him on standby.

"Look everyone! David's here! Brook, I got you a present!" Her arm was around David as she was leading him over to me. I glanced at Cade and I noticed his mouth tighten.

This is fucking great, I thought. "Now, you can get laid!" Wendy giggled when she said the words, flinging them loudly from the other side of the room. Her eyes were hard as they met mine: her face sobering, and her mouth tightening as she looked at me.

I could feel the hairs on the back of my neck start to prickle. *That bitch,* my mind screamed. *She knows, or at least suspects and she's going to do whatever she can to make trouble between us.* She let go of David, and went to Cade's side, gazing into his face as he took in the scene in front of him.

"Hey, babe." David came toward me and threw his arm around my shoulders, pulling me toward him so he could plant a kiss on my stunned lips. "I missed you."

I groaned internally, knowing Cade was taking this right in his gut.

He looked Cade straight in the face, gloating openly with his arm still draped possessively over me. "Cade." He nodded in his direction. "How's things over the pond?" He smiled, but I thought it was more like a jeer.

"Brilliant," Cade said through his teeth. "I can't wait to get back there, actually. I've got a lot going on, working on some new music with my mates and promoting two other films." He ran his hand through his hair. "If you'll all excuse me," he said, and went out the balcony door.

My heart sank. I knew he was seething, and I tried to move away from David, but his arm tightened around me as he felt my resistance. I was royally pissed at Wendy for inviting him, but I couldn't say a damn thing about it. I didn't know what to do.

Obviously, I wanted to get the hell out of there, but if I left, I wouldn't see Cade anymore tonight. I couldn't stay because David would be hanging all over me. Damn him! Didn't he know that he wasn't "on duty" right now? To make it worse, David kissed me. I'd promised Cade, no kissing during this damn charade, and now with Wendy acting like a fucking bloodhound, I wouldn't have the chance to talk to him.

Wendy made a beeline to follow Cade out, and my hands clenched at my sides. I didn't know how we were going to get through this. I, for one, couldn't stand it for one more minute.

"I'm not feeling so well," I said as I put a hand to my head. "I need some air." I made my way toward the front door and in doing so, I moved away from David.

"You need me to come?" he asked.

"Um, no. Thanks." I shook my head almost imperceptibly. That's the last thing I needed. "I'll be okay and back in a few minutes." I made my way out the front door to the porch.

Jen followed me. "Damn Wendy! That girl is like a bitch in heat."

I felt sick to my stomach. "I've never told her how I felt about him, but I wonder if she figured it out?"

"Come on, Brook!" Jen pressed her lips together and paused before she continues. "She knows about you and Cade. She asked me about it at the wrap party, but I played dumb. I told her she was crazy, but it was clear that she was more than suspicious." My friend shook her head. "I always thought she was a big fame whore, but it's becoming apparent she's just a whore, period. She only wanted to be your friend because Cade was always hanging around you. He'd be the biggest conquest of her life: frigging front-page news. She'd make sure of it."

"No, Wendy and I were friends before the movie. We met through David a couple of years ago. We all hang out together." I went to her defense. She'd worked with Martin on a small indie move when she was still in school." I shook my head quickly. "She might even be the reason I got the audition for *The Future or Our Past*, the first *Remembrance* film."

"Yeah, well, you can bet she took advantage of your friendship during filming. She still is using you to get to Cade. How did it make you feel when she was around David all the time?" Jen was perceptive. "Before, I mean?"

Jennifer's face was filled with concern. I looked down and shook my head again. "Um... to be honest, I never gave it a thought. We were all just friends. Wendy's pretty wild, she does some wacky shit, and I guess, she used to be fun. I never worried she was after David." My voice trailed off as I realized the minutes were ticking by with Wendy outside with Cade.

"With friends like that, you don't need enemies. Maybe David wasn't a big enough fish," she said pointedly. "Cade is more like a whale."

I felt the bile rise in my throat at the thought of Wendy's red fingernails all over Cade. "I'm feeling sick all of a sudden. I just really want to go home. I'm not used to alcohol and uh... what's going on out on the balcony, and David here... Ugh!" I closed my eyes; I really was going to puke. "It's too much."

"What about Cade? You know nothing is going on out there, Brook. He completely adores you. You don't want to leave without talking to him, do you? Isn't he flying to England, tomorrow?"

"It might be easier if I just text him later."

She rubbed my arm. "This is going to upset him. Go out there, and put that sleazy bitch in her place."

I sighed in defeat. "I can't, Jen. This isn't easy for either of us. I don't want to follow him around like Wendy is doing. It's just not me." I sighed. "Even if I wanted to, there's no way I will."

She pursed her lips. "I'll go tell him you're leaving, and I'm sure he'll want to come say goodbye," Jen said.

I smiled weakly. She was a savior. "If you insist," I said softly with a smile, "and Jen? Thanks."

She nodded with a small smile, as she went back into the house and toward the balcony. I followed, found a table off to the side by the window, and sat down to look out onto the street.

At that moment, David came over "Want a ride home?"

I hesitated. "I guess, maybe? I'm not sure. I want to say goodbye to everyone first." My brow crinkled, and he lit a cigarette. "Thanks for giving me a little space, before." I smiled at him weakly.

"Sure. Okay, let me know when you're ready." He moved off to mingle and talk to the other guys. Maybe he and I would be able to be friends after all. I hoped so.

Chapter 13

Daydreams & Desire

Caden

WENDY WAS INCESSANTLY annoying as she rambled on about mindless shit, always touching me, leaning in, panting all over me with her inebriated breath. *Bloody hell!* How was I ever going to untangle myself from her, and get a chance to talk to Brooklyn?

Brook. My heart swelled at the thought of her.

Last night, and this morning, had been absolute perfection. Making love with her was more than I imagined; the passion between us was beyond anything I'd ever experienced, but, I realized, just being able to be in the same room with her was enough. To be immersed in her real world was amazing. My life had become so commercialized, and my own family so far away most of the time, that just the normalcy of spending time with her family, seeing her joking with her brother, or laughing with her mum was indescribable.

This morning waking up with her in my arms made it real. I was finally a part of her life as I'd wanted for so long, and it was better, and more, than I'd expected. My throat felt thick as emotion washed over me. I blinked in surprise.

Hearing Brook say she loved me and only me, gave me a type of natural high like I'd never known. It would have been so much easier on both of us if we'd only been honest about our feelings months ago.

After the first time, we'd made love in London, and she'd resolved my past torment by admitting that she hadn't allowed David to touch her since she met me, was such a gift. I understood her loyalty to David at the time, however. She wouldn't be the person I loved if she could have cut him loose without remorse.

I closed my eyes at the memory. She was so damn beautiful and sexy, and more, the love in her eyes glowed. I swallowed the lump in my throat as I told myself how lucky I was.

I felt a tug on my arm. "Cade!" Wendy whined. "You're not listening! Don't I look pretty?" She fished for compliments. Her immaturity was such a stark contrast to Brook's personality, even though she was closer to my age than Brook's. *Jesus*. She left me utterly cold.

"Wendy, you always look nice," I dismissed and took another drink of my beer. I looked up as Jennifer approached, thankful for the interruption with Wendy.

"Hey, Jen," I said, relieved to have someone else join us. I wanted any excuse to get away from Wendy. "How have you been? You look great." I smiled and gave her a hug.

"Hi, Cade. You look, um, very happy." Her wry expression was quickly replaced with a knowing smile. I smirked at her. Did she know? "Hi, Wendy," she said.

"What's going on in the other room? Has Dawson kicked Ethan's ass on PlayStation baseball?" I asked, but wanted to know what was going on between David and my girl.

"Dawson is bad-ass at baseball and karaoke, but Ethan is better at football and the fighting games. The testosterone is really thick in there!" She folded her arms and leaned on the rail.

"Wendy, you look like you could use another drink." Jennifer looked pointedly at her empty glass, and I knew it was a ploy to help me out. Jen was smart and intuitive, and I liked her. She was one of only a few up-and-coming actresses that treated me like a normal person. That was one thing I hated about Hollywood, and working with newcomers.

"You should go get one. I'll keep Cade company," she said sweetly, her smile mockingly innocent. I almost choked on my beer.

"I'll go in for one when Cade is ready." Wendy glanced between Jennifer and I, her agitation showing on her face.

"You don't have to wait for me, Wendy. Go ahead." I nodded in the direction of the door, practically begging her to leave when her lower lip came out in a pout. I didn't give a damn. Clearly Jennifer wanted to talk to me without anyone listening, but that wasn't going to happen if Wendy had her way. I looked at Jennifer over Wendy's head and widened my eyes as I ran a hand through my hair.

Jennifer's mouth twitched, trying to hold back a laugh. "Um, you know Brook isn't feeling well, I think she's going to leave soon. I thought you might like to say goodbye, since we won't all be together again for several weeks," she said quietly.

"What's wrong with her? She looked great when I saw her earlier." I said as I patted her arm, looking intently into her face, trying my best to determine whether Brook was really ill or this was just Jennifer's way of giving me an excuse to get away from Wendy. "I do want to check on her before she goes. Um, thanks, Jen."

I moved quickly to the door leading from the balcony into Ethan's condo, before giving either one of them a chance to answer.

"Cade, wait." Wendy began to follow me, but Jennifer grabbed her arm.

"Great dress, Wendy. Who's the designer?" she started a conversation to keep Wendy occupied as I made my escape.

My eyes searched for Brook and found her sitting at a small table on the far wall looking out the window; clearly lost in her thoughts. Sadness haunted her delicate features and I ached to take away her pain. Thankfully, David was talking to Noah on the other side of the room, so I made my way over and pulled out the chair next to her. She looked up, her eyes lighting up as I sat down.

"Hey," she murmured, a smile coming to her lips. I could see her visibly reign in her reaction to me, and I hated she needed to.

"Mind if I join you, sweetheart?" I asked softly. I wanted to take her in my arms and whisk her out of this crowded apartment, and back to her room to make slow love to her, but that was impossible with the confines of the damn contracts hanging over our heads.

"Jennifer said you weren't feeling well and were leaving soon." I sighed. "I wish... " I let the words fall off. Brook's hand reached out to touch me, but then she stopped abruptly, once again remembered the illusion we were forced to create.

"That you could leave with me?" She read my mind, her eyes languid pools. "I know. Me, too." She took a deep breath, her hand tracing patterns on the tabletop, watching her fingers move. "I'm just feeling like I don't want to be here anymore. I'm not having a great time because it isn't like it was on set. Even though you're here, I can't be with you."

She raised her beautiful blue eyes as sadness crept back into them. I could easily stare into those eyes for all eternity.

I ran a hand through my hair, and looked at her a few seconds before I spoke. Drinking in everything about her, the dark blue blouse that brought out the pink tinge to her pale skin plunging between her perfect breasts, where I could imagine her heart beating. Her hair flowing in disarray around her shoulders, and her open mouth as she lightly ran her tongue over her lips.

I leaned in a little and lowered my voice, knowing my eyes had to be burning with desire as I looked at her. She looked so fragile; so soft.

"I want," I let out a breath and dropped my head, shaking it slightly before raising my eyes back up to meet hers. "I want to tell the entire fucking world that I love you. I want to be able to take a hold of you and say to them all; we're leaving now because we can't wait another bloody minute to be alone. And, I want to make love to each other until we're panting and breathless. Just once more before I have to go."

I watched her face for her reaction. Her jaw dropped slightly and her lips parted, eyes growing darker, and her cheeks flushing with heat as she drew in her breath in an audible gasp.

"I get hard just looking at you from across the room, Brook. I want you so much, I just—" I sighed. "Right now, without even touching you, you can make me—" my breath caught in my throat as my hand on the table clenched into a fist.

Desire surged through her as I said the words, her lids drooped to half cover her eyes, her breath came in short bursts, her mouth opened and she bit her lower lip. It was palpable and visible, and it made my own heart and body quicken in response.

"Cade, stop." She was breathless. "Stop making love to me with words when we can't do anything about it. It makes me insane." Her voice thickened as she spoke and she ran a hand through her gorgeous blonde hair. I wanted it to be my hands in the silken strands, grasping, pulling her face back to kiss her.

Seeing the way my words affected her, I just couldn't stop.

"I want to make love to you with my hands, my mouth, my body. To worship you until you scream for me to stop." My mouth went dry just thinking about it.

Her mouth open, she tried to speak and couldn't. Seconds passed and she tried again.

"You know I feel the same way. I'd rip your clothes off right here and now if I could. She let out a shaky breath. "I'll never get enough of you. E-ver." She punctuated the words by saying them slowly, her breathing getting notably shallower, and her eyes were liquid fire.

My erection was straining in my jeans to the point of getting uncomfortable, my heart pounding in my chest, my breath coming faster. I felt like a starving man, never dreaming in my life before Brook that this degree of longing, desire, lust, and love was even a remote possibility. Body and soul, I was aching; writhing in beautiful agony.

At that moment, Ethan walked up and pushed against my shoulder, breaking the invisible bubble between Brook and I. Always the perfect host, he sat a new beer in front of me and handed Brook another glass of white wine. Guiltily, we both sat up straighter in our chairs, away from the close conversation we'd been engaged in. I could feel the heat rising in my face, and could see the blush infuse Brook's cheeks as well. She lowered her head so that a curtain of hair fell around her face.

He leaned down and spoke softly near my ear, but loud enough for Brook to hear. "Get a room," Ethan said dryly and chuckled as he walked away. I laughed as he left, but Brook's eyes just widened.

She ran a hand through her hair again, tearing her gaze away from mine to look over the room. "It's hopeless." She sighed. "We suck at hiding our feelings. It's our damn job, and we can't do it. How hilarious is that?" She raised her head, but a small smile danced on her lips. "I mean, seriously?"

I noticed the soft sheen of perspiration on her forehead and was concerned.

"Love, are you really sick?" I asked. I was aching at the thought of her leaving, but I wanted to make sure she took care of herself. I tried to calm the reactions of my body, slow my breathing.

"My stomach is a little upset, and my skin feels hot." She placed the back of her hand on her cheek. "I didn't want to sit here and think about Wendy trying to latch onto your junk all night." Her lips twitched, in an attempt to keep from bursting out laughing.

My face broke into a big ass grin. God, I loved this woman; gorgeous, with a great sense of humor as well.

"Hmmm," I said. "Now, that's one visual I could live without!" She had me laughing out loud.

"As could I," she retorted cryptically, her head cocking to one side as she bit her lower lip and giggled, her shoulders shaking as she laughed.

"You know no one will be doing that except you, yeah?" I was rewarded with the beautiful smile broke out on her face. "You look hot tonight. Extremely hot, Ryan's not the only one who loves that color on you." A devilish little smile splayed on my mouth.

She smirked. "Well, that's 'cause I *am* hot!" She let out her breath in a soft snort as was her custom when she was making fun of something.

"Hmmph! You have no idea."

Her eyebrow arched and her lip twitched in the start of a devilish grin. I could feel my heart beat faster again at her words. She really knew how to get me going, but I laughed softly under my breath.

Unfortunately, Wendy chose that moment to bounce over and put her arm around my shoulders, shattering our perfect moment to bits; *end of intimacy with Brook; more annoying Wendy.* My mind and body protested.

"So, um I'll see you when you get back from London, then for the *Entertainment Weekly* photo shoot next month?"

Brook rose from her chair.

"Oh, are you leaving?" Wendy looked at Brook with wide eyes. I could tell what she was thinking. "Yep, that EW shoot will be a blast. We're ALL gonna be there!"

Jesus, not only did she have to ruin this moment, she had to remind us that she would ruin that as well.

"Yay!" Brook said flatly.

She and I hadn't made plans for the night, so I didn't know if I was supposed to have Denise's driver take me back over to her house, but I knew that's what I wanted. Even just to hold her in sleep or take care of her if she felt ill, I wanted my arms around her. I decided to call Denise and figure out a way to be with her later.

"Do you have a ride home?" I asked, as I untangled Wendy's arms from around me and placed them at her side, my focus on Brook.

"Oh, I'm sure David will take her. Won't he, Brook? Maybe he can, um, give you a little prescription," Wendy said sweetly, looking pointedly at Brook, her eyes widened in an overly obvious attempt at silent communication. She didn't want Brook asking me for a ride.

"Shut up, Wendy. You're drunk," Brook said as she glared at her; her eyes hardened, and her mouth tightened with anger.

"Is that what you want?" I asked.

Brook paused, then sighed, as she directed her words to me. "Um, yeah, David offered. I think I'll have him drop me off, and go straight to bed. I'm not feeling so good." She made sure I knew that she wouldn't be receptive to any of David's advances, should he make any.

I rose to take a hold of her arm as she turned to go. I pulled her in to hug her goodbye. Surely friends are allowed to hug when they weren't going to see each other for more than a bloody month. It tingled where she touched me as her arms wound around me.

It's been four hours since I've held you like this, I thought.

I squeezed her then ran my hand up and down on the small of her back. Her hand slid up over the top of my shoulder to the back of my neck and curved around it; her face turned in toward mine as it rested on my shoulder. Mmmmm, I thought. She smelled delicious, and felt so warm and soft in my arms. It was all I could do not to kiss her madly in front of this room full of our friends.

"Bye, Brooklyn. I hope you feel better, soon." I spoke for Wendy's benefit, hoping Brook knew I wanted her to call me when she arrived home. "Let's keep in touch, okay?" I looked into her eyes. *I love you. Don't go!* My mind and heart were screaming.

"Yeah. For sure we will." Her hand slid down my chest from behind my head, then she was turning and walking away from me. ";," she said.

At that moment, I realized that I'd always feel pain seeing her walk away from me. Even though I knew she loved me, and that she was mine, I still felt my chest tighten. I dreaded the minutes until we'd be together again.

She walked over to David and talked to him for a minute, then went around to say goodnight to Ethan and the others. After a while, she made her way to the door where David was waiting for her. Her eyes searched for mine one more time, and the corner of her mouth lifted in a little smile as they left for the night.

After they were gone, Wendy came on full force. She even tried to sit on my lap when I was sharing a drink with Ethan and a couple of the guys from the crew. Dawson and Jennifer were leaving, and so I shoved Wendy off so I could say goodbye to them. She was hammered, and I tried to cut her some slack; telling myself that it was the alcohol causing her to make such a complete ass of herself.

I was itching to leave, so I called and asked my manager to send a car. Even though I had moved back to the table I'd shared with Brook and had my back turned to Wendy, she overheard my conversation.

She ran a hand down the back of my head causing an automatic move away from her. "Where are we going, lover?" she asked suggestively.

"Look, Wendy, I'm really tired, and this jet lag is a bitch. I just want to go back to my hotel."

"Sounds perfect." She leaned down and tried to kiss me. I grabbed her wrists and held her away from me.

"Wendy, you're a beautiful girl, but this is not going to happen. Let's just keep it as friends, shall we?" I tried to sooth the blow.

"But Cade, we don't have to tell anyone. It could be just for the pure physical release. I'm great in the sack; I bet you are, too. We could take care of each other." She pouted up at me.

How could I say I just wasn't interested without hurting her feelings?

I wanted to tell the truth, but I knew that Brook wouldn't want me to. I found another way to be honest.

I ran my hand through my hair as my phone vibrated in my pocket. I knew it would be from Brook. "Look, I've got a clause in my contract that says I'm not allowed to get involved with co-stars, okay? You've got the same clause; we all do."

"Sure doesn't look like it keeps you off Brook. You practically fucked her with your eyes tonight." She was angry.

"How I feel about Brook is none of your business." I was positive my anger was showing on my face, so I made an effort to relax my expression. "Brook has become one of my best friends, and I'd trust her with everything. That's all you need to know." I was extremely uncomfortable so I made a move to leave. In this one instance, I was grateful for the clause in our contracts. Even if I wasn't involved with Brook, or if Wendy didn't wear on me like an exposed nerve, I'd never consider even a fling with her. She couldn't be trusted not to run off and prattle to the press.   "My car should be here now, so I'll see you next month."

Wendy's hand still gripped my forearm, but she made no move to stop me as I turned, her hand falling away.

I went over to Ethan; who was speaking to James, one of the actors cast for the next film, and told them both goodbye. Ethan walked me to the door with a hand on my shoulder. "What was Wendy's problem, dude?"

"Oh, she's inebriated, and she tried to get me to take her back to my hotel for a shag." I shrugged and rolled my eyes when he smirked. Naturally, most men would jump at the opportunity to be with Wendy. "I guess I'm just exhausted, and don't want to deal with that rubbish tonight."

Ethan's brows rose. "Yeah, sure, you're tired." His eyes were smiling as he nudged my shoulder with his. "Tell Brook I said 'hey.'" He laughed, as my eyes grew larger. "If you talk at all, that is." He gave me one of those brief man-hugs that despite my obvious Americanism from being in the country for four years, still felt odd. He was laughing, and still unable to overcome my surprise at his intuitiveness. I was speechless.

I simply nodded, my mouth quirking at the corner. "See ya," I said, slugging his shoulder as I walked out to find my car waiting for me.

I pulled out my phone to read Brook's message.

Sorry I couldn't stay. But I love you, want you, need you...
Miss you. :(

My heart jumped in my chest. After all the months of hoping for those words from her, I was still surprised.

I closed my eyes, and leaned my head back as I gave her address to the driver. It was two in the morning, so I asked him to circle around to make sure there weren't any photographers lurking. I wanted to surprise her, so I called Nathan.

"Yeah?" His voice was sleepy.

"Nate, it's Cade. Sorry to wake you, man."

"Hey Cade, what's up?"

"Um, can you let me in through the pool entrance? I'm going back to London tomorrow evening, and I hoped to surprise Brook. She said she didn't feel well, and I wanted to check on her."

"Yeah. I'm sure she'll want to see you. David dropped her off about an hour ago, and she went straight to her room. What's up with that? I thought you and her... were, well..." Nathan's voice trailed off.

"Yeah. We have to keep up the illusion that she's still dating him for the studio. It's all hushed up bullshit. You can't tell anyone."

"No problem. When will you be here?" he asked.

"About five minutes. Will you meet me out by the gate?" I was getting anxious.

"Yeah. My mom's home, so you're gonna need to be quiet."

"No problem. Thanks."

As I crept quietly up the stairs to her room, I could already feel my heart begin to beat faster. I moved the door handle so slowly, so I wouldn't let it click then quietly opened the door.

She lay sleeping on her side in her bed, the covers pulled up around her slender form and one pale arm curled around them. Her left hand rested between her face and the pillow, and her dark lashes fanned her cheeks.

She looked so innocent and beautiful with her hair splayed out above and behind her head, and my fingers itched to run through it. I moved to the far side of the bed and quietly removed my clothes, laying them over the chair in the corner, before lifting the edge of the duvet and sliding beneath the cool sheets. The heat around her radiated out and urged me closer.

I moved nearer to Brook, my head propped on one arm as I lay on my side. She was facing away from me as my fingers traced lightly down her arm.

"Cade…" she sighed. My heart swelled, almost to the point of bursting. *She really does love me*, I thought. Now I knew exactly how Ryan felt. There was a scene in the movie very similar to this. I sighed softly, kissing her shoulder, and the side of her neck with my open mouth.

"Yes, my love?" I whispered near her ear. She turned her face toward me over her shoulder, but still in her sleep. "I'm here." I kissed her velvety soft cheek.

She rolled on to her back and I saw the black lace and chiffon thing she had on. She was hoping I'd come back here tonight. I smiled with a huff. Mmmm. I could feel the throbbing begin, my cock responding to her need. "I want you so much, love."

I ran a hand down the flat plain of her stomach and then further down the slope of her hip and leg.

"Mmmm, are you real or a yummy dream?" Brook murmured through her sleep, but slowly waking under the ministrations of my hands on her body.

"So real," I whispered against her shoulder. "I couldn't stay away." Her eyes half opened as she turned fully toward me, my hand brushed up the line of her breast, then down the side of her ribcage to her waist, my fingers curling into the soft silk of her gown. I brought her leg over my waist and pressed my hardness against her. She caught her breath. "Mmmmm. You feel wonderful."

"How did you get in here?" She was staring sleepily into my eyes now, her hand making lazy traces on my jaw.

"Magic." I smiled as she touched two fingers to my lips and shook her head slightly.

"Uh uh. Having you here is the magic." She smiled languidly, and then placed a small, open-mouthed kiss on my lips. She tasted amazing. I felt I could kiss her forever.

"Nate let me in," I whispered, as I took her mouth in the soul-scorching kiss I'd been dying to give her all evening. I groaned as Brook began to return the kiss with equal fervor, her tongue moving into my mouth, as mine dove into hers. My hand moved over her hip and down her thigh, the silk of her gown sliding up as my hand retraced its movement in reverse.

"I'm glad you're here," she whispered as her fingers ran up my chest and around my neck.

"Where else would I be? Every second without you, aches." I placed small kisses down her neck, over her collarbone and shoulder.

"I've been dying to touch you and kiss you like this all evening," I said softly. I leaned over her and let my hand roam over her body; between her breasts, over her flat stomach, and further down to the hem of her nightgown; knowing I was teasing her and loving her reaction.

"This is beautiful," I breathed, as I bent to her lips again. "You drive me crazy, Brook. You are so, incredibly sexy." Her back arched as she pressed her body up toward mine.

I inched the gown up until her black silk and lace panties were within view. My breath caught as I moved down enough to kiss her tummy and rib cage. I dragged my lips and tongue in small kisses that moved from the band of those delicious panties upward until I could take her hard nipple into my mouth. I wrapped my hand around her firm breast, as I suckled and nipped at the taut peak. Her moans of pleasure drove me wild. As impatient as I was to sink into her slick heat, I wanted to give her everything, to wring every breathy moan of pleasure from her.

"Cade," she said softly, her hand moving in my hair to cradle my head. Her touch was the only thing that mattered to me in this moment, or forever and like a lifeline, it brought salvation. My heart pounded and my dick throbbed as I looked upon my beautiful Brook.

"I want to taste you," she breathed. Her words stopped me dead in my tracks. Oh, God. I didn't know if I could bear it, and for sure not with the silence needed because there were others in the house. Her mum allowed us time last night, but as far as she knew, we only talked and slept. Tonight, Brook's mother was completely unaware of my presence, so we had to be careful. She was young, and though I was only five years older, I knew they wouldn't approve of us making love in their house. Regardless of the risk, it would be impossible to stop.

My lips left her breast, but my hand remained, teasing and gently squeezing the nipple.

I kissed her neck with my open mouth, letting my tongue press her skin and then trailing a path to her mouth, as I moved over her and spread her legs with my knee, finally pressing my hardness into her softness. It was incredible. She was so warm and giving, and I was drowning in our kisses and the way her hands felt on my body.

"Oh, babe. I love you, Brook. You'll never know how much." I lifted my head to look into her eyes, and they were drunk with love and desire.

"Yes, I do." Her voice was low and thick. I shivered as her hands moved down my back, her nails lightly raking. "I want to leave marks on you. I want everyone to know you're mine," she breathed.

The desire rushing through me nearly made me unable to move. I was shaking and she was trembling.

"You own me, Brook. I could never want anyone else ever again." I took her lower lip and tasted it like it was wine. I felt out of control as the kiss deepened, my hands roaming her body, seeking the heat between her legs. I felt the wetness seeping through the silk, and immediately, she began to arch against my hand.

Brook panted my name and pulled at my shoulders to bring my face up to hers. My hand slipped under the waistband of her panties, until I found what I was searching for. She pulled in a breath and her stomach contracted.

"Uhhh," she moaned as my fingers found entrance to her body. She licked my top lip and drew it between hers, sucking. Oh, God, I couldn't take it; it was sweet torture. My mouth took hers in a deep kiss. I couldn't get enough, and never would.

Her fingers pushed me back into the mattress as our mouths

parted. "Do you want to be on top, honey?" I whispered through the haze of passion that engulfed me.

"No. I want to taste you, Cade. I told you." She sat up and I could see through the black nightgown; the panties, her perfect body, her navel, and nipples clearly visible under the lace. I was mesmerized by her tousled hair and glistening lips; her breasts heaving as her breath came in excited pants.

"Can you lay back for me? Let me do this for you, baby." She was kissing my neck, then moved lower to press her mouth to my chest and stomach. When she reached the edge of my boxer briefs, she looked up, but her mouth and hands never stopped what they were doing, her palm pressed and rubbed over my cock.

A low groan erupted from my throat. She pulled my boxer briefs down, and my dick sprung free, standing strong and erect for her view as she slid them down my hips, and off my legs.

She grabbed my ankles and slid her hands up the length of my legs, her nails raking lightly as she moved up my body, pausing to place wet kisses on my thighs as she moved closer to the object of her quest.

I held my breath and stared at her as she licked down the shaft, and around the head. My eyes closed and my head fell back when her hot mouth surrounded and enraptured me. Her hand was moving at the base, she sucked and licked until I thought I would explode. I had a good deal of experience with women, but because it was Brook; the act was a thousand times more intimate.

"You're so beautiful," she whispered against me. Time had no meaning as I lost myself to the sensations she was creating with her mouth and tongue.

I began to pant, my heart pounding and my hips thrusting as she took me in almost to the back of her throat. I knew I would come within seconds if I didn't stop her. "Mmmm…" she moaned as she swirled her tongue around and continued sucking, her little hand working at the base, in time with her mouth.

"God, Brook!" I groaned, but I let her continue, relishing the exquisite feelings that were running through me until I knew I was at the edge. "Baby, you have to stop now. I won't be able to keep quiet if you make me come. Fuck, this is amazing, but you have to stop." She brought me to the brink, and I could feel the pre-cum leaking from the tip of my dick, the sensation tightening my balls and building. I was gasping for breath, my pulse pounding. She felt so fucking incredible.

Brook looked up at me, and her beautiful eyes took in what she was doing to me. " Are you sure?" she murmured, as her mouth went back to the sweet torture. I could only take it for a couple of minutes before I sat up, and put my arms around her, dragging her up and rolling her onto her back.

My hands went to the hem of her gown and drew it up her body, sliding up the sides of her hips, her breasts and raising her arms above her head as I removed it, and flung it aside. Then, I kissed her stomach as my teeth found the band of her panties and dragged them down.

The scent of her arousal made me swell and throb to the point of pain. "Brook, what you do to me, God, I want you," I whispered against her stomach as my hand finished removing the black silk.

My knee slid between hers as I spread her legs wide. Brook gasped as I reached between us and found the sensitive little nub, hard and silken evidence of her desire. She was hot and wet and I knew she wanted me badly. It was all I could do to keep from plunging into her and pumping hard, but I wanted to bring her to the edge before entering her, as she had me.

I moved my fingers in little circles, pressing gently until she was moaning my name breathlessly. "Remember, love, we have to be quiet. Shhh, baby," I whispered as I pleasured her. She was trembling, her legs shaking as she bit her lip.

"I love you," she breathed as her hips rose to tempt my hand. This was the moment I'd been waiting for. My mouth took hers as I slipped inside her and it was heaven. Her warmth engulfed me as I moved inside her body, my thrusts getting stronger as she panted out my name, and matched me thrust for thrust.

The sound of my name on her lips as her arousal grew did something to me deep inside my gut. I'd never wanted anyone so much, but I needed the moment to last. I wanted to memorize all of it. Her body was writhing underneath mine, and I could feel the trembling of her limbs that meant she was getting close. Both of my hands cupped her head and her fingers clawed at my flesh as I moved inside her, my body digging deep into hers.

"Cade... Cade... Uhhh... Oh, God, don't stop."

"Let it go, Brook." I felt like I was begging. I needed her to come. "Let your love flood over me, I want it all," I moaned as I felt her body start to convulse around mine. She clenched and pulled on my dick with her sweetness and I could feel the beginning of my own orgasm, her nails raking down my back and her fingers pressing into my ass to urge our bodies closer. My entire body tensed as sensation washed over me, wave after wave as I exploded inside her.

"Uhhnnn... Jesus, Brook," I moaned as I came. "Oh, God!" I kissed her mouth as my body moved and rubbed hers. Her back arched, and her muscles clenched around me, over and over again, in quick succession. I kissed her neck and shoulder. "Oh, my love," I whispered against her skin, her body trembling, when she whispered my name again.

We were both breathing hard as we descended from the climax. I felt her shudder and quake as the last spasms ran through her.

My body was still coming down, but the emotion was so strong. My throat tightened and my eyes stung. "I love you, Brook. I love you, so much." I could never say it enough. Never enough. "Don't ever forget that."

"I won't," she said softly.

I brushed the hair off of her beautiful face, and placed a whisper soft kiss on her lips, my mouth moving slowly, playing with hers, and my nose nuzzling hers.

Her arms were wound around me and I her nails lightly traced over my back, sending more shivers down my spine. I moved to her side and pulled her in to rest on my shoulder, her arm across my stomach as we lay spent and exhausted.

I kissed her forehead, my hand running through her hair, splaying it on her back. It's softness raining like silk across my skin where it fell on my chest. I closed my eyes. This was paradise. We lay silent in the afterglow of our lovemaking. I thought she'd fallen asleep again, but then her voice whispered in the darkness.

"So um, I guess Wendy didn't get her wish tonight, hmmm?" Brook lifted her head and looked warily up at my face.

"Honey, you're not jealous of Wendy are you?" I scoffed. "She's harmless."

"More like... ruthless," she said her voice strained. "She wants you bad. She," Brook began hesitantly, as if it was something she wanted to tell me but thought she shouldn't. "Well, she taunts me with it, like she knows about us."

"So what if she does? Is the world going to end?"

"Maybe?"

"Never."

"She wants you. She told me. She told all of us."

I huffed, wondering how Brook could think I'd even give her a second look. "I could never want her, sweetheart. This is needless worry. Yes, she put the moves on me, asked if she could come back to my hotel, but you are the one I want. Only you. You know that, so please stop this."

My fingers skimmed her cheek as she looked up at me. We were wrapped up together, my hand in her long, luxurious hair, as I gazed down into her face. "You trust me, don't you?"

I hugged her close, and she rested her head back on my chest. "Yes." I felt something hot on my chest and realized she was crying.

"What is it, Brook? Love, tell me." I said softly.

"I'm usually this tough bitch that never gets hurt, but ever since the final weeks of the shoot, I've been an emotional wreck. I'm sorry." Her voice broke with her tears. "I've never been jealous before. I hate it."

I smiled to myself. She was jealous, and my heart sored. "Oh, love, it's okay. I'm an emotional wreck, too. It's all I could do not to rip David's bloody head off for kissing you tonight," I said against her forehead. "We're going to get through this babe, and then you're going to marry me, remember?" My voice deepened. We'd joked about it enough, but I was never more serious. She nodded on my chest and her arms tightened around my body.

"I'm scared of all the time apart. You're leaving tomorrow and..." Her voice was thick, and the hot tears fell on my chest in a steady stream.

"The time apart will be horrible. I'll hate every second, but it won't change what's between us. I think being away will make me love you more. You'll never be off my mind. Brook, you have to believe that, please? No amount of distance or time will change that."

I tried to lighten her sadness as I held her. "Think about how tightly we'll be wound when next we see each other," I attempted to tease her, "we'll make love for a week straight." My fingers ran down her spine and she trembled.

"I don't want you to go," she cried harder, and her arms tightened around me. "I miss you so much. It hurts so fucking bad, and you're still with me."

"I know sweetheart. I don't want to go either. I never want to be away from you." I sighed as I stroked the hair on her back. "It's sheer hell, but we both have commitments and the time will go fast. I'll call you every day, I promise." I ran my hand up and down her back to soothe her, but my own heart was breaking. "I love you more than anything. Only you."

Chapter 14

Picture Perfect

Brooklyn

THE ENTERTAINMENT WEEKLY shoot was today. Finally.

The last four weeks had dragged by even though I had the audition and several promotional events for *Remembrance* to keep me busy.

I spent some time with Noah, another of my cast mates who played Mike Turner in the film, Wendy, Jennifer, and even David, to pass the time. David had become a good friend now that he wasn't trying to get me into bed or bash Cade, and he could be fun at times. He'd come over a couple of times to hang out with Nate and have dinner with my family. My parents loved him like a son, and to be honest, our relationship hadn't changed that much, we were always more friends than anything else.

I still wasn't ready to go out in public with him, though. I didn't want to risk any more misconstrued pictures. I made sure not to discuss Cade with David around because there was no sense rubbing salt in a new wound. I wanted the best for David and for him to be happy with his life.

Cade and I had been in touch daily, either by text, Skype or the phone, though he still didn't trust David, and I sensed his anger and anxiety when we spoke. I missed him terribly, but I was secure that he loved me. His words on our calls were enough to make my heart beat faster and keep a smile on my face.

Denise, Cade's agent, had arranged the EW shoot, and it was in the middle of some farm about fifty miles north of L.A. I thought it strange that the setting had little to do with the movie, but she said it was about establishing a connection with the actors, more than the actual plot of the film. I shrugged. What did I know? She'd rented one of those huge Hummer limos, and we were all driving up together. Cade was flying into LAX around 10 AM, and we were picking everyone else up at the Pinnacle studio headquarters first.

On the way, Denise went over with me again the need to be only on friendly terms with Cade. Her rant was similar to that of my agent and manager. Like I didn't get an ear full that day in the restaurant.

"I know Denise, okay? We both do." I made an effort not to roll my eyes and smile at her instead. "I got this."

I was nervous, yet extremely excited at the prospect of seeing Cade, but tired from a sleepless night. I felt like a five-year-old on Christmas, counting the hours until I'd see him.

Everyone settled inside the limo, and we were on our way to the airport. Jennifer sat next to me with Dawson on the other side of her. The seats wrapped around the interior of the car, so we were all facing each other. Wendy was talking to Noah, practically oozing all over him. Noah was good-looking; fairly tall, built, blonde and tan. He started his career as a fitness model, so he was cut. *Leave it to her to find the hottest guy in any situation.*

"Noah, you're looking good there, buddy." I smiled at him.

Pleasure lit up his face at my words, and his blue eyes sparkled. "Thanks." He smiled. "Even still, I don't get the girl." He winked at me. "At least on film." He was clearly flirting.

I smiled at him. "You never know," I teased back to keep the illusion alive. Denise's eyes met mine in approval.

"Brook, why are you so giddy today?" Wendy asked. Her eyes narrowed as she looked at me. I pulled my sunglasses down from the top of my head and back on to cover my eyes from her curious gaze. Giddy? Did I appear giddy despite my efforts to tamp it down?

About two weeks after Cade left, she'd told me that she'd approached him at Ethan's party, but he didn't seem interested. She'd been totally tanked that night, so I tried not to hold it against her.

Cade was ridiculously hot. What woman wouldn't want him? I reasoned, telling myself to back off of Wendy's infatuation, and if I acted pissed off, it would be too obvious how I felt.

Despite some tense moments, we remained friends and went shopping or to lunch occasionally. She did try to get me to confess to a relationship with Cade, on occasion, but I always insisted he and I were only friends. Obviously, she was still suspicious because rarely did she pass an opportunity to dig me for dirt.

"I'm happy, Wendy. This is my first photo-shoot. It will be fun, won't it? I'm excited!"

"Fun for whom? Denise said the group of us wouldn't be taking that many pictures, but that most were of you and Cade. The rest of us will just be hanging out sweating and covered in dust all day. *Joy*," she whined annoyingly. "At least, Cade will be here, and I can watch."

I mentally shook my head at her. Five minutes earlier she'd been draped all over Noah, and now she was gushing about Cade.

I decided to ignore the last part. "I'm sure they'll have a trailer and air conditioning for you, Wendy," I said calmly. "Where are Gavin and Sarah? They're part of this shoot, aren't they, Denise?"

She was sitting up front with the driver and turned to answer me. "Yeah, they're meeting us out there. Gavin's oldest daughter had a dance recital this morning and Sarah's parents were visiting. They're joining her on the shoot, so the three of them will pick up Gavin and arrive together."

"Mmm," I said. The actors needed for Julia's parents would be cast if the first movie did well.

Wendy turned to her left and began talking excitedly to Madeline Sinclair, the woman who played a smaller role in the films, and the guys were discussing the possibility of doing a second film in the series. Jennifer and Dawson were lost in their own little world, their conversation clearly private.

I looked out the window at the planes landing and taking off as we made our way to the international terminal where we would pick up Cade. The butterflies in my stomach were getting to the point of making me nauseous, and my hands started to sweat.

I'd spoken with Jeanne earlier and was told that bodyguards would meet his plane and escort him to the curb where he would join us. His bags would be delivered directly to a hotel in Beverly Hills. He was only in L.A. for two days before he had to go to New York for a book signing with the author of the series, and Martin Deering. His schedule was on fire.

I would have my own signings here in L.A. later in the week when Martin came to LA. Pinnacle was doing a good job of covering the country, and that meant that Cade and I would be split up for at least half of our appearances.

I tried to keep my demeanor calm as we neared the terminal.

Denise was watching me for signs of blowing our cover, and she raised her eyebrows at me. I sighed, nodded slightly, and bit my lip. We pulled up and waited.

"Cade's plane landed ten minutes ago. He was in the first class cabin so he should be here soon," Denise said as the driver of the limo got out and stepped around to be ready to open the door.

I was sitting at the back with Jennifer and Dawson, but Wendy readied a place next to her by telling Noah to move over. She was sitting opposite the door, which would be the natural place Cade would gravitate toward when he got in.

Jennifer nudged me. I looked at her and she winked, making me wonder what she was up to, but I continued to play it cool and didn't respond to the gesture. She turned over her cell phone, acting as if she was checking messages, but held it low on her lap so I could read the message. The sunglasses hid my eyes from view as I did so.

It was from Cade.

Get me next to Brook if you can.

Joy flooded through me, and I felt my face break into a smile that I could not contain, no matter how I tried. I looked down and played with the strap of my bag as I tried to get my face under control.

"There he is!" Wendy squealed.

What was she, fucking fourteen, now?

I was annoyed and feeling decidedly snarky at her comment. "Wendy, maybe you'd like to grab your little autograph book and hop out to join the screamers?" I retorted flatly. Her eyes narrowed and her nose wrinkled as she glared at me.

Game on.

I saw Cade coming out to the curb, flanked by three massive bodyguards, paparazzi following and cameras flashing. My heart thumped inside my chest. He was so gorgeous; I could barely breathe. I sank down a little further in my seat and tried to get control of the fluttering I felt in my stomach.

Fans and paparazzi lined the curb and were following him out of the double doors in droves. "Cade, stop, please! Center for the camera, Cade!"

It was madness as the cameras continued to flash a million times a minute, and many fans vied for his attention, asking him to sign pictures of himself from other movies. I wondered how anyone knew he was coming into town since we'd barely started promoting the film. I found this much attention a little weird. Especially since they seemed to know what airline and time he'd be here.

Dressed in gray pants, white t-shirt, and converse tennis shoes; he was gorgeous even without trying. His dark golden hair was in perfect tousled disarray as usual, and I wanted to get my hands into it. He carried a jacket and his duffle. Always gracious, he posed for some photos with fans and signed a few autographs amid the screams.

My eyes drank him in as I watched through the window. He spoke briefly with the driver, gave his bag to one of the bodyguards, and then the door was flung open as he came inside.

His eyes searched for me in the group, and Jennifer scooted over to make room for Cade between her and me.

"Cade!" Wendy called. "I saved you a seat," she said as he took the one next to me.

"Oh, sorry, Wendy. This one was closer." He winked at her and grinned devilishly.

His thigh burned against mine. I wanted to fling myself into his arms and press my mouth to his. I knew it was impossible, and I'd have to be satisfied to have him this close to me for the two-hour drive. At least, I could smell him and feel him pressed into me. He flung his jacket across his lap, some of it falling over mine. He surprised me by grabbing my hand underneath it, his thumb rubbing across my wrist. My heart thumped and my mouth went dry at his touch.

"Hey, everyone. It's nice to see all of you." His face was flushed and he ran his free hand through his hair.

After some small talk about his flight and various projects we were all working on, Noah moved over to talk to him. "Cade, when do you think they'll make a decision on the rest of the series? Have you heard anything?" he asked anxiously.

"Um, yeah." Denise was now seated in the front seat next to the driver, and the window between there and the rear of the limo was closed, and Cade glanced in her direction. "My agent said she spoke with the studio and they won't commit until after the U.S. premiere of the first film is past. They're waiting to see what the box office is that first weekend before they make a decision. She feels there is a better than fifty-fifty chance it will go into production, Noah." This movie was Noah's first break, as it was mine, and he was anxious for the other films to be made. I was, too, but for different reasons. Cade leaned back on the seat and toward me slightly, his shoulder pressing into mine. Then, he squeezed my hand under his jacket.

Wendy looked sullen from her position opposite me; I almost felt sorry for her. *Almost.*

I knew she still had that annoying crush on Cade, and had called and texted him several times when she and I were on our shopping trips. It always made my stomach lurch, but I wasn't aware that Cade ever picked up or responded. I made sure never to ask him about it because I didn't want to come across as insecure or mistrusting.

I was so happy to see him, but it was hell to make small talk when I wanted to hug and kiss him. Mostly, I just listened to the others. "Brook, are you okay? You seem quiet," Cade asked.

Wendy bristled at his show of concern for me, her face hardening. I threaded my fingers through his under the jacket.

"Yeah, I'm fine. I'm just a little tired, I guess. I tossed and turned all night." I smiled. "I'll be fine for the shoot." "Tossed" was one of our secret words. It meant *I want to kiss you.*

He smiled in understanding of what I said, his eyes glinting with amusement.

"I understand."

I smiled back. "I'm dragging a bit as well. I hate trans-Atlantic flying. The time change wears on me, but luckily, it will hit me tomorrow rather than today."

"Well, if you'd stop staying out late and partying before flying here, you might fare better," Wendy interjected. It was obvious that she was feeling pissy as she watched him.

Cade frowned and his mouth set. I could see his annoyance.

"I'm working on some new music with Dan, so I wasn't out too late. I sincerely hate to disappoint you, Wendy, but thanks for worrying about me." Her eyes hardened on her face as he paused.

Then he turned to me as his features softened. "I can't have Brooklyn putting me to shame in these photos because my ass is dragging." His thumb caressed the top of my hand under the jacket, and a brilliant smile split across his face.

I had to look down because I couldn't keep from smiling. I let my breath out in a whoosh. Cade heard it and realized that I knew what he meant. "Shame" was another of our code-words; it translated to "I want to make love to you." His thumb continued its caress on the side of my hand, my skin burning where he touched me.

I remembered the day by the pool when we came up with our list of words and worked to memorize our secret language with each other. It was a lot of fun, and we were laughing the whole time. It was ridiculous how happy I was just to have him sitting next to me.

I looked up and met his gaze. "Um, well... I don't think I'll be putting you to *shame* Cade. You're the experienced one and look gorgeous, as always." I said the word back to him so he'd know I wanted to jump his bones as well. This was hilarious. He tightened his hand on mine.

"You will if I'm lucky." He grinned at me. I couldn't help myself; I laughed out loud. Many pairs of eyes turned toward me as they tried to understand what was going on.

My left hand went up to cover my heart as my eyes rose to meet his again, a smile still on my face.

It was going to be a great day. I couldn't wait to get my hands on him. Cade dropped his head, ran his hand over the back of his neck and cleared his throat, obviously trying not to laugh as well.

"Didn't we have enough of your private little jokes during filming, you two?" Wendy clipped.

My smile fell away as I glared at her. I couldn't see Cade's expression as his face was averted to gaze out of the window, but his hand continued to stroke mine under the jacket. He was better at letting shit roll off of his back.

The window in front whizzed as it rolled down. Denise turned in her seat to send Cade and I a look. *What?* I mouthed at her as I felt my eyebrow shoot up. She had no idea why we were laughing.

So what? Couldn't I even laugh now? Jesus.

Cade inhaled deeply. "Did you want something, Denise?"

She cleared her throat. "We're almost there."

"Good."

When we got to the location, the handlers moved us off in two groups; the men to one trailer for wardrobe and the girls to another. Hair and makeup application would take place in another trailer, but we wouldn't be separated.

Cade and I had the most to shoot so they would be starting with us.

The field was enormous and empty except for a few trees in the background, the trailers, and one large tree in the foreground with a swing on it. I looked down at the black strapless dress they dressed me in. It was edged in lace, which I felt sure it would get full of the weeds that seemed to be everywhere I looked. Plus, I felt like it was slipping and I'd always be pulling it up, but whatever, I wasn't the creative director. I decided to leave on the bracelet Cade had given me. It went with the movie, and I'd just say it was a prop if anyone asked. I wanted something real in these pictures, so when I looked at them, they'd have a personal meaning.

They did my hair in tousled windblown style, but they let me wear my own shoes, which were converse tennis shoes similar to the one's Cade had on. They weren't exactly elegant with the dress, but the length kept them from showing, and they were good for the terrain.

When I walked out for the first set of shots, I saw Cade was already waiting; his back was to me, and his arms wrapped around his body. He was in a black suit, and they had just touched up his hair a little. He looked like a God; a true movie star.

My breath stopped and my pulse sped up.

If I hurried, I might be able to talk to him a little in private as they readied the cameras. They had a portable stereo playing contemporary rock in the background, so hopefully, no one would be able to hear our words.

"Hey you," I said as I walked up to him. He turned and looked me up and down. I could now see the suit was a tuxedo and he had sunglasses on; every bit the epitome of a movie star. Holy fuck. I couldn't breathe.

"You take my breath away. You're gorgeous. I want to kiss you so badly, Brook." Cade's eyes were intent. "I can't stand it."

"I know. Me, too." I took a shaky breath. "I wish. Mmmmm." I pushed a small strand of my hair back off of my face.

"At least, we get to touch today, and I can look at you all I want." He smiled his crooked grin and my heart stopped. "I love you, Brook."

"I love you, more," I said, licking my lips, and added in a whisper, "You look hot."

"You're gonna kill me, woman," he groaned.

"That's not *exactly* my plan for you." I smiled sweetly, even though I was feeling devilish. Denise was watching us, damn her. I pushed the sunglasses the wardrobe girl had given me onto my face.

Cade laughed at my words; raising his eyebrows. "I can't wait for you to follow through on that one, babe."

"Cade!" Denise shot him a warning look.

"Buggar off, Denise," Cade dismissed her.

I laughed under my breath but turned my back to the woman.

The photographer took us through several poses, some just standing near each other and leaning in toward each other. In the same series, there were some that I reclined on a chaise lounge under a big tree and Cade stood behind it, looking off to one side. Then, he was told to sit next to me and take my hand. He brought it to his mouth and the camera clicked over and over as shivers ran down my spine.

Once we touched, we couldn't seem to let go of each other. When they adjusted our hair or the lighting, our hands were locked together as we hung onto each other for dear life.

Later, they asked Cade to sit behind me, and I leaned back against him, my head on his shoulder, or my face turned to rest my forehead on the side of his jaw.

His cologne enveloped me as he cradled me to him. His hand reached over his to poke at me gently in the ribs.

When the photographer reloaded, I wanted to turn into him and hold on tight, but the most I could do was to wind my arm up and around behind his head, so my fingers twined in his hair while we waited. I did get to cling to him during some of the shots, which I thoroughly enjoyed.

For the next set, they had him sitting on the end of the chaise while I stood behind him, my hand on his shoulder. His hand came up to hold mine as we looked into the camera. I was able to lean on him and feel him breathing, his warmth burning through my body where we touched. I wanted to kiss the back of his neck.

"Okay, Cade, just bring your right hand to your face as you lean into it. Brook, sort of wrap around Cade a little more. You may have to sit behind him."

I did as I was told, and the crew moved in and situated us as they wanted. It was hot, and the arid wind blowing made this the shittiest place for evening dresses and tuxedos, but I assumed the contrast was the point. As I looked into the camera, my heart was pounding, and my brain screaming; *You want me to hold him? No problem, since I love him more than anything.*

Finally, they decided to move Cade and me inside a tent for the next series of shots. It was filled with rich fabrics and pillows, like a luxurious scene from The Arabian Nights. They removed Cade's jacket and tie, unbuttoned his shirt and pulled it from his slacks, and tousled his hair more. With me, they changed me into a slinkier silk dress that was very sexy and on the verge of being lingerie. Cade's eyes widened when they brought me back out.

We started with me lying back on the pillows and Cade posed to look like he was crawling over me on the bed, our eyes staring into each other's. We were so lost in the moment, that we didn't hear them tell us to move to the next shot.

"Guys," the photographer said. "Hello? Brook, Cade, next shot please."

I felt my face burn in embarrassment, as he moved off of the pillows. Cade turned away to run both hands through his hair.

The last one was worse.

"Okay," the photographer said, "I think we've got some good shots, but I just want to try one more thing. Cade, remove your shirt and then lay on top of Brook. I want your head on her chest. I want to get some real intimacy," she said.

Huhhh! My breath left in a rush. Wendy, Jen, and the boys were all standing off to one side watching, but that didn't stop my heart from pounding. My eyes drank in his bare chest and Cade's deep blue eyes met mine as he began to do as the photographer and director instructed.

When he settled down on my body, I wound my fingers through is hair automatically. Cade's heart was beating against my chest.

Oh, babe, I missed you. I didn't mind the heat and the dust because we were able to touch and get close.

"Think you can handle some *real* intimacy, honey?" He leaned in toward me; his voice was low and husky, as he settled down on top of me.

I laughed. "Um, yeah. I'm an *actor*, remember?" I teased.

"Oh, right." Cade smiled.

"Okay, so how are we going to do this, then?" I asked. "Is this good?" I directed my question at the photographer, conscious of Denise's, and everyone else's eyes, trained on Cade and me.

Cade pressed his hips into mine; his movements so subtle, nobody could tell, but I felt his erection pressing into me.

"I think this is my favorite pose so far." Cade smirked. My breath whooshed out of my lungs at his words.

The stylists fiddled with our hair as we held the position, each passing second was pure torture. Finally, the photographer was giving us instructions.

"Brook, bring your left knee up alongside Cade's hip and waist, keep your hand in his hair and turn your head toward me. Cade, nuzzle into her, or something." He complied by running his nose up the side of my cheek.

"That's good, but hold it." The camera fired off for sixty seconds.

Now, move down her body to nestle against her, Cade. End with your head on her chest and looking toward the camera. I'm going to be shooting as you move, so make the whole thing look real.

"No problem," he murmured as they started to shoot. I almost forgot that we were in the middle of a desert with twenty or thirty people watching. He was all that existed.

For the final few shots, as we looked at the camera, I wondered if the whole world would be able to see the love and desire in these pictures. Finally getting our hands around each other for the first time in a month, I tingled everywhere he touched me.

The photographer reversed our positions so I was draped over the top of Cade, my leg hooked over his, and his arm bent at the elbow so his hand could play with a strand of my hair.

"Okay, Cade, lean your cheek on Brook's forehead, and then both of you look at the camera. Try to look sexy and smoldering, you know what I mean." She laughed as she instructed the assistant to turn on the fans.

Oh yeah, I know what you mean. "We got this," I said under my breath, and Cade sighed as his arms tightened around me.

My heart was pounding at being this close to him, and I knew the longing I felt would show on my features. My fingers trailed down his bare chest, as I looked right into the lens, my mouth opened slightly. Click, click, click; the cameras flashed.

I raised my head, and Cade reached up and softly nuzzled and kissed the underside of my jaw as his hand slid down my thigh, now bare, because the silk had hoisted up my leg. Um, not supposed to do that. Click, click, click; the camera went off again.

"Sorry, couldn't resist. You're so delicious and I'm just... starving," he whispered as he slid me down his body until my feet touched the ground and his eyes burned into me.

"Yeah, I'm going off of my fast today, too," I said softly for only his ears. I felt my skin prickle and goosebumps ran down my arms, despite the hundred-degree temperature, and my mouth went dry.

"Mmmm," he said as I lifted away from his body and ran a hand through my hair, trying to get a hold of my emotions.

"Are we finished?" I asked the photographer.

"Just about."

They asked Noah to join us, and told him to take my hand and pull me away from Cade, who huffed under his breath and I laughed softly.

"Are they serious?" Cade asked.

"It's part of the plot, ba— er, Cade."

He laughed out loud at my slip up.

"Sober faces!" The photographer shouted above the music.

Cade was the embodiment of professional, but toward the end, we were getting tired.

"Hey, can we wrap this up? Parts of me, that I'm too gentlemanly to name in the presence of women, are beginning to chafe."

I started giggling so bad we had to pause. Noah joined in the laughter, as well.

"I'm so sorry," I gasped through my giggles. The photographer looked at us sternly as we made fun of her idea. "Sorry," I said again as I tried to get control of my giggles.

Cade grinned and winked at me. "Well, it *is* bloody ridiculous, isn't it," he said to the photographer; his British accent making me swoon. "It's got to be forty degrees out here."

"Forty? It's over one hundred, Cade," Noah said.

Cade nodded. "Exactly, mate. Forty, Celsius."

Thankfully, they brought the rest of the cast out and took a series of shots in various poses. Cade and I were not side-by-side, and Wendy weaseled her way near him. I should have laughed, but she was blatant and the heat boiling under my skin only made the temperature more unbearable.

After that, we changed again and took a few shots with the entire cast in various groups, then the photo of all of us together. Wendy stood next to me with her arm around me, even kissing my cheek during the shoot. It looked like we were friends to everyone else, and would to the world in the photos, but she whispered, in my ear; "You are one lucky little bitch." I wasn't sure if she meant the photos with

Cade or she knew something more. I was just happy when we were done.

I glanced at Cade as I made my way toward the trailer where I would change back into my street clothes. He smiled as he hurried into the men's trailer with the rest of the guys. They were all joking and laughing with each other. He looked so happy; my heart thumped in my chest.

As I walked toward the women's trailer, Denise stopped me. "Brook, can I talk to you for a minute?"

"Yeah, what's up?" I looked into her face. She had a ruddy complexion and blondish-red hair. She was fit, and attractive, but not beautiful in a conventional sort of way. She looked at me sternly.

"You and Cade are going to have to rein in some of the looks and laughing. And, what is up with that kiss?" she wanted to know.

"Denise, it was a peck, for God's sake. It's *acting*. You know, for the shoot." I made a hand gesture toward the field where we'd just been. She knew I was lying out of my ass, but there was nothing else I could say. "We were only doing what they told us to do!"

"We'll have to make sure that shot doesn't get published. You need to be aware that everyone is watching you. Wendy is watching Cade like a hawk! Her reputation for being a paparazzi sympathizer is not something we want to mess with." She sighed in frustration.

"Well, the term I've heard her referred to is *fame whore*, but your term is more politically correct." I cringed and Denise nodded emphatically.

"Exactly."

"About that," I said. "Can you do something about her coming on to Cade all the time?" I asked. "Doesn't her contract state the same as ours? If so, can you please point that out to her manager? It's one thing for Cade and I to have to hide our relationship, but I don't want to be subjected to that crap all the time."

"Brook, if we do that, it might look like you're jealous, and we can't have any eyebrows raised for any reason. Besides, it will just make her worse. You understand that don't you?" She lit a cigarette.

"Yeah, I guess." My voice was resigned. "But she looks at him like she wants to lick him from head to toe. I'm so fucking sick of it." I sighed and threaded my fingers through my hair.

"You'll have a lot of time to deal with all of this, so you'd better get used to it. I'm fairly sure the second movie will go into production, and so we'll be doing this dance all over again. You have to learn to deal with women like Wendy. Cade is crawling with them." She put her hand on my shoulder. "I can ask Cade to tell her to back off, and that he's not interested in her that way."

"He already has! She's relentless." I sighed heavily and dug the toe of my shoe into the dirt, dust instantly clouded around my feet. "What's the plan for the rest of the night?" I was anxious to hear the managers' plan for getting us together.

"Cade has a suite at the Regent Beverly Wilshire, and we've arranged to cater a meal for all of you there. After that, you'll all arrange rides home on your own." She paused. "And, Brooklyn, you *must* go home. You can't stay with him at the hotel, okay? The paps are watching you now, too."

"Ugh!" I groaned as my head fell back. "You don't know what you're asking, Denise. I haven't been with him in over a month! Jesus!" My brow furrowed.

"Oh, believe me, I know, Brook. Cade's been hammering me with it. I'm sorry. Let me think about it, and I'll see what I can figure out, but we really can't risk you being seen leaving the hotel in the morning. We need to protect your contracts."

"I know. I'm sorry, but it's so unfair. We're frustrated."

"It will work out Brook. I can see how much you love each other, but that's just the problem. *Everyone* can see it when you're together. It oozes right out of both of you.

I smiled and shrugged. "We can't help it. Cade makes me happy." I hugged her. "I guess I'd better change. Wendy will be ragging on my ass if you're all waiting on me," I said as I went in the trailer. "Unless she can hang out with Cade."

"Well, hurry then, because he's given me clear instructions to keep that one away from him."

Chapter 15
Too Close for Comfort

Brooklyn

CADE'S SUITE WAS beautiful and large, with twelve-foot ceilings and long draping tapestries in shades of mauve and cream. It was more like a luxurious apartment than a hotel room. Pinnacle was footing the bill because this was a promotional obligation for the film. They had a nice spread of grilled meats, cold shrimp, fruit and vegetable trays, and a variety of different breads and desserts set up buffet style on the table by the balcony.

Dawson brought his guitar with him, and he'd probably want to have another of the many jam sessions that were one of our usual activities up in Vancouver. I made up a small plate of food and found a place on the corner of one of the sofas. Cade had gone into the bedroom to remove his jacket and get his guitar. I watched Wendy follow him in there, and my stomach tightened. Dawson was next to me and heard my deep intake of breath.

"Don't worry, doll," he said. "He's not interested in Wendy." I'd figured Cade had shared his feelings about me with Dawson, and this confirmed it.

"Oh?" I said innocently, then, smiled. "And I would care, why?"

"Yeah right, Brook. Okay, if you want to play it like that." He grinned back at me.

"The worst part is, I have to Dawson. We both do." I frowned.

"Jen and I have the same issues with our contracts, but we work around it. I know it's easier for us because we live in the same city and the press doesn't hound us like they do you two, but we've worked through it. You will, too." He looked at me seriously as my eyes strayed toward the entrance to the bedroom when Cade still didn't emerge. Dawson put a hand on mine. "He's telling her to sod off right now. Trust me," he said in a British accent and laughed.

"I hope so Dawson..." I was sure sadness filled my eyes, but I offered a weak smile.

"Brook. Come on. He only has eyes for you. I've never seen a man so crazy about a woman, seriously." I felt tears prick at my eyes as I tried to blink them back. "I give him all kinds of shit about it." He smiled warmly and covered my hand with his.

"Thanks, Dawson." At that moment Cade came out of from the bedroom carrying his guitar, his eyes searching mine. He offered a wry grimace as Wendy followed him out.

"See? Told ya," Dawson whispered at my side, squeezing my hand.

Wendy looked upset as she went to the wet bar for a drink. Cade set his guitar down, got a plate of food, and moved toward Dawson and me. "Mind if I join you?" he asked, the smile on his lips reaching his eyes.

"Not at all," Dawson replied. They talked a lot about Cade's music and what he was working on with Daniel. Dawson had a band called *Insane Interference*, so he and Cade enjoyed jamming together after our long days on the set. When Cade's friend, Daniel, or Dawson's band members visited during filming, they all played together. It was during these sessions that Cade started to teach me to play guitar, and what led up to him buying me one for my birthday earlier this year.

"Did you ever see the final notes on the piano scene?" I asked. It was in the next movie and one Cade might be allowed to write a song for the film. I'd heard he'd been asked to submit one or two.

"Yeah. I hear they are leaning toward a song by someone established in the industry. I'm trying not to be pissed." I saw the disappointment in his eyes, as he took a bite of his sandwich. Shit.

"But that song you wrote was so beautiful! I'm sorry. I don't want to see it wasted." I felt my lower lip pout out a little.

"It wasn't wasted." He took my hand. "You stayed with me that entire day while I composed." He leaned forward so only I could hear him. "That was for you, not the movie, love. Always for you." He touched my chin with his finger.

My breath caught in my throat as I looked at his beautiful face and my eyes started to burn. I blinked. The moment was getting too intimate so I decided I needed to move away from him for a bit. I hated this fucking charade.

"I think I'll toss this back and get another drink. Want something? Dawson, how about you?" I asked. Feeling about him as I did, it was impossible to keep the love out of my expression. He looked up at me as I stood and smiled.

Yes, I want to kiss you, too. I saw it on his face.

"I'm good," Cade said as I made to leave. *Yes, you are,* I thought.

Dawson shook his head indicating he didn't need anything from the bar.

As I moved across the room, I told myself I needed to socialize with everyone there so that no one would be suspicious. I saw Gavin talking to Sarah and I wanted to say hello.

I went across and gave them each a big hug. "I'm so glad to see you both," I said as Gavin kissed me on the cheek.

"How did things work out in London?" he asked quietly. I glanced at Sarah. From her smile, it was clear Gavin must have filled her in on the details.

"Really good. Thanks so much for your help with that." I gave him a big smile. All of my close friends seemed to know about us, which made things a little easier. They also seemed willing to keep the secret from the public.

I spoke with them for a while longer, asking about the recital his daughter had earlier that morning and talking with Sarah after she introduced me to her parents. They were only staying for a day or two longer, so she was leaving the party early.

"Cade looks so happy, Brook. So do you," Sarah whispered in my ear as she hugged me goodbye. I hugged her tighter. "A far cry from how miserable you both were at the wrap party."

"Yeah. We are." A big smile spread across my face. "Really happy."

The phone rang, Cade answered it, and a few minutes later went to the door of the suite. He took out a folded bill as he walked to the door. Handing the bellman the money, he returned with my guitar. As he walked over to me to give it to me, his crooked grin stopped my heart.

"What? How is this here?" I asked as my eyes widened.

"I figured you'd want to join us tonight." He smiled. "I'd like you to, if you want, and knew you'd need this, so I sent the driver to get it from your house." He shrugged.

God, he was so incredible.

"Thank you, Cade. That's… very thoughtful." My heart was melting and at the same time, I was speechless. Gavin and Sarah smiled and she raised her eyebrow at me, a wry grin landing on her mouth.

Wendy got up and huffed onto the balcony. Cade shrugged again as we both watched her leave. I set the guitar down and decided to go after her. The last thing we needed was her leaking to the press and we used to be friends. Maybe I could still salvage that.

"Hey Wendy, are you going to hang out for the jam session? I guess we're gonna start in a few minutes."

She whirled around and turned hard eyes on me. "What the fuck is up with you and Cade, Brook? I want to know!" Her voice was elevated enough to carry inside.

Her response startled me. "Nuh... Nothing." Her confrontation was more than I expected. "I've told you. We're good friends, Wendy." I looked at her seriously.

"Why are you lying?" she practically screamed at me. "You eye fuck each other all the time! I see the way he always finds a way to touch you, and now he makes a point to get your stupid guitar delivered? And what about, David? Have you suddenly forgotten about him?" She was furious.

"No. I'm not lying, Wendy." I swallowed the lump in my throat. "Cade and I are very close, but Dave and I are still together," I lied through my teeth.

She didn't look convinced. "Very close, as in *fucking*?" Her thin brows shot up as emphasis.

"I can't believe you're asking me that," I said. "He's my best friend." I spoke quietly, hoping she wouldn't press me for more.

She looked at me for a long moment. Her eyes were hard and she was breathing fast. "Why won't Cade give me the time of day, then?" She slammed down the vodka in her glass.

"He likes you, Wendy. He talked to you a lot on the way back from the shoot." I was stammering because I didn't know what to say that wouldn't give it all away. "I guess, I just don't understand what you expect me to say," I said tightly.

"I'm asking you to tell me the truth. Why doesn't he want me? Aren't I pretty or sexy? What does he want that I don't have?" Her tone was bitter. "If you're best friends, he tells you everything, right?" She spat the words at me. I still heard the disbelief of my explanation in her voice.

"Wendy, Cade and I talk about a lot of things, but he doesn't talk to me about you in that way. He's way too much of a gentleman to discuss women in those terms. I um, I wouldn't know the answer to those questions," I said hesitantly.

In a way, I felt sorry for her. I knew how I'd feel if I found myself in love with him and he didn't return those feelings. I wanted to find out if she was in love or just lust.

"I'm sorry you're upset."

"You're my friend, right, Brook?" She looked at me pleadingly, deciding to change her approach.

"Yeah, of course," I told her.

"Then help me figure out how to get him." Her voice was begging. *Oh, God.*

"What exactly do you want from him?" I asked, not really wanting to know the answer.

"Fucking him will do to start with." I cringed. "He's just so damn hot, I can't help myself," she said and pulled on her cigarette. "And if I can get him in the sack, that ups my chances of getting more."

My lips pressed into a tight line. I looked at her for a minute and then shook my head and let out an angry breath.

"What?" She asked, exasperated.

I was pissed and I knew my face was flushing. "There is more to Cade than just being hot, Wendy. You should try to get to know him. He's an old soul, very deep and intellectual. He actually cares about people and thinks about things. Try to be less superficial. That isn't what he's about," I said honestly and hoped the love wasn't dripping off my words.

I couldn't believe I just told her how to get close to the man I adored. I felt sick to my stomach.

"Wow." She raised her eyebrows and she nodded as she held her cigarette. "That's heavy shit, Brook. Can you talk to him for me? See if he'll open up?" Her voice was low and I could see the wheels turning behind her eyes. "Maybe set us up?"

"I'm not going to help you treat him like a piece of meat, Wendy. I care about him." I told a little piece of the truth. "But yeah, I will see if I can find out his feelings." Since I already knew what they were. "You can't get mad at me if he isn't in a place you want him to be, and you can't ask me to stop being his friend. That isn't up for negotiation, okay?" I was hoping that I'd tell her he wasn't interested and she'd drop it.

"Okay," she said shortly. "Wait here," she said as she ran back into the room.

What was she up to? I was looking out over Beverly Hills and Hollywood, the lights of the city were pretty, and I got lost in thought. I ran my hand through my hair and shook my head.

"Hey," Cade touched my arm softly. "Wendy said you wanted to talk to me; that it was important." His eyes were hungry as he looked at me. "Are you okay, love? Is something wrong?" He leaned on the rail close to me; his face turned toward mine.

When I didn't say anything, his brow crinkled. "Brook, tell me what this is about," he said softly.

I took a deep breath. "Wendy has been drilling me about my relationship with you. I had to tell her that we are just good friends and that I'm still with David."

Cade's jaw set and his eyes hardened, sparkling almost black in the dim light.

"I didn't know what else to do. I wasn't prepared for her to press me. I'm sorry." My eyes were pleading for his understanding.

"Is that all?" he asked. "I'm not angry, babe, but I bloody well hate this."

"No, that's not all. She wants me to help her get you in the sack, to find out why you won't take her up on her offer."

He groaned and he leaned both elbows on the railing of the balcony. He paused for a second to shake his head and let out an angry breath.

"Just tell her the fucking truth, Brook. If you don't, I will." He was upset, his blue eyes flashing, as he ran a hand angrily through his tousled locks.

"Cade, you can't. Denise told me today that Wendy has a reputation for connections with the paparazzi. She tips them off to photo ops, and they spin the story in her favor. She is probably responsible for all the paps at the airport today. We can't risk her knowing the truth. Not now."

It was getting out of hand, and I sighed.

Cade turned and studied me, his eyes intent on my face. "I just want to love you, to be with you and not hide it. That's all. Why is that so bloody difficult?" I could read the pain on his face. "I'm so angry about all of this!"

I softened my voice, hoping to ease his angst. "Look, I'm really looking forward to this jam session. I want to hear you play for me." I smiled. "We'll figure out what to tell Wendy later."

His eyes were intent on mine as he reached out to run his hand down my arm. "Do you trust me, Brook?" I nodded slowly. "I'm going to handle it once and for all, okay

"Yeah. What will you do?" I trusted him completely but was worried about his methods.

"You don't have to worry about it, but I will take care of it, I promise." He took my hand, "Come on, love, time to have a good time. Forget about her," he said as we walked back in.

Wendy looked at me anxiously and I smiled, hoping she would wait for another time to confront me about my conversation with Cade.

He let go of my hand and went to pick up his guitar. Dawson already had his and was tuning it on the opposite couch. Jennifer came to sit next to me and brought mine with her.

I watched Cade as he started to play, and knew it would all be okay somehow. I let myself get lost in the intricate strains of his acoustic guitar. Just like the day in the piano studio writing music, he amazed me every time he played an instrument.

He was truly gifted. He had perfect pitch, and could play practically anything by ear. He was so perfect. And he was mine.

Chapter 16

Only You

Caden

WHEN I COULD, I stole glances at Brook and watched her play and sing with us. I asked her to play again the song she did in London, and Dawson and I played with her. Her face was glowing, her eyes full of love as she sang it, I found myself not playing at times. When I bought it for her, shortly after our goodbye in Vancouver, I never dreamed she'd learn to play it. It made my heart swell knowing it meant as much to her as it did to me.

I loved to see her so happy. She was laughing most of the night, except when Wendy decided to interrogate her, and I saw her face tighten. After our conversation on the patio, I mulled over how I was going to handle Wendy, but one way or another, I *was* going to handle it.

It was almost midnight, and I was ready for the night to be over, at least with this room full of people. I wanted to be alone with Brook. I was leaving the next evening, and I needed as much time with her as I could get. I really needed to consider getting a place in L.A. Most of my business was here, my agent was here, and now Brook was. It just made sense.

"I'm really tired, guys. It's 8 AM London time, and I need to get to bed. Does everyone have a ride home?" I asked.

Wendy was, of course, the first to speak. "I don't have to leave yet, Cade!" she said coyly.

Always tuned in to her, I noticed Brook stiffen at her words. She turned to put her guitar away, and my jaw clenched. This ridiculous shit caused her pain, and I was bloody well going to put a stop to it. Now.

Everyone filed out one by one, and when everyone was gone except Wendy, Dawson, Jennifer, and Brook, I spoke. "Brook, I've called my car to take you, Dawson and Jennifer home. Wendy, let's get you a cab."

My plan was for the media to see Brook leaving with Jen and Dawson, and then sneak her back into the hotel through the garage entrance after the other two were dropped off. It also gave me the needed time to talk to Wendy alone. I would make my point this time, once and for all.

Brook's eyes looked up anxiously as she wondered what I was planning. I hugged Jennifer goodbye, and spoke with Dawson briefly, before taking Brook's hand and walking her out behind them.

"Trust me, love. See you in half an hour," I whispered to her as she left. She only nodded as I blocked Wendy's view with my body and handed Brook the key card to my suite

"Okay Love you," she said softly. I wished I could kiss those sweet lips, as my fingers brushed her cheek, but had to content myself with knowing she would be back in mere minutes.

"Me, too."

After the door had closed, I turned back to Wendy, who was already unbuttoning her blouse and walking towards me.

"I'm so glad you came to your senses, Cade," she said as she started to run her hands up my chest and around my neck, then trying to pull my head down so she could kiss me. I stopped her, pulling my head back and out of reach of her mouth.

I took her wrists in both of my hands to still their movement on my body and pulled them down to her sides. "We have to talk," I told her sternly. Her full breasts were visible but it didn't arouse me at all. I was angry that she would corner Brook about our relationship and then presume that I was hers for the taking. It was going to stop, now.

"Please button up your shirt, Wendy. I told you before that this isn't going to happen, and I meant it. It *will never* happen, do you understand me?" She frowned and I could see that she was hurt by the harshness of my voice.

"Why?" she murmured.

"It's simple." I took a breath. "I'm in love with someone else." I emphasized the word and waited for her reaction.

"Brook," she said without hesitation, her eyes shooting daggers. My gaze never wavered as I looked at her. I'd hoped I wouldn't have to admit whom, but I'd do whatever needed to be done.

"Yeah, and I don't want you asking her about my relationship with her again. That is between her and me." I let go of her arms and walked away from her.

"But, she's with David. You're a fool, Cade. She's been dating him for two years, but they've been close twice that long!" I could see her anger and jealousy flush her face. "She told me tonight that she's just your friend! She told me how to get you to be with me! That I should get beyond your looks and learn more about you." She laughed cruelly.

"That's all you are to her... a good *friend*." She threw Brook's words from the MTV interview in my face.

I sighed and then shrugged. "None of that matters. It doesn't change my feelings. My heart doesn't want anyone else. I've fought against it all these months, and I'm not going to bloody do it anymore."

She turned and started to button up her blouse, embarrassment burning her cheeks and flushing them bright pink.

"So what? Doesn't your body want anyone else either?" She sneered at me. "You would waste a chance with me or anyone else, and wait around in the hope that Brook will suddenly wake up and realize she's in love with you?" she asked astonished.

"Yes." I nodded. "I'll wait forever if I have to. The connection between us is undeniable. So I'll wait, and I won't screw up my chances with her for a meaningless one night stand." My tone was matter-of-fact. I wanted her to fully understand what I was saying; that she meant nothing to me.

"Yet, you sit here and know she's fucking David?" She laughed in my face. "Oh, you disappoint me, Cade. You're really pathetic. I thought you were more than Brook's lap dog." Her face was incredulous. She paused for a moment and then apparently decided to change her approach.

She walked toward me and placed her hand on my chest as she looked up at me and pouted. "I wouldn't have to be a one night stand, Cade. I want to know you, *and* fuck you." Her voice was barely a whisper, but she emphasized her meaning.

Jesus, does she think that would turn me on? I took her by the shoulders and pushed her back from me.

"Enough, Wendy! I'm done with this!" I said harshly. "Finished."

"What is it about her that's so special?" She practically screamed at me. "She's a nobody in this town! What is it about her that has you acting like an idiot? I'm sexier than her! She's boring!"

I sighed, but remained calm, then turned and moved to lean against the back of the couch across from her. Jesus, where to start.

"Wendy, of course, you're desirable. There is no denying you're a beautiful woman," I tried to soften the blow, "but this thing with Brook; it's so much more than physical. I find her beautiful, desirable, yes, but talented, insightful and able to read me. She knows me better than I even know myself... she looks right into my soul, we can talk for hours. She's amazing, just... she's everything." I looked right into Wendy's eyes as I said more than I intended, my gaze never flinching, as I crossed my arms in front of my body. "I can't explain it any better than that."

"Well, you're going to feel like a jackass when she stays with David. I really think you're wasting your time, Cade, and missing some really great sex." She got her purse and headed for the door. "You'll be sorry you made this choice." It sounded like a threat as she walked out of the suite, but I didn't care. "In more ways, than one."

"Wendy!" I yelled at her. She was clearly startled and turned back toward me. "If you fuck with me or try to hurt Brook in any way, you will regret it. You might be able to cause us some momentary discomfort, but I can make sure you don't get cast. I have a lot of influence. Do you understand me?"

She glared at me and then stormed from the suite, slamming the door behind her, leaving me to sigh heavily. I ran my hand through my hair and went to take a shower. Thank God that was over. Maybe now, Wendy would leave Brook the hell alone.

I stripped off my clothes and let the hot water rush over my body. I was exhausted. I shouldn't have let everyone stay so late because the eight-hour time difference was really dragging me down. It was 8:30 AM in London, and I hadn't slept for more than twenty-four hours. I had been too anxious about getting to Brook to be able to sleep on the plane.

I leaned my head on the wall of the shower and reminded myself that, in a matter of minutes, I'd have her in my arms.

I loved her, and I'd risk everything for her. Fame, whatever... it didn't matter. My breath left in a rush as the realization smacked me. I had enough bloody money to last a lifetime, and the celebrity lifestyle wasn't all it was cracked up to be.

Thinking how sexy she'd been today at the shoot, her eyes smoldering as she looked at me, and tonight her eyes full of pain when Wendy made it clear she wanted me, only served to increase the protectiveness I felt. I couldn't believe how just sitting next to her in the limo today could make my heart race faster. And, our little word game was *brilliant*. I loved it, and the memory of it made me smile, happily.

"Hey, handsome." I heard Brook's soft voice and opened my eyes as I raised my head to see her standing right outside the shower door, her beautiful blue eyes glowing, a small smile on her lips as she took in my naked body through the glass.

I flung open the shower door, put my arms around her and quickly dragged her in beside me, fully clothed. Then I moved in slow motion. "Hey, yourself," I said in a whisper against her lips before my mouth latched onto hers in a slow, deep kiss.

"God, you taste so good," I moaned as I pulled her lower lip into my mouth, licked her top lip with my tongue, as I pressed her body against the tiles with mine. My mouth teased hers as I spoke. "I've missed you, so much, love." I bent my head to take her lips in a wild kiss. Tasting, sucking, nipping and she matched me kiss for kiss, responding with the same desire I felt for her.

I was starving for her, feeling like I hadn't kissed her in years.

"Oh, Cade, I love you so much, I can't breathe," she whispered as she kissed my neck. I started stripping off her sodden clothes. Her breasts were visible above the white lace bra, as I unbuttoned her shirt. I wanted to taste every inch of her skin; my hand moved to cup her perfect breast.

"I've missed you," she whispered, her mouth searching for mine. She found it as my hands were undoing her bra and then moved to cup both of her pert breasts, the nipples hard in my palms. Her skin felt like silk. "I hate being away from you."

My erection was already pulsing on her stomach as my hands moved to the button on her jeans as I made short work of it and the zipper. The wet fabric clung to her curves, and it took some effort to move them down her hips. I bent to the task, trailing kisses on her breasts, sucking her nipples until I couldn't stand anymore. I moved lower to her flat stomach above her frilly white panties. When her hands twined in my hair, it only made me hungrier. I loved it.

"Oh, babe," I groaned against her body. "You're so beautiful."

My hands went to knead her ass as I pressed my mouth to her over her panties and then pulled them off. I kissed her pubic mound and slowed my pace. "God, Brook, I can't live without being with you like this." She moaned and leaned against the shower wall, as I raised one of her legs to rest on my shoulder and kissed and licked her hot flesh. She was so sweet.

She tasted so good; I wanted to devour her. Her body was visibly trembling and she moaned in pleasure as my mouth continued to assault her. "I want my tongue inside you," I groaned, my erection so hard, it was to the point of bursting.

We were so hungry for each other, and I knew I had to have her now. The urgency we felt overwhelming us both.

I picked her up and carried her into the darkness of the bedroom. We were both dripping wet and I didn't care. I lowered her to the bed and followed her down, my mouth never leaving hers as I settled into the cradle of her open limbs, which folded around my body to cage me in her embrace.

I could feel her hand on my ass, pulling me closer, she was rubbing her body against the length of my hardness, her other hand clutching at my back and her hips arching into mine. "Brook…" I gasped.

"Cade, I want you inside me. I need you," she whispered as her arms tightened around me, and her heels dug into my ass. "I don't want to wait another minute," she begged. "It's been too long… Please don't wait."

"Oh, sweetheart, I love you." I lowered my hand to the spot between her legs that I knew drove her crazy to find she was slick with need. She moaned against my mouth and raised her hips toward mine. I used my hand to pleasure her for a few delicious moments as I kissed her mouth. She was moaning against my mouth, and I couldn't take another minute of waiting.

I moved in between her legs, rubbing the head of my dick up and down her wetness until it slipped inside her. She was so hot and tight. I closed my eyes as I lost myself in her body and our love.

I pushed in slowly, feeling her stretch around me and she gasped.

"Uhhhh…" I groaned as I started to move inside her. The need we both felt at the long separation spurred us into deep thrusts, her hips rising to meet mine each time as I drove deeper and deeper into her. I kissed her neck and jaw as my hands played with her nipples. She was moaning against my mouth as her pleasure grew, her hands moved into my hair again, as she pulled my mouth back to hers, her tongue and mine intertwining as we kissed. Sweet Jesus, I was drowning in her. "God, Brook... I can't get close enough."

The little mewling sounds she made as I loved her were the most beautiful, arousing things I'd ever heard and when she added her voice, "Mmmmmm, Cade... You're making me come... Huh, huh, huh," as she panted softly with each thrust, then sent me over the edge. I felt my muscles tighten as my own climax overtook me.

"Oh, Brook!" I moaned into her mouth as I spilled deep within her body. "I love you so much, babe." Her fingers were raking down my back pushing my ass to bring me into her deeper, even at the end. Her body clenching mine, she was squeezing every last drop of ecstasy from me. I thrust with each spurt until I lay spent.

My body was damp and trembling as we both came down from the heights of our mating. I could feel her body shaking as well, and I kissed her mouth softly, her eyes opened to stare straight into my soul. I brushed my knuckles across her cheek as I continued to move within her body.

"Mmmmm..." she groaned and kissed my shoulder with her open mouth, sucking and nipping.

"You're so beautiful, Brook." I stared at her in amazement. Her wet hair was in disarray framing her face, her cheeks flushed and her eyes pools of love. I felt emotion well up within my chest and my eyes pricked with tears. "I've missed you so bloody much."

She saw the tears in my eyes and reached up to touch my face. "Cade, what is it?" she asked softly. "Are you ok?"

"I'm *incredible*. I never want this moment to end. I love you more than words can say." I put my forehead against hers and her arms tightened around me.

"I know how you feel. You're... everything." Her hand ran tenderly through my hair as she said the same words that I'd used to describe her to Wendy earlier. I felt as if my heart would burst in my chest. I pulled her close and kissed her temple.

We'd left the shower running and the entire room was engulfed in steam, and hot like a sauna.

"Be right back, love." I pulled out of her and went into the loo to get a towel and shut off the water. As I returned, she was lying naked to my view and I stared in amazement at the site.

Her white skin was translucent in the soft light from the cracked bathroom door, her blonde hair splayed around her head on the pillows. My eyes traveled over her breasts; round, and creamy, with light pink nipples, her flat perfect stomach, and the slight swell of her hips, the soft triangle of curls at her sex, and the long beautiful legs... and finally, her face flushed with the aftermath of our lovemaking; her blue eyes soft and sated.

Life couldn't get any better than this. Everything I needed was lying on that bed.

I bent with the towel to wipe the remnants of our shared fluids from between her legs.

"Uhhh..." Her back arched as I watched her, and her eyes burned into mine, her body still ultra sensitive after her orgasm.

I dried myself, threw the towel aside, and then crawled into bed next to her, laying on my side to stare into her face. I took her hand and brought it to my lips, as I kissed it softly she looked unwaveringly into my eyes.

I bent to kiss her mouth in a series of soft, sucking kisses and didn't think I'd ever get enough of her. She ran her fingers lightly along my jaw. "Do you like me better as a brunette? Like Julia?"

"Either way, you're gorgeous." My fingers reached out to stroke into the silken strands. "After the audition when you were blonde, it was sort of a shock to see you darker, but still, it's this face." I touched her nose with the tip of my index finger.

"Cade, you need to sleep, baby," she whispered.

"I don't want to waste one precious minute of my time with you, sleeping," I said seriously. She smiled softly in response. Our fingers playing, our hands ghosted each other's for a moment before intertwining.

"You have to, or you'll get ill. I'll stay with you for a while, but I need to leave before dawn. The car is waiting for me downstairs." My arms went around her in protest.

"No. I want you to stay."

"We have to be careful, Cade. Denise already read me the riot act today." She kissed the tip of my nose and I decided I'd have to have a talk with Denise. What the hell was she doing talking to Brook like that? "Tomorrow you can come to my house. I'm supposed to grill out for my family and I'd love for you to be there, okay

"You mean, today?" I asked and she nodded, my fingers tracing up and down her back and hip. "Okay, I'd love to, but can't you sleep with me for a while? I haven't had a good night's sleep in, oh I don't know, a month?" I teased her. She kissed me softly again. "I have to leave again tonight, so can't you stay with me now?" I begged.

"Mmmm. I want to."

"I don't ever want to leave." I gathered her close to me and we lay together stroking and lightly kissing each other for a few minutes then I decided to tell her about my conversation with Wendy.

"Okay. Stay forever." She smiled and nuzzled into my neck.

"Brook..." I began.

"Hmmmm?" she said. I could hear the sleep in her voice.

"I told Wendy it wasn't going to happen between her and I, so you don't have to fret about it anymore, okay?" I began. Her eyes opened and she propped up on her elbows so she could look into my face, her eyes still sleepy. "I told her that I didn't appreciate her asking you about our relationship, and she wasn't to do so again." I was lost in her eyes, my fingers touching her, stroking wherever I could reach.

"What did she say?" she asked quietly, lifting a hand to the side of my face; she brushed her thumb along my jaw.

"She wanted to know why I didn't find her attractive."

"And?" Brook pressed.

"And, I said I did find her attractive, that she was quite beautiful."

Brook's eyes widened. "Oh, you did, did you?" she asked, suddenly wide-awake.

"Uh huh." I kissed her hand again, smiling because I couldn't help myself. My girl was jealous, and my heart soared. "But that it didn't matter in the slightest," I paused for a beat, "because I was in love... with you."

"Cade, no you didn't," she accused.

"Oh, yes, I bloody well did." I brushed her hair back tenderly as I continued. "Then she wanted to know what was so special about you, and I told her that you can see straight into my soul. So now will you stop worrying? Please?" I asked softly as I kissed her mouth. "I only want you, will only want you, and I told her so in no uncertain terms." I deepened the kiss and moved down to nibble down her neck.

I wrapped my arms around her as I heard her sigh. "She's going to make trouble; I can feel it." Brook's voice was wary. "I don't trust her. Did she say anything else?"

"She told me that you were in love with David and that I was a fool." I yawned. "She said that you told her how to get me."

"Hmmmm," she said. "That's not exactly the way I remember it. I told her that she wouldn't win you over with sex. That you were deep and there was more to you than that superficial bullshit." Her light blue eyes glowed as she looked at me, still stroking my face.

"Well," My hand ran up her body lightly causing goosebumps on her skin, "if I wasn't already in love with you, I'm pretty sure you could win me over with sex." I laughed softly.

"Oh really?"

She was so adorable. Her mouth quirked and her brow arched. "Without a doubt. It's pretty damn amazing, isn't it?" I smiled, kissing her lips tenderly, and brushing her hair back.

She stared into my eyes, right into my soul again, I thought. "Mmmmm, I'll say." She smiled softly and nodded gently. "It's because I love you so much," she whispered.

"And, because I love *you* so much. So stop worrying about Wendy." I placed another soft kiss on her luscious mouth and pulled her close to my side. "This..." I raised my arm to wave over our entwined bodies, "Is the only thing that matters." I turned and pressed my lips against her forehead, and just before we drifted off into an exhausted sleep, tangled together under the sheets, I said, "You're all that matters to me. Only you."

Chapter 17

Goodbye Again

Brooklyn

I AWOKE TO the song Cade had written for me, as my phone alarm went off. It was 4 AM, and I needed to get out of Cade's hotel before daylight. His arm pinned me to the bed but I lifted it slightly, trying not to wake him, and then made my way to the bathroom to retrieve my soaked clothes.

Oh, crap! What was I going to wear? I blushed as I recalled how he'd peeled them from me in the shower. I closed the door, leaving it cracked, then turned on the light. It dimly illuminated the room where Cade was still sleeping.

I found a plastic bag in the closet the hotel provided to send out dry cleaning, and put my wet clothes inside. I found Cade's bag and rummaged through it until I found a pair of gym shorts and an old gray t-shirt. I knew he wouldn't mind if I borrowed them, so I quickly got dressed. The clothes were loose, but I tied a knot in the shirt so that it fitted my waist.

How in the hell was I going to sneak down to the garage without anyone seeing me, I wondered. I found a piece of paper on the desk and wrote him a note.

C-

Thank you for the beautiful evening. I had to borrow a pair of shorts and a shirt, sorry. I'll give them back when you come over later. Call me when you wake up.

Love you with my whole heart.

Yours,

-B

I laid the note on the pillow I'd used, tiptoed around and knelt down on his side of the bed to look at him. He was lying on his stomach, spread eagle on the bed. Even in sleep, and dim light, he was so beautiful, more than beautiful. My heart filled with sadness at his impending departure, even as it ached with love. I bent toward him and placed a soft kiss on his mouth, part of me hoping he'd wake up to give me a proper kiss goodbye. "I love you," I whispered.

"Brook," he whispered. He stayed asleep though his eyelids fluttered. I sighed and brushed his hair off his forehead. I hated leaving him.

I picked up the bag containing my clothes, and then my purse, trying to sneak out of the room as quietly as I could. He wouldn't hear the door to the suite close as I left because I'd closed the one separating the bedroom. I rushed down the hall, found the stairs, and ran down twelve flights to the garage. Peeking my head out of the stairwell door, I saw the limo waiting where I'd left it three hours earlier. No one was around, but I still crouched down and ran between the parked cars and the wall until I reached the limo. I opened the back door and flung myself inside, breathing heavily, not from exertion, but from sheer terror at being caught.

"Home, Miss?" the driver asked nonchalantly, as if waiting hours in garages and having young women jump inside his car were normal.

"Yes, please. Thank you for waiting, Shane. I didn't mean to be so long."

"That's okay, Miss. Mr. Carlisle told me you might be all night." He smiled at me.

I guessed Cade's driver was in on the secret and decided to give him a big tip. Shit, everyone knew, it seemed, so what the hell were we sneaking around like this?

When Shane dropped me off at home, I tiptoed into my room, and peeled off the shorts, but left Cade's T-shirt on as the memories of our evening together flooded my thoughts. I could still smell him on my body and hugged a pillow, wishing it was him instead. As I lay there in the dark, yearning for him, I wondered if I'd ever really get used to the intensity of my feelings. They were so wonderful, but at times, extremely painful.

The evening when he would be torn from me again, was only hours away, and I dreaded it. The weeks apart were like torture. I'd gotten the lead role in a new dystopian fantasy film, so at least, I had that to keep me busy. I was going to spend some time with the cast over the holidays, but that was months away. Fantasy and sci-fi weren't genres I spent a lot of time reading; so I made plans to rectify that, particularly of this writer since the movie was another book adaptation. I also wanted to watch some of the director's films and spend some time researching the cast and the producers. Jeanne insisted I get to know their body of work in advance to prevent me from looking like a moron when we all hit the set.

Cade arrived later in the morning, and we spent time with both my parents and my brother. My dad seemed to love him as much as my mother did, and I breathed a sigh of relief. I had been slightly worried because my dad had been even more reluctant because David cried on his shoulder when we'd broken up, and always allowed me to include him on all of our family vacations. When I really thought about it; it was more because Dad treated him like a son than because he was my boyfriend. It had been slightly uncomfortable at first, but Cade engaged him in conversation, and soon, I was able to relax.

I watched as Cade said goodbye to Mom, Dad and Nathan. "It was good to meet you, finally, sir." He shook hands with my dad and then hugged my mom. "Thanks for everything, Mrs. Halloway."

"Cade." She looked at him sternly. "Diane," Mom told him and smiled warmly. "I thought we covered that the other day."

"Yes, ma'am. Thank you, Diane." He smiled at her. "It means so much to feel welcome in your home."

He turned and gave Nate a hug. "Good to see you, man," he said.

"Yeah, next time, I'll kick your ass on guitar hero. I'm going to practice my butt off." Nathan smiled warmly.

"I'm already looking forward to it." He put his hand on Nate's shoulder.

Cade took my hand as we went out the back door, and into the garage. Our fingers laced together, and my head rested on his shoulder as we walked. He raised my hand to his lips, and brushed his mouth across the back of my knuckles.

When we made it to Jeanne's waiting SUV, he turned to me and I bent my head, pressing the top of it against his chest, taking a deep breath as I struggled to control my emotions. I was working hard not to cry and let him see how sad his leaving made me. My hands went to the sides of his trim waist, and I sucked in my breath, feeling my resolve quickly slipping, my eyes already blurring.

He rubbed both hands down my arms and back up again as he kissed the top of my head and rested his cheek against it. Cade sighed heavily, and when I raised my teary eyes to his, he took me in his arms.

Jeanne had come to take him to LAX, and she waited inside her car, behind the closed garage door. His bodyguards would meet them at the airport drop-off, and get him safely on the plane to New York. The paparazzi would be suspicious of Denise's or any other strange car hanging outside my house, so Jeanne graciously volunteered to help, despite the interruption to her evening.

My arms wrapped around his neck as I clung to him, breathing in his scent, my whole body began to tremble with my grief, and Cade bent, tightened his arms and lifted me off of the ground, as he held me closely against him.

"Oh, babe," he whispered as we hugged goodbye. Jeanne tried to avert her eyes, and left the radio playing, so we had more privacy. "Don't forget, I love you more than life." He set me down and raised a hand to touch my face. I started crying, and his fingers caught my tears. "Shhh. Don't cry, Brook."

"Cade—this is so hard!" My body was shaking as his arms tightened around me again. His hands were fisting on my back, gathering my shirt in them, as he held me close, his face buried in the side of my neck. "I can't take it," I sobbed into him. "I won't survive doing this over and over... I... I feel like I'm dying," I cried, gasping. His face moved into the curve of my neck as he kissed it with his open mouth. He was silent, but I felt him struggling. "I'm s-s-sorry I'm such a mess." My voice cracked on a sob.

His voice was low and laced with emotion as he finally spoke to me. "Brook, the next time I come back, we'll have more time together. You know we have a lot of the promotional stuff beginning, so we'll be together for longer, I promise."

He held me in silence for a time, kissing the sides of my face and my temple, waiting for me to say something. When I didn't, he continued his voice breaking a little. "It's bloody hard. It's killing me, too. The pain of being apart is the worst I've suffered in my entire life, but it's worth it because you're mine. Do you hear me?" he said, his voice thickening, but urgent. "You're mine," he said again.

"Oh, God, Cade," I sobbed. "Will this ever get any fucking easier?" I said as tears squeezed from my closed eyes. My hands went into his hair as my grip tightened around him.

"No, love, I don't think it will. I'm so sorry." He pressed his lips to my forehead as his hands came up to hold both sides of my face. His blue eyes were wide and sad, one thumb brushing my cheekbone, and the other my lower lip as it trembled. "Honey, I have to go. I love you, so much. You're everything to me." He kissed my mouth in a wild hungry kiss. Our mouths melted together, and our tongues dove into each other's mouths, both of us giving and taking with equal fervor. We couldn't get enough, both of us reluctant to let go, but finally, he dragged his mouth from mine across my cheek.

"I love you," he choked out, at the same time as he pulled my arms from around his neck. "I'll miss my flight."

"I love you, Cade." He kissed my wrist and then put his hand behind my neck, pulling me forward to kiss my forehead again, before getting in the car with Jeanne.

I reached for him again, and he took my hand through the open window. As she backed out of the garage, once again, his fingers slipping from mine as we parted. My body shaking, I brought my arms around my chest to try and stop the pain.

Caden

AS HER FINGERS fell from mine, I watched Brook standing in the garage shaking, tears streaming down her beautiful face. Then, as she wrapped her arms around herself in pain, her mother came to take her in her arms and hug her. When Jeanne backed out, it was all I could do not to jump out of the car, and run back to her.

"Jesus Christ!" I groaned as the garage door closed. Both hands fisted on my forehead as I bent over in agony of my own. I felt like I'd been punched in the gut, my lungs fighting for oxygen. I closed my eyes as I tried to swallow against the lump in my throat. "AGHHHHH!" The sound ripped loudly from my chest, pain shredding my heart and lungs.

Jeanne glanced at me, visibly shaken by the outburst. "I'm so, so sorry, Cade," she said in a soft voice. "I wasn't sure this was real, given the circumstances, but my skepticism was misplaced."

I looked out the window at the dark night sky, lost in my misery. My throat ached, my chest painfully tight, and my eyes stinging. I couldn't breathe.

"Yeah. She's turned into my whole world." It was a simple explanation.

Jeanne was quiet for a few minutes as we drove out of their neighborhood, through Hollywood and Beverly Hills on our way to the airport. I continued to stare out the window, my eyes seeing nothing but Brook standing in that fucking garage, and her tear-stained face haunting me.

"If it brings you any comfort, I've never seen Brook like this before either. She's young, but she's usually so strong. When she said goodbye to David, it was never anything like this." She stopped abruptly probably thinking she shouldn't have mentioned his name.

"Maybe it's because we don't see each other for weeks or months at a time. Or maybe it's that I'm halfway across the fucking world," I moaned.

"Or, maybe she just loves you more." Jeanne reached for my hand and gave it a little squeeze.

"Seeing her in that much pain and knowing it's because of me, it tears my heart out," I said quietly. "Maybe I shouldn't have told her how I felt."

"You don't cause her pain, Cade. Obviously, she loves you, so, of course, it hurts her when you leave. It's not your fault. You know that. You're suffering just as much as Brook is," she said softly.

I leaned my head back on the seat. "I know." My voice was almost a whisper. My eyes closed as my chest constricted again.

She didn't speak for a while, but when she did, her voice was quiet. "How did it happen?" she finally asked as she turned on to the expressway.

"What do you mean?"

"Well, when did you two..." She began and let her words fall off.

"Oh." I nodded in understanding. "Hmmph." I let out my breath and sat up at little straighter in the seat. "Um, I guess the moment we met," I said quietly as she glanced at me and her eyes widened. "When she walked in the room at the audition, I was drawn to her immediately. Denise had shown me photos of the top five contenders for the role, but when I actually saw Brooklyn for the first time, it was like electricity shot through my entire body." I ran a hand through my hair, and let it remain at the back of my neck for a minute while I paused, and remembered. I flushed, thinking that for a grown man to admit such weakness, especially, in this industry, might seem idiotic. Everywhere I went, beautiful women were dripping from the walls everywhere.

"Continue. If you don't mind," Jeanne murmured.

"We had this intense connection right from the beginning. When I looked into her eyes, it was like I'd known her all my life, loved her all my life, and when our lips met the first time, I knew." I smiled at the memory. "She was better than me. She tried harder to fight it, but we were drawn to each other, intensely attracted, just, fascinated, I suppose. I wanted to spend every minute with her," I paused. "That hasn't changed."

"Really? Surely, you've had reactions to other actresses." Jeanne was probing; her protectiveness about Brooklyn apparent, and I respected her more for it.

"Not like Brook."

"That's incredible."

"Yeah. It's been... " I searched for a word to do the feelings justice, but there wasn't one. "Amazing," I said and then took a ragged breath. "A mixture of heaven and hell, the greatest joy, such unfathomable ecstasy and yet, the most unbearable pain I've ever experienced in my life."

"It's like the book series."

I huffed softly. I'd made the comparison myself, many times, even trying to convince myself the rush I was experiencing was just getting into character.

"When she told us that the two of you were in love, you should have seen her face. Her eyes glowed with it. Naturally, I was worried."

I smiled through my sadness, but I nodded. "I'd convinced myself we'd never be able to be together because of her situation with David. Now that it has, it seems like a miracle. I still sometimes wonder if I'm dreaming." I felt my mouth quirk. "All those months, dying inside when he came on location, I tried to convince myself that I'd never have her. I knew that I was torturing myself by wanting to be near her, yet I couldn't drag myself away. I hated myself because I couldn't stop the overpowering need for her, and part of me didn't want to stop."

I took out my cigarettes and paused before lighting one. "Do you mind?" I asked. When she shook her head, I continued. "The brilliant part was that she wanted to be with me, too. It was like neither of us had a choice."

"What happened?" she asked. "That's if you don't mind sharing."

"No, Jeanne, that's okay. Being able to talk about Brook was like a balm to my aching heart. I blew out the smoke after taking a drag on the cigarette. "We spent time with the script; at first, talking about how we wanted to develop the characters. We watched movies and read the books together. Basically, we spent weeks inseparable. Thinking back on all the time we spent together made my heart lurch in my chest.

"Martin had a very specific idea of how he wanted the characters to be played, but Brook and I disagreed with him. He wanted us to be fluffier, and such gibberish. After reading the series, we wanted to play the characters with all the pain that had to be in such an impossible relationship; two people who wanted more than anything to be together and couldn't."

I physically grimaced. Life was imitating art.

"Then, the utter anguish of being forgotten by the one person you live for." I paused, swallowing. My voice was introspective when I continued. "We re-wrote every scene, rehearsed for hours in private, and argued tirelessly with the directors and producers." I took a drag off of the cigarette. "We took a lot of grief, but Brook was like a dog with a bone and I found it incredible to watch. I sat back and watched her work Martin over until she finally got him convinced, and the movie will be so much better because of it. We made the relationship real." I stared out the window at the passing billboards and lights as the traffic and streets passed by.

"There was like this unspoken unity between us. Like this was something we were always going to do together, and we did. Every step of the way." I paused and took another drag. "Off set, we spent most of our time together, too. Watching movies, talking, playing music. She loved listening to me play the guitar and we fell asleep together many nights after spending the evening running lines for the next day's shoot." I looked at Jeanne. "We went out with the cast a lot as well, but the tension between us was bloody palpable. Everyone noticed how we gravitated toward each other and sometimes it was just easier to stay in together instead."

She didn't say anything, so I continued, "The fact that she was still technically a minor those first months kept me from even kissing her except in rehearsal or during filming. But as the end of the shoot came near, her birthday came, and went and I couldn't bear the thought of not seeing her every day." I pinched the end of the cigarette off and pushed it back into the pack, and replaced it in my jacket pocket. Jeanne was still silent as I glanced at her.

"That's when I knew. I spent the last two weeks trying to figure out how I was going to say goodbye to the one person that I couldn't live without." My mouth quirked at the memory of those last weeks in Vancouver... I had been completely miserable. Lost.

Jeanne just drove and let me talk. "Every time that David would show up, I disappeared, avoiding everyone, except on set. Especially Brook. She always came to find me; then, how was I supposed to hide how bloody miserable I was? It was as if my pain, were her own. She just—" I stopped and shook my head in amazement. "She knew I needed her. Even thinking I'd never have her, knowing she cared was enough at the time."

I let out my breath, "I know it must sound ridiculous and rather pathetic to you…" I let the words drop on a half-assed laugh. "Especially given who I am."

"Not at all." Jeanne put a hand on mine. "It's beautiful, Cade, and seeing you together, I can see you're being honest. I'm so sorry that you have the damn contract restrictions. I wish there was a way to get out of them."

"Yeah, I'm ready to tell them to sod off. Seriously, I'd chuck it all to end this madness," I sighed. "The money, fame, even the next film, none of it, is worth this. The pain I feel when I have to leave her fucking devastates me every time. There are no words to describe the pain."

Jeanne pulled up to the curb at Virgin Atlantic and two of my regular bodyguards were waiting on the curb to surround me once I was out of the car. She hugged me in the car so that paps wouldn't see her, and then be able to connect me to Brook.

"Have a safe flight, Cade. Everything will work out, honey." She tried to reassure me, but my heart had fallen and was sitting like lead in my stomach. Sadness enveloped me.

I got out of the car, and opened the back door to get my carry on, as the guys unloaded my case from the rear hatch.

"Jeanne, I want to thank you, sincerely, for helping us have time together despite the contracts. I can't tell you what it means. Every second we have together is like gold."

Cameras were already flashing. I hated this shit. I leaned in the open door further, so I could talk to her without the press hearing my words, as my bodyguards stood between them and me, arms spread to keep them at bay. It was difficult because of the screaming fans and the paparazzi yelling at me for a photo op. The dark windows would help hide Jeanne's identity from the press. Brook's career was only starting, so that helped tamp down suspicion, but it would only be a matter of time, and I knew it. I threw my bag over my shoulder, ready to go into the terminal.

"Thanks for listening. It helped." I patted the top of the door over the open window, after I shut it. "Take good care of her. Tell her not to forget about me." I knew sadness was evident on my face, but I consciously changed my expression stoic and shoved on my sunglasses.

"I will, I promise," Jeanne said. I could barely hear her amid the din, but her eyes were sympathetic. "But she knows, Cade. She knows."

I stepped between my guys and turned amid screaming fans, flashing cameras and pushing paparazzi to go into the terminal where I would board the plane that would take me the three thousand miles to New York City and my next role. Three thousand miles away from my heart, New York to the West Coast, the same distance that separated Boston and L.A.

So, bloody ironic.

* * *

AFTER I WAS ushered through security and settled into my first class seat, the entire portion of the plane, reserved for my team to ensure privacy and discretion, I decided to check my phone before I turned it off for the flight. There was a message from Brooklyn.

"Mmmm," I sighed. I was happy to see her name already on the screen, but my chest hurt uncomfortably, and I felt like my skin was crawling. I prayed, I'd get some sleep during the flight.

Seeing Brook was always completely amazing, but what followed, was pure heartbreak. Remembering her trembling in the garage as we backed out was too much for my aching heart. I pulled up her message.

I'm sorry I cried so much. I'll try to be stronger. I love you.

My heart thudded in my chest as I felt my throat constrict.

I'll call you when I land in New York. I love you with all my heart. Don't forget to remember me.

I pushed send, and then dialed Denise.

The next time Brook and I would see each other was when I came to L.A. next month for the Vanity Fair shoot and Comic Con. I decided to call my manager.

"Denise, it's Cade." I had an agent in Los Angeles and one in London.

"Hi, doll! Did you have a nice time in L.A.?"

" Yeah, it was nice to be here. I'm on the plane, waiting to taxi out."

"Okay, well when you get to the hotel, you'll find your press packet in your room with your itinerary, and the contact numbers for your transportation to and from events, and everything..." Filming was scheduled for Wednesday, but until then, I had two days of press junkets.

I was bored with this conversation; I already knew the drill. "Listen, Denise, I need a couple of things."

"Sure, what can I do for you?" she asked.

"Well, who is getting photographed for Vanity Fair next month?" I asked. I was remembering what Wendy said about all of us being there, and was hoping we wouldn't have to deal with her bullshit again.

"All of the main cast, and Noah," she said. "Why?"

"Can you see if you can just have Brook, Noah, me and only a couple of the others? I don't want Wendy McFarland on that shoot."

"What's your problem with her?" Denise asked cautiously.

"She's been coming on to me, and frankly, I don't want to subject Brook to that nonsense. Brook said you mentioned Wendy has a reputation for calling the paps to tip them off; she gets more publicity that way. If that's true, just keep her away from me. I don't want even a rumor getting out that she and I are seeing each other, and more importantly, I don't need any press around if I'm going to keep my relationship with Brook a secret."

"Yeah, I see your point. Okay, I'll make sure she's contained." She laughed. "Cade, you will always have women chasing after you. Brook will need to deal with it."

"I'm really oblivious to it, Denise. I just want some form of normalcy and will do whatever I can to keep Brook from being hurt."

"Don't say her name loud enough for anyone to hear Cade! Good God! You have to be so careful." She paused when I didn't say anything. Bloody hell, now I can't even talk about her in an empty airplane compartment?

"Speaking of Brook, did you get to spend any time with her after the photo shoot? Jeanne said she was going to work it out, but I never heard." Even though she was my manager, Denise had also become a close friend.

"Yeah, Jeanne has been great. We only had the one night. But um, it was... incredible, wonderful. It's leaving that kills me, you know?" I closed my eyes.

Her voice was full of understanding. "I'm so sorry, Cade. We're all working to get something done so maybe the two of you can have some time alone somewhere, extend your next L.A. trip, perhaps. There's a lot of press to do, and Martin called and said there are three scenes he needs. That means you may be here as long as two weeks."

"Well, maybe that's a blessing in disguise. Which scenes? Are they reshoots?" I wanted to know.

"Um, I think they're all new, but I can't remember what they are right now, sorry."

"Are they sending us back up to Vancouver?"

"No, they're scouting locations in LA." The flight attendant began going over the in-flight safety instructions, so I wanted to finish the call.

"Listen, Denise, I need a favor, if you don't mind," I said hesitantly.

"Okay, what?" She was eager to help me. She'd been my manager since I was twelve, and I could always count on her for anything I needed.

"Well, I need to go to Tiffany's while I'm in New York, but no one can know. Maybe you can go for me, or arrange a time when the store is closed when I could meet with only the manager? I'll need to pay in cash, so there isn't a paper trail."

"Um..." Her voice was wary. "What exactly are you buying at Tiffany's, Cade?"

I smiled, but I knew all hell was going to break lose as soon as I said it. "An engagement ring," I said softly.

Silence. I waited.

"Cade!" Her voice was panicked. "We can't have Brooklyn parading around wearing a damn engagement ring unless it's from David."

"Fuck David," I growled at her. His name was the last one I needed to hear. He'd be rammed down my bloody throat enough in the next months.

"You can't be seen buying one. Is that clear?" Her voice was stern.

I was annoyed at her resistance. "Look, I'm in love with her, and by some miracle, she loves me, too. We aren't telling anyone and she won't wear it until we can come out with our relationship, but I need to buy this ring. I need to know she's mine." My voice was low and serious. "Will you help me, or not?"

"If she isn't going to wear it, can't it wait?" she almost begged.

"I'm not giving it to her until I'm back in LA, so we have a month. I'm going to be in New York, so I thought I could get it while I'm there." I paused and sighed. "Doing this will help me feel less separated from her, less miserable. Right now, I'm sick with it. You want me to function, don't you?" I tried to lighten the mood with light teasing.

She sighed on the other end of the phone. "Okay. I'll see what I can do, but I'm sure as hell not letting you go in anywhere to buy it. I'll have to figure this out and get back to you." I could hear the reluctance in her voice, but she knew I was serious.

"I appreciate it, but I want to pick it out myself. It has to be perfect."

"Cade! You barely know her."

"I'm not going to argue about it."

"God, you're impossible! I'm only doing this because I love you," she said tightly, but I knew she was probably smiling.

"I know. What would I do without you?" I was the last to board the plane, so the flight attendant's announcement was beginning.

"Not a whole hell of a lot!" She laughed.

"I've gotta go, they are making me shut down my phone while we take off. I'll call you when I get to New York. Thanks for everything." I rang off and settled back in my seat as my phone buzzed in my pocket. Brook's message flashed on the screen before flipped the phone to airplane mode.

I won't forget. I love you, more.

I sighed and closed my eyes. She loved me, more? That was impossible.

Chapter 18

Stolen Moments

Brooklyn

I KEPT BUSY during my time without Cade, working on my upcoming role and also reading a couple of scripts Jeanne had given me to look through for future jobs. I still couldn't commit to anything, though, because we didn't know if we'd be doing the rest of the Remembrance Series, so I needed to keep my calendar relatively clear in the spring. *Army of Two* was slotted to begin filming in the summer months, but if I was going to be a successful actress, I needed to get more projects lined up beyond that.

David and I talked and were on pretty good terms. I sensed he was still hurt, but agreed that being friends was something we would always have, and really, what our entire relationship had been based on. It was still awkward, but I was hoping that over time it would get easier. I had some appearances with Cade coming up that David would be attending with me, per our arrangement, and while it was apparently necessary, it would be weird for all of us.

I saw Jennifer and Wendy a couple of times. We all met for lunch at a sushi bar about a week earlier, and to give Wendy credit, she didn't even mention Cade once. I would have thought it strange except I knew about the conversation in his room the last time he was in LA.

She was angry that the Vanity Fair shoot had been changed only to include Cade, Noah, Sarah, Gavin and me. That magazine was a big deal and promotional powerhouse, so she had other reasons to be disappointed, beyond not seeing Cade.

Call me selfish, but I was glad I wouldn't have to deal with the possibility of her attitude. It would've been odd seeing her reaction around Cade when he'd told her he wasn't interested in her. I was sure it hurt her, and I felt a little bit guilty though I still felt real jealousy at her blatant attempts to seduce him. I knew her well enough to know that his discouraging words wouldn't deter her forever.

Cade texted several times, but we only spoke a few times a week on the phone or Skype. It probably would have been more often, if we didn't get so sad when we said goodbye. It seemed we were in touch a little less as time went on. Another one of our unspoken communications; it kept us sane.

His sweet words coming from my phone reminded me he was thinking of me, but made me anxious for the time we would be together again. Most of the messages were filled with love, but some were a little bit naughty, too. I giggled at the thought. He either had my heart swelling, or my body aching. I loved it, either way.

The distance was getting a little bit easier to bear, or maybe it was just time passing that made me acclimate. I told myself that the real test would be the next time he'd leave me, but I wouldn't let myself think about that, and shifted my focus to seeing him.

He was coming in tomorrow and would be in L.A. for two full weeks. I longed for some time alone with him, but we would also be doing additional scenes for the film, which would take several of those days, some mall appearances, and a couple of interviews on radio and entertainment TV. This was life after our private little filming bubble popped, I thought ruefully. It was likely to get even more maddening as the premieres came closer, the first of which would be at the end of October in Rome. The schedule would be brutal, but at least, I'd be seeing much more of Cade. I was missing him more than I let myself admit.

Jeanne was on her way over to discuss the schedule for the weeks to come, and take me to the VF shoot. I wondered what she and Denise came up with to allow alone time with Cade.

We were lucky that we had so many people we trusted working to help us maintain our contracts with Pinnacle, and help us to see each other under the radar. It wasn't ideal, but it was better than nothing. I could sense Cade's frustrations when he and I talked. I worried that he'd do something rash, not caring about the contracts or future work with the studio.

I hadn't seen my manager since that day she came to take Cade to the airport a month before, but we'd maintained close contact on the phone and through email.

Jeanne and Ken were the business end of my career. They handled all the mundane stuff like finding jobs and negotiation of contracts, which left me to the part that I loved. Acting. She arrived dressed in a business suit and I smiled brightly.

"Hey!" I said as I jumped in the front seat of her SUV. My cheeks felt heated; I was flushed and excited.

"Hi, honey," she said as she leaned over toward my seat and hugged me. "You look really good!! Much happier than the last time I saw you." She gave me a squeeze.

"Um, yeah. Sorry about that. I never mean to be such a mess, but..." I began.

"Oh, that's okay, Brooklyn." She looked at me and as she put the car in reverse and starting to back out. "I want to apologize for doubting that yours and Cade's relationship was the real thing."

"It's, okay." I shrugged and shook my head, surprised by her admission. "I guess it was evident by the way I fell apart before, huh?"

"And, by Cade's reaction in the car on the way to the airport." She paused as she searched my face. "He was pretty much a mess. He really loves you, Brook, and I decided then and there, I was going to do whatever I need to do to help the two of you see each other." She smiled.

I wondered what she had planned, pleasure at her words racing through me.

"After the shoot today, you guys have three days before any of your other commitments and so we're sending you off together."

My breath caught in my throat and I felt my stomach lurch. "What?" I gasped out.

"Denise and I worked it out. You can't travel together, but she's got him booked on a flight for Vancouver tomorrow morning," she used her hand to make quote marks in the air, "to visit Daniel, who has a concert up there. And you will be staying home all weekend. Poor thing, he's got what amounts to a day-long plane ride, just to keep up the illusion, and you... You're going to get so *damn* ill." Her eyes sparkled, a big smile on her lips.

I couldn't help the giggle that burst out.

"We've chartered a plane to pick up Cade at a private airstrip and fly him down to meet you in San Diego. My parents have a bungalow down there by the ocean and I've managed to get it for you."

I felt my heart leap inside my chest. Did she just say what I thought she said? Three days alone with Cade?

"Really?" I couldn't believe it was possible. She nodded, and I wanted to hug her. "Oh Jeanne, I'll never be able to thank you!! Ahhhhhh!" I screamed.

"Well, don't get too excited. You won't be able to go out site seeing or anything like that. Cade is too recognizable, but there is a pool and gated grounds, and I've had the refrigerator stocked with everything you'll need."

I was practically jumping in my seat. "I'm so nervous. Why am I nervous?" I fell back against the seat laughing. "I'm so happy! Thank you, Jeanne. I owe you big time!" I squealed. "Oh, my God! Does Cade know?"

"Yes, he's known for a while, but he wanted to surprise you." She was as breathless as I was.

"What? How could he keep it from me? He must have been dying to spill it! I think I'm going to torture him later." I laughed.

"Yes, I'm sure you will," she said knowingly.

We pulled up to the studio and she grabbed my hand to stop me from bounding out of the car. "We've got to go in, but I haven't told you what will happen today. There are several costume changes because they are shooting for more than one issue. One set will be you and Cade, with the other cast members; another will be just you and Cade in the rain."

She ran through it fast but I was so excited I hardly heard a word she said.

I didn't understand why not much of it matched the movie, but I was so excited to get inside, I didn't care. "Is Cade already here?" I was breathless as she nodded, quickly.

"Okay, I need to calm down," I said. I grabbed Jeanne's hands, ready to squeal. "What the hell is wrong with me? I'm jumping out of my freaking skin!"

"Just take a deep breath Brooklyn. Remember you have to keep your feelings under wraps, no one can see it," she said calmly as she gripped my hands harder. "Can you do this?"

"Yeah." I closed my eyes and tried to steady my breathing. "Yes, I can do it," I said more forcefully. "I can!" I looked at her, then burst out laughing. She smiled and raised her eyebrows.

"Cade will already be in makeup, so you go to wardrobe and then meet me in the makeup room. I'll make some excuse to get everyone out of there for five minutes so you can say hello to Cade in private. But I'm serious, Cinderella! Five minutes!" she exclaimed with a smile.

I put my arm around her as we walked into the studio, the green screen was there for the shoot and they would put some backgrounds in later. "I love you, Jeanne. Thank you." I hugged her again. "I really mean it."

She smiled. "Off to wardrobe now." She shooed me away and as I walked, I made a conscious effort not to look around in search of a particular pair of blue eyes or full head of golden hair. Even though I knew I wouldn't see him, I had to force myself to rein it in.

A few minutes later, I came out of wardrobe in the dark blue dress they'd given me for the first part of the shoot; my stomach was fluttering in anticipation. It was all I could do not to run down to hair and makeup.

Sarah, Gavin, Noah, Jen and Ethan would arrive in about an hour, joining Cade and me for some shots after we'd taken several alone. *Alone...* What a beautiful word.

I remembered Cade's from earlier that morning, as heat rose

under the skin on my face. He had a habit of sending a text once a week or so, that showed the days, hours and minutes until he'd be with me again. I thrilled at this morning's version because it was now down to hours, minutes and seconds.

3 hours, 26 minutes, 13 seconds, until I get
to see those beautiful blue eyes.

I shook my head and smiled softly to myself. He was so amazing. How could any one person be so incredible?

My breath caught as I stopped on the other side of the door where I would finally see him after so long. Jesus, I was shaking but had to stop. I had to stop. I took a deep breath and fanned my hands out in front of me. "Okay," I told myself. "Breathe."

Then, inhaling, I opened the door to the makeup room and saw him sitting with his back to me, an overly excited girl working on his hair. She was talking about a film he'd done a couple of years earlier, barely taking a breath. His eyes met mine in the mirror and he smirked at me, the corner of his mouth lifting in a crooked grin as our eyes locked on one another. Every inch of my skin vibrated as I looked at him. He was so beautiful. Always so flipping beautiful. On film, I'd always found him striking, but when he was looking at me, for me, he was unlike anything I'd ever seen.

Jeanne put up her hand to stop the makeup artist's chatter, then she began talking to him, and he nodded at something she said. As I was ushered into the seat next to him, she kept her promise to clear the room. I could almost feel the heat radiating off of his skin. His eyes were flashing fire at me as we looked at each other in the mirror.

I dropped my gaze so as not to give too much away. I had to bite my lip to keep a huge smile from splitting across my face.

"Mary, Jason," Jeanne called to the makeup artists. "Can I have a word with you outside? I want to talk about the look for the last set," she said. "Can you help me find the stylist?" she asked them, and then looked pointedly at Cade and I. "If you two will excuse us," she raised her eyebrows at me, "We won't make you wait too long." I knew she was reminding me of our five-minute limit as she opened the door and followed the artists out.

The minute the door closed, we were both out of our seats and in each other's arms.

"Jesus, you feel so good, love." He held me tight, breathing me in, his arms pulling me tight against his chest. I could feel his hands on my back and waist, pressing into my body. Closer, I wanted to get closer.

My arms went around his neck, into his hair, and tears pricked at the back of my eyes; my throat tightening. "I love you," I whispered as his mouth closed over mine in a hot, hungry kiss. We devoured each other, our lips sucking, nipping and tasting each other. My breasts burned through my dress as he pressed me closer.

"Brooklyn, baby, I'm dying. I've missed you so bloody much," he groaned into my neck and then took my face in his hands to look in my eyes. "How much time do we have?" he asked, his dimples showing as he grinned at me.

"Ugh!" I groaned, "Not long enough, never enough. Only five minutes," I whispered against his mouth and sucked his lower lip into my mouth. He drew back his lips clinging to mine and then looked in my eyes.

His thumbs brushed my cheekbones as he placed a soft, teasing kiss on my lips, and then ran his finger across my lower lip, his other hand still holding the side of my face. I felt devilish as I reached out and flicked his finger with my tongue and then drew it into my mouth, gently sucking, my eyes boring into his, as I slid my mouth down the length of it and then back up.

"I want to kiss you, and hold you, but I want to look at you."

"Mmmm," I moaned. I sucked his finger like I would have another part of his anatomy, and knew he imagined that I was. "Cade, I want to..." I let the words drop off as my eyes remained locked with his, staring deeply into their blue depths. They were glazed over in passion, I could see how much he wanted me, and I loved him so much I thought my heart would explode.

He was so handsome; I never wanted to stop looking at him.

He drew in his breath and I knew the reaction his body was having.

"Oh, God. You're so mean to me! So blissfully mean." His voice was low and husky as he leaned his forehead on mine. "I'll make you pay later, I promise." He warned, but he smiled as he kissed the palm of my hand with his open mouth, his eyes still locked on mine. "My baby," he groaned and placed one last kiss on my mouth, his thumb gently tracing my chin. "They'll be coming back in so we'd better behave for now."

He took a deep breath, and motioned for me to return to the seat. After placing his hands on my shoulders and running them down the length of my arms, and kissing the top of my head, he took his own chair again, and just in time.

He was barely seated when the door opened. Mary came back to resume work on Cade's hair.

"What the hell? What happened to your hair?" She was clearly upset. "Look at this!" She motioned to the back that was all messy.

Oh shit!

My hands had messed up his newly coiffed hair as I got lost in our kisses. He glanced at me in the mirror and I felt my cheeks burn. I concentrated on not laughing. Just breathe, I told myself.

Cade's mouth moved to speak but then shut again. He smiled a huge shit-eating grin.

"Uh, yeah." Cade flushed. "Sorry, I have a bad habit of running my hand through it." His eyes met mine in the mirror, and I bit my lip and bent my head to hide a smile. He shrugged.

It appeared some of the fan girl enthusiasm was now taking a back seat to her annoyance. "Sorry?" Mary asked.

"Yes. Bloody, sorry." His mouth twitched, as she started messing with the ruined parts, shaking her head.

I struggled not to burst out laughing.

"Yeah, they gave me pictures, and I had it fucking perfect," she huffed. "Shit," she said as she went back to work to repair the damage.

Jeanne was shaking her head, and trying to hide a smile, as Jason went to work on me.

Chapter 19

Anticipation

Brooklyn

THE PHOTO SHOOT went well, and as a group, we planned on having dinner at CUT, Wolfgang Puck's steakhouse in Beverly Hills. Naturally, I sat next to Cade during dinner and though we made sure to keep it very platonic, his hand would rest on my knee, or he would grab my hand under the table once in a while. He was constantly touching me in some way, and my heart was thrumming. I glanced up at him as he chatted with Ethan and Gavin, never missing a beat as he spoke of the details of his new film.

It made my pulse race when his fingers would lace with mine and he'd hold on tight. All the while the dinner continued, everyone ate, talked and laughed, around us.

I spoke to Jeanne again as I changed back into my street clothes, and she said due to a very early flight tomorrow, Cade wouldn't be able to come to my house, and of course, because of the paparazzi, I wouldn't be able to go to his hotel. I tried not to be disappointed though it wasn't easy. There had to be times when he was in town that we did what was necessary to firmly establish the illusion; which meant he be seen going back to his hotel alone and checking out before his flight, the following morning.

My heart squeezed a little at the thought, but I knew we'd have the next three days together, the longest time we'd ever had to be alone. Three, bliss-filled days, in the arms of the man I adored. I could live through one more night without him - *barely*.

He went to the bathroom and sent me a text before we all got ready to leave.

Tonight will feel like eternity without you in my arms.

My knees went weak at his words. He was so damn romantic. He knew exactly how to turn my insides to mush. It was surprising. He was only twenty-three, and most guys at that age just wanted to get laid and didn't give a crap about the girl's pleasure. It amazed me how attentive and invested Cade was.

Noah was standing next to me, so I wasn't able to return the message right away. "Brooklyn, it was good to see you." His voice was warm and he had a smile on his face, his arm coming around me to pull me into his side.

Cade walked back into the room at that moment and I saw him stiffen slightly. He didn't think I was flirting with Noah, did he?

"Um, yeah, you, too." I nodded. "Are you still hitting the gym every day? Your character wasn't written so beefy, was he?" I tried to make small talk as Cade rejoined the group.

"Yeah, four hours every day." He flexed his biceps in front of me. "This is who I am. They knew I worked out before I was cast."

"Wow," I said. Considering this was his first film, his comment convinced me he that his main thing was fitness modeling, and it would likely remain his focus. "Well, you look great."

"Thanks!" His eyes were excited. "No option."

I smiled at him weakly, a little bereft of what I should say. He was confident, I'd give him that but it came off a little conceited and then there was the issue of the other, taller man walking toward us. "I see."

"If you want, I can work you out. Like a personal trainer." His face broke out into a huge smile as he nudged me with his shoulder.

"Oh? All of us? Cade looks like he works out, too." I wanted to include him in the conversation, so he had a clear picture of what was going on.

"Uh, yeah, right." Cade's mouth twitched sardonically.

Jeanne came up and told me it was time to leave.

"I'll just say goodbye to everyone and meet you in the front?" I asked.

"Okay, Honey," she said. "Cade, it's good to see you again." She hugged him goodbye.

"It's always a pleasure, Jeanne." He flashed a drop-dead smile at her. She grinned and patted his arm as she left.

I said goodbye to Gavin and Sarah, then Noah gathered me up in a big bear hug. He took me by surprise when he lifted me off of the ground and twirled me around. "See ya, Jules," he said fondly, using a nickname for my character in the film.

"Yeah, see ya." I smiled tightly as he finally put me down. I glanced at Cade, who was watching intently from where he was standing about twenty feet away. He was speaking to Ethan, but excused himself and came over to me.

"So Cade, I guess I'll see you in a few days for the extra scenes?" I went through the motions because Noah was still near us. I reached out to touch his stomach in a casual way, like a little punch.

"Yes, I think the first one is on Tuesday." His eyes bore into mine. I wondered if he was upset that Noah hugged me?

"It's really good to see you." My eyes were soft and full of love. Though I hope he could read them, I was nervous someone else would, too.

He pulled me into a hug and it was all I could do not to throw my arms around him and pull his face down for a kiss.

"You, too. I'd like to spend more time with you guys, but I have an early flight." His mouth sported a small smile as he released me, which silently told me he wasn't upset by Noah's hug. "Noah, you're not in any of the new scenes, are you? Anyway, it was good to see you." Cade put out a hand in offering to Noah, who took it and shook it firmly.

"Good to see you, too, Cade," Noah replied.

"It's okay that you have to call it an early night," I said so Noah and the others could hear. "I'm not feeling very well. I think I may be coming down with something." Cade's hand went to my forehead and then he brought the back of his hand to my cheek.

"Yeah, you're warm." He played along. "You should get home and go to bed. I'll call you tomorrow to see how you're doing."

"Have a safe flight to Vancouver and tell Daniel I said 'hi,'" I said, as I turned to leave.

Jeanne was smirking at me when we climbed back into her SUV for the trip back to my parent's house. "You guys are good."

"It was a lot easier because I know we'll be together tomorrow." I sighed. "Is it real, Jeanne? I feel a little out of control of myself." I shook my head. "But, I really couldn't give a damn," I said incredulously.

Jeanne was on the interstate back toward my parents' neighborhood. "He loves you; that's for sure."

"It was weird because other than the minute or two in the makeup room, we didn't have any time alone to talk, but it's enough just to be in the same room with him." I shook my head at myself because I realized how true that statement was. "Even when we have to leave each other, even though it hurts so damn bad, I wouldn't change a second of it, Jeanne. Does that make any sense? It's just... the love is so indescribable, that I want to feel *everything* with him."

"I understand, Brook. You're very lucky. Both of you."

We sat in silence for a second, and then I remembered Cade's text, and that I needed to reply. "He sent a text, and I wasn't able to respond earlier, can you give me a minute?" I pulled out my phone as she nodded as I started to type.

Eternity is ours. Only one more night until the mad, mad love begins. xo

I hit send, my heart thundering in my chest. "I feel so, I don't know, giddy, I guess. Just being with him, Jeanne, I have a high. I know it's pathetic, isn't it?" I laughed.

"If only I could be so pathetic," she teased. "Brook, I have one more thing to tell you," she said hesitantly.

"Yeah?" I waited. "What?"

"There's another surprise for you, when you get to the bungalow tomorrow, okay?" She smiled at me as my eyes widened.

"What is it?" I demanded as excitement coursed through me.

Jeanne shook her head. "Oh, no! I can't say. Cade would kill me! He's really very romantic, isn't he? Jesus, I'm jealous!"

My eyes widened at her words. "Yes, he's amazing and sexy, and brilliant and talented! I can't believe he loves me, or that he's even real."

"Brook, come on. If you heard him talk about you when I took him to the airport..." her words fell off for a moment as she shook her head. "Just listening, not only to his words about the way you met, the connection, left me breathless, but the reverent way in which he said them..." She trailed off and shrugged. "Well, it was like a fucking romance novel." She let out a small laugh and I burst out laughing. Happiness was like a drug and I couldn't get enough.

"Really?" My heart swelled and I knew my face was lit up like a Christmas tree. "I've never felt anything like this!"

Jeanne nodded in understanding, a smile spreading across her face. "Well, you're young, Brook, and I'd be remiss if I didn't watch out for you, but Cade is genuine. It's obvious how he feels about you."

"I feel like my heart will just explode with it, you know? He's like oxygen; I can't breathe without him. I know I sound ridiculous." I laughed softly. "Jeanne, can I tell you something? I'm just dying to talk about it!"

"Oh, sweetheart. I'm so happy for you. Of course, you can tell me anything. I'll take it to the grave." She laughed.

I hesitated and bit my lip, then turned toward her in the front seat of her car and looked down as I felt myself blush.

"When we make love, it's so incredible. Just beautiful, you know?" Jeanne smirked at me. "He knows just how to touch me, and he makes love to me with his words as well. He cares about how it is for me. It's so amazing... it's brought us both to tears before." I sighed, emotion welling up in my chest and making my eyes burn and my throat tight. "I sometimes think he's a dream, and it feels so good, it hurts. Now I sound like a romance novel!" I tried to laugh, but only managed to blink and swallow.

"Brook, on the way to LAX, Cade made a similar statement. He told me that you're his whole world, that he can't believe you love him in return, and that you do, is a miracle that must be a dream." She beamed at me.

I looked at my hands as tears filled my eyes. "He asked me to marry him," I said softly. "And, I just have to." I shrugged and wrung my hands. "There is no other choice but to be with him forever." I smiled through my tears. "I just love him so much I can't even put it into words."

"Save me a seat in the front of the church, okay?" Her eyes were glistening with tears, too.

I let out a small laugh as I wiped the happy tears from my face, and nodded. "Yeah, I promise," I replied.

When I got home, I began packing my bags, and even though I needed to sleep, I was aching to talk to Cade. As if he read my mind, my phone started playing his song. I couldn't get to my phone fast enough.

"Hey!" I breathed into the phone.

"What are you doing?" he murmured his voice low.

"Um, I'm packing," I laughed.

"Don't pack too many clothes, love." I could hear the lazy smile in his voice even though I couldn't see his face.

"Well, okay, I won't. Mmmm, I miss you," I said softly as I snuggled into my bed.

"Me, too. It was hell not being able to touch you and kiss you tonight. I wanted to all day. It's worse than when I was in New York."

"You managed under the table a little, which felt amazing. Just to be in the same room with you calms me down... and makes me very excited." I laughed shortly.

"Oh, love. God, I bloody hate being this close and not being able to hold you. More, when you say that type of thing," he groaned.

"Caden Michael Carlisle," I teased him. "I'm going to make you come so hard tomorrow night; you won't ever want to leave me." I heard his sharp intake of breath, and I smiled gently.

"Brook." He sighed deeply. "I love you so much," he said so softly I could barely hear him, but there were tremors in his voice. "I dream of making love to you, of holding you, and just talking to you. I love your voice, the velvet suppleness of your skin beneath my hands and lips, the scent of your arousal. Mmmm. Then, to feel your body move in response to mine... Christ," he groaned "And when you make those little sounds in your throat when I'm making love to you, when you moan my name, you drive me insane."

His words left me breathless. "Stop. You have to stop. I'll never get used to this longing, Cade." I sighed; my heart beating faster.

"Yeah, isn't it brilliant? I can't believe I'm going to have you to myself for three whole days. It will be heaven," he said softly. "It will fly by in a flash. It can never be enough, love. Never enough." His voice was velvet smooth. I pictured him running his hand through his hair, and his muscled chest and abs bare above the sheet at his waist while he lay in his bed.

"I'll take what I can get, and be thankful for every second." My voice was trembling. "You should. Um, you have an early flight, and you'll need to be rested tomorrow night, I promise." I gave a throaty laugh.

"Witch..." he said, but I knew he was smiling. "I can't wait to be with you. You've got me hard just talking like this on the phone." He let out his breath.

"That's because you love me," I breathed. I lay down on my bed and curled up in a ball under the covers.

"It is Brooklyn." Longing filled his words. "You're so beautiful. You were gorgeous today. Even after the rain, sopping wet."

"I do know. I feel the same way," I promised him.

"Just don't forget how to say that." His voice was low and throaty.

"How to say what?" I didn't understand his meaning.

"I do," he said.

"Oh, hon…" My eyes flooded with tears and my voice throbbed. "*I do*, I will, I want, I wish, I love you. All of it, I'll never forget. I'll tell you all the time, I promise. I hate hiding it."

"You make me very happy. Okay, have sweet dreams, and I'll make them come true tomorrow evening, right?"

"Mmmmm, yes," I whispered into my phone. "I'm kissing you goodnight, right now. Can you feel it?"

"I can always feel you, Brook. Goodnight, my love."

"Goodnight." My body was visibly shaking as I hung up the phone. I lay there for a minute thinking of all he'd said, then started planning how I was going to make good on my promise to give him the orgasm of his life the next night. I smiled, got up and resumed packing my suitcase.

Shorts, tanks and camisoles, as well as lacy underwear, bras, and the skimpy lingerie that I'd ordered online over the past month, and three bikinis. I was determined to rock his world if it was the last thing I did.

I took a bath, shaved my legs and got into my old sweat shorts and wife beater for sleep. As I settled into my bed, my hand lovingly touching the bracelet, now back around my wrist as I tried to relax and drift off to sleep. Easier said than done, my mind and heart were racing as I contemplated the events of the next three days.

Chapter 20

Suprise, Suprise

Brooklyn

CADE WAS FLYING needlessly to Vancouver to make our charade real. He then would be picked up at the airport and by his friend Daniel Mayfield and driven to a private FBO so he could take the chartered plane all the way back down to San Diego. A whole fucking day wasted. I could barely stand it!

We were meeting at the bungalow Jeanne had arranged for us to use for the weekend. All of my friends were told I was ill, and my mom, dad, and Nathan were all covering my tracks, telling anyone who called that I was too sick to talk or see anyone.

I could hardly sit still for the two and a half hour drive from L.A. Jeanne was driving me down, and I wanted to get there early so we'd have enough time to get anything I might need before Cade's arrival around 6 PM.

She was going to pick him up at a private airfield near the west side of the city and bring him to me. She was our only transportation, so she made reservations to stay in a posh hotel while we were here.

Our return plan the coming Monday would take Cade back to the airstrip where he'd do it all in reverse, back to Vancouver, meet up with Daniel again and have him drive him to the airport in full view of the paparazzi. God, it was such a drain.

Jeanne would be driving me home, but I wished Cade could drive back with us. The damn paparazzi stalking our every move made it impossible for his departure from Vancouver to be avoided. Cade's weekend with Daniel had to be believable, on the back-end as well.

As hard as I tried, I couldn't get Jeanne to spill what Cade's other surprise was. It was driving me crazy, but knowing who was behind it, it would probably be mind-blowing.

I was so excited I couldn't sit still in her leather seats.

I planned on making a nice dinner for the two of us. It would give him enough time to clean up and relax before my plan to seduce him.

There was zero chance I'd fail at that one, I thought with a grin and I bit my lip to stifle a laugh.

"What are you smiling about?" Jeanne asked with a laugh. "As if I couldn't guess!"

"I'm so happy, Jeanne. I can't thank you enough for this weekend. I don't know how to repay you."

"You don't have to, Brooklyn. I'm happy to do what I can to help you two lovebirds."

I grinned at her. "Well, I'd ask you to thank your parents for me, but you didn't tell them, did you?"

"No. They believe that I'm using the house with two of my friends. Ken and Denise agree we have to keep this a secret, even from family. The pilot flying Cade down is about sixty-five, and we figure he won't have a clue he's a movie star." She winked at me.

When we got to the house, I was pleasantly surprised by how

isolated it was.

It was on the beach but had its own pool with a high wall and locked gate that ran around the five acres of property that went with it. The tropical climate created lush gardens with pathways, landscaped with fountains and bubbling brook through it. I gasped as I took it all in.

"Wow! Jeanne, this is perfect. We can actually go out for walks and no one will see us?"

"That's the idea." She smiled. "The best I could do for you."

"Thank you." My eyes were pricking and blurring. I blinked away the tears as I hugged her. "I really mean it."

"Brooklyn, I know we're new at this, but you're like my own daughter. I love you and want you to be happy. It's evident that Cade is the key to that, and vice versa, I might add," she replied.

When we went into the house, I found the surprise. The house was filled with white flowers, roses, freesia, and others. Light, ethereal bouquets scattered throughout.

"Oh, my God!" I gasped as I walked into the living room.

The bungalow was quaint, with rattan tables, and large, fluffy couches in a light yellow. A fireplace stood on one side of the room, and Italian marble lined the floors and kitchen counter tops. There was a large lanai that ran around the entire house, filled with wicker furniture with plush yellow and white cushions and a small glass table and chairs. It was screened so that we'd be able to enjoy dinner or breakfast outside if we wanted.

"It's so beautiful!" I gasped in wonder.

There was a trail of white rose petals on the floor leading from the front door down the long hallway to the master suite. No doubt part of Cade's surprise; a path of flowers to the bedroom. I was slightly in shock at his thoughtfulness. Amazing.

The bedroom had light blue walls and a large four-poster bed with a thick white duvet and lots of pillows strewn on it. A mosquito net draping down from the ceiling covered the entire bed. There were white rose petals all over it, even scattered over the top of the comforter. Wow!

"Did you do this?" I asked her incredulously.

"Nope." Jeanne shook her head and smiled. "Cade asked Denise to do it, and I helped her, that's all."

A hundred candles were strewn throughout the rooms in many different shapes, heights and sizes. I could imagine how elegant the room would be with all of them lit after dark.

Off to the side of the bedroom, there was a big bathroom with a huge whirlpool tub, a double shower with crystal clear glass doors and several multi-level showerheads. More candles and more lush bouquets of white flowers were on the counter and the bedroom dressers.

"Your parents have a beautiful place. I'm sure we're going to love being here. Thank you so much, Jeanne," I said again.

She shrugged. "My pleasure, honey." She went to the closet and brought out a large white box tied with a ribbon. There was a card on the top.

"This is the surprise." She smiled as she set it in front of me.

"I thought the flowers were the surprise." She shook her head.

"Did he want me to open it now or wait for him?" I asked as she handed me the box.

"Now. He knew you'd be here a while before he could get here and he wanted to give you something. If you'd like, I can leave while you open it."

"No, that's okay," I said as I ran a hand lovingly over the card, and went to sit the white sofa in the corner between the full windows on both walls.

My Love, was written on the front of the envelope in Cade's rough writing. My heart beat faster as my fingers traced over the words.

My hand was shaking as I opened the card and flipped it open.

Brook,
Will you wear this for me tonight,
and make my dreams come true?
I love you more than anything.
Yours forever,
Cade.

I read the words aloud so Jeanne could hear.

My throat constricted, and tears started to well in my eyes. "Would you look at me? It's like I'm a rain machine. I can't seem to stop crying."

"They're happy tears, honey. I'd be crying, too, if the man I loved wrote those words to me. Especially, if he were *that man.*"

I looked at her as I brushed a tear off of my cheek and smiled. I started to giggle through the tears. "He makes me so happy! He's just amazing! Isn't he?" I asked incredulously.

Jeanne nodded and laughed out loud, taking a seat on the bed next to the box.

I ripped open the ribbon and removed the lid off of the box, and gently lifted the edge of the tissue paper that was around the contents. Inside was a beautiful French lace and silk chiffon negligee that must have cost a fortune.

My hand touched the delicate fabric and lifted it from the box. The purest white, the bodice had sheer chiffon cups that plunged in front to a sparkling lace inset that wrapped around the waist and then the sheer material of the skirt belled and flowed to the floor in translucent shimmers.

The back was deep and open, with only slight spaghetti straps coming over the shoulders and straight down to just below the waist. Princess darts in front and back would make it fitted through the waist and hips, before flowing down in soft folds to the floor.

The deep V in back was edged in a continuation of the lace from around the waist. There was a matching lace duster that went over it, also glittering in iridescent sequins, the sleeves sheer silk until below the elbows, and then billowing out in a drape of lace to the wrists.

I blushed as I realized that wearing the gown without the coat, every part of my anatomy would be visible through the sheer material.

"It's just gorgeous, isn't it?" I breathed, gently touching the delicate lace. She nodded "Did Cade pick this out?" That would be heart stopping.

"Yes." I looked at her as my eyes widened in amazement.

"He told Denise what he wanted it to look like and they had it made just for you. He even knew what size you needed, and how long it should be because of your height, Brook!" She shook her head in amazement. "He's really something."

She sighed and fanned a hand in front of her face a few times. "It almost makes *me* fall in love with him." She laughed. "And the flowers, champagne and candles were all at his request."

I laughed at her display, and then I laid the nightgown gently back in the box and moved it into the bathroom to set it on the chair in there until it was time to put it on later.

"Wow. Just... wow!" I stopped and shook my head. "He doesn't think he's romantic, but he just... leaves me breathless." I ran my hand through my hair, my face glowing and flushed.

It was 3 PM so I wanted to check what was in the fridge that I could use to make dinner but then I wanted to text Cade. My heart felt like it would fly from my chest and my feet barely touched the ground. In a very short time, we'd be together for three whole days.

I found some rib eye steaks, makings for a salad, some French bread and new potatoes and started planning my meal. The bar was stocked as well with several nice wines, Cade's favorite beer and some champagne.

"Is this all for us?" I asked. "I don't want to use something that I'm not supposed to."

"Brook, you're welcome to everything here. This is all for you guys. I tried to think of everything," her eyes were sparkling at me, "that Cade didn't, that is." She grinned at me. "But, that wasn't much."

Caden

I TOOK MY black duffle bag out of the back of Jeanne's SUV, then went around to the driver's side to hug her before she climbed back up into the truck. I had been with beautiful women a lot of times, but my heart was pounding a hundred miles per hour as I anticipated Brooklyn waiting for me on the other side of the door.

"Thanks again, Jeanne. You're a good friend. I'll never forget this," I said after I'd hugged her. "Truly."

"Glad to do it, Cade. See you Monday. Enjoy yourselves." She smiled brightly then drove off. I turned and walked up the path to the door; I could feel my heart beating in my chest. I could hear some Latin music coming from the house as I opened the door. Setting my bag in the hall, I looked around anxiously for Brook. I was an hour early so she wouldn't be expecting me yet.

The flowers I'd ordered were strewn around the rooms and sprinkled the carpet down the hall as I'd asked.

I smiled. I was a grown man and I was feeling almost adolescent. Tonight was going to be like a dream, and the next three days; pure heaven.

I would finally get to be with her, uninterrupted, no distractions, no obligations, and no need to hide our feelings because other people were lurking.

I followed the music and found her with her back to me as she chopped something on a cutting board in the kitchen. Dressed in frayed jean shorts and a jade green bikini top, her hips undulating to the music in what looked to me like a samba or salsa step.

She's so damn sexy, I thought, as I drank in her bare back, shoulders, and firm round buns. My mouth twitched as I leaned against the door jam and crossed my arms. As much as I wanted to go in there and sweep her up in my arms, I was enjoying the view too much.

Her feet were moving in what looked like choreographed steps, her hair swinging across her back as she swayed... *Hmmm,* I thought, *when did she learn to do this?*

She was singing to a Jennifer Lopez song and then she set down the knife as she continued to dance, really getting into it. I smiled and raised a hand to my mouth to stifle a laugh, leaving the other crossed on my chest as I watched her.

She did a pivot turn and froze when she saw me standing there.

My grin split into a bright smile.

Her face lit up when our eyes met, and then she covered the ten feet separating us and threw herself into my arms. I caught her easily as she jumped in my arms, her legs winding around my waist.

I crushed her to me as my mouth took hers in a hot, wet kiss.

Mmmmmm," I moaned into her mouth. "I've been waiting a hundred years for this."

My hand went to the back of her head to bring her mouth back to mine as I continued to kiss her for several more minutes.

Finally, she pulled her head back to look into my eyes and then raised her right eyebrow at me. "How long have you been here?" she asked accusingly, but she was smiling.

"Not long enough." I grinned back. "Where did you learn to do that? It was very sexy." I started to kiss down her neck lightly with my open mouth. I felt her tremble as the goosebumps appeared on her skin. My hands were holding her to me, at her waist on both sides.

"My trainer insisted that Latin rhythm was good for my core. She said it tightens the stomach muscles, your ass and legs," she said as her head tipped up to rain kisses on my jaw.

"Remind me to send your trainer a gift," I teased. "As long as it's not *Noah*."

She laughed and tightened her arms around me, her face twisting wryly. "Ah. You aren't jealous of Noah, are you?"

I inhaled the scent of her skin, but ignored the question. "Mmmm, you're so delicious. I've missed you, babe."

I walked over and sat her on the marble island in the middle of the kitchen, pulling her tight against my body. Her legs were on either side of me, heels digging into the back of my thighs, and her arms still around my shoulders; felt amazing. I kissed her again and again, as my hands pulled her pelvis flush against mine. I couldn't stop. I was starving for her. My hands skimmed her body and wound in her hair as I slanted my mouth across hers in a deep kiss.

I felt myself start to throb and tighten in my jeans. I pushed into her heat, my hands at her hips pulling her closer.

She moaned on my mouth. "God, Cade, don't start," she begged.

"Why not?" I whispered against her open mouth as she gasped.

"Because I'm making dinner now, and," She kissed me again deeply, "I've got plans for you later." She drew back and looked in my eyes. Her lips quirked as she rubbed the tip of her nose with mine then placed a series of feather-light kisses on my face and mouth.

"You do, hmmm?" I smiled and pressed against her again, taking her mouth softly with mine, sucking on her lips, first the top, then the bottom. My arms wound around her, pulling her close to my chest. "That sounds perfect."

"Ugh..." Against her will, she pressed closer to me and nipped at my lower lip with her teeth. "Yes," she said softly. "So why don't you get a beer, a shower and relax while I finish up?"

"Do I have to?" I asked, practically begging, my hand going to the side of her face as I kissed the opposite cheek and temple, moving back to the curve of her neck where I licked her skin and then breathed softly where it was damp.

She shuddered against me, as my other hand pressed her more firmly against my hardness as I moved on her. I breathed in her scent and moaned. God, I love those sounds.

"Yes! You have to. Please?" She placed a soft kiss on my mouth. "Pretty please, with sugar on top?" Another kiss. "I promise it will be worth it." More little kisses... as her mouth ghosted against mine. She was driving me wild, and I wanted more.

I took her mouth, my tongue diving into the warm orifice and hers coming to meet mine. I was starving for her, my hands roaming up and down her back, pushing on her ass to bring her tighter against my body. The heat radiating from her was literally burning me alive as her hands went to my hair and she pulled my mouth even closer to her own. The intensity of her response sent fire trailing through my veins.

I broke off the kiss and moved away abruptly, kissing her hand.

"If you insist." I smiled wickedly as I knew she was left panting for more. I'd be bloody well damned if I'd be suffering the next couple of hours alone.

I grinned at her. She was so beautiful, her eyes alight with passion, her hair wild, and her breasts heaving as her breath came in spurts. I left her sitting on the counter with her bare legs spread on the edge of the counter her hand moving to her hair.

She was so gorgeous. I wanted to go back and take up where I left off, who was I to not give her what she wanted.

I watched her with intent eyes as I walked to the refrigerator to get a beer. I knew she could see the naked longing in my eyes, but I was going to enjoy every last moment with her.

It had been so long since we'd had any time to just hang out, talk, or share a meal alone. I wanted to savor every second of this weekend.

"What are you making for dinner?" I leaned my back against the counter by the refrigerator, as I looked that the herbs and various types of greens she was chopping on the board.

"Um, Grilled steak with béarnaise sauce, roasted new potatoes with parsley butter, mixed greens with dried cranberries, almonds, feta and poppy seed dressing," she said offhandedly as she hopped down off of the island.

I smiled at her. "Sounds good, love, but I'm more interested in um, what's for dessert?" Her eyebrows raised as her breath caught in her throat. Her eyes lit up with a devilish gleam.

"Fresh strawberries and cream," she said softly then ran her tongue across her lips and then her teeth came out to bite her lower lip as she raised her eyes to mine.

She resumed her chopping as I watched. She was an amazing cook on top of it all. *Mmmm, I thought. Strawberries and cream just like her skin.* What more could a man want in a woman? She was beautiful, smart, funny as hell and she cooked; in more ways than one. Am I a lucky sod or what?

I smiled to myself.

I let out my breath in a small huff as I shook my head slightly and then took a drink of the beer.

"What?" she wanted to know.

"Nothing." I grinned. "Did you get my gift?" I walked up behind her and kissed her shoulder softly. Goosebumps ran down her arms as I moved to kiss her neck.

"Mmmmm." She put down the knife and turned to face me. Her hands went to my chest as she leaned into me and my arms moved around her. "Yes, it's just gorgeous. I love it." A seductive smile on her lips, her eyes limpid with love. "Jeanne said you designed it for me, it's so insanely romantic. You overwhelm me." Her arms slid up my chest around my neck and into my hair, before tugging gently. It drove me crazy, and Brook knew it.

"No, I'm going to be overwhelmed when you wear it," I whispered as I bent to her mouth and brushed it with mine.

"Um," she began and then returned my kiss, her mouth as soft on mine as mine was on hers.

"Yes? What is it?" I murmured as I trailed my mouth across her cheek.

"It looks," she hesitated. "Well, it looks…"

I nuzzled her neck and breathed in her scent, a heady mixture of soap, shampoo and musky perfume. I knew what she was asking. "Like a bride?"

"Yes." She looked in my face and raised her hand to my jaw.

"That's the idea," I said softly. I was drowning in the blue depths. "Can we pretend a bit?" I begged against her mouth as I gave in to kissing her again. "It's my highest wish." I sighed and rested my forehead on hers, sliding the back of my knuckles along her cheek.

"Anything you want, you know that," she said in return as she surrendered her lips to mine. After another series of intense kisses, she finally pulled back and put her head on my chest, and kissed it softly.

"Why don't you get a shower while I finish up? I'll get ready before we sit down for dinner." She placed another super soft and sensual kiss on my mouth, her tongue darting into my mouth as she teased me, pulling on my lips with her own.

"Brook. " My arms tightened around her as I buried my face in the curtain of her hair. "I love you." I pulled back and shouted into the room surrounding us. "I love you!"

We laughed together, then sobered, our eyes intent on each other.

Brook kissed my neck and then ran her mouth down my chest, trailing a path with her tongue and it scorched my skin through my shirt, her breath hot on my skin. Her hand moved around to squeeze my ass as she smirked playfully up at me. I smiled down at her as her eyes flirted with mine.

"You're so damn sexy, I don't know if I'll be able to wait until after dinner." My thumb traced her lower lip as I stared at her mouth.

She offered a sexy smile and raised her lazy, half-lidded gaze to mine.

"You *will* wait. And be glad you did," she promised as she raised her right eyebrow and patted my butt once more, smiling slightly. "It's just as difficult for me, I promise. Now, off to the shower with you, babe." Her hand ran down my arm as she turned back to her work on the meal. "Maybe you should make it a cold one?" she suggested.

"Bloody hell! No way," I moaned as I picked up my bag and made my way down the hall, her soft laughter following me as I went. *Brilliant.*

Chapter 21

Dreams Fulfilled

Brooklyn

CADE CAME OUT of the shower shirtless in black silk pajama bottoms, and my heart skipped a beat.

"You're hotter than hell, do you know that?" I asked him in astonishment as I stared at his perfect form. His body called to me like a siren song. His muscled arms, chest and the six pack across his taut stomach.

Mmmm... It was all I could do not to go to him and touch every inch of his skin. His beautiful face was so intense with desire; my skin burned as he looked at me.

Holy fuck. Cade's mouth quirked and I thought he was the sexiest thing I'd ever seen.

"As long as you think so," he said softly; simple words made sensual by the man saying them. "Can I help with anything, love?

"You can open the wine so it can breathe for about an hour before dinner." I nodded toward the bottle of Cabernet on the counter. I had a bottle of Dom Perignon in the refrigerator for later and I smiled to myself at the thought of the evening to come.

"What are you thinking about?" Cade asked, his eyes following every move I made. He moved to pick up the corkscrew and the wine.

I had the sauce ready for the steak, the salad was finished, and the potatoes were in the oven roasting. "I'm just happy to be here with you like this." I lifted my gaze to his.

"It's a dream," he agreed, his blue eyes smoldering.

My heart lurched. He always said the most perfect things. "Cade," I shook my head in wonder. "You're so perfect." My shoulders shrugged. "I can't believe you love me," I breathed.

He put down the wine and took me in his arms, whispering into my hair.

"Of course, I do. More than anything." He kissed my lips softly and then took my face in his hands as he stared down at me. "More than my career, or even my life. I don't want you ever to doubt that, Brooklyn. I know you think I'm this star, but I'm just me. All of that isn't who I am, and to me, it's you. You're the perfect one." Then his mouth closed over mine in the sweetest, softest kiss I'd ever felt.

I sighed dreamily. "I love you more than that."

"Hardly," he murmured against my mouth, distracted slightly by the direction of his thoughts. "Don't you have something to do about now, beautiful girl?" He smiled sheepishly and squeezed my butt with one hand.

"Before dinner?" I was surprised, despite the touches, kisses, and love words.

"If you don't mind."

"Okay." I blushed and nodded as he brushed his knuckles against my cheek.

"Can you handle watching things? The potatoes have a timer and will need to be taken out when it goes off. The steak needs to go on the grill in about thirty minutes, and then four minutes on each side for medium rare. Can you handle that?" I teased.

"Yeah. Of course." He kissed me again and brushed his thumb along my jaw. "Down the hall with you now. Go make my dreams come true."

"I'll try," I breathed as my hand came up to touch his face. "You might also want to find some music. There is an iPod dock so I'm sure you've got some favorites, huh?"

I hugged his waist and placed a few open mouth kisses along his chest, my mouth soft on his skin. He shuddered.

"I have something in mind for tonight, yes." His hand at the back of my head ran through my hair making me tremble. I left him and walked down the hall, my heart pounding in my chest.

After my bath, I found some clips and bobby pins and pulled my hair up on top of my head, leaving some tendrils falling on both sides, a soft pile of curls at the crown. I took a large open white rose and some baby's breath from one of the arrangements in the bedroom and pinned it to the left side of the upsweep. Placing a few more pieces of the baby's breath here and there throughout my hair, I was satisfied with it and knew Cade would appreciate the extra effort.

I took special care with my makeup as well, choosing some silver eye shadow to sweep underneath my brows and some smoke gray to outline my eyes. Soft pink blush and shiny gloss on my lips made them look wet. Cade's diamond bracelet shimmered on my wrist, and diamond drop earrings were my only other jewelry.

He wanted me to look like a bride, so I'd do my best for him. I didn't wear a necklace so my skin would be unobstructed to his exploration. I had some new Giorgio Armani perfume, and I sprayed it lightly over my whole body. My skin was smoothed with matching body lotion, the delicate, but musky scent floating all around me.

I needed to be everything he wanted. To assault all of his senses, touch, sight, smell, taste and give him everything I had.

I put on the gown and looked at myself in the mirror.

It was completely sheer except for the lace inset that shimmered around the waist. The translucent fabric was glowing against my skin, where it skimmed my curves. Every part of my body was clearly visible underneath. My nipples, the blonde curls on my sex, like I was completely naked... yet, better somehow.

I smiled as I realized he'd designed this nightgown. It was so flipping intimate.

My heart stopped in my chest and swelled at the thought of his tender and passionate lovemaking. My stomach tightened and the heat rushed lower between my legs. I took a shaky breath as I took the duster and slipped it on.

Completely made of lace, except the sleeves until midway between my elbow and wrist, it would cover the nakedness beneath during dinner. A white satin ribbon was woven in and out of the shimmering lace around the empire waist, and I tied in a bow beneath my breasts. The deep V of the neckline echoed that of the nightgown underneath, giving a hint of what was to come when it was removed.

I smiled as I looked at my reflection. I removed all of my rings and bracelets, letting the gown be the focus. The princess seams fitted to my body below my breasts, through the waist and skimming the hips before flowing out, and a little longer in the back to sweep the floor.

Wow.

Incredibly, he thought of everything. My stomach fluttered as I lit the candles in the bedroom and the bathroom. I went to the door and hesitated. I felt the butterflies in my stomach and took a deep breath.

As I opened the door, I heard soft strains of music coming down the hall. He had chosen a soft, romantic playlist, and the candles flickered throughout the rooms.

The steaks were done and resting on the counter and Cade was at the glass sliding doors, looking out on the ocean view as the sun went down.

"Hey..." I said softly, my heart thumping loudly in my chest as he turned to me.

Caden

I WANTED TO find the perfect moment.

The engagement ring that I'd gotten on my trip to New York last month was in my pocket, waiting. A three-carat oval solitaire surrounded by smaller brilliant diamonds, in platinum, the band thin and also encased in the smaller diamonds. The stones were flawless. I thought a diamond that size would look bigger and on seeing it, considered a larger one, but realized that Brook might even consider this one too much. Besides, it wasn't about the ring, and I was certain she wouldn't care if it were made of glass. Still, considering my situation and success, and I didn't want her to think I wasn't serious.

It was simple, yet exquisitely beautiful. Just like Brook. It was perfect for her. I'd known right away when I'd seen it, that it was the one.

"Hmmph," I let out my breath; it had been similar to the moment I saw Brook for the first time. I ran my hand through my hair as I stared out toward the beach. It was a beautiful evening, which I knew would only get better. I was uncharacteristically nervous. I shook my head at myself. Crazy. I'd been with more sophisticated women; older, too. Yet, Brook had me in knots.

"Hey…"

Her voice, so sweet, seductive, and beautiful, sounded behind me. I braced myself for the sight that would hit me when I turned around, but nothing could have prepared me for the vision she made.

My breath stuck in my throat, and my hand went to cover my wildly beating heart.

She was absolutely incredible. Her hair was piled up with flowers in it, whispering tendrils that were soft and sexy, falling down the sides of her perfect cheekbones to her chin. The white silk and lace gown flowing and glistening around her, the hint of her small, perfectly round breasts showing from the deep V of the neckline, my bracelet shimmering as she gently touched her hand to her throat. The shadows from the candles dancing around her collarbones and her beautiful face left me breathless.

She was perfect; love shining in her shimmering blue eyes, her lips glistening as she licked them nervously, and a becoming blush on her cheeks.

I just stood frozen to the floor and stared, trying to speak, but no words would come out, and then my vision blurred as tears filled my eyes. The emotion I felt for her, was almost more than I could bear. She turned slowly so I could see every part of her.

When she faced me again, I found my voice.

"My God," I said finally, my hand lifted and then returned to my pounding heart, my throat tightening as I struggled to find adequate words.

"Brook. You're more beautiful than I ever imagined possible.

Just— indescribably breathtaking. Thank you." She was the only woman I'd ever shed a tear for and I blinked as one rolled down my right cheek, despite my attempts to keep them at bay.

She moved toward me, and as she got closer, her arms opened.

"Oh, Cade, I love you, so much," she whispered as her arms went around me. I gathered her close against me as the soft scent of her perfume enveloped me. I bent my head to her shoulder and held her heart to mine, as emotions overwhelmed us both.

I drew back and saw that she was crying, too. I wiped the errant tears from her face.

"I wish we were married already. If I lose you now, I won't survive," I whispered as I took her lips in a soft kiss, both of my hands gently cradling her face. My mouth lifted and I nuzzled her nose, my open mouth hovering over hers. "So, so beautiful," I whispered.

"In my heart, I'm yours already. I'll always be with you, if you want me," she whispered against my mouth as her hands crept around my neck into my hair. "You're like a dream. I never thought... " Her words trailed off.

I caressed her back, and arms, and then let my hands cup her face as I kissed her. The kiss started with gentle tenderness, but became deep and passionate, both of us holding the other with reverence. It was surreal.

I felt my chest constrict, so full of love that it physically hurt.

"*If* I want you?" More tears squeezed out from my closed eyes. "I've never wanted anything or anyone so much in my life. I love you, Brook. Only you; from the moment I laid eyes on you. I'm lost."

My arm shifted underneath her knees and I lifted her to carry her with me to the couch. Her arms went around my neck and she looked into my eyes.

I sat down and settled her onto my lap, just holding her and looking at her for a time, before my forehead came to rest on hers briefly. I savored the moment before I moved back so I could look into her eyes, gently playing with a tendril of hair at the side of her face. "I want to give you something."

"You've already given me so much. There's nothing more I need." She gently stroked my cheek and placed a soft kiss on my chin. "You've become my whole world," she whispered.

My heart constricted painfully as my arms tightened around her and I kissed her sweet lips again. "Maybe I need it, then... " I said softly, the words trailing off.

I lifted her to place her on the couch and then got down on one knee before her. I took her left hand in mine, while I pulled the ring box from the pocket with the right.

She gasped on seeing the velvet box in my hand and her eyes widened as she looked from the box to my face.

"I know you've already said yes, but I want to give you everything, take care of you, wake up each morning holding you in my arms, to make love with you, talk to you and share my life with you." My throat ached and my voice deepened while I spoke. "To tell the world you're mine. I love you with everything I am."

My eyes looked up at her, in her white lace gown, her features full of love, her eyes liquid and thought she was the most beautiful thing I'd ever seen. I swallowed back the lump rising in my throat, trying to burn every curve of her face, her expression, the sparkle of the gown in the candlelight to my memory.

"Will you do me the great honor of becoming my wife?" My voice was thick as emotions overtook me. "Brooklyn Marie Halloway, will you marry me?"

She was trembling and her eyes were glistening with tears as I opened the box.

Her right hand went to touch my face as she bent to place a whisper soft kiss on my mouth. Tears slipped from her eyes and her hand trembled where she touched me.

"Oh, my God. Yes." She nodded and reached out to cup the side of my face with her hand. There was no shrieking, just love. "Nothing would make me happier. I love you, more than anything."

I took the ring from the box and slipped it onto her left hand, then raised it to my lips and kissed it.

"It's just perfect, so beautiful. I love it," Brook said, though I didn't think she'd even looked at it. Her glistening eyes were still locked with mine as she brushed her right hand through my hair at my temple.

"You make me so happy, sweetheart. I'm the luckiest bastard on earth." I smiled at her and she laughed at me through her tears.

Then she was in my arms as I gathered her up and stood, lifting her with me.

I kissed her gently, my mouth coaxing, and her's; trembling. This was the biggest moment of my life. Bigger than landing my first breakout role, bigger than anything I'd ever experience again. Except maybe someday, if we had a child together. I was young to consider it, but I could see it in my future as clearly as if it had already happened. I'd never been more certain of anything.

I moved my hands to her face as I kissed her eyes, her nose, her cheeks and finally taking her lips in a long deep kiss, our mouths moving on each other's. I inhaled her breath and leaned my forehead on hers.

"Oh, love," I sighed. My heart swelled at the thought that my ring was finally on her finger. "You're really mine, now."

She kissed my neck and collarbones, her hand sliding down my chest as her head rested on my shoulder. My hands gently rubbing and kneading her back; I was savoring each, and every second. We held each other in silence for a few moments.

"Will you dance with me?" I said. I'd turned on the stereo while she was getting ready, and it filled the room softly.

Brook laughed lightly, her hand trying to brush the tears from her cheeks. "Of course. I'd love to," she whispered against my chest. I took her right hand in my left, and my other went behind her back, while her fingers played the hair at the back of my neck, as we swayed slowly to the music.

In all the time we'd spent together, this was the first time we'd danced. Our characters had an emotional scene in the next film where our characters had a make-out scene on a dance floor after a long separation. "I can't decide if this is good practice for the film, or filming was good practice for this." I teased, with a smile.

She shook her head as she nuzzled into my neck. "It doesn't matter. It's perfect either way." I could feel her smile against my skin.

Thank you, God, for this moment, for this beautiful woman, for the time with her, and for the future we'd have together and mostly for her love, I prayed silently.

I held her close to my chest and rested my cheek against hers; my head bent toward her to breathe in the scent of her shampoo and skin. I couldn't help it; I finally bent to kiss her mouth hungrily as our bodies moved together. Having her in my arms like this, knowing she was mine, filled me with pride and emotions I couldn't describe. I felt protective, elated, infatuated, and fascinated.

As the song ended, her hand slid from behind my neck down my chest. I took it and brought it to join the other, holding them both together between us.

She looked up at me in silence.

I kissed her temple and hugged her close. "I love you so much, Brook. I love you," I whispered as if I'd never said the words before. Maybe I was afraid she wouldn't believe me, but I couldn't stop saying it. I dragged my mouth down to her neck and pressed a hot kiss to the curve.

"Mmmm, that feels so good," she breathed. We danced without speaking, reveling in the feel of each other as the music softly played on.

As it ended, Brook reached up and placed a series of soft kisses along my jaw line and I wanted to forget all about dinner, but she finally mentioned it.

"We better have dinner before we get side-tracked." She smiled up at me and I had to agree that if I had my way, we'd forget dinner all together. "Are you hungry?"

"Mmmmm." I placed more soft kisses on her neck. "Starving," I said suggestively and smiled against her skin.

"Then will you pour the wine, babe? I'll get everything else, okay?" Her lips curved a little as she moved out of my arms and made her way to the kitchen.

I couldn't take my eyes off of her as she went to get the meal.

I had placed some candles on the glass dining table along with the wine and as she brought the plates to the table, I devoured her with my eyes. The flickering light glimmered off her skin; so breathtaking and elegant. The soft tendrils of hair that framed her face were so soft, sexy that I wanted to reach out and touch her.

The food was beautiful on the plate and smelled delicious. I pulled out her chair to help her get seated before taking my own, and I poured the wine. I knew she'd taken great care with the meal she made for me and my heart swelled.

I sat at her right and stared at her, my face was serious. She blushed and looked down at the diamond now firmly on her finger. The bracelet glimmered above it on her wrist, and it was profound. It was like living a scene from the movie we had yet to shoot, but it was more. It was real.

"Is everything okay, Cade?" she asked hesitantly. She reached out a hand to softly touch my face. Her eyes searched mine.

"Perfect," I said, as I took the hand on my face and kissed it. "Just incredible. I don't ever want this to end, Brooklyn. I can't seem to take my eyes off of you, and I never want to stop looking at you."

My thumb brushed back and forth on the top of her hand as she blushed from my words.

"For the rest of my life?" She raised her shoulders in a little shrug, as she said a line from the second book. I felt like I'd memorized those books, mostly because they symbolized more time with her.

I swallowed and nodded. "Yes."

"A year ago we were sitting up all night with scripts." She smiled softly. "And here we are..." her words dropped off as she looked at her hand again then her eyes moved up to meet mine, "Engaged," she let out her breath and smiled tumultuously.

My mouth twitched at her response. Brook's incredulity suggested she thought it impossible that I would ever be with her, but I saw it in reverse. "Yes. It's a bloody miracle," I said softly, not letting go of her hand, my eyes studying every detail of her face. "More like a dream I never believed would happen."

"I'm sorry it took me so long to admit my feelings. I've always loved you. The intensity of it scared the crap out of me. I just didn't know how to handle it, but I wouldn't change one of our moments together. Not one second," Brook replied.

"I know, honey. It's okay. You were worth the wait, love." I smiled because I couldn't bloody help myself. "I treasure every memory, too." I let go of her hand and raised my glass. "A toast; to us. Forever," I said softly.

"Forever." She smiled and touched her glass to mine before we both took a sip. "When did you get the ring? It's incredible, but unexpected. It's kind of soon. Not that I ever expected it, I mean." She flushed; apparently embarrassed that she might have considered it. She was adorable as she glanced at her hand, then into my eyes.

"When Jeanne drove me to the airport, I felt like my heart was ripped out and left bleeding at your feet in the garage. I felt like my soul had left my body."

"Me, too." She reached out and touched my hand softly, a soft throb in her voice. My fingers closed around hers. "It hurts so much when you leave."

"I had to do something to feel closer to you, to ease the ache I felt and the pain I saw in your expression. So, I decided to use the time apart to search for the most beautiful ring I could find, so you would know for sure how I felt. This is it for me."

"Oh, Cade, I knew that already. Never has someone made me feel more loved, or wanted." She raised my hand to her cheek and pressed her face to my palm then turned into it and kissed it. "I didn't need a ring for that."

I smiled, though bittersweet pain shot through my chest. "I know, but never doubt it, Brook. Please," I begged.

"Not possible," she said softly. The look on her beautiful face said everything. The meal was really delicious. We took our time eating and talked about many things. "Every woman in the world will hate me when we come out with this."

I grinned at her. "Who cares what they think, if you have me?"

She told me about *Army of Two*, her movie that was scheduled to shoot next summer, and I told her about a new script I was asked to read. We talked about my music and our friends, fond memories of our time on set, sharing what was going through each of our minds and hearts at times during filming, and the gut-wrenching events of our goodbye afterward. Reliving it hurt and sent me to cloud nine at the same time.

I loved being with her, sharing her thoughts, sharing her food, laughing with her, gazing in her eyes, but the looming separation was eating away at my heart like acid. It never occurred to me that in falling so deeply in love, it would hurt like so much hell.

I couldn't believe how beautiful Brook was in the negligee. She stole the breath from my lungs each time I looked at her. More than once, she caught me staring at her.

"What?" She'd asked several times over the course of the evening, but I just smiled and shook my head. The last time, she persisted. "What, Cade?" Her eyes sparkled at me and I wanted to drown in them. "You keep looking at me like you've never seen me before."

"Maybe I haven't. You're just so gorgeous. I'm sorry, I can't help myself." A beautiful flush took purchase on the apples of her cheeks and her eyes softened as she reached for my hand.

"Are you blushing because your future husband loves you more than anything?" I asked softly as my finger touched her chin.

"No." Her hand came up to hold mine and then she kissed it. "I'm blushing because I can't believe it." She smiled gently, as she moved to my side; her luscious pink lips curving up ever so slightly, and her hand ran down the back of my head, through my hair.

"Are you finished?" she asked.

"Yes. It was delicious, thank you."

When she came to remove my plate, my hand ran down her back and slid around her waist as I got up from the table.

"It was fun. I love doing things for you." She was so graceful as she moved to place the plates in the kitchen and I found myself unable to look away. "Do you want dessert now?" she said, glancing up at me as she walked to my side.

My mouth lifted slightly at the corners in a smirk.

"Um, not yet," I said. I had moved to the sofa and grabbed her hand as she passed me. I pulled her onto my lap. She curled into me, like she was meant to be there. One of my hands went around her back and the other traced up and down her thigh. The lace fell away and I could see the sheer material underneath, the creamy skin of her knees and thighs visible through it.

"I told you I'd be overwhelmed," I said lifting the fabric and rubbing the silk between my fingers. "Mmmmm," I said as I kissed her neck with my open mouth, my tongue running down to her delicate collarbone. "You're so beautiful. A vision and you smell incredible," I whispered into her temple. "More than I could ever ask for," I breathed against her skin.

She shivered as my mouth moved to hers. The music continued to play softly in the background, the candles flickering and dancing off the walls. While my body reacted of its own violation to her nearness, my heart and mind were content just to hold her.

"I can't believe you're here with me when you could be with anyone."

My heart swelled. "Believe it, Brook." I laid my head on her shoulder in the curve of her neck as she snuggled into me and her arms wound around my shoulders. "Just being with you is all I'll ever need."

"Cade," she breathed out my name, and ran her hand up and down my forearm until then her fingers found mine. Our hands opened and intertwined with each other, and I wanted to melt right into her. "I miss you so much when we're not together. These moments are so perfect, but it hurts."

My other arm tightened around her as my eyes closed, her words were enough to wreck me.

"I know, me, too. I can't breathe when we're apart," I said against her hair. "Being famous is inconvenient, but if not for my life, we wouldn't have met. That's how I keep it in perspective."

"I know." She nodded against the side of my neck.

"I love being with you like this; the passion between us is staggering." I kissed her mouth, teasing hers to come to life beneath mine, dying to show her proof of my words. I placed several searching and clinging kisses on her luscious mouth before I continued, my hand tracing lightly up and down her back. "But, I don't want you to think that the physical stuff is the most important to me," I said hesitantly. "If I could never make love with you again, I'd still want to be with you, always. I'd still want to marry you... "

She shivered as my hand ran down her arm and back up again. My hand moving to cup around her face, my thumb brushing her chin lovingly as we kissed, our tongues making love to each other, feeding the electricity between us.

Brook waited for a second to answer, and then pulled back so she could look into my face. The blue depths were darker in the low light, but still full of love; languid, but serious.

"Cade, I know that, baby." She shook her head so slightly I almost missed it, and then kissed me so tenderly, her lips tasting and savoring mine. Her hand fluttering on the side of my face, she drew back and looked into my eyes.

"The love makes the passion that much more intense... and sex, so mind-blowing. All you have to do is look at me and my skin vibrates." She made me smile as she rubbed a thumb on my lower lip. Her lids dropped, and her mouth fell open in desire.

"I have to admit," she teased with a secret smile, then brushed her lips against mine, her hand lifting to the back of my head again, "you *are* the sexiest, hottest, absolutely yummiest man I've ever seen, and I simply can't help myself. I just want to take you down and have you." Her mouth came to hover over mine as she finished speaking, "Constantly," she whispered against my mouth. "But, I love you, too."

I couldn't hold back another second and I closed over her lips in a deep kiss, sucking, tasting, devouring. Our tongues warring with each other, her hands moving to delve deep in my hair and my hand coming up to cover her breast through the lace. I felt the nipple harden in my hand. Her touch, her mouth on mine, her scent... she drove me insane.

And her words... Jesus, they were like a lit match tossed into my soul.

I knew I'd never love anyone or want anyone more in my entire life. The passion between us was like a living thing. I felt myself throb and harden underneath her.

"Brooklyn, you are so sexy. I'm mad for you," I breathed against her neck.

She felt my arousal underneath her as she sat in my lap, and moaned against my mouth. She sucked on my lower lip as she pulled her mouth from mine.

"That works for me," she breathed and smiled. "Grab the

champagne and glasses, okay?" she said as she got up and walked toward the bedroom.

She didn't have to ask me twice. I went to refrigerator and found the Dom. The anticipation was more than I could bear, and I couldn't pop the cork fast enough and splashed champagne on the kitchen floor as it exploded from the bottle. I grabbed the flutes she'd left out on the counter and made my way down the hall, determined to make this a night neither of us would ever forget.

Chapter 22

Of What Dreams Are Made

Caden

BROOK WAS STANDING near the head of the bed, the netting shrouding behind her like an ethereal veil, as I poured the champagne. I offered her a glass and she took it, raising it to her lips to take a sip but never taking her eyes off of me.

My heart thundered in my chest at seeing the ring glint on her hand around the glass, sparkling in the candlelight. I felt so possessive, and I could see the raw hunger in her gaze. It did amazing things to me. If the situation weren't enough, the desire in her eyes made it more intense. I took a swallow of my wine, and stepped toward her, but she put her hand up to stop me.

Her eyes were on fire as she set her glass down, then took mine from me gently, and placed it next to hers on the dresser. Her stare burned into my flesh as she slowly pulled on the ribbon bow below her breasts to open the lace of her gown. I watched, my body throbbing and my mouth falling open as she slowly slid the sleeves down her arms.

The sheer gown beneath showed every curve, every nuance of her beautiful, slender body. The lace at her tiny waist accentuated her perfectly round breasts above it, with her pink nipples taut and her hips swelling below it. Brook's bare arms and shoulders shone golden in the candlelight.

My breath caught in my throat. "You're just," I paused, "stunning, my love." I was paralyzed; yet my body was shaking, my mouth felt dry and my breathing sped up.

She moved forward and took my hand, while staring intently into my eyes, then raised it up and placed a wet, open mouth kiss on the palm, sucking slightly as she pulled her mouth away. Her eyes never left mine. It was powerful and sexy as hell, her little pink tongue softly hinting at what was to come.

"God, Brook," I said, my voice heavy with desire, my hands itching to touch her. "I'm going to burst."

"That's the idea," she said softly as she pushed at my shoulders gently. Obviously, she wanted to take the lead, and I let her, helpless.

"Will you lay back on the bed for me?" she whispered as she ran soft kisses across my chest. Her mouth closed over my left nipple and she sucked and nipped at it.

My erection strained in my silk pajama pants, aching; it was so engorged it hurt. I tried to put my arms around her to pull her close, but she held me off. I looked at her and tipped my head, my eyes questioning.

"You don't get to touch me until I say so." She smiled and raised her right eyebrow. "Okay?" she asked as she bit her lower lip.

She was so incredibly sexy. "I'm not sure I can do that. It's... not possible," I breathed out. I shook my head slowly as the words ripped from me. "I can't, Brook."

"You have to trust me. I promised you something, remember?" She laughed a small throaty laugh. "Last night on the phone, remember what I told you?"

My head fell back as she ran her tongue across my collarbone and kissed me again. I tried to think through the passionate haze, to recall what she meant. "I can't think just now," I groaned.

"I said I was going to make you come harder than you ever had in your life… and I will. I promise. I want you to forget every woman who's ever touched you, but me." Her hands moved to the tie at the top of my pajama pants. She continued to suck on my nipples and run kisses on my chest as her hands made swift work of the silk ties. I reached for her, my fingers grazing the side of her supple breast.

"No, Cade," Brook whispered, pushing my hands away. She bent to the task of removing them completely. As her head came level with my dick, she ran her tongue up the shaft.

"Baby, I can't breathe."

She continued to lick and suck for just a moment. "I love you," she whispered against me. It was so amazingly intimate, her warm breath fanning out on my body. My eyes opened, to see her rising to push me back toward the bed, again. I stepped out of the cloth heap at my feet and did exactly as she wanted because I was helpless to do anything else.

I leaned back on the pillows and pulled myself up toward the headboard, the mosquito net all around the bed adding to the bridal ambiance of the evening.

As I watched, she turned from me to gather something from her suitcase. The back of the negligee was just as beautiful as the front, with the low back dipping to well below her waist. The two dimples above her butt were visible above the lace opening. Her slender form was so perfect; her ass round and firm, her shoulders slim and smooth, and her long legs, clearly visible through the sheer silk, were toned and tight.

My mouth watered at the site. *My god*, I thought. *Is she real? Is this real?*

Her hands moved to her hair as she removed the clip and the pins, the flower fell to the carpet as her hair cascaded down her back, still with bits of baby's breath scattered through it. I yearned to put my hands in it, to pull her head back so I could ravish her mouth. The waiting was painful paradise.

She turned toward me, her hair falling softly around her delicate features, her smoldering eyes, never leaving my face.

"Are you going to do everything I say?" She smiled softly as she said the words.

"Anything. Just come to me," I begged.

"All in good time," she said softly. "Lay on your stomach, Cade."

I did as I was told, and she climbed on the bed. I felt her straddle my back... I could feel the heat emanating from her feminine core. "Brook, I can feel you. God, you're so hot," I groaned. "You're killing me."

"So, you know what you do to me, then. See how much I want you?" she asked softly as she pressed her groin tighter against my ass, grinding against me. She bent to kiss the back of my neck. Her open mouth burning hot against my skin, her hair tickling me as it sent shivers down my spine. The muscles in my stomach tightened in response to her words.

Her hands touched me then, warm and smooth. "I want you to relax, honey," she coaxed as her hands began kneading the muscles of my shoulders, back, and neck. I realized that she had oil and was giving me a massage. It was torturous perfection.

"I don't deserve you," I said softly as the delicious sensations flooded over me. "That feels wonderful."

"Mmmm..." She continued her ministrations for several minutes, down my arms, legs, butt cheeks, stopping to place kisses here or there or whisper love words against my skin. She massaged behind my elbows and knees and it felt like heaven.

No one had ever touched me like this before and I savored her strong, yet gentle fingers as they moved over me. Her nails raked gently down my back, over my butt, and down my legs, sending shivers up my spine. She moved to my feet and I protested the absence of her on top of me.

"Shhhhh..." she said as she worked over me for a few minutes more. When her hands stilled, she spoke, "Turn over, Cade," so softly, I could barely hear. When I did, she'd see the evidence of her effect on me, but I did as I was told.

"Okay, remember, you can't touch me. Promise?"

"Ugh!!!!" I groaned. My body curled up toward her, as instinct took over and I reached for her.

"No," Brook said softly, moving my hands to my sides. She straddled my thighs as she repeated all of the same techniques on the front of my body, rubbing and squeezing my legs, arms and chest, carefully avoiding the one part of my anatomy that screamed for her touch. I tried to run my hands up her thighs, squeezing and pulling her closer, but she pushed them away. "Cade... *no* touching," she whispered.

"Why? I want to feel you. Please," I begged.

"Not yet. Patience." She bent to kiss my mouth so softly if felt like a whisper. " I want to please you. You have to trust me." She licked my upper lip with her tongue and then pulled on my lower one with her teeth, her hands still kneading the muscle on my shoulders and chest, her actions visceral.

I opened my eyes to find her straddling my legs, her body clearly visible through the beautiful gown, the skirt pooling between her thighs, hinting at the treasure there, the candlelight casting a soft glow on her body. Her eyes were glazed over with passion and her mouth fell open in desire.

She was like an angel, so ethereal, so unreal, exquisite, and mine. My heart swelled to the point of bursting. Completely mesmerized, I couldn't tear my eyes away.

"I love you, too, Brook. Don't ever leave me, please."

"Not possible. You're burned into me," she promised, using words from the

movie script as her hands ran lightly over my chest, giving me a new series of shivers.

"Cade, you have to tell me when you're getting close. Promise me you will stop me before you cum, but I want you on the brink." She cocked her head to one side and bit her lip. "Promise me, baby," she said again.

I already felt like I could come and she hadn't even touched my cock, my body was humming. "Okay. I'm yours. Do what you will. I promise. You're so fucking beautiful, Brook. I can't believe you're real right now."

"I'm so real, and just for you." She smiled a sexy little smile, as she put some more oil on her hands and warmed it before bringing her hands down around my screaming erection.

"Oh, God," I moaned as she worked over me, her hands moving up and down, over and around the head until the throbbing intensified and the sensations threatened to overcome me. I'm not sure how long her hands moved on me because I was so lost in the sensations, lost in watching my beautiful Brook. "Ahhhhhh..." I groaned. I felt the pre-cum start; some was dripping from the head. I hissed and I sucked in my breath.

"Mmmmm," she said as she bent to lick it off. "You taste so delicious," she said as her hands kept on with their sweet torture, her breath like fire on my body.

"Brook..." I was panting. "Okay, Brook, stop now. I'm only seconds away from exploding. Love, you have to stop."

Her movements on my engorged cock slowed and ceased. She moved to my side, her head on my chest, she reached up and kissed my jaw and into the curve of my neck. I was breathing hard, my heart racing, my throbbing body screaming for release.

I struggled to control myself, to not throw her on her back and push into her body with my own. "Can I touch you now?" I said breathlessly.

Her hand was on my chest. "Only a little. Hold me while you calm down."

I didn't need a second invitation as my arms closed around her delectable body. One hand rubbed up and down her arm, the other running up and down her back and hip. As a couple of minutes passed, I felt my breathing even out, my erection start to subside slightly.

"Did that feel good?" She smiled against my skin.

"So good it almost killed me," I sighed.

"That won't do. I need you alive." The lilt in her voice made me smile softly as I rolled onto my side and rested my head on my fist. Looking down at her, I stared as I traced her body with my fingers. My hand ghosted over her nipple under the sheer silk and I felt it tighten and grow beneath my fingers. Her body was so responsive to my touch and I loved it.

"No touching me to pleasure me, Cade. You promised." She moved away from me and handed me the champagne. I took it, though I didn't want it. I wanted her.

"But...why, Brook? You're driving me insane. I love tasting you, smelling your arousal, making you moan and quiver beneath my hands. Jesus, I want you so much." I tore my gaze from her body up to her eyes as my tongue came out to dance over my lips. "Jesus, just thinking about it is too much."

She touched my face gently as my eyes flashed to hers. "Exactly. For me, too. It's my turn to take care of you." Her eyes were penetrating as she took a drink from her glass and then set it aside to return to lie beside me on the bed.

I stopped and looked down at her. "You are so perfect. Brook, all of those months, wanting you... I love you."

"I know." Her lips curved into a smile, but I could see sadness in her eyes. "I'm sorry I put you through that."

"Don't. It's over. Everything is brilliant now. Let's just focus on this."

Brook nodded. "You're right." Her tone turned seductive. "Are you ready?" She kissed me again, her mouth soft then demanding, then softly pulling away. I groaned in frustration, and she let out a soft impish chuckle and reached to remove my glass to the bedside table.

"Ready?" she asked. "Are you calm enough now so I can start again?"

I raised my eyebrows. "Again? Yes, please." My mouth lifted at the corners in the beginning of a smile.

"Yes, but the same rules apply. No touching, and tell me when you get close. So, so close, my love." She bent over me and breathed on my body, starting to kiss my neck and chest; her hand reached for my penis and I felt it surge to life in her hand. I groaned.

"Mmmm, yummy," she breathed as her mouth moved down my chest and stomach toward my erection. Worshiping my body with her mouth as she moved lower, she had me tense with anticipation.

God, it was so sweet. Her mouth was hot on my skin as she licked and teased down the shaft of my cock. My breath caught in my throat. After a few minutes of teasing me, and searing me with her hot breath, she had me twitching for release, begging her to take me in her mouth.

"Brook." I commanded. "Oh, God... Please, babe." My hands ached to feel her body but instead fisted in the sheets as my body arched toward her. Her eyes rose to meet mine and I could see that she was going to give me what I wanted.

Her hot mouth closed around my engorged member and she licked and sucked for all she was worth, devouring me with her delicious mouth until I thought I would explode. She ran her tongue around the head and sucked, then drew me in to the hilt, taking me in as deep as she could, her hand curling around the base. Her mouth and hand moving up and down were driving me wild as she leaned over me. I watched her glistening lips move on me; her beautiful face taking me in and it was so erotic I almost lost it.

"Uhhhm, love, you're so good, it feels fucking unbelievable," I moaned as my hips thrust toward her.

"I can taste you, Cade," she breathed against me. "That means you're getting close, baby."

I could feel the orgasm building, but her words punched it up. "Brook, uhhhh..," I was panting in time with her movements as she took me into the warm recesses of her mouth, her tongue and lips surrounding me in delicious heat and sensation. "Huh, huh..."

She took one last long stroke and then sucked a little on the head, her lips getting lighter before she stopped. She placed a wet, open mouth kiss on my stomach below my navel and then one on my chest on her way up my body.

"Cade, you're so beautiful; just amazing. I love the way you taste."

My cock was so hard I thought it would burst, bobbing toward her, aching for the release that I was being denied. "Good God, love, how long are you going to torture me? I want to touch you, taste you... *now*." I was out of breath as she brought her lips to mine. I took them in a deep kiss as my dick throbbed in protest.

"We have to wait a little," Brook commanded gently.

I moaned deep in my throat, my hands reaching for her body, but her hands closed around my wrists. I was panting as I fell back against the pillows, letting her hold me down. "I don't want to."

"Just a little. Then you can touch me." Her mouth moved softly back and forth on my chest, teasing my nipples with a series of butterfly kisses, and my abdominals contracted against my will.

My hands twisted out of her grasp and lifted, finally flowing over her curves beneath the delicate silk. I was determined as I pulled her closer to me. "It's my turn now. No more waiting."

I couldn't stand another minute of not touching her, worshiping her in return. I sat up and pulled her with me to the head of the bed. I lifted her on top of me until she was straddling my lap as I leaned back on the headboard.

I took my time, pulling the strap of the gown over her shoulder until her left breast was bare. My hand softly teasing the tip; I reached around her waist and pulled her to me, then bent to take it into my mouth. I licked and sucked until she started moaning. I pulled on it with my lips and sucked some more. She smelled of perfume and salt, and tasted like ambrosia on my tongue. Now that I was in control, I could afford to take my time and give back a little of what she'd put me through.

"Uhhmm... Cade," she murmured as her head fell back. I laved the nipple, sucking, teasing, my tongue pulsing against it as I felt it stiffen and rise in my mouth as my arm wrapped tightly around her. Her hair fell like rain over my arm, around her back and I melted. She was everywhere, in my heart, my hands, on my mouth. It still wasn't enough.

I felt my body echo hers as it stiffened even more, throbbing to find release, wound so tight from all of her teasing that I thought I'd explode any second.

My arm tightened around her again, my mouth still wild on her breast as I drew her lower body tighter against mine. She was sweltering hot and wet. I lifted the fabric of the skirt of her gown, my hand searching for its moist prize.

Her clit was full and erect. I let my breath out when my thumb found it, her hips started to move, of their own volition, into my hand as I took her mouth hungrily with mine.

"Uh, Cade, it feels so good," she said against my mouth. "But I don't want... huh, huh... mmm... to come without you." She was gasping, as I moved my thumb for a few more seconds and then my fingers slipped inside her and I felt her muscles constrict around my fingers. My heart was racing. I was in so much love and lust my eyes blurred. She was tight and it made me even harder, swelling to the point of pain. "Please... Please," she was begging, "not without you."

"Brook, I need to be inside you, baby. I'm starving, drowning and only you can save me." I wasn't sure if I was begging for release or baring my soul. Probably, it was both.

I lifted her with the arm around her waist, as I moved the skirt of her gown up with the other, and then lowered her beneath me on the bed, my mouth still connected to hers. I kissed her passionately and she met my demands, her tongue warring with mine. My breath was coming faster and my heart was full.

"You taste so amazing."

When I lifted my head, the candles illuminated her face and I thought I'd never seen anything more beautiful in my life. Her eyes were liquid with love and passion as she drew me into the blue depths. I wanted this to last forever, so I slowed my pace.

My knee parted her thighs, spreading her legs wide with my own, as my hand brushed her hair back. Settling down into the cradle of her body, I kissed her long and deep, sucking her tongue into my mouth and feasting on it as I found her opening and started to enter her.

She moaned into my mouth as she moved to sheath the full length of me; hot; wet, and tight. I closed my eyes at the ecstasy of the sensations as her fingers wound in my hair, cradling my head.

"Oh Brook," I groaned against the curve of her slender neck. It was always like the first time with her. "Mmmmmm. You feel so incredible; like you were made just for me," I breathed as I kissed her again. "Nothing else will ever feel this amazing. God."

I started to move slowly within her, as I looked down upon her face. Her head turned to one side, her mouth open as she panted my name, her long hair like silk on the pillows above her head.

"I am, Cade... Cade... Uhhhh... we are."

I kissed her cheek and dragged my lips to her neck where I sucked and licked as my body drove into hers in long, slow, purposeful thrusts. My hand came up to her breast where I teased and tweaked her hard nipple. Her hands were roaming lightly up my back making my skin tingle until her slender fingers wound in my hair.

"I love you, Brook." I put more pressure with my thrusts but didn't increase the speed. I wanted to be deeper, deeper inside my baby... "Mmmmm, you're mine forever," I murmured as I felt the orgasm starting to tighten my muscles as it was building.

She brought her knees up as I sank deeper into her body. She pulled my mouth back to hers and sucked my lower lip between her lips before I took her mouth completely in a soul-wrenching kiss.

She turned her face toward me, looking up at me; then her eyes closed and her back started to arch. She brought her hips up to meet my thrusts, her teeth biting her lower lip. I was mesmerized by her flushed skin and lost expression. My hand went between our bodies and touched her clit, my fingers moving in small circles again and again.

"Ohhhhh, Cade..." She moaned my name against my mouth. Her eyes opened and then her arms were going around my neck, into my hair, and sliding her tongue into my mouth as I felt her body clench and convulse around mine, and I answered her with mine. I sucked on her mouth like her body was sucking on mine.

"I love you..." she said and then moaned my name. "I love you, Cade."

Her beautiful voice, her lithe body writhing under mine, her face drunk with passion, her insides grasping around me, so hot, I felt myself start to come. I tried, but I couldn't stop it.

I groaned as my mouth closed over hers in another hot kiss, my tongue delving into her mouth, sucking on her lips and her response driving me insane with desire.

I felt her hands rake down my back, she threw her head back and I knew she was starting to climax. I thrust into her harder, deeper, and she was making the sounds that drove me wild.

"Mmmmm... uhhhh... Cade. Cade, oh, my God, can you come with me?" Brook's voice throbbed.

"I'm there, Brook. I'm there. You got me." I felt my body tense, and then I exploded deep within her body. It was so fucking strong, my whole body trembled and shook, spasm after spasm racked my frame and I took her mouth in kiss after kiss.

"My God." I was gasping, my body twitching as the waves of pleasure continued, and her body pulled my orgasm from me in powerful spurts. My chest heaved against her, my hands pushing the tendrils clinging to her skin by a sheen of sweat, away from her face, I felt her hands ghost down my back to my ass.

I was exhausted as I collapsed into the pillows beside her head, my hand going up to cup her cheek and I kissed the other side of her face.

My body still moved within her softly, slowly as if it had a mind of its own. I could still feel her contractions as her orgasm subsided. I brushed back her hair from her damp brow and stared down at her perfect features. I nuzzled her neck, my hands framing her face as I rested on my elbows above her.

"Brook..." I whispered. "Oh, honey." I kissed her mouth softly, sucking her upper lip into my mouth and I felt her breath fan out warmly on my face.

My eyes opened slowly to see her cornflower blue ones watching and languid. She ran her nails down my back and I shivered.

"So, did I?" She smiled at me as she kissed my temple and then my chin.

"Mmmm, babe that was earthshattering. Mission accomplished, I'd say." I laughed softly, nuzzling her neck and cheek, kissing her open mouth once more before I moved to her side and pulled the strap back into place over her shoulder.

"It doesn't hide much, even when it's on." She grinned at me, both of us still panting.

I waggled my eyebrows at her with a grin. " I know. I chose well," I teased. She nuzzled into my neck and I felt content and sated. I ran my hand down her body, stilling when I crossed her flat stomach.

I lay beside her; studying her features, looking at her perfect form as emotion overwhelmed me. I knew my features were thoughtful, relaxed and satisfied as my hands traced lightly over her body. I bent to place a soft, teasing kiss on her moist lips.

Her hand was on me, too, rubbing up and down my arm and then reaching out to touch my face, as her face turned serious. Her fingers brushing away the hair at my temple then fluttered down to brush across my chin.

"I can't stop touching you." It was the simple truth. I'd never be able to.

"Never stop." She lifted her head toward mine, asking silently for me to kiss her. I brought my mouth to hers and our lips brushed against one another. "Thank you for all of this."

"No." I was contemplative, backing away, my eyes locked with hers. "Thank *you*, love. You're so much more than I could ever deserve. There are no words." I brushed her cheek with the back of my hand and then cupped her chin.

I stared at her as if I'd never see her again, taking in every curve of her face and body. I bent to kiss her luscious lips, brushing her mouth with mine again and again.

"Brook…" I began.

"Hmmm?" her hand moved down to run soft fingers across my forearm as my hand lay on her stomach.

"Well, we never really talked about this, but well… are we safe, to make love like we do?" Her eyes widened a little, but she nodded. "I should have asked before, but I don't think straight when I'm with you."

"Of course, Cade. I'd never risk that. I'd never try to trap you into anything." Her brow wrinkled as her hand stroked the skin on my chest.

I started. She has the wrong idea. I shook my head. "No. I know that. I trust you. But I want you protected. You're so young."

"We both are," she said softly, her fingers still tracing my arm.

"Yeah, I guess." My hand came up to cover hers and bring it lovingly to my lips. I'd never considered children before and maybe we did have years to think about it, but if it happened with Brook, I would embrace it.

"It's been so amazing between us, that I never even thought about the consequences. This thing between us is so earthshaking, it always takes over the moment."

I stared down into her aquamarine eyes as she listened to what I was saying. She was sated by our love, so languid, glowing, as she watched my face, and softly caressed my forearm.

"But, I think we should talk about it," I said and then hesitated. This was a serious conversation and I rubbed my hand lightly on her tummy. "Um…" I stopped.

"Cade, what is it?" she whispered. I hesitated because of this new, powerful desire that had risen within me. "Just say it."

I was totally unprepared for the intensity and complete and utter astonishment I felt at this new need of mine.

My heart pounding in my chest, I knew that I wanted to give her the world and more. She had become my entire life.

"Brook." I bent to kiss her mouth, brushing mine back and forth across it before kissing her more deeply, and then a few more, soft, sucking kisses.

"I would give you anything you asked. Would you do the same?" I whispered against her luscious mouth, she rose toward me, her lips searching, seeking mine. I took her mouth wildly with mine, my tongue diving into her mouth, I sucked on her tongue, tasting, teasing.

She reached up to brush the hair from my forehead as she sucked my lower lip into her mouth, before again brushing my lips with hers.

"Yes, anything." She nodded and I could see the questions in her eyes, her brow crinkling a little above her nose. "Anything." She smiled softly as she said it again.

"Would you give me... a child?" My eyes never left her face as I asked.

She gasped and her eyes grew wider.

"Not right away, obviously," I assured her.

"But, I thought... you wouldn't want that..." Brook began, shaking her head, her brow furrowed.

I placed a finger on her lips to still her words.

"I didn't think I did either, but this thing between us is so profound, I find myself in unfamiliar territory. A place I never thought I'd be. Maybe I'm thinking about it because of the books—the movies."

I stopped for a second and moved my hand on her stomach below her navel again. I watched her looking at me, her hair like silk fanning out behind her head, her blue eyes soft.

"But, nothing would make me happier. " I stopped and lifted her hand to my mouth to softly kiss it, noticing the beautiful engagement ring on her delicate finger. My heart felt like it would burst within my chest: it was so full of her. "I want that with you." I raised my eyes to meet hers and smiled. *"Someday."*

Her beautiful eyes filled up with tears as she looked at me. I moved to lie on my side, propping up on one hand while the other went back to her smooth stomach and lightly rested there.

"It would be irrefutable proof of the love between us; and the world would know it," I said, my voice growing deeper as emotion surged within my chest. "I can't wait to see a beautiful little girl with your face and my eyes, or to see my baby son suckling at your breast would be the most incredible, powerful thing I could ever imagine." I watched her expression soften and her lips tremble, her eyes becoming even more liquid. "I love you so much I feel a little ridiculous, like I'm making an utter ass of myself."

The tears fell softly from her eyes as she looked into mine and shook her head. "Brook, don't cry. I'm sorry." I kissed the tears from her cheeks. "You're the love of my life," I vowed.

"Cade, don't be sorry that you love me like that. You make me so happy." Her hand covered mine and pressed it against her where it rested above her womb. "Nothing would give me more joy. It's amazing to know you want to share that with me." Her voice cracked as a sob broke from her chest. "I love you," she whispered, and I bent to kiss her again softly, the fingers of my right hand twining with her left. "More than I ever believed it was possible to love anyone."

I rested my head against hers, and sighed deeply. I felt like I was living a dream.

"Just not for about ten years, okay?" She laughed though the tears on her face.

"Okay, honey, sure." I smiled and laughed with her as my arms closed around her and we both laughed out loud. "Whatever you want. Anything," I promised, and meant every word.

Chapter 23
Morning Glory

Brooklyn

I AWOKE IN the dark, many of the candles burnt out and only a few of the larger ones still flickering. Cade was curled up against my body from behind, his hand around my waist and coming up to cup my breast. I inhaled the scent of him all around me as I closed my eyes, remembering the ecstasy of the evening before.

It was magical and unbelievable; the stuff dreams are made of.

Thinking back, I remembered his beautiful eyes, glistening with tears when he looked upon me in the negligee for the first time, and again as he knelt to place his ring on my finger. I closed my eyes as I remembered his velvet voice telling me he loved me and that I belonged to him in the middle of our passionate lovemaking. His touch made my body sing. The reverence in his voice when he admitted that he wanted our child filled my heart to the point of bursting. It was surreal. Never in my wildest imagination would I have dared hope that Caden Carlisle would be mine. Not only that, he'd proposed and told me he wanted a child with me. *Holy fuck.*

I never thought I could love someone this much. It mirrored the intense relationship Ryan and Julia shared in the books, and in our film.

My eyes stung with tears at the memory of the months since the end of shooting, and the pain we'd suffered during our separation. All of the longing and worry that had built up inside as I'd wondered if we'd still be "us" when we finally had time to spend time together again had been for nothing.

I listened to Cade's steady breathing, the warmth of his breath on my shoulder and neck. There was nowhere else I'd rather be.

He's so perfect in every way… How could such a man even exist, let alone love me?

My heart beat faster and my arm tightened on top of his. I brought his hand up to my face and pressed my lips to it. Part of me was afraid that this was too good to be true, that something would happen to shatter the perfection in front of me, but I tried to push those feelings away.

I would cherish these precious moments and days with Cade, memorize every second and pack it away in the recesses of my heart so I could relive them when we were apart.

Usually, I was beyond all of this romantic stuff, even thinking at times that it was all bullshit or something that only existed in movie scripts, but never in reality. I never thought in a million years that I'd want to have children either. Even though it would still be years, Cade had changed my mind in a matter of seconds..

He was perfect; a gentleman, respectful and caring, not to mention beautiful. It was no wonder every woman he met wanted him.

My stomach lurched a little at the thought of all of the women that would chase him and surely all of the tabloid rumors that would be conjured up just to sell magazines. It wouldn't be easy, but being with Cade would be worth the turmoil.

He was worth everything.

I was content as I lay next to him as he slept, his warm arms around me, feeling protected and safe from anything bad that could happen.

If only the studio didn't have such utter control over our lives. I knew I shouldn't think of it that way; it was because of this movie that we'd met, but the restrictions they placed over our lives and time together, sucked. And, the pain Cade would suffer when I had to pretend to be with David was regrettable. Even though it was a ruse, I hated putting him through that, and there was much more of it to come.

Jeanne told me yesterday on the phone that David would be flying with me to Rome for the premiere of *The Future of Our Past* in October, and Cade would be joining us directly from London after visiting his family. No doubt, Cade would torture himself the entire time I was with David; at least, until he was holed up with me in my hotel room after the red carpet and the interviews were finished.

The worst part of the secrecy was the lying. I hated it and it was risky. I hated pretending I was with David when my heart was screaming for Cade. I hated that he suffered because of it, but so did David. Mostly, I hated not being able to be open with our feelings for each other, hated we couldn't just be natural with each other. It was bullshit.

I also worried about all of the screaming women and surely all of the actresses that he'd be in contact with over the next few months. I shivered as the thought left me ice cold. This thing with Cade was fragile and filled with variables, which scared the living shit out of me. I was terrified. If I ever lost him, it would devastate my life.

I didn't give a damn about what people thought about me, but everything was different now. Celebrity changed everything, but if I had my druthers, I'd rather stand my ground. Cade gave me all I wanted and he knew what I needed before I did. No negotiation necessary. There was a strange tightness building within my chest at the turn of my thoughts. I was a pile of mush under his hands; one word from him could take me to heaven, or plunge me to hell. It was a precarious, yet glorious place to be.

Amazing, and scary.

My fingers traced up and down the strong forearm that was wrapped around me. Cade stirred slightly and his arm tightened more when he pressed his lips into the back of my head in a series of kisses that continued down my neck to the curve of my shoulder, as he lifted the curtain of my hair out of his way.

"Mmmm...," he breathed against the side of my neck. "Here you are, as if in a dream." His body mirrored mine, both of us lying on our sides. He was plastered up against my back, and yet I wanted him closer. I felt the soft caress of his lips run across my shoulder and I smiled at his words. "I was afraid to wake up."

"Don't. It's the middle of the night." I turned toward him and wrapped my arms around him while his slid around me. "I could get used to this, babe." I kissed his chest and rested my head down to snuggle into him.

"I wish," he murmured into my hair and kissed my temple, his fingers lightly caressing my shoulder and arm. "Last night was amazing, my love. You're a little sex kitten, Brook. I think I'm stunned."

He smiled as his index finger ran down my cheek and I smiled at the same time as I shook my head. "No, you aren't," I scoffed.

"Yes, I am. It was absolutely brilliant. Just the thought if it gets me going all over again." He pressed into me so I could feel the proof of his words.

"It's all your fault." My fingers were drawing circles on his skin low on his stomach, and I never wanted to stop touching him.

"Well, then I'm more talented than I gave myself credit for," he said, his fingers lightly running up and down my back gave me chills, goosebumps rising all over my arms.

"You are very talented, for which I am eternally grateful." I kissed his mouth lightly, and his stomach growled. "Should I get you something to eat? Are you hungry?"

He laughed out loud. "Is that a trick question?" I looked up into his grinning face with a smile of my own. The darkness of the room and the remnants of the candlelight cast soft shadows on the classic planes of his face.

"No, because I'm starving, too." I touched his face and then moved to get out of bed. He grabbed me around the waist.

"Not so fast," he murmured as he pulled me back toward him and wrapped his arms around me. "It feels too good to be with you like this. I don't want it to end yet." His hand came to the back of my head and grabbed a handful of my hair. He tugged gently, bringing my head back as his mouth took mine in a hot, soulful kiss, his tongue entering my mouth. I moaned as I opened my mouth to him, giving him complete access and my tongue came into his mouth as well.

He was so delicious, so sweet.

I wanted more kisses, more touches, more Cade. I responded with everything I had, my mouth begging his to deepen the kiss as I sucked on his tongue. He groaned, giving in to what I wanted as his mouth hardened on mine and I felt his hand move to my hair and pull me closer.

"Brook," he said softly as he nuzzled into my neck and kissed it softly with a series of wet, hot kisses. He sucked gently on the skin with his open mouth, sending electric shivers through my entire body.

I felt my body begin to open as my hips involuntarily rose to press into him, the heat beginning to pool between my legs. He groaned at my movement. "I want you." He pressed into me, and I felt his already hard erection on my stomach as he moved. "Is that okay?" he said as his mouth hovered inches above mine.

"Yes, please." I smiled softly at him. I ran my fingers through his hair at the back of his neck as I urged his mouth back to mine. "I really love you, you know?" I whispered just before his mouth engulfed mine again.

His fingers were grazing the skin of my arms and back, one hand finally coming up to slide to the back of my head and twine in my hair. We kissed madly, passionately, our bodies grinding against each other through the thin silk of my gown and his pajama bottoms.

Cade groaned into my mouth as desire surged between us. His hand on my leg gathered up the fabric of the skirt of the negligee until it was exploring my bare thigh, and moving up to lightly graze my core, as I parted my legs for him. His hand fluttered softly across the tender flesh and my body arched of its own volition up to increase the pressure. "I'm already so hard, Brook."

"You know just how to touch me." I raised my head toward his, seeking his mouth with my own. When he pulled back, I whispered against his mouth. "You make me want you so much."

He pulled me onto my side so I was facing him as he hitched my leg over his hip, his hand on my thigh burning into my skin, and causing trembles through my body.

"Hearing you say that, knowing it's the truth... I can't get enough.

I never want to leave this house."

The blue depths of his eyes were intense. His mouth brushed mine, the heat of passion momentarily replaced by pure love. We were mesmerized by each other, our breathing deep, eyes locked. My hand glided up his muscled arm over his shoulder, to cup his cheek.

I bit my lip as I gazed upon his beautiful face, my thumb brushing back and forth on his lower lip and then his jaw line, the little bit of stubble that I loved beginning from growth overnight.

"Cade," I said his name and I knew the love was dripping from my voice. "I just... want you so much." His arms gathered me close as his mouth found mine, taking my lower lip between both of his.

"I'm yours," he said against my mouth and then his kiss became more passionate as he pulled me close. "But, I want you more. God, so much more." He rolled me over onto my back and pressed into me again as his hand brushed my hair back. I brought my arms up to circle his back and shoulders.

I lost myself in his kisses and our glorious lovemaking. All thoughts beyond my hunger for his mouth, his body, and his love were completely forgotten.

The remnants of the candlelight bathed us in its golden glow as once again he made me his.

Caden

I WOKE TO the sun streaming in the windows of the bedroom, casting rays that reflected off of the walls. My arms reached out for Brook in the bed beside me, as if by habit. I smiled to myself thinking that after only this short time together she was already a fixture in my life.

My arms searched the empty bed beside me as I opened my eyes. I could smell her scent on the sheets so I knew that I hadn't dreamed the entire night before. I placed my hand over my eyes as I remembered the deliciousness of the evening and night we'd shared together.

As usual, every moment with her was ecstasy, utterly unbelievable. I took a deep breath as I buried my nose in her pillow and then dragged my naked self from the bed, grabbing my pajama bottoms as I went into the bathroom.

Her negligee was in the box again, I noted sadly, and decided I'd buy her bloody drawers full of that stuff. It was a delicious thought and I grinned, picturing it in my mind.

She'd been so beautiful last night; I'd been left breathless and entranced. I huffed in astonishment. And how she teased me for hours before letting me make love to her.

Every delectable moment of our time was burned into my brain. I couldn't remember ever being so happy and I knew there was a shit-eating grin spread across my face, but I couldn't bloody help it. I got out of bed and went into the bathroom, noting the shower was damp, so it appeared Brook had already made use of it. *Damn, a missed opportunity.*

The wonderful smells emanating from the kitchen drew me from the bathroom and down the hall. She was dressed in a backless blue halter and frayed jean shorts, standing at the stove and frying bacon from the smell of it. She heard me approach and turned toward me.

"Hi, sweetie." She was smiling as she glanced up into my face. "Are you hungry?" She set a cup of coffee in front of me and then went to the refrigerator to pour me some orange juice.

I watched her ministrations as she moved around the kitchen and I imagined that this is what it would be like if we were married. I ran my hand through my hair and sighed as the joy of it washed over me.

She was taking care of me like only Brook could.

"Yes. Starving. You wore me out, love." I smiled crookedly at her as I swooped her in my arms and kissed her sweet mouth. "Feel free to do it as often as you like, from this day forward."

"I think that might be arranged," she laughed softly as she nuzzled into my shoulder. My heart swelled as I held her and kissed her shoulder.

"What are you cooking?"

I felt so much delight just being here with her. She moved out of my arms to dish some food on the plates that were waiting on the counter.

"Um, well, I made bacon and scrambled eggs with herbs, lemon muffins and we have the strawberries from last night's dessert, which well, obviously went uneaten."

I sat down on one of the stools at the kitchen bar, and she brought me a plate filled with the luscious offerings. She smiled; her eyes radiating pleasure.

"Lemon, huh?" I smiled broadly. A lock of hair fell haphazardly over my forehead and I used my right hand to push it away.

"Yep. And, we have some champagne left if you'd like some in your orange juice?" I sliced open a muffin and loaded it up with butter. It smelled divine.

"No I'm good, honey," I said as I dove in and took a big bite. It was hot and the flavor exploded on my tongue. "God, Brook, this is really delicious," I said with my mouth full.

She laughed out loud at me. "What'd you expect, Cade? Pop Tarts?" She placed another plate next to mine and went to get her coffee before coming to join me.

"Um," I swallowed. "I wasn't sure what to expect, I suppose." I leaned over and kissed her mouth. "You're full of surprises." My fingers brushed her cheek and she leaned her face into them. "I'm very happy, Brook. Thank you."

"Well, don't worry, I'll let you make me Cinnamon Toast Crunch or Fruit Loops tomorrow morning." She was laughing at my food preferences, her eyes dancing with mischief. Left on my own, I'd live on Diet Coke, cereal and sandwiches and she knew it.

"Hmmph." I smiled back at her. She was so gorgeous: her hair still damp from her shower.

She forked some eggs into her mouth and looked at me for a moment. "I love doing this stuff for you, okay?" Her eyes were soft as she looked at me and she touched my face. I nodded and dug into my plate with relish.

"I love you, baby girl," I said and winked at her. She smiled and put her hand on my forearm to give it a squeeze before letting go to pick up her fork.

"I was ravenous myself, you know. All that sex really takes its toll on a girl." She raised an eyebrow as she took a drink of her coffee and smirked at me. "But hey, I'm not complaining."

I laughed. "Eat up, regain your strength. You're going to need it," I teased.

"Promises, promises..." she sighed, teasing. A sweet smile was dancing across her lips and I bent to kiss her again. I couldn't get enough of her and knew I never would. I placed my left hand on her knee as she sat beside me.

"What do you want to do today?" I asked, really wanting to know the answer. The prospect of being able to be with her like this precluded any preference as to what we'd be doing. I studied her features as she thought about it.

"I don't know, since we can't leave the grounds, I guess, go for a walk or lounge around by the pool. What about you?"

"I really don't care as long as I'm with you." My hand took hers and brought it to my lips. "I might make use of the piano for a bit, if you wouldn't mind." Her eyes lit up at my words. I knew she loved to hear me play. We'd spent hours sitting side-by-side on a piano bench laughing and messing around.

"I think one of the scenes we have to reshoot is that one in the bedroom, right? We could practice," I said, tongue in cheek. "The real piano scene isn't until the next film."

"Yes, I know, Ryan. It's me, Julia." Brook rolled her eyes at me. "You have to learn the song for that scene, but it will take about thirty seconds, so what do you want to do after that?" she said and then nudged my shoulder.

Brook was always telling me how talented I was, but for me, music was a natural thing. Normal: not extraordinary. It gave me a rush that she thought I was special, though. I reached out to brush my hand along her jaw.

"Well, I could make love to you…"

Her eyes came up to mine and burned into me. What started out as a joke became very serious. I got up and moved to Brook, turning her on her stool and picking her up in my arms, her arms and legs wrapped around me.

"Or, you could make love to me."

I kissed her deeply, my tongue moving into her mouth as her arms found their way around my neck to pull my mouth closer. She was as hungry for me as I was for her. The breakfast forgotten: I carried her down the hall.

"Or," she whispered against my mouth, "We could make love to each other."

God, she was perfect. The moment was perfect. Our love was perfect.

Chapter 24

Sunrise On The Beach

Brooklyn

THE WARM BREEZE was blowing in from the open window and was stirring the curtains and the mosquito net around the bed. Cade was sound asleep after another long and glorious lovemaking session. God, he was as good at it as I'd imagined he'd be. He brought my body to new heights each and every time he touched me.

I was lying on his chest and could hear the steady beat of his heart and the gentle rise and fall of his chest beneath my cheek. It was so perfect. Too, perfect.

It was dark, the moon shining in through the window, the only light. My mind had been racing since I woke from a dream and since, I couldn't go back to sleep. Being here with him like this, I didn't understand why I'd have a bad dream unless it was just anxiety at our impending departure. I woke up sweating with my heart beating wildly, the dream leaving me unsettled. It was ridiculous really. I mean, we were together, so why in the hell was I having nightmares about losing him to someone else?

It was strange. I couldn't see the face of the woman taunting in the dream, but she felt familiar. We were standing on the red carpet at one of our premieres, laughing and signing autographs when suddenly someone took his hand and pulled him away from me. The woman was ambiguous; I didn't know what she looked like, what color her hair was, just that she was beautiful. My mind filled with flashes of Cade moving further and further away from me.

"Cade's mine now. You've had him long enough, and he doesn't want you anymore." Her sultry voice still haunted me, even though now; I was wide-awake.

The worst part was he didn't protest. He didn't tell her that he loved me, just let go of me and went with her, to be absorbed in a huge mass of screaming women. I woke up panting and frantic. I pushed my damp hair off of my forehead.

"Hmmph..." I let out my breath in a whoosh. *What, am I going fucking crazy?*

After how loving he'd been and how often he tells me his feelings, having this dream was completely unexplainable. The expression in his eyes whenever he looked at me told me that he was mine.

Forever.

So what the fuck? I shook my head to clear my thoughts. I wasn't going to be one of those insecure idiots. He was who he was, and women would want him and be blatant about it, so I'd better get my head on straight.

Still, the emotions that flowed over me as I thought about him, touched him, and made love with him, did scare me. I felt a little out of control and that was not like me. I was always in control, which was why I'd fought my feelings for Cade for so long. I didn't want to be out of control of my heart or my life. Loving him was something I couldn't control.

I moved away from him gently so as not to wake him, and lie there staring at the ceiling. I glanced at the clock. It was 3:30 in the morning. I turned on my side to again look at the beautiful man beside me, the moonlight streaming in from the windows casting an eerie bluish glow about the room and across his features.

At the sight of him, love rushed over me and my heart beat faster. I reached out my hand to brush back the lock of hair that fell across his forehead. Loving someone this much could be dangerous.

Maybe the dream was my conscience telling me to be careful, be prepared for the worst. How could I ever be prepared for losing him? I wasn't prepared for anything about him. I shook myself again.

The gentle way he came in and took over my heart, my very life, was completely beyond my control, unstoppable. My heart would not be denied when it came to him; he was completely irresistible. And that was just the problem.

Cade was irresistible. No question. He was good through and through which meant more than his looks or even his talent. Not just to me, but soon, to the whole frigging world.

I tossed in the bed and finally decided to get up. Trying to sleep was hopeless in my current state. I didn't want to wake him so I decided to go for a walk. Maybe it would calm me down and help me put some things in perspective. I pulled on some lace panties and Cade's discarded T-shirt from the floor beside the bed. It was way too big and hit me halfway between my thigh and knee.

I sighed at the memory of taking it off of him, kissing his stomach and chest as I pushed it up his arms and over his head.

God, he was so delicious. Just thinking about our lovemaking brought a flush to my skin and made my panties damp.

His scent on the shirt engulfed me as I padded out of the bedroom and into the living room to look out at the ocean view. I knew it wasn't really a good idea to leave the gated grounds, but my tumultuous thoughts left me feeling claustrophobic. I wanted to walk on the beach and clear my head. Surely, at this time of the morning, there wouldn't be anyone to see me.

Cade probably wouldn't wake up while I was gone, but I left him a note on the pillow, just in case, though I wrote it in the dark, so it was most likely a scribbled mess.

Couldn't sleep. I'm going for a walk on the beach. The breeze feels so beautiful.

I'll be back before you miss me.

Yours,

~B

My hand twined in the silken strands of dark gold hair at his forehead and pushed it off his face again, then kissed his temple.

That hair. Even in sleep, he was so damn sexy.

I grabbed one of the big beach towels from the bathroom so I'd be able to sit on the beach without getting sand inside my underwear.

That would be bad. Very bad. I laughed softly to myself.

Opening the sliding glass door as quietly as possible, I made my way across the patio by the pool and through the grounds toward the back gate, cursing myself that I hadn't worn shoes. The path was uneven and even though worn down, had many rocks that weren't that visible in the moonlight. *Shit.*

After I'd passed through the gate to the beach, the soft, white sand was a pleasure between my toes. It had been a hot day and the sand still held some of the warmth, and the breeze was strong enough to blow my hair off of my face. It felt cool and soft against my skin.

The full moon reflecting off of the ocean's gentle waves made a peaceful scene where I could stop and reflect on the many changes that had occurred in my life recently.

If our film did as well as we all thought it would, my life could change forever. It was already bad enough that Cade and I had to sneak around to keep our relationship a secret, but it was only going to get more difficult.

I tried to keep the situation in perspective. *What if I'd never auditioned for that movie? I wouldn't have met Cade and none of this would have happened.*

Hell, I didn't even want the role in the beginning. When Jeanne called and said she'd set up an audition, I hadn't read any of the books and I had no experience so had little hope of getting cast, but she insisted that every failed audition was one step closer to the one that would make my career. I didn't find the premise that motivating either.

Best friends, secretly in love, fight their feelings despite impossible obstacles.

Big deal, I'd thought. It had been done a hundred times before. I was more interested in doing little independent films with meaty characters. I didn't care about box office pull, and I didn't want to get typecast in romantic fluff. For me, it was all about content. But I read the script and it wasn't fluff. The pain made it more interesting.

So when my agent forced the issue, I did as she asked. After I understood the complexity of the characters, and especially after reading with Cade... I wanted the part. We clicked. Getting into character with him was as easy as breathing... Despite how intimidated

I should have been by even being in the same room with him.

Martin made me do the love scene and the coffee shop scene and, the connection with Cade was immediate and undeniable. The scenes just fell out of us. He made my heart beat faster even then.

I felt he would change my life, and he did. In more ways than I even knew at the time.

I put the towel on the beach and sat down, bringing my knees up to rest my chin on my crossed arms.

Cade.

My heart expanded just thinking his name. I was still getting used to the overwhelming emotion and now this ridiculous new fear of losing him. My head knew it was dumb, given how much he had done to show he cared. It was completely nuts to worry like this, when he made me feel so loved.

The waves lapped at the shore about twenty feet in front of me, but other than that and the breeze rushing through the trees further in along the line of homes, there was no sound. I noticed the moon's reflection off of my engagement ring, making it sparkle and shimmer on my hand. I reached out in front of me and admired it. It was so simple in design, yet so exquisite. It was such a perfect choice.

Everything Cade did was always so perfect. I inhaled deeply. Would this bubble burst?

"I was getting lonely up there without you," Cade's velvet voice spoke behind me and I jumped a little at the sound. "Sorry, love, I didn't mean to startle you."

I turned toward him and reached my hand up to him and he took it. I pulled and he came down to sit behind and around me. His knees were at my sides as he put his arms around me and pulled me back against his chest. I leaned into him and put my arms around his knees on both sides.

He buried his face in my neck and placed several soft kisses down the length of it, making my skin tingle and a shiver run through me.

"Are you cold?" His arms tightened as he spoke.

I shook my head.

"Are you okay? Is something wrong?" His tone was worried because I hadn't spoken.

"No, babe. I'm just thinking. I couldn't sleep." My voice was soft. "I didn't want to wake you." I snuggled into him a little more. "But, I'm glad you're here."

"I reached for you in the bed and when you weren't there, I was worried about you. You should have woken me, love. I don't want to waste this time sleeping anyway."

"You're so sweet to me," I whispered against the skin of his neck as I turned my face toward him, my head resting on his shoulder. I shrugged. "I'm sorry I keep saying it."

"Brook. I know you, too well." He placed a kiss on my forehead. "Something's bugging you. What is it?"

I sighed. He did know me. My hands traced light patterns on his legs below his knees. He rested his chin on my shoulder. "Yeah, it scares the shit out of me."

Cade hesitated, the movements of his hands halting. "What does?" he asked cautiously.

I shrugged in his arms. "This. All of it."

"It shouldn't. I'll always protect you. You know that, don't you?" He asked softly. The love in his voice almost vibrated on my skin.

"Yes," I said, gently. I turned sideways in his arms so I could look in his face.

His eyes were intent as he looked at me. "So, tell me then." He bent to place a soft kiss on my mouth and then another. His lips were only inches from mine when he whispered. "Tell me, sweetheart." He kissed the top of my nose.

"Oh, it was just a bad dream. Silly really. I just couldn't get back to sleep." My hand went to his bare chest and slid upward around his neck as my head rested on his shoulder. His hands began to move rhythmically while he rubbed circles on my back. "You make me feel so safe and loved. I'm just..." I turned my face into the curve of his neck. "Well, a little bit scared something will happen to tear us apart. Nobody wants us to be together."

He breathed in sharply and his hand went to the back of my head to tilt my face toward him.

"Brook. Stop. Babe... *We* want us to be together, and that's the only thing that matters. This is just the beginning of our story. Don't you know how special this is? Do you think everyone loves like this?"

I flushed. Again, life was imitating art. Those words were the title to the third book in the series. "No, but you can't know what will happen, Cade. You can't see the future," I breathed.

"I know that I love you more than anything in this world, and nothing or no one, will ever change that, Brook. I won't allow anything to come between us." His head bent to take my mouth in a deep, slow kiss. He tasted so damn good. "I'll always be with you, I promise." He raised his head to look into my eyes and brushed my lower lip with his thumb. "What can I do to put your mind at ease?"

"Just love me," I said simply.

"That's easy." Cade's mouth lifted on one side in a crooked grin. His gaze moved to my mouth and then he returned his lips to mine.

His tongue teased my lips apart and then slid across mine as he deepened the kiss. Our lips moved together so perfectly, sucking and tasting the other. Kiss after kiss, he eased my fears, his hands roaming my body and moving up beneath his T-shirt that I wore. I wanted to get closer. Needed to be closer. The need between us was always so potent and overwhelming.

Cade's arms went underneath me... he lifted and turned me toward him in one smooth motion, like I weighed no more than a feather. Suddenly I was straddling his lap as his hands ran up my rib cage to the side swells of my breasts. His thumbs brushed against both nipples bringing a series of soft moans from my lips.

"Babe..." His voice was low and husky. "I love you so much, it hurts."

I wound my arms around his shoulders, one hand moving into the hair at the nape of his neck. I pulled back from the kiss but he didn't want to let me go, his mouth moving forward to follow mine, his lips hovered over mine. I opened my eyes and nuzzled his nose with mine. His blue eyes were burning into mine as he gazed at me through half closed lids.

"Brook, kiss me. Make love with me." Somewhere between a command and begging, his words melted my fears. I pulled his mouth back to mine and kissed him back with all I had. His hands moved to my bottom and pulled me tighter against him. God, I could feel his erection pulsing through my panties as we continued to kiss passionately. I ground my hips into his and he groaned into my mouth.

There was no sound except our breathing... the soft moans and kisses, beyond the soft lull of the waves and the gentle breeze. We were completely alone on the stretch of white beach; it was like we were the only two people on Earth and that God had made this place just for us.

My senses were flooded with his scent, his taste and how he felt beneath my hands and pressed intimately into my body. Love overwhelmed me as I let myself feel everything. His ardent kisses on my mouth, his hands on my body, his warm breath on my skin and his hardness rubbing against my most sensitive place until I felt I had to have him or die trying.

I wanted him, and I wanted him here and now.

"Cade... Oh, God, I want you so much. Right now. Please," I begged against his open mouth. His kisses deepened and became more intense as his tongue slid so beautifully against and with my own. Our mouths were moving; mating with each other's, pulling and tasting for what seemed like hours.

I felt him move the hem of the t-shirt up and start to bring it up my body. I lifted my arms for him and he removed it completely, throwing to the side, and ran his arms back down the length of mine, to go to my rib cage and to cover my breasts. I couldn't help myself; I arched my body into his hands. God, he felt good.

His eyes burned my flesh as his gaze roamed my breasts and up to my face again.

"Bloody hell. You're so beautiful in the moonlight. Oh, my God." His hand reached out to touch my breast; so soft and gentle; as if I would break beneath his hands. My nipples hardened and grew even more beneath his touch.

Somehow we ended up lying down on the towel facing each other as we continued to kiss and explore each other. He groaned as he turned over me, the kisses continuing to burn on my mouth as he pulled me to his chest. Skin on skin... it was glorious.

My hands found the top of his shorts and I undid the button and slid the zipper down. As my hand reached inside and found his smooth hardness, he groaned as he took my mouth in another earthshaking kiss. Somehow, I managed to take his shorts down with my foot as my hands feathered over his back.

His hands were like silk on my skin, leaving a trail of fire in their wake, as he took my leg and hitched it over his waist. His hand slid around my back to pull me closer as he found my opening with his body. He slid into me, filling me with one thrust and I gasped at the pleasure of it.

"Believe you are mine. I'll never let you go," he whispered against my neck as his mouth sucked and nipped at my delicate skin. The sensation sent shivers through my entire body. He thrust into me again and again... I couldn't get close enough to him. I began to move my hips with his and squeezed my muscles around him. "You feel so damn good."

I raked my nails down his back as my head fell back and he bent to place wet, open mouth kisses on the skin of my shoulders and neck as he moved within my body. His fingers finding the place I needed him to touch as his hand went between our bodies to pleasure me.

"Uhhh... Oh, Cade. Don't stop."

"Never," he moaned as he took my mouth again. My hands fisted in his hair as we kissed madly, my body beginning to tense as I felt the orgasm build. "Brook, I can feel you getting close. Oh, God. It's perfect how your body fits me so perfectly."

Our movements increased in intensity as we both got closer and closer to being overcome. It wasn't long before he had me spiraling over the edge. "I love you, Cade. Uhhhh..." I whispered against his mouth as I came.

His head fell to my shoulder as his body thrust into mine and held as he spilled into me. He jerked with each spasm of his body. "Fuck, Brook! Brook." He fell against me, his breathing hard and fast.

Our arms wound around each other and pulled each other close as our breathing calmed. I placed several kisses on his sweat-dampened shoulders and neck and brushed the hair back off of his beautiful features.

His love-drunk eyes opened as he brushed his knuckles against my chin over and over. His blue eyes burned into mine. "See how much I love you? Do you think I could be like this with anyone else?"

Cade waited for my answer. "Do you?" His hand at the side of my face lifted it so he could look in my eyes. His eyes were languid and serious, as he stared into mine.

I knew I'd never feel like this for anyone else, and I had to believe it was the same for him. I was so overwhelmed that I couldn't speak, so I slowly shook my head, and raised my hand to touch his jaw, the stubble soft against my fingers. *So sexy.* I shook my head.

"Then trust this, please."

He bent to kiss my mouth as he pulled me closer. As I snuggled into him, there was no more need for words as we remained wrapped around each other for what could have been hours. Time ceased to matter.

I felt content just to lie in his arms. As the sun began to come up, Cade finally spoke. "Let's get you back to the house, minx." He kissed my forehead and the side of my temple.

He stood and put his shorts on and handed me back his t-shirt and my panties. He pulled me up and watched me dress then picked up the towel. I squealed as he caught me by surprise and pulled me in for another passionate kiss and then another.

"Up you go." He lifted me onto his back to give me a piggyback ride to the house. I snuggled into his back and wrapped my arms around his neck. He took my right hand with his and brought it to his lips.

"This is like Julia and Ryan," I murmured in his ear as he walked up toward the house.

"No, it's us. It's us, Brook, okay?"

I closed my eyes and nodded against his back. "Yes."

He loved me. My heart was certain.

Please join Cade & Brooklyn
when their story continues in...

More Than
FAMOUS
Famous Novel-Two

About the Author

Kahlen Aymes is a USA Today bestselling author who writes steamy romance novels that cross genre lines between New Adult, Adult Contemporary, and Erotica.

Kahlen has been on several bestseller lists including Barnes & Noble, Amazon, Smashwords, Publisher's Weekly, iBooks and USA Today! She began her writing career without ever planning on publishing a single word and won multiple awards in the world's second largest fan fiction community, including BEST Author, BEST RPF, Best All-Human that Knocks You Off Your Feet, and several others! Her readers encouragement and support are what prompted publication.

Her interests include reading, as well as writing, theater arts, cooking, roller skating and going for long walks. She is the proud mom to one teenage daughter and two golden retrievers, who basically rule her world.

With a strong love of writing and romance, and you can count on her to deliver strong, relatable characters, deep and detailed plots, sexy love scenes, and emotion overflow!

Connect:

Facebook: https://www.facebook.com/kahlen.aymes.author?fref=ts
Goodreads: https://www.goodreads.com/search?utf8=
Twitter: @Kahlen_Aymes
Pinterest: https://www.pinterest.com/kahlenaymes/
Booktropolis Social https://booktropoloussocial.com/index.php?do=/

Visit Kahlen's website for merchandise, signed books, Julia's recipes, missing scenes, events, Kahlen's Blog, and series playlists: KahlenAymes.com

News/Giveaways & Eclusive Ecerpts/ Book Disscussion

Sign Up:Kahlen's Newsletter: http://eepurl.com/RuW4X
Join: Kahlen's Book Babes on
FB: https://www.facebook.com/groups/252301134873105/

Request an eBook autograph at: http://www.authorgraph.com/authors/
Kahlen_Aymes

Literary representation and rights information: McIntosh & Otis Literary, Inc.
353 Lexington Avenue • New York, NY 10016
Tel: 1-212-687-7400 • Fax: 1-212-687-6894 • Email: info@mcintoshandotis.com

Other Books By Kahlen Aymes

The Remembrance Trilogy & Prequel
(Also, coming soon to Audio)
Prequel: Before Ryan Was Mine
1. The Future of Our Past
2. Don't Forget to Remember Me
3. A Love Like This

The After Dark Series
(Also available on Audio at iTunes & audible.com)

1. Angel After Dark
2. Confessions After Dark
3. Promises After Dark

The FAMOUS Novels
1. FAMOUS
2. More Than FAMOUS
3. Beyond FAMOUS

Coming in 2016-17
One Step Closer
Covered in Raine
Soulmate
Unfinished Business
So Damn Beautiful
Stripped

Rockin' After Dark